STARFIST: FORCE RECON
BOOK II

POINTBLANK

STARFIST: FORCE RECON
BOOK II
POINTBLANK

DAVID SHERMAN & DAN CRAGG

BALLANTINE BOOKS • NEW YORK

A Del Rey Mass Market Original

Copyright © 2006 by David Sherman and Dan Cragg
Excerpt from *Flashfire* copyright © 2006 by David Sherman and Dan Cragg

All rights reserved.

Published in the United States by Del Rey Books, an imprint of The Random House Publishing Group, a division of Random House, Inc., New York.

DEL REY is a registered trademark and the Del Rey colophon is a trademark of Random House, Inc.

ISBN 0-345-46059-6

Printed in the United States of America

www.delreybooks.com

OPM   9 8 7 6 5 4 3 2 1

Dedicated to Master Sergeant Ray Ytzaina, USA (Ret.)
Korea, Vietnam
1933–2005

PROLOGUE

A heavy explosion shook the walls, causing a fine cloud of dust to fall gently onto General Jason Billie's desk. That was immediately followed by several *wump-wump-wump*s as friendly coastal batteries answered the enemy cruiser firing several kilometers out on Pohick Bay.

"Missed again!" Lieutenant General Alistair Cazombi grinned. The artillery dueling was getting to be a daily occurrence for the army cooped up on Bataan. General Billie never batted an eyelash as he brushed the dust off his desk. *He's getting used to the bombardments,* Cazombi reflected.

"Would you have a cigar, General?" Billie shoved the humidor across the desk.

Now that's unusual, Cazombi thought, *the supreme commander offering anyone except his chief of staff a cigar. What's he want this time?*

"No, thank you, sir." Billie raised his eyebrows at the refusal. "You issued an order against anyone smoking in here, don't you recall? The air-filtering system can't handle all these men smoking, much less exhaling, down here," Cazombi elaborated.

"Ah, yes. Well, General, I never intended that order to apply to *senior* officers." Billie sighed, helping himself to a Clinton. Soon a foul blue cloud of tobacco smoke rose up between the two generals. "These are exquisite smokes, Alistair. Sure you won't have one?"

1

"Positive, sir. I prefer Davidoffs, when they're available. Besides, if my men can't smoke, I don't think I should." It had become a standing joke among Cazombi's small staff that when he came back into his office smelling of cigar smoke, it was a sure sign he'd been in to see the supreme commander, as General Billie preferred to be called.

Billie inclined his head and regarded Cazombi through the smoke. "RHIP, General," he intoned.

"I'd rather not, thank you just the same."

Goddamned prig, Billie thought, shifting his cigar from left to right in his mouth. Then: "We've got to find out what the hell he's up to." Billie nodded toward the sound of the naval bombardment. "What kind of an intelligence network did you have before I got here?"

"I didn't. I was a depot commander, remember? I had neither the personnel nor the mission to set up an intelligence network. General Sorca's division G2 had someone planted in Ashburtonville as I recall. A female sergeant. She was able to develop some pretty reliable intelligence before she disappeared."

"Umpf. An enlisted person, and a *female* at that? I've never put much stock in human intelligence, Alistair. Too damned impressionable. What we need is electronic surveillance."

"Lyons's damned antisatellite lasers have been playing hell with Admiral Hoi's string-of-pearls, sir, and our aerial reconnaissance flights have been very costly in men and machines. We need someone to go in there and knock those guns out. I'd call for immediate deployment of Force Recon elements—"

"General, don't tell me you've fallen for that Marine poop-and-snoop propaganda!" Billie snorted. "What we need is eyes-in-the-skies. You'd think Task Force 79 would have fixes on those guns' emissions and could take them out when they fire! Damn, what good is that fleet up there to us?" Billie puffed exasperatedly on his Clinton.

"The enemy are using laser cannon with passive sensors, they're undetectable until they fire. Somehow, they seem to have an inexhaustible supply of the guns. Take one out, and another crops up somewhere else. You have to admit, they've been effective. You've seen the reports from Admiral Hoi and your own G2's evaluations, sir."

"Yes, yes, yes—" Billie snorted impatiently. "I know all that, I've read the reports. But damn! Where's the innovation up there, Alistair? Where's the original thinking, eh?"

"If the Combined Chiefs hadn't disbanded the army's long-range reconnaissance units, we could send our own men out to—"

"Humpf." Billie gestured with his cigar. "That was a very wise move, General, as you should know. We had to reduce our budget, and with all the money we'd been spending on technology, it was only logical to eliminate the costs of maintaining human intelligence programs. Pure and simple."

General Cazombi suppressed a sigh. "As I recall, sir, that was done because the Chiefs envisioned combined operations that would rely on Marine Force Reconnaissance so the army's Rangers and so on were considered a redundancy."

"Um. Yes. Well. Hmmm." Billie puffed on his cigar in silence for a while, sidestepping the direction the conversation had taken. Like all conservative army officers, General Billie harbored a deep distrust and resentment of any elite unit, regardless of service affiliation.

Cautiously, as if scratching it, Cazombi put a hand to his nose to suppress a violent sneeze he felt coming on.

"General, I want you to get on this problem," Billie said at last. "Get in touch with Admiral Hoi in his 'ivory starship' up there. Goose him to find a way to take out those guns, *before* they kill his satellites." As if the enemy were listening, a series of powerful explosions shook the command post.

"Jesus!" someone exclaimed.

"First thing I want Hoi to do is eliminate that goddamned naval presence out in the bay," Billie said, banging a fist on his desk.

"General, consider it done." Cazombi got to his feet and saluted. Yes, and he knew *exactly* how to do it.

Office of the Deputy Commander, Coalition Forces, Ravenette

"Sir, you've been in with the supreme commander again," Brigadier Ted Sturgeon, Confederation Marine Corps, observed wryly.

"Yes, Ted, I have. As soon as this campaign's over, I'm burning every piece of uniform and clothing I've been wearing down here," Cazombi chuckled. "But our supreme commander has given me a task, and I want you to help me with it."

"You name it, Alistair."

"It's an easy one, Ted, and I hope I'm not insulting your Marines by asking them to do this for me. Just go out there, behind the enemy lines, find those damned antisatellite laser batteries, and knock them out. While you're at it, look around a bit. See what Lyons is up to, count noses. Maybe even pull off a few raids and ambushes, get the enemy off-balance. Then come back here and tell us everything we need to know about his capabilities and intentions and the deployment of his forces. Think you can handle that?"

Brigadier Theodosius Sturgeon, commander of the Thirty-fourth Fleet Initial Strike Team, stared at his friend silently for a long moment. "Aye, aye, sir," he responded, and made as if to leave.

"Ted? Have a cigar?" Cazombi reached into a cargo pocket and withdrew a portable humidor. He opened it and shook out one Davidoff Anniversario. "It's the last of Cazombi's Zombies, Ted, and I'd like you to share it with me on this momentous occasion."

"Thanks, Alistair, but General Billie issued an order—"

"Oh, we won't *smoke* it, Ted! Heaven forbid!" Cazombi produced a small cutter and sliced the cigar in half. "Seems a sin to treat such an exquisite cigar this way, but we can sure chew on it. While you're doing that, chew on what I just said. How do you think we can do all that?"

"Force Recon."

"Precisely! Ted, I'm surprised at how goddamned smart you've become since you first met me."

"But we don't have them. And before they can be deployed, we've got to get the supreme commander's approval to conduct the missions. I think under the present circumstances, that is not going to be forthcoming."

"Wrong. I just got that authority directly from General Billie. He told me to get with Admiral Hoi and figure out how to take out the laser guns that've been shooting down his satellites. He didn't say *how.* I have sent a message to the fleet commander, using my authority as General Billie's deputy, requesting help from Fourth Recon Company. Once they have completed their first mission, I'll let General Billie know what I've done. Nothing succeeds like success, Ted, but if he doesn't like it, let him fire me. What do you think of them apples, Brigadier?"

"I think I am truly astonished at how devious you have become since you first met me," Sturgeon answered. They laughed long and hard and chewed happily on their cigars.

CHAPTER
ONE

Planetfall in an Undisclosed Location

None of the watchers on top of the shore cliffs paid any particular attention to the meteorite that briefly flashed down through the sky before it plunged below the horizon.

The AstroGhost stealth shuttle dropped far enough out to sea that the diffused flares of its braking engines, fired at five thousand meters altitude, weren't visible from land. A ship at sea, seeing the diffused flares, might be excused for thinking a meteorite was breaking up in the atmosphere. As soon as the juddering of the firing brakes began to smooth out, the AstroGhost popped a drogue chute. The chute tore off after only a few moments, but it was enough to cut the descent velocity; then the AstroGhost turned its descent from straight down to a velocity-eating spiral, which further slowed its fall. At five hundred meters, it gained a stable orbit and lowered its loading ramp. A Mark 8 Skimmer, a specialized version of the standard hopper troop tactical air carrier used by the Confederation Marine Corps, slid out of the Astro-Ghost's bay and fell a hundred meters before firing its engines. In another moment it demonstrated how it got its name by staying barely high enough above the waves to avoid raising a rooster tail. The Skimmer was fully loaded with the Marines of first and third squads, second platoon, Fourth Force Recon Company, and their gear. Staff Sergeant Fryman, second platoon's first section leader, commanded. The nine Marines were wearing chameleon uniforms but the screens of their helmets were up, allowing their faces to be seen.

Fifty kilometers offshore, well out of sight of any watchers on the shore cliffs, the Skimmer stopped, hovered, and lowered itself closer to the top of the ocean swells. Staff Sergeant Fryman didn't bother checking his men to make sure they had all their gear; it wouldn't have been possible in the cramped quarters of the Skimmer; besides, he and the squad leaders had done that before they'd boarded the Skimmer. Instead, he stood out of the way and closely observed through his infrared screen as first squad, then third squad, acting by feel, each lowered a chameleoned Sea Squirt out of the Skimmer's hatch, then followed the Sea Squirts into the water. Each squad leader mounted his Sea Squirt and operated its controls to extend transparent, bullet-shaped tubes, one on the top, and four more along its sides. The squad leaders slithered into the open ends of the top tubes, their men into three of the side tubes. The gear the Marines weren't carrying on their persons was secured in the fourth tube on third squad's Sea Squirt.

When the last of his Marines was wet, Fryman gave an ungloved thumbs-up to the Skimmer's crew chief, closed his own chameleoning, and followed his men into the water. The Skimmer gently backed off as Fryman paddled to the farther Sea Squirt, first squad's. He slipped into his tube, plugged into the rebreather, took firm hold of the grips, and said into the all-hands circuit, "Squad leaders, report."

"First squad's ready," Sergeant Bingh replied.

"Third squad is go," Sergeant Kindy said.

"Let's do this thing."

Sergeants Kindy and Bingh, the two squad leaders, had already assured themselves that their men were secured inside their tubes, their rebreathers hooked up. The squad leaders took the controls and sent the Sea Squirts on a shallow dive path to five meters' depth, where they leveled off, and, using inertial guidance, directed the Sea Squirts toward the distant cliffs. In minutes, they were moving at twenty-five knots; third squad's Sea Squirt was at wing position, a hundred meters to the left and fifty meters behind first squad. Everybody settled in for the long ride.

A standard hour later, Fryman signaled Bingh and Kindy, and the squad leaders began slowly edging their Sea Squirts toward the surface. When Kindy looked over the side of his Sea Squirt through the light-gatherer screen of his helmet, he could see the sea bottom slowly rising toward them. At another signal from Fryman, the squad leaders brought the Sea Squirts to a stop on the bottom with the tops of their upper tubes a meter below the surface of the ebbing tide.

The Marines slid backward out of their tubes and gathered their gear, then paddled to where they could kneel on the bottom with only their heads above water and observed the shore—half with their infra screens, half with light gatherers. The squad leaders took a moment before exiting to key the "wait" instructions into the Sea Squirts, which headed for a designated hiding area in deeper water as soon as the Marines were all clear.

While the nine Marines were assembling, Fryman gave the beach and cliffs close behind it a scan with his motion detector. No one there. "Hit the beach," he ordered.

Keeping only their heads above water, the Marines advanced on a line, propelling themselves with their fingertips and toes against the sandy bottom. When the water was shallow enough that they were almost on their bellies, they rose to their feet and surged forward, past the waterline and across the shallow, boulder-studded beach, to the foot of the cliff. Water streamed off their water-repellent chameleons.

Fryman took a minnie from his waist pack, turned it on, and placed it against the cliff face. The minnie felt about for tiny irregularities in the rock that would give it purchase, then began scampering upward. The miniature reconnaissance device was disguised as a type of rodent common to the cliffs in this area and would easily fool any casual observer. As dark as the night was, a casual observer wouldn't even notice the unnatural assemblage hanging off the rodent's hindquarters. Two more, similarly disguised, minnies followed the first.

The cliff at that point was a little more than thirty meters high. It took the minnies only a few minutes to reach its top, where they skittered about in a most rodentlike manner, looking at their surroundings and into the middle distance in visible light, infrared, and amplified visible. They raised their noses and sniffed at the air, seeking airborne chemicals that would telltale hidden watchers. Then waited for instructions.

At the foot of the cliff, Fryman studied the data his controller comp received from the minnies. Satisfied there wasn't anybody directly above the Marines, he transmitted new orders to the minnies. Still rodentlike, the minnies skittered about until the assemblages on their hindquarters hung at the edge of the cliff. A faint whirring was the only indication they were doing something unrodentlike; the thin lines the minnies lowered down the cliff were almost invisible in daylight, completely so in the dark. Except for the weights on the ends of the lines, which had markers visible in ultraviolet.

Fryman and the squad leaders watched through UV lenses for the lines and caught them when they reached the bottom of the cliffs. Working rapidly but carefully, they attached lightweight grasping cables to the ends of the lines. On a signal from Fryman, the minnies skittered away from the edge of the cliff to small boulders they could anchor themselves to and towed up the lines. Fryman and the squad leaders let the cables trail through their fingers. When the tops of the cables went over the cliff top, they tightened their grips and the minnies stopped reeling them in. The three Marine leaders twisted the cables *just so,* and the top ends frayed and splayed out, to grip the rocky ground as firmly as a clinging vine.

The Marines attached a climbing grip to the cables and headed up, half climbing, half towed by the grips. When the first three reached the top, they rolled away from the cables into defensive positions and let the climbing grips drop back down for the next three Marines.

In moments, all nine were atop the cliff. Their objective was right where they expected it to be, spreading out two hundred meters to their left and fifty meters from the cliff edge. They'd studied the latest images of the objective right before boarding the AstroGhost to make planetfall; nothing they could detect from the cliff top indicated anything in it had changed. They'd rehearsed the mission several times before leaving for it and had studied it constantly during transit. Each of them knew exactly what he had to do and how to do it. Staff Sergeant Fryman said, "Let's do it," into his helmet comm, and the nine Marines rose up and headed toward their objective.

Half an hour later, eight of them returned. They gathered the minnies, then rapelled down the cliff. The last Marines down twisted the cables *just so;* the tops of the cables released their grips on the rocky cliff top and fell over the edge. While the cables were being gathered, the squad leaders signaled the Sea Squirts to come out of hiding and pick them up. In a few more minutes, the eight Marines were back in the Sea Squirts, heading for the rendezvous point with the Skimmer that would transport them to the AstroGhost, which would return them to the starship that had brought them.

As for the ninth Marine in the party . . .

Staff Sergeant Fryman quietly drew the camp chair from under the camp table and comfortably settled himself in it before he took off his helmet. He sat quietly for a moment, gazing on the man sleeping on a cot so close Fryman's knees almost touched its side. He checked the time, watched the seconds tick off, then gently reached out and shook the man's shoulder.

"Hmmpf? Wha—" the man began. He began to sit up before he realized someone was next to his cot, in a position to block him.

"Sir, I'm Staff Sergeant Kazan Fryman, Fourth Force Recon Company. It's my pleasure to inform the colonel that in"—Fryman glanced at the time—"eight seconds your command post and operations center will be destroyed."

"What!" the man roared, leaping out of his bed. But before he could do anything, there was a rapid series of explosions nearby, culminating in a flash-bang inside the tent of the commanding officer of the Confederation Army's 525th Heavy Infantry Regiment.

"That one killed you, sir," Fryman said with a grin, thinking, Gotcha, doggie.

CHAPTER TWO

En Route, Halfway to Cecil Roads

It was a night of phantasmagoria in the top-floor bar of the Hotel Victoria. But it didn't start out that way.

Sergeant Jak Daly had departed Camp Basilone in good order. The process of clearing base was one he'd done before. After twelve years in the Corps, getting those personal belongings he wasn't taking with him into storage, turning in his field gear, clearing all the hand receipts he was responsible for, updating his medical and personnel records, and getting clearances from a dozen other places around the base—even places he'd never visited like the sports locker—were routine. But by the time he reported to the base transportation office to get his tickets, his name had to be deleted from all the fields in the clearance system or he'd have to get last-minute checkouts, always a pain in the nether regions.

Because Daly had to report in to Arsenault in six weeks in order to catch the next OTC cycle, and no military vessel was available that would get him there in that amount of time, he was booked out of Halfway on a merchant ship, the SS *Accotink*. She would drop him at Cecil Roads, where he'd catch an Earth-bound cargo vessel, the SS *Miomai,* which would drop him off at Arsenault on the way and in time to report for his course. His orders specified he'd report in to OTC in dress reds, but while in transit he was to wear "appropriate casual business attire."

One of his last stops was the Navy Times Bookstore, where he stocked up on the vids and readers he'd amuse himself with on the long voyage to Arsenault (and during whatever free time he might have while at OTC). Among these were the military classics *All Quiet on the Western Front, Charlie Don't Live Here Anymore, The Soldier's Prize,* and all twenty-two volumes of the Starfist series, books he'd read when a boy but ones he wanted to read again because they had convinced him he wanted to be a Marine someday. He also got copies of all the popular vids based on the Starfist novels.

Next he visited the navy finance office, where he drew, in cash, his travel pay, and finally the local Navy Credit Union, where he drew his account down to only a few hundred credits, to keep it active against his return. The rest of the money he took with him in cash and a debit chip that would be good anywhere in Human Space. Daly did not like to travel with only "plastic" money; he liked the feel of security cash gave him. He'd have a forty-eight-hour layover at Cecil Roads before catching the *Miomai* so who knew what use he might find for the money. Besides, during the months he'd be in Officer Training College he'd be authorized liberty at Oceanside, and he did not plan to go third-class.

It did not take Daly long to discover that the SS *Accotink* would have been better named the SS *Neanderthal.* The captain was a taciturn man who spent most of his time in his cabin. When he was on deck, he gave orders using as few words as possible. The first mate was a morose slob who never seemed to change his work clothes, and the crew amused themselves when off duty playing cribbage in the galley until all hours. They played for money, a decicredit a point, and made it clear the game had been in progress since the vessel had left her home port and Daly was not welcome. That was just as well because often fights erupted when someone pegged too many points on the board. The ship's cook was a woman—at least Daly thought she was, or had been once—and the food she prepared was indifferent at best. He laid the crew's bad temper to her cooking.

Sergeant Jak Daly breathed a sigh of relief when the *Accotink* at last docked at Cecil Roads and he was able to catch a shuttle to the surface. That is when he took a room at the

Hotel Victoria, which happened to be the lodging most convenient to the spaceport. "It's clean and reasonable," a porter informed him, "and within walking distance." The man gave Daly the once-over. He could see Daly was no space bum and guessed from the way he was dressed and his haircut and just the way he carried himself that he was a military man between assignments. "How long you gonna be here?" the porter asked.

"I have a forty-eight-hour layover," Daly replied. "I'm due out on the *Miomai* on third day this week."

"Miomai?" The porter nodded. "I know her. Good ship. She's got good clean lines too. Wait'll you see her. The captain and crew are okay. Passenger accommodations too." He paused and regarded Daly speculatively. "Looks to me like you been around, son, but I'll tell you anyways. The Victoria's on the Strip, end closest to the port here. But stay away from them clip joints." The porter nodded affirmatively and shuffled off.

Cecil Roads was a busy port and the streets outside the surface terminal were full of traffic. A huge sign glittering a few hundred meters outside the main gate announced the location of the Hotel Victoria, and Daly, carrying his handbag—the rest of his gear was being transferred to the *Miomai* (he hoped) and he'd retrieve it once he was on Arsenault—started walking in that direction.

The porter had been right, Sergeant Jak Daly had been around, he'd seen port-town strips like this one before. They were not like the strips outside the military bases he'd been on. Those places were full of the youth and life of the fun-loving sailors and Marines who crowded into the beer joints, tattoo parlors, bordellos, and restaurants to enjoy their hours of liberty. But this place was depressing, peopled with the flotsam of Human Space, the most depressing of all those who eked out a living serving the transitory space bums who sought temporary forgetfulness there. And the most depressing of these were the women. At least the transients who hung out in the bars and flophouses could get out of the place, back to the familiar surroundings of their ships and

the company of their shipmates and, who knew, maybe somewhere a home waiting for them. This place, even from the
street where he was standing, only beckoned him to leave as
soon as possible.

Given the sleazy neighborhood it occupied, the Hotel Victoria was not bad, so he took a room on the tenth floor, just
below the penthouse restaurant. His only plan was to sleep,
eat, and read until the *Miomai* was ready to depart. It was
morning in that hemisphere of Cecil Roads when Daly arrived. He had skipped breakfast aboard the *Accotink*—
wisely since the cook's breakfasts tended to remain on one's
stomach for quite some time. So after unpacking his bags
and washing up, he stretched out on the bed for a while. As
he lay there, his stomach began to rumble, and he decided to
try the Victoria's restaurant.

The breakfast was quite good, although the bacon and
eggs were clearly ersatz. Daly sat at his table for some time
after he'd finished his repast, the only diner in the place, enjoying his coffee. The restaurant consisted of a small dining
area, a dance floor, and a comfortable bar.

"Place picks up at night," the waitress informed him conversationally as she cleared his table. "We even have a live
band." She gave Daly a sidelong glance. She could see he
was no space bum: neatly dressed, closely cropped hair.
"You in the army or sumptin'?" she asked.

"Nope." Daly smiled and rolled up his left sleeve to reveal
the Eagle, Globe, and Starstream tattooed there. "Marines,
ma'am."

"Well, we don't get many Marines in here," she replied
speculatively, then, almost as an afterthought, said, "We stop
servin' at twenty-one hours, but the bar stays open all night."

"Thanks." Daly fished out his wallet and laid several bills
on the table. "You keep the change, miss." He got up and
nodded politely at the waitress, who could not help grinning
at the tip, or noticing the wad of credits in his wallet. She
watched him as he strode over to the elevators.

On an impulse, she followed him over. "My name is
Maria," she informed him. "Thanks for the tip. Most of the

bums who eat in here only give me a hard time." She smiled
self-consciously.

Daly regarded Maria curiously. "My name is Jak." He extended his hand. Is she coming on to me? he wondered, and
grinned to himself. He could see she'd been a pretty woman
at one time, but now she looked old enough to be his mother.

"Well, this place begins to pick up after dark, Jak, and I
just wanted to say," she glanced over her shoulder at the bar,
"I just wanted to tell you, be careful who you sit with if you
come back up here tonight." With that she hurried back to the
table and noisily began to clear it. Daly stared after her, then
shook his head and called for the elevator. He had no plans to
go back there that night.

Hotel Victoria, Cecil Roads

Daly spent the rest of the morning stretched out on his
bed, reading. He picked up the first volume in the Starfist series, *First to Fight,* and read the opening lines. How true to
life these novels were! After twenty years they still rang true.
He scrolled to the author's pictures and studied them for a
while, wondering what had happened to them all those years
ago. They sure had their stuff together when they wrote these
novels, he thought. He continued to read and at some point
dozed off. He awoke with a start. The sun was down. He'd
slept away the entire day! He stretched luxuriously. Maybe
he'd call room service and watch a movie the rest of the night.
From far away came the *thump-thump-thump* of a base drum.
It must be the band in the penthouse restaurant. He picked up
the reader. He'd left off at the liberty scene near the end of the
book. Suddenly he was overcome by a wave of nostalgia. He
realized he was homesick for Camp Basilone! "Aw, screw it,"
he said aloud. He got up and dressed. He'd go up to the bar,
have something to eat, a few drinks, listen to the music, and
relax.

Jak Daly liked live music, and the band, incongruously
called The Dead Socks, was certainly "live." But their female
vocalist was pretty good and their repertoire was pretty catchy.

One song in particular made him smile and keep time to the music with his fingers on the bar:

"We were havin' sex, aft n' before

"When Death come a-knockin' at muh door . . ."

"Lonely?" Daly was startled by a fairly good-looking woman climbing onto the stool next to him.

"Not particularly." He did not appreciate the interruption, but he looked her over anyway. Barfly he thought. In Sergeant Daly's code of conduct, if a woman sat next to you in a bar and spoke to you, you were obligated to be polite to her. "Have a drink on me," he offered.

"Thanks. Henri—" She signaled to the bartender, a painfully thin man with a narrow face, long nose, and pencil-thin black mustache, "gimme a Yellow Basher with a twist of grimmick leaf."

Daly threw a bill on the bar. "You know good stuff," he commented. He had no idea what this Yellow Basher might be and had no intention of switching from beer, but he thought it was the thing to say under the circumstances. When the drink came, they saluted each other. Daly sipped at his beer. "What's your name?"

"Zephyr. Yours?" Zephyr's eyes had widened when Daly had withdrawn his bulging wallet to pay for her drink, and he had not caught the glance that had passed between her and the bartender when he served it. Daly told her his name. "Let's get a bite to eat," Zephyr offered. "They've got a private room in the back. We can get to know each other better there." She gave Daly a significant look.

Daly suppressed a slight twinge of annoyance. He'd come up to the bar to enjoy himself and now this intrusion. But he was hungry and this Zephyr wasn't a bad-looking woman for one in her profession. Besides, Sergeant Jak Daly was not the kind of man to tell any woman to go take a flying leap. So he gave in to circumstances and what he knew was the woman's objective—to cadge some drinks and a free meal off a lonely space bum—and accompanied her to the back of the bar where they entered a private booth.

The booth measured about four by five meters. In the middle was a table flanked by two comfortable benches long enough that Daly could have stretched out fully on either of them. He suspected that's just what they were for, but the cushions looked clean. Once they were inside, a sound-proofed panel slid closed behind them and they were cut off from the rest of the bar and restaurant. The music from The Dead Socks came to them muted through the soundproofed panel. They both had access to small consoles on which were the food and bar menus from which they ordered. Daly noted a key marked Privacy Sign, which he deduced correctly could be pressed to insure they were not disturbed; another indication of what the little room's main purpose was. The food was served by a waiter. Henri, the bartender, delivered the drinks. Daly brought his unfinished schooner of beer, which he intended to make last the evening, but Zephyr eagerly ordered Yellow Bashers one after the other.

Zephyr maintained a steady torrent of talk throughout the meal. "I'm from Euthalia," she informed him at one point between bites of steak and potatoes. She ate with so much gusto Daly wondered if she might not be starving. He tuned out most of her blabber, concentrating on the meal, only offering an occasional "Um-hum" or "Oh, yeah?" to be polite. The steak, from cows bred on Cecil Roads, as Zephyr proudly informed him, was quite good.

"So what do you do, Jak?" Zephyr asked, spooning some soup and slurping it eagerly.

"Me? I'm in the Marines." Daly, who had by this time endured over an hour of Zephyr's nonstop chatter about everything but anything revealing about herself, knew this question was coming. He looked at his watch. It was past 21 hours, time to call it a night. "And you, Zephyr?"

"Marines?" Zephyr echoed. She punched in an order for two Yellow Bashers on the console and almost immediately Henri appeared, as if he'd just been waiting with them in hand right outside the booth, which Daly suspected he had been, as with many of the things Zephyr had ordered during the meal. "Our Jak here is a *Marine,* Henri, did you know that?"

"Ah?" Henri said. "Have you ever killed anyone?" He smirked as he served the drinks. Daly felt an urge to flatten the man's thin nose. The soup had just been served, a viscous brew with chunks of meat floating in it. At least it was hot. Maria described it as a "speciality of the house" and encouraged him to taste it. Mentally, he turned up his nose instead. It was high time to finish the stupid meal and go.

"And what do you do, Zephyr?" Daly asked again, after Henri closed the panel behind him. He sipped cautiously at the Yellow Basher, just to be polite, and wondered how much the farcical meal was going to cost him. The drink tasted quite horrible and left a strong medicinal aftertaste. He made a face and shoved the glass aside, not even trying to hide his disgust.

Maria grinned at Daly, sipped her drink, and answered, "Me? I'm a whore, just a fucking whore, Jak, ol' boy."

Daly found himself startled at the frank admission. He stared at Zephyr in surprise. "Well, I—" he began, but the entire room began to go out of focus and his tongue refused to form words.

Zephyr burst into laughter when she saw the expression that had come over Daly's face. "Yeah, just a whore, Marine," she sneered, "and I make my livin' rolling dudes like you. And my name ain't Zephyr, either, you stupid bastard."

Daly could only make out blurry movements and heard someone else talking, but the voice sounded tinny and far, far away. He thought it belonged to Henri and he thought it said, "Do you think he got enough of it?"

Then Daly's head plunged straight into the soup. He'd gotten enough of it.

CHAPTER
THREE

Havelock, Near Camp Howard,
Marine Corps Base Camp Basilone, Halfway

Sergeant D'Wayne Williams ambled, relaxed, along Princeton Street in Havelock, a liberty town outside Camp Basilone on Halfway, though most everybody other than a Marine would call his amble a march. And the people who knew him best would easily recognize that he wasn't really relaxed. One reason he wasn't truly relaxed ambled/marched at his left side, Corporal Harv Belinski. Another ambled behind him, Lance Corporal Santiago Rudd. A third reason ambled next to Rudd, Lance Corporal Elin Skripska. Any more than the most cursory glance would reveal that both Belinski and Rudd walked gingerly, and Skripska kept casting concerned glances at them.

The reason Williams was uneasy with these three Marines was that he was new in Fourth Force Recon Company, and he was the new squad leader for the three Marines ambling along Princeton Street with him. Before his most recent tour as a squad leader with Seventeenth Fleet Initial Strike Team, Williams had served as senior reconman with Eighth Force Recon Company, so he knew coming in that there would be a certain degree of unease and even tension with a new squad leader. But there was more than the usual amount of tension this time, because he was replacing a well-liked squad leader who'd been killed on the squad's most recent mission—on which mission Belinski and Rudd had also been wounded, which explained their gait. Williams didn't know much about that mission beyond that it was a raid conducted by the entire second platoon, and that the platoon had suffered heavy casualties.

It was a Force Recon tradition that a new squad leader coming in from outside the company took his new squad on liberty at his own expense soon after joining the squad. This was a mechanism for him and his men to get to know each other and begin getting comfortable together. The basic Force Recon operational unit was the squad. The four Marines of a Force Recon squad went alone and unsupported into the most dangerous places the Confederation military sent anyone, and they had to go in and return undetected. To be detected meant they couldn't accomplish their mission—and probably got them killed in the bargain. So the Marines of a Force Recon squad had to be closer than Marines in a squad or fire team in a FIST; they had to know each other better than Marines in other kinds of units did. They had to *know* exactly what each of their squadmates would do in any situation. Their lives depended on that intimate knowledge.

Williams also needed to find out what had happened on that platoon-size raid, a raid that saw six Force Recon Marines killed and ten wounded; he'd never heard of a platoon-size Force Recon mission that had suffered so many casualties. Williams needed to know what had gone wrong. His life, and the lives of his men, might depend on his having that knowledge.

"How's this place?" he asked, pausing in front of a bar-restaurant whose sign announced it as The Unfouled Anchor.

"It's fine by me, boss," Rudd said, "as long as you're paying."

Belinski and Skripska agreed, so Williams led the way in.

About the same time that Sergeant Williams was finding out why The Unfouled Anchor was fine with his men "as long as you're paying," the eight Marines of second platoon's first and third squads were settling into a side room at the Snoop 'n Poop, a much less costly establishment that catered to the Force Recon Marines, and a favorite of second platoon. Neither Sergeant Wil Bingh nor Sergeant Him Kindy had to pick up the tabs for their men. Bingh had been third squad leader on the recent deadly mission, and Kindy the assistant squad leader of first squad—the two squads had swapped positions in the platoon. Third squad's, now first squad's, Corporals Gin Musica and Dana Pricer had both been wounded on that mission; Lance Corporal Stanis Wehrli was the only member of the squad who had come through unscathed. First, now third, squad's only casualty was the first Marine killed in the raid, but Kindy nonetheless had two new men, Corporal Ryn Jaschke and Lance Corporal Hans Ellis. Kindy had been promoted to squad leader when his squad leader on that mission, Sergeant Jak Daly, was accepted into Officer Training College.

Pitchers of Onofre Ale, a local brew, were delivered to the room by two reasonably attractive young women dressed in mock female Marine dress reds, scarlet jackets over navy blue skirts. But the Confederation Marine Corps would never authorize uniforms cut the way these were. The jackets started off right, with high stock collars covering their throats, but went seriously awry from there. The sleeves were too short—one woman's jacket had short sleeves, the other's had three-quarter length. The bodices, well, the bodices gaped wide open in a broad horizontal oval from just below the collar to halfway down the slopes of the women's breasts. The jackets were cut away a couple of inches above the solar plexus. And the backs were deeply scooped from just below the collar, so it was only the shoulders that kept the bodices up. The only modification to the skirts was they stopped well short of mid-thigh.

Needless to say, not many female Marines patronized the Snoop 'n Poop; many of the female Marines who pulled liberty in Havelock preferred Chesty's Place on Fort Nassau Boulevard, where the serving staff consisted totally of young men garbed to display their muscles.

It was rumored that several of the Snoop 'n Poop serving staff were off-duty female Marines. A large percentage of the servers were tough enough that many of the male Marines who patronized the establishment believed the rumors.

That evening, while the eight Marines of the two squads

appreciated seeing their waitresses, the appreciation was more in theory than active. They gave their food orders and waited politely, quietly, for a moment while the ersatz female Marines left the side room, closing the door behind themselves, then whooped into laughter.

Jaschke was the first to regain enough control and breath to be able to speak. "We did it!" he said. "We showed them!"

Bingh and Kindy stopped breathing for a moment and exchanged a glance, then looked at Jaschke and burst into even louder laughter.

Jaschke saw they were laughing at him, spread his hands, and asked in an offended tone, "Did I say something funny?"

Pricer, sitting next to Jaschke, slapped him on the back. He shook his head, gasping to try to gain control of his breath, and leaned forward. When he was finally able to speak, he shook his head again and said, "You had to have been there," then doubled over with more laughter.

Jaschke now looked confused as well as offended—he *had* been there, so why was he being laughed at?

Kindy managed to pull himself together and leaned across the table to grasp Jaschke's forearm. "Don't sweat it, new guy. When you've been here awhile, you'll know that we didn't do it, we didn't show anybody—not until the Skipper says we did."

That set off another peal of laughter around the table, wiping away any trace of mollification from Jaschke's face. "But didn't you see the shit-eating grin on Staff Sergeant Fryman's face when he rejoined us?" he demanded.

Now Bingh had regained control. "New guy, our section leader is a new guy, too. He doesn't know yet, either," he declaimed.

Jaschke looked at Ellis, the only other Marine in the room who was new to Fourth Force Recon—and the only other man who hadn't started laughing again at Fryman's being another new guy. Ellis just shrugged; he looked as confused as Jaschke.

Finally Bingh, the senior man present, sat erect, sucked in

a deep breath and held it for a moment, then bellowed, "Shit-can the grabass, people!"

There was a brief roar of laughter at that, which cut off when Bingh reached out and smacked Wehrli on the back of his head. An instant later, Kindy stopped laughing and did the same to Corporal Mikel Nomonon. Everyone stopped laughing, though it was an obvious struggle for most of them.

Corporal Gin Musica almost lost it again when the door suddenly opened and their waitresses reentered with trays of food, but he choked his laughter back when Bingh glared at him.

As soon as the waitresses were gone again, Bingh growled, "By the numbers, people. Eat!"

Kindy couldn't help laughing at that, but was the only one who did, so he quickly stopped. They ate in silence for several minutes.

Sometime later, when the edge was off his appetite, Bingh cleared his throat and said softly, "I wish I could have seen the expression on that doggie colonel's face when Staff Sergeant Fryman told him his HQ was wiped out."

"He must have been pissed something fierce," Nomonon said.

Bingh nodded. "I overheard Staff Sergeant Fryman telling Gunny Lytle the doggie tried to overrule him, but the referee who followed him into the colonel's tent had already radioed in his report on the action."

Kindy chuckled. "And you heard what the Skipper said when he debriefed us."

Commander Walt Obannion, the commanding officer of Fourth Force Recon Company, told the squads who'd run the raid in the training exercise that the commander of the Con-federation Army's 525th Heavy Infantry Regiment had lodged an official protest. Exercise Sea Eagle had pitted the army's Eighty-sixth Infantry Division against three Marine FISTs in a force-on-force training exercise in Camp Basilone's huge train-ing area. The Marines relished the opportunity to go up against a larger, better-equipped, and more heavily armed force and fight circles around it. The army relished the opportunity to put the Marines in their place by kicking their asses all over the training area.

The army hadn't expected the Marines to insert Force Recon elements into the exercise and declared that the use of Force Recon was outside the scheme of the exercise, so the results of its actions should be discounted. The raid conducted by the eight Marines having dinner in the Snoop 'n Poop had so thoroughly disrupted the army's operational plans that the three FISTs were now close to defeating the division, despite still being outnumbered five to one on the battlefield.

"Did they really think we wouldn't use every available asset?" Musica asked rhetorically.

Wehrli snorted. "Shit, they probably thought the Raptors already gave the FISTs an unfair advantage."

Pricer shook his head at the army's obtuseness. "I'm surprised the army hasn't figured out that having our own aircraft is one of the things that makes Marines more effective fighters than anybody else."

"Semper Fi, brother," Bingh said, and held a hand up for Pricer to slap. Bingh turned solemn and asked, "You understand why they picked us for that exercise, don't you?"

Most of them nodded, but Jaschke and Ellis looked blank. Bingh looked at them and explained.

"The three of us"—he gestured to indicate himself, Musica, and Pricer—"were wounded on our last op. It was a test to see if we'd recovered enough to go on live ops. Sergeant Kindy is in his first command as a squad leader; they wanted to see how he'd handle it. You two"—Bingh pointed at Jaschke and Ellis—"and Staff Sergeant Fryman are new— Fryman's been in Force Recon before, and he's been a platoon sergeant in a FIST, but this is his first assignment as a Force Recon section leader. They wanted to see how the three of you would function. The only ones of us who *weren't* being tested, who were just being trained, were Nomonon and Wehrli." Bingh grinned broadly. "I think we passed."

"OOO-RAH!" they roared, and clanked mugs.

Later, after they finished eating, and after they'd drunk

several more pitchers of Onofre Ale, the eight Marines of first and third squads, second platoon, Fourth Force Recon Company, went in search of female companionship. The two sergeants and a couple of the corporals had steady lady friends whom they went to see; the other four split into pairs and went on the prowl.

Headquarters, Fourth Fleet Marines, Camp Basilone, Halfway

As late as it was, Lieutenant General Ramses Indrus, Commanding General, Fourth Fleet Marines, his operations officer Colonel Lars Szilk, and Commander Walt Obannion of Fourth Force Recon Company were still at work. They weren't planning a new Force Recon mission, they were doing something of far less importance to them: they were dealing with some very upset army officers. Indrus, flanked by Szilk and Obannion, sat on one side of a conference table. Opposite him was Lieutenant General Thom Kratson, commander of the Confederation Army's XI Corps, who was on Halfway to observe the training exercise. To his left were Brigadier General Lusey and Brigadier General Judite, respectively the corps G3 and assistant division commander of the Eighty-sixth Infantry Division; Major General Nikil, the commander of the Eighty-sixth wasn't present, he was still engaged in the exercise. On Kratson's right was his chief of staff, Major General Olgah. Colonel Evava, commander of the 525th Heavy Infantry Regiment, sat next to Major General Olgah. The four army generals and the colonel were furious.

Even though there was only one flag officer among the three Marines, they weren't any more intimidated by the seven stars opposing them than they were by being outnumbered five to three.

"My Marines were within Standard Operating Procedure, General," Indrus patiently explained for what felt like the thousanth time, but probably wasn't more than the twentieth. "Fourth Fleet Marines Headquarters received a request—"

Kratson slammed a hand on the tabletop and thundered,

"Force Recon wasn't in the Marine Order of Battle for this exercise. You cheated by introducing them!"

Indrus looked at him blandly and continued almost as though he hadn't been interrupted. "—received a request from the FISTs engaged with opposing forces for a Force Recon raid. It is Standard Operating Procedure for such requests from a multiple FIST operation to be honored by this command if such assets are available."

"But—"

Indrus raised his voice to ride over Kratson's objection. He knew what the army general was going to say, he'd heard it several times already. "The operational plan for this exercise stated that no reinforcements were available within twenty-five light-years, I know that. But the op/plan also stated that it was within eight lights of a Fleet Marine Headquarters. FMHQ, as I'm sure you know, is where Force Recon companies are based. My staff, on my orders, held off on opening the request for thirty hours, to simulate transit time via drone from the area of operations to this headquarters. After 'receiving' the request, they wrote and issued an operation order to Fourth Force Recon Company. The selected squads took the normal time to prepare for such a mission. They then delayed four days before making planetfall, to simulate the transit time from here to the area of operation."

Indrus folded his arms on the tabletop and leaned forward. "Let me tell you a story, General," he said conversationally. "Way back, when I was a young lance corporal in Thirty-eighth FIST, my company commander told me something, not in a company formation, but just him and me in his office. He said, 'Lance Corporal, there's no such thing as a fair fight. One side or the other always has an advantage. When you get into a fight, it's up to you to find the advantage.'

"My Marines didn't cheat, General. They found an advantage and didn't copy the opposition commander on their plans."

Kratson's lip curled at Indrus's story. He then took a deep breath and made a valiant, and almost successful, attempt to sound reasonable. "General, I'm not saying my soldiers should have been copied on your plans. But you stepped outside the normal limits of Force Recon's functions. Force Recon is tasked to aid the Confederation Army, allied forces, and Marine forces commanded by a major general or higher. You—"

Indrus held up a hand to stop him. "Not quite. There is no requirement for a Marine major general to put in a request for Force Recon. Force Recon may be tasked in *any* multiple FIST mission. The commanders of the three FISTs facing the Eighty-sixth Division consulted, then the senior of them put in the request. As per doctrine. My command honored the request, as our tasking allows." Indrus turned for the first time since he'd sat down to the man sitting alone at the end of the table, a Confederation Navy commodore with a referee's brassard on his sleeve. "Am I right, sir?"

Commodore Petrch tapped a query into his console, read what came up, and nodded. "That's right, sir," he said. "NavReg 94, section 42b, paragraph five. 'On a multi-FIST operation, in the absence of a higher-ranking officer, if the FIST commanders are in concurrence, the senior among them may request that the appropriate Fleet Marine Force detach a Force Recon element(s) to provide appropriate assistance.' " Petrch looked at Kratson. "The Marines were operating within the rules, sir. I have to find against Colonel Evava."

Kratson jerked to his feet. "We'll see about this," he snapped. He spun about and stormed from the room, knocking his chair over as he went. The other four army officers hustled after him.

The three Marines and the commodore sat looking at the doorway for a moment, then Indrus rose to his feet. "It's been a long day, gentlemen," he said dourly. "I believe we are entitled to a drink." He turned to Petrch and added, "Commodore, I would invite you to join us, but I'm afraid that would give the impression of impropriety, and the appearance of impropriety is something we need to avoid at this juncture."

"I thank you for the thought, General," Petrch said, also rising. "You're right about the appearance of impropriety,

though there is none. Now I should get back to my duties. By
your leave, sir?"

Indrus nodded and Petrch left. "Gentlemen," Indrus said
when the three Marines were alone, "Flag Club. My treat."
He didn't say anything to Szilk or Obannion, but internally
he was seething at Kratson's obtuseness; that kind of thinking on the part of a general could lose a campaign. When the
enemy introduces an unexpected element, a commander
doesn't complain about it, he deals with it.

The Peepsight, Havelock, Halfway

The snipers of Fourth Force Recon Company seldom frequented the Snoop 'n Poop with the rest of second platoon.
The favorite watering-cum-dining salon of all of Fourth Force
Recon Company's snipers was The Peepsight, on Matthews
Avenue. The decor of The Peepsight was clearly designed to
appeal to expert marksmen: an astonishing array of targets,
designed for an equally astonishing variety of individual weapons, adorned the walls; shooting trophies rather than bottles
lined the shelves behind the bar and served as lamp bases on
the tables; match-conditioned shoulder weapons were mounted
on the walls above the targets; recorded sounds of sniper weapons, whether the almost inaudible humm of the M14A5 maser,
the blast of the M2Z midrange sabot rifle, or the loud boom
of the long-range M111 fin-stabilized rifle, echoed randomly
from speakers placed throughout the main room. The M111's
boom was always accompanied by a bright actinic flash from
hidden LEDs.

Fourth Force Recon Company's snipers weren't the only
patrons of The Peepsight—the place would quickly go out of
business if they were. After all, a customer base of twenty-
eight people, some of whom were always off-planet at any
given time, simply wasn't enough to sustain a bar-restaurant.
Base personnel also frequented The Peepsight, most of them
from Camp Howard or Camp Hathcock, two of the smaller
"camps" that made up the eighty-thousand-square-kilometer
establishment called Marine Corps Base Camp Basilone.

Those Marines pulled liberty in Havelock for the same reason the Marines of Fourth Force Recon did—it was conveniently located to both. Some went to The Peepsight because its food and drink were high quality and reasonably priced. Some because of its weaponry décor and its military ambience. Others because the presence of the snipers made them feel more like real Marines than like the pogues the combat-arms Marines considered them to be. Yet others were sniper groupies. Whatever their reasons, the snipers didn't scare them as much as the reconmen of Fourth Force Recon, which was why they were at The Peepsight rather than the Snoop 'n Poop.

The snipers had their own corner of the main room, and a stretch of the long bar was unofficially reserved for them, and just about everyone knew to vacate those places when the snipers came in.

Of course, except for the snipers not many of The Peepsight's patrons knew what a peep sight was.

So it wasn't surprising that The Peepsight was the place where Lance Corporal Bella Dwan was most likely to be found when she pulled liberty in Havelock.

As usual when she was there, Bella Dwan sat more or less alone, nursing something pink in a tall glass. The "more" was because nobody much engaged her in conversation. The "less" was because Sergeant Ivo Gossner, her team leader and spotter, sat at the same table with her, though he engaged with snipers at other tables far more than he did with her. Dwan didn't feel at all put out by being virtually ignored by the other snipers. She seemed interested in nothing but weapons, marksmanship, and kills, while the other snipers indulged in a much wider range of conversational topics.

Bella Dwan was petite and pixie-faced, with tight, blondish curls haloing her head. She looked like your best friend's favorite kid sister, the one you felt protectively brotherly toward. Until you looked into her eyes. *Nobody's* favorite kid sister had eyes like that. They were cold and hard and looked as if she were painting a pretty sight-picture on you, were only waiting for a vagrant breeze to blow its course before squeezing the trigger and ending your miserable life.

Everybody at Camp Howard and Camp Hathcock knew about the Queen of Killers and knew to stay out of her way.

But then there were those who might be called sniper groupies.

"Hi, Bella," a tall, muscular, blond man said, sitting down at Bella Dwan's table without asking. He was in civilian clothes, but his way of holding himself and his high-and-tight haircut marked him as surely as would a uniform as a Marine. "Evening, Sergeant," the tall Marine said to Gossner. He either didn't see or chose to ignore the warning look Gossner gave him and turned his attention back to Dwan.

"It's really nice to see you back," Blondie said to her. He'd tried to make conversation with her before. With the other snipers too, but mostly with Dwan; often enough that they all called him Blondie, and none bothered to find out or remember his name or rank, though if pressed they'd allow he was probably a corporal. "We missed you." He waved vaguely at the other patrons. "And you too, Sergeant," to Gossner. Gossner turned away from Blondie, Dwan hadn't yet looked at him. "That must have been some mission you were on. I mean, just the two of you. You were gone for weeks. Nobody"—again he waved at the room—"has heard anything about it. Where'd you go? What did you do?" He paused to let her answer, or for Gossner to say something. When neither did, he continued.

"You know, usually when a sniper team goes out, we all know all about it by the time you get back. This time, nobody knows squat, and we're dying to find out what you did. So where'd you go?"

Gossner looked at him briefly, muttered, "You just said something more true than you realize," and looked away again.

Conversation among the other snipers ebbed, then died, as Blondie talked, and they all started listening. Many of them hoped that Gossner or Dwan would say *something* about the assignment. All any of them knew was that the mission was so tightly held that the pair weren't allowed to say *anything* about it. None of them had ever heard of a Force Recon mission so secret that those who went on it didn't ever tell anybody else in the company. And *all* of them were watching and waiting to see how Dwan would deal with Blondie's pestering.

"Come on, Bella, you can tell me, sweetheart." Blondie put his hand on Dwan's wrist. The hush in that corner of the room seemed to suddenly suck in its breath. Blondie didn't notice. "Come on, we're just a bunch of pogues, you know that. We have to live vicarously through you. Tell me."

Dwan looked at the hand gently holding her wrist and murmured, "Move it."

Blondie jerked his hand back as though it had just been jolted by a thousand volts of electricity. "Uh, oh, sure, Bella. I didn't mean anything by that. Just being friendly, you know that."

She finally looked at him and her lips curled into what would have been a sweet smile, had it extended beyond her mouth.

Blondie looked relieved but Gossner tensed; he had a good idea what was coming.

"It's so good to have you back, Bella," Blondie said. "I like you, I like you a lot. You know that, don't you?" So did a lot of other men—at first meeting; one look into her eyes backed most of them off. But Blondie wasn't looking into her eyes, he was focusing on her lips. "So where did you go? What did you and the sergeant do?" He grinned what he thought was the grin of a harmless, trustworthy man.

"I can't tell you," Dwan said softly.

"Ah, you can tell me, Bella. Please?"

Dwan lowered her eyelids as though she were thinking it over. Then she looked into his eyes and said just as softly as before, "Yes, I could tell you. But then I'd have to kill you. And everyone else who overheard."

"Oh, you don't mean that, Bella, do y—" He lifted his gaze a few inches from her mouth to her eyes. Death was looking back at him. His throat suddenly thickened and his voice harshened. "Ah, listen, ah, Bella, ah, Lance Corporal Dwan. I-I'm sorry I bothered you. No harm meant." His chair scraped and fell over as he pushed back and to his feet. He hastened away.

"Damn," one of the other snipers whispered. "I was hoping she'd say something."

"Be glad she didn't *do* something," one of the others whispered back.

CHAPTER
FOUR

Sergeant Major Maurice Periz had a problem with two of his Marines. The problem wasn't something they had *done*. The problem was that he didn't *know* what they had done. Periz was the senior enlisted man of Fourth Force Recon Company, and as such he believed it was his mission to take care of his Marines; to look out for their interests when they got into trouble; to be intermediary between them and higher command; to take care of their welfare in general. He also firmly believed that, to accomplish his mission, he had to know everything his Marines did—at least everything they did in the course of their duties, if not everything they did even when off duty. As sergeant major, he was involved, at least peripherally, in the planning of every mission his Marines were sent on.

With one exception.

Two of his Marines had recently returned from a mission on which he'd been closed out of the planning. Totally. Completely. He hadn't even been told where the two Marines were going or the nature of the mission.

Well, he could guess at the nature of the mission—the two Marines were a sniper team, so obviously they had been sent somewhere to ply their trade. But where and against whom?

Commander Obannion, the company commander, had told him he was better off not knowing where they went and what they were doing. He even forbade Periz to question the snipers about the mission.

33

This mission was so wrapped in secrecy that Periz just *knew* there would be serious repercussions if word of it was ever made public. If that happened, he wouldn't be able to take care of his people because he didn't know what they had done.

So he *had* to know.

Sniper Range, Camp Hathcock, Halfway

Lance Corporal Bella Dwan was doing what she most often did when she didn't have other required duties: she was on the range at Camp Hathcock, honing her already considerable skills with her M14A5 maser. As was normal when Dwan was on the range, Sergeant Ivo Gossner was spotting for her and overseeing the bank of automated sniper targets. As both her superior and her team leader, he should also have been coaching her, but Dwan's skill with the maser far exceeded Gossner's, so he did little coaching. Indeed, he agreed with her assessment that she was the best shot with the maser in all of Human Space; he even acknowledged that she was the best overall sniper he'd ever seen. He didn't agree, though, that she was the best with all the sniper weapons. He himself was her equal with the midrange M2Z sabot rifle and somewhat better with the long-range M111 fin-stabilized rifle. Not that he'd say that in front of her, of course. Like other Marines, he was wary of her—particularly in the aftermath of their last mission.

The range was where Sergeant Major Periz found them.

Targets briefly appeared here and there, at distances ranging from two hundred to four hundred meters. Some poked around the sides of obstacles, others appeared in the windows of mock-up buildings, a few were completely out in the open. They were in sunlight and in shadow, or half and half. None stayed up for more than four seconds. In the brief time Gossner and Dwan had to spot them, she had to draw a sight-picture on the target and fire, holding her aim for the three-quarters of a second required to kill at four hundred meters. Some targets dropped out of sight before Dwan could shoot them, and others before she locked on for the required time. Still, she "killed" about 75 percent of her targets. Periz watched for a while. As often as he had seen Dwan shoot, he was still impressed by her ability with the maser.

But Periz wasn't on the range to observe, he was there to get some answers. He waited until Gossner was finished recording one of Dwan's shots and the two were seeking another target, then called out their names.

"Good morning, Sergeant Major," Gossner said, standing and coming to an easy attention at Periz's approach.

"Sergeant Major," Dwan said as she rose into an approximation of attention.

"That's some good shooting, Lance Corporal," Periz said, looking downrange and shaking his head in semidisbelief.

"It's why I get the big bucks, sir," Dwan said. Gossner nudged her with his elbow. She elbowed him back, harder.

"Is the maser what you used on your last mission?" Periz asked.

Dwan looked away, almost turned her back on him. Gossner looked uncomfortable.

"Come on, tell me about it. I'm your top sergeant."

"Sir, we're under strict orders not to say anything about that mission," Gossner said.

"That's all right. I'm your sergeant major, you can tell me."

Now Dwan did turn her back and folded her arms under her breasts.

"I know that, sir," Gossner said, "but our orders were very clear, we aren't to speak to *anybody* about that mission."

"Buddha's blue balls, Sergeant! I'm not just *anybody*, I'm your sergeant major! You *have* to tell me!"

Dwan spat.

"Nosir." Gossner stood at a rigid attention, eyes straight ahead, face expressionless.

"Sergeant, you *will* tell me about your last mission. That's an order!"

"Nosir, I will not."

Periz stepped close to Gossner and leaned in so his face was inches from the other man's. "Refusing an order is insubordination, Sergeant. You *will* tell me or I'll have your ass up on charges for insubordination!"

"Sir!" Gossner's voice thickened. "There are many things the sergeant major can do to a sergeant, but the sergeant major *cannot* bring a sergeant up on insubordination charges for refusing to tell the sergeant major something the sergeant was expressly ordered by much higher authority *not* to tell the sergeant major."

Periz drew back, still glowering. Gossner was right, and Periz knew it. If he wanted to, he could make life miserable for the junior man, but that went against his grain; making Gossner's life miserable wouldn't be taking care of his people. But he still had to know what Gossner and Dwan had done. So he'd find another way to do it.

But a sergeant major doesn't simply back off from a sergeant and a lance corporal; just backing off after making a threat could cost him respect. He continued glowering.

"We'll see what I can and cannot do, Sergeant," Periz growled. "You just watch your ass, both of you. I *am* going to find out what you did." He spun about and stalked away.

When his footsteps faded, Dwan turned around and looked after him.

"He can't do anything to us for not telling, can he?" she asked.

Gossner shook his head. "There are a lot of things he can do, but he won't do them. I think he knows we'd be in deep shit if we broke security on that mission, so he won't punish us. Remember, his top priority is taking care of his people; punishing us for obeying orders isn't taking care of us. But he's going to keep trying to find out until somebody very much higher steps on him." Gossner paused, then softly added, "I only hope he gets stopped before he lands in Darkside."

Camp Howard, Halfway

The relationship between Fourth Force Recon Company's commanding officer, Commander Walt Obannion, and Sergeant Major Maurice Periz had cooled sharply as soon as Periz had been frozen out of planning for, and even knowledge of, the mission Gossner and Dwan had been sent on. But enough time had gone by that the freeze was thawing. It was only a couple of weeks after Gossner and Dwan had returned from the mission when one morning Periz joined Obannion for the commander's morning run, one they'd made together for as long as both men had been with the company.

But Periz wasn't about to stop trying to find out about that mission.

Daybreak the morning after Periz had confronted Gossner and Dwan on the sniper range found him and Obannion moving effortlessly along Camp Howard's track. That morning they were on the medium course of three, fifteen kilometers of winding trail that led over undulating terrain, through woods and marsh, over alkaline flats. The trail was marked, but not cleared where it went over a rubble-covered stretch of broken rock. The last kilometer and a half was along a sandy beach. Some days Captain Qindall or Captain Wainwright, respectively the company's executive officer and its operations officer, or other members of the headquarters element joined them. But that morning, they ran alone.

They were more than ten kilometers into the run, breathing easily, flowing sweat keeping their bodies from overheating, legs pumping smoothly. In another fifteen minutes they'd begin walking to cool down, then shower, replenish lost fluids, change into garrison utilities, and eat breakfast before heading for the company office.

"I gotta know, Walt," Periz said, breaking the companionable silence in which they'd run until then.

"What do you gotta know, Morrie?" Obannion replied.

"What did Gossner and Dwan do?"

Obannion closed his eyes for a few paces—that was the last question he wanted to hear from Periz. He opened his eyes and said, "You've known from the beginning I can't tell you that."

"Dammit, Skipper." Periz shifted into more formal mode.

"I'm top dog in this company. I *have* to know what my Marines are doing. I *have* to know what their missions are."

Obannion didn't say anything for another fifty meters. When he did, he also adopted a more formal mode. "Sergeant Major, I know you have to know what your Marines are doing. I also know that I'm under strictest orders not to divulge what their last mission was to *anyone.* Unfortunately, 'anyone' includes you."

"Dammit!" Periz snorted, but didn't say anything else for a couple of hundred meters.

"Come on, Walt." Periz relaxed back to informality. "We've been together for a long time. Hell, we were squadmates way back when we first joined First Force Recon Company. You know I have the need to know, and you know you can trust me."

"I know that, Morrie. But, dammit, the security lock on that mission came from very much higher-higher. I *can't* tell you!"

Periz snorted. "Sure, higher-higher. I'll request mast with General Indrus—I can do that you know—he'll tell me." *Request mast,* the right to go to any commander up the chain of command, with a problem or question.

Obannion shook his head, certain that Periz would see it in his peripheral vision. "The orders came from higher then CG, Fourth Fleet Marines. He's under the same nondisclosure orders I am."

Periz blinked, then shook his head. "I know the Sergeant Major of the Marine Corps. He was my first sergeant when I was a gunny in Eleventh FIST. Hell, it's his fault I'm a sergeant major today instead of a captain or even a commander. He's the one who taught me that taking care of my Marines is more valuable than leading them. I'll go to him. I can't take care of my people if I don't know about their missions."

"Drop it, Morrie," Obannion snapped. "This came from higher than the Commandant."

Periz clamped a hand on Obannion's arm and slowed to a

walk, dragging his commanding officer with him. He stopped and turned to face Obannion.

"What in the nine levels of Hades is going on here?" He was almost shouting.

Obannion stared into Periz's eyes, his jaw working as he decided what to say. Then he said slowly, "Morrie, that mission is so secret that I doubt there are twenty people in all of Human Space who know about it." He stared into the sergeant major's eyes for a long moment, then worked his jaw again and said, "Morrie, it carries a Darkside penalty. If word about that mission gets out, *everybody* who knows about it goes to Darkside."

That stunned Periz. He let go of Obannion's arm, heaved a deep breath, and asked, "How high up does the penalty go?"

"I don't know. Maybe as high as General Indrus. Maybe higher. I *do* know that it includes everyone in Fourth Force Recon Company who knows about the mission. I won't put you in that kind of jeopardy, which is what would happen if I told you what that mission was." Abruptly, he turned from Periz and broke off the running course, heading straight for his quarters.

Periz stood staring after him for a moment, then shook his head and muttered, "This isn't right." Darkside was a prison world. Some of its inmates were sentenced to Darkside after a formal trial, others were condemned to Darkside via extrajudicial actions. Darkside was a life sentence, nobody ever left it. The worst criminals were consigned to Darkside, people too dangerous ever to be returned to society. So were people who knew secrets the government couldn't risk being released to the public. "This isn't right at all," Periz muttered. Slowly, he began trotting at a tangent to his company commander's path, toward his own quarters.

CHAPTER
FIVE

An Alley, Cecil Roads

Sergeant Jak Daly, his head throbbing like an FTL drive, awoke in a dark alley somewhere behind the Strip. He tried to sit up but the throbbing in his head grew so intense at the effort that he had to lie back down and catch his breath. "Ohhhh," he groaned. His stomach heaved violently and he rolled to one side despite the intense pain in his head and vomited up the previous night's steak. Once that ordeal was through, he managed to get to his knees and then, using the building beside where he lay to brace himself, painfully got to his feet.

Daly steadied himself against the wall, breathing in the cool morning air. It was morning, the light had grown considerably brighter since he'd regained consciousness. "The oldest trick in the book," he muttered, holding his head with his free hand. The pain and nausea began to subside a little so he ventured a few faltering steps. When he discovered he could stand without leaning against anything, he stepped out into the alley. He stood there for a long time, growing more confident of his balance. After a while he reached for his wallet. It had been stuffed carelessly down inside his tunic. It was empty. No surprise there. His wrist chronometer was gone too, that was to be expected.

Daly stood there holding the empty wallet and swore. "That bitch and that fucking bartender," he muttered. They'd slipped him a Mickey Finn special and rolled him like a common drunk. Fortunately, he'd left most of his money and his debit card in his room the night before, but he was still out over a thousand credits, a month's pay for an NCO in his grade and with his time in service. *A thousand credits.* It wasn't so much the loss of the money as the way he'd lost it that upset Daly the most. How could he have fallen for such a scam? Him, a Force Recon Marine, a combat veteran, a man who always sized up his environment before making any move.

His only goal just then was to find his way back to his hotel room and get better. Since he could clearly see the remains of the meal he'd eaten last night on the ground behind him, he reasoned this must be the morning after his arrival, which meant he had another day before he could get off the planet and be on his way again.

Hotel Victoria, Cecil Roads

"My god, sir, looks like you had a hard night," the hotel clerk exclaimed as Daly walked into the lobby of the Hotel Victoria.

"That isn't the half of it," Daly muttered as he headed for the elevators. Then he turned back to the clerk. "What time does the night clerk come on?"

"Eighteen hours, sir."

"Will the clerk who's on tonight be the same one who was here last night?"

"Yes, sir," the man answered, checking his console. "Name's Delaney."

"Good." Daly nodded and headed back toward the elevators. He had nearly twelve hours to get himself back into shape. The *Miomai* didn't leave until the next day. That would leave him all night to take care of what he had to do.

Daly found his room in order. The Hotel Victoria used old-fashioned digital codes to open the locks on its doors. That meant Zephyr and Henri hadn't been able to get the code out of him and that the hotel management, which could override the security system, wasn't in on the scam.

Daly stripped off his clothing, took a long, hot shower, then he did what any smart Force Recon Marine would do under the circumstances, he ate a hearty breakfast and went to bed.

Feeling human once again, Sergeant Daly stepped into the lobby carrying his bag. The lobby was empty at that hour. A stocky, red-faced man who he assumed must be Delaney, the night clerk, stood at the desk. On a hunch Daly greeted the man in Irish Gaelic. Without looking up, the man responded automatically with a welcome in the same language. Then he looked up and his red face turned even redder.

"Ah, Mr. Daly!" He straightened up and stepped back from the counter a pace. "You are from New Cobh, I take it? I didn't know." New Cobh had been settled by a group of unusually dissident Irish, and for two hundred years it had been compulsory that every schoolchild there learn Irish Gaelic as well as Standard English.

"I am, Mr. Delaney." The two faced each other silently for a moment and then shook hands warmly. "I'm from Lake Carra. You?"

Delaney nodded, "New Mallow."

"I need some information, Mr. Delaney."

"You shall have it." Delaney nodded.

"Last night—"

"Ah!"

"Last night, did you see me leaving here in the company of the bartender, Henri I think his name is, and a woman, possibly a frequent visitor to the bar upstairs? Name of Zephyr—or that's the name she used last night. Buxom lass, auburn hair, fair complexion, but she had a mole on her right cheekbone and—"

"Yes, Mr. Daly, I know them and you did leave here with them, but not quite under your own power, if you know what I mean. You appeared to be quite, well, you know—"

"Yeah. Well, we had a simply great time last night, Mr. Delaney, and I'd like to join up with them again tonight. Where can I find them, can you tell me that? I've been up to the bar and Henri's not on tonight and the bartender who is claims he doesn't know this Zephyr."

Delaney regarded Daly carefully for a moment, making up his mind, then he leaned across the counter. "Bad people, Mr. Daly. I'm sorry you got hooked up with them. Why would you ever want to have any more to do with them?"

Daly shrugged. "I left my watch in the woman's flat, Mr. Delaney, and I want it back."

"Well, my advice, Mr. Daly, is forget them. They're trouble."

"No, Mr. Delaney," Daly said carefully, leaning in toward the clerk and speaking in a conspiratorial tone, "it's *I* who am trouble. Now tell me what you know about these people."

On the Streets of Cecil Roads

Outside, the sun was well above the horizon. The bartender's name really was Henri, although Delaney didn't know his last name. Henri worked occasionally at the Victoria, but his real employment was as a pimp for women like Zephyr, who operated under several names: Esmeralda, Connie, and others. Delaney did not know where they lived, but he gave Daly the names of several joints along the Strip where they might be found after 18 hours. Daly smiled to himself. Pinning these two down would be like hunting the legendary vampire who slept in the day and prowled at night, except Sergeant Jak Daly was just as deadly in the day as he was in the dark—and *very* good at finding his objective at night.

Daly's shuttle to the orbital station was due to leave at 8 hours the next day. That would give him a good twelve hours to find the pair and the rest of the day to get ready. After his conversation with Delaney, Daly checked out of the Hotel Victoria. If he finished his mission early, he planned to spend the rest of the night in the lounge at the ground terminal until the shuttle was ready to depart.

Daly's plan was simple. He had the names of four bars on the Strip where Henri and Zephyr were known to hang out. He'd simply rotate among the four. In each place he'd find a spot to hang out, nurse a drink, remain inconspicuous, and wait patiently for his prey. If they were taking a night off, well, he'd leave in the morning as planned and just chalk the whole thing up to experience. But something told him he wouldn't have long to wait.

The first place on his list was called the River Queen and it was a dump. He didn't remain there very long. Toward midnight as he was reading *Rally Point* in a dark corner of a bar called Aces Up, he finally spotted Zephyr. He put the book into his travel bag and slid farther back into the corner of his booth. The man with Zephyr was not quite sober. As they took places at the bar, the man drunkenly announced, "I'm six months out from Carhart's World and ready to have some fun!" That meant the poor jerk had six months' pay in his pockets. Zephyr wouldn't need knockout drops to relieve this man of his hard-earned cash. In a few minutes they moved to a booth where Daly couldn't see them, but he could see the door, and when at last Zephyr got up to leave, he followed her out. Her latest victim, oblivious to her sudden departure, snored happily in his booth.

Zephyr walked quickly down the street and disappeared into a doorway about a block from the Aces Up. Daly caught her and Henri as they were gloating over the drunk's wallet. For just a brief instant the pair stood there like feral beasts caught in the bright lights of an oncoming car, totally unprepared for what was about to befall them. Daly had the lean and sinuous strength of the typical Force Recon Marine, was quick on his feet, and an expert in unarmed combat.

"Hi!" he announced cheerily as he drove his fist straight into Henri's sharp little nose, smashing it with a satisfying *crrrrrunch* that sent blood and snot flying in all directions. Daly's fist proved to be the last thing Henri saw that evening. Daly pivoted smoothly, grabbed Zephyr by the throat, and slammed her up against the wall. "Let's see what you have there," he said, snatching the drunk's wallet from her hand.

"Urk, urk, urk!" Zephyr gasped.

"Sorry, I don't usually treat ladies like this. You owe a certain gentleman snoozing away back at the Aces Up some money, ma'am. I presume it's in here?" he shook the wallet in his free hand. The light in the doorway was too dim to inspect its contents, so he slid it inside his jacket. He shoved Zephyr roughly into a corner where she collapsed, gasping for breath. "Stay right there," he told her. "Now we attend to the money that you owe me." He rolled Henri onto his back and swiftly checked his clothing, removing a fat wad of bills. Henri groaned. Daly slammed his head hard into the ground. "Now"—he stood up—"there is the little matter of my wrist chrono, lady. Where is it?"

"I-I—it's at home," Zephyr gasped, scuttling fearfully as far into the corner as she could get.

"All right, keep the goddamned thing then, and every time you look at it, you remember me, lady. And you tell your 'manager' here, if I *ever* see either of you two again, I'll personally rip your fucking guts out." He rammed his fist one more time into Henri's smashed nose for good measure and left them there.

On his way to the port Daly stepped into the Aces Up and gently replaced the drunk's wallet.

The following morning Daly boarded the *Miomai* without incident. When he counted the wad of bills he'd taken off Henri, he found it contained more than four thousand credits.

Several times during the next few days Jak Daly wondered what the Tac officers at OTC would say if they knew how he, a potential ensign, had conducted himself on Cecil Roads. Well, they'd never know. But he knew what Sergeant Major Periz would say: "Damned fine job, Marine!"

Sergeant Jak Daly leaned back and smiled.

CHAPTER
SIX

On Board the <u>Miomai</u>, En Route to Arsenault

The *Miomai* was a "happy" starship because she and her crew took after their captain, Hakalau d'Colacs, known throughout the space lanes as Happy Hakalau because he was always in a good mood, all 140 kilos of him. He was an inveterate trencherman who thought everyone else should enjoy their food as much as he did, and his officers and guests dined sumptuously at his table, an ordinary spaceman's table in one corner of the ship's galley—not his cabin. Mealtimes were an occasion for socializing, during which he'd hold forth with torrents of commentary interspersed with good-natured gibes at members of the crew who happened to be dining nearby. His highest form of compliment was to refer to someone or something as "monstrous fine."

Only one other passenger besides Daly felt like eating at the first meal after the *Miomai*'s jump into Beamspace. He was an older, balding, heavyset government contractor returning to Earth for another assignment. He introduced himself to Daly as Bok—"call me Bokkie"—Merrifield. Besides Captain d'Colacs the only crew member to join them was the first mate, a man named Heming, who did not say much but who laughed often at Happy's jokes, which he really seemed to enjoy, not just because his captain made them.

Captain d'Colacs returned from the server with a heavily laden tray. "Monstrous fine!" he said of his food as he eased his bulk onto a stool and sorted out his silverware. "Arh, Mr.

Daly, Mr. Merrifield, I'm pleased you could join us. The lubbers usually don't take too well to food after their first jump."

"We've been jumped before," Merrifield said, laughing, winking at Daly, who grinned at the innuendo.

"Mr. Daly, are you a military man by any chance? I ask because you have a certain military air about you, and"— Captain d'Colacs shrugged as he forked a piece of steak into his mouth—"we're dropping you off at Arsenault."

"Yes, sir, I'm a Marine."

"Marine?" d'Colacs roared, and all the heads in the galley turned toward him. "Well, goddamned monstrous fine to have you on my ship, Mr. Daly." He extended a huge paw and shook Daly's hand vigorously. "Say, you feelin' poorly, lad?" He nodded at Daly's tray, which contained only a salad, a small portion of meat, and a bottle of water.

"No, I'm just fine, sir. I don't believe in eating very much when I can't burn it off."

"Eat, lad, eat, you've got to keep body and soul together." Captain d'Colacs laughed. "Well, Mr. Heming there and I are old navy men, aren't we, Heming? How 'bout you, Mr. Merrifield," he said, nodding at the contractor.

"I was in the army, Third Silvasian War. What do you do in the Marines, Mr. Daly?"

"I'm in Force Reconnaissance, sir."

Merrifield raised an eyebrow and nodded at the others. "No wonder he looks so lean and mean."

"Ah, this is monstrous fine," Captain d'Colacs enthused around a mouthful of potato. "Tonight at my table we're all old ex-military farts, just like being back in the fleet again! Well, excuse the expression, Mr. Daly, that does not include you, of course." The captain laughed. "You're no recruit, Mr. Daly, so are you going to Arsenault as cadre or attending some advanced specialty school?"

"Asshole!" Merrifield exclaimed. "How well I remember *that* goddamned place!"

"Arh, we've all been there! We have that in common!" Captain d'Colacs grinned. The others laughed and nodded in agreement. Arsenault, the Confederation's military training world, was known throughout the services as Asshole because that's what it was like there.

"Ah, no, sir, I'm going to Officer Training College. And if you gentlemen will please excuse me, I'd like you to call me Jak. This 'Mr. Daly' stuff can wait until after I'm commissioned."

"Spoken like a true gentleman! Monstrous fine! Gentlemen, raise your glasses to Mr. Daly!" They toasted. "And, Mr. Daly, let me tell you, this ship is carrying more than four thousand metric tons of fresh fruit for the troops on Arsenault. Yes, we stopped at Summerville's Gardens and loaded up on the stuff." Summerville's Gardens was the name given to a world developed by agribusiness and noted for the fine fruits grown there and exported throughout Human Space. "So you won't get scurvy while you're on Asshole," Captain d'Colacs roared.

The meal continued in an atmosphere of warm camaraderie, the four of them trading stories about their times in their respective military services. While alcohol consumption was permitted on most commercial vessels and the *Miomai*'s galley boasted a full cooler, the captain and his first officer drank sparingly. So did Daly, who got a beer after he'd finished his meal. But abstinence did not apply to Mr. Merrifield. The more he drank, the more loquacious and amusing he became until everyone in the galley was doubled over from his ribald stories and jokes. Finally Captain d'Colacs, wiping tears of laughter from his eyes, excused himself, which was the sign that the meal was over.

"Jak, ol' buddy," Merrifield slurred, draping an arm drunkenly around Daly's shoulders, "I have a lit-mus test I apply to every new man I meet. You know what that test is, Jak? That test is if he's ever forn, er, *worn* a uniform. Far as I'm concerned"—he shook his head gravely—"any man's been in the service, no matter what kind of an asshole he might be otherwise, he automatically, *auto-ma-tick-lee* gets ten points in my book. Yessir! Ten, count 'em! But Jak, ol' buddy, you get *twenny*!"

Besides Daly, the *Miomai*'s passengers consisted of a Scientific Pantheist minister, two Catholic nuns, a family of six returning home after a long tour with a mining company on a world far out on the borders of Human Space, and Bokkie Merrifield.

The minister, a tall, spare, middle-aged man named Durand Eastman, claimed to be a member of the Rochester Synod, and although he maintained that the sect did not proselytize, several times he engaged Daly in conversation over beer in the galley. "When you look out the observation ports, Jak, aren't you awed by the power and beauty and, yes, the *mystery* of the natural universe? To us this represents 'divinity,' but not in the Western, theistic sense. We belong to this universe, Jak, with all its wonders. We are one with all the life in it and with nature, which is all one great unity."

Daly, raised a Catholic, merely said, "Sounds reasonable to me."

The two nuns, Sister Bartholomay and Sister Henrietta, were nurses returning from missionary work on a newly established colony on Fitzhugh's World. They became concerned about Daly, not because he was a lapsed Catholic, of which he made no secret, but because to them he looked too thin and undernourished, and when finally he departed the *Miomai,* they pressed a basket lunch into his hands. "Jak, you will positively collapse before you finish your training if you don't eat properly," Sister Henrietta told him. "Cook prepared this for you under our supervision," she added proudly. Profoundly touched, Daly politely returned the food, telling the sisters that the Marine Corps absolutely forbade its officer candidates to bring—and here he slipped up—"pogey bait" onto the OTC campus.

The crew of the *Miomai* was a hardworking coterie of space bums with dirt under their fingernails, but they adopted Daly as if he were one of their own. Most of them, like their captain and first officer, had seen some military service, and they often referred to their starship as "the old sailors' home."

But it was the children of Parks and Latta Ontario— Charlotte, ten; Glen, eight; Edith, six; and Josephine, four— who became Daly's best friends. "I don't mind kids," he told their mother. "After all, what are Marines but big kids? Taking care of yours is actually good leadership training for me." Normally an uncontrollable mob of noise and bedlam, the children became docile in Daly's presence and listened with quiet fascination to the tales he told them of his adventures in the Corps. And when Josephine found out that Daly was leaving the *Miomai,* she was so upset she hid in her cabin and wouldn't come out until Daly went in and talked to her. "I'll see you in the Corps!" she exclaimed bravely when Daly at last picked her up and gave her a big farewell hug.

Bokkie Merrifield, none the better for the whiskey he'd been drinking all that day, exclaimed, "Zhak, when you get out of the Corps, come see me. I'll be sheaf—*chief* executive ossifer of my own company by then, if m' liver holds out, an' I'll hire you, m'boy! Remember! There *is* life after retirement!"

So when the time came at last for Jak Daly to depart the *Miomai,* it was almost like saying good-bye to his own family. Captain d'Colacs extended his massive paw as Daly prepared to board the shuttle that would take him to the surface of Arsenault.

"Ensign Daly," he said, "it's been a pleasure to have you aboard my ship. Let's do it again someday."

"To that, Captain, I say a hearty 'Aye, aye, sir!'" Daly paused for an instant before turning to go. Life aboard the *Miomai* reminded him poignantly of his own boisterous clan back on New Cobh. "Well, Captain"—he came to attention and delivered a smart salute—"it is time for this Marine to get his arse down on the Arsehole."

CHAPTER
SEVEN

Lieutenant General Indrus was no longer as stoic about it as he had been the first time he'd sat down with Lieutenant General Kratson to discuss the complaint lodged by Colonel Evava and seconded by Major General Nikil. Not only did Indrus feel, as he had the first three times the army had insisted on these sessions, that his time was being wasted, this time he was angered by Kratson's latest pronouncement: the XI Corps commander had forwarded a formal complaint to the Commandant of the Marine Corps and to the Combined Chiefs of Staff. Further, Kratson had forwarded a formal complaint against Commodore Petrch to the Chief of Naval Operations for, as the complaint alleged, "misinterpreting" the rules of the exercise.

"Well, sir," Indrus said, standing, Colonel Szilk and Commander Obannion standing with him, "if you have already forwarded your complaints to the Combined Chiefs and the CNO, I see no point in—" He stopped and looked toward the door of the conference room at the sound of its opening. A captain from the Operations section stood in the doorway.

"Excuse me, sir," the captain said, "but Comm just received a Most Urgent, Immediate Attention." He held a crystal extended in his hand.

"Give," Indrus said, reaching a hand out. The captain stepped forward and gave him the crystal. "Excuse me, gentlemen," Indrus said to Kratson and his followers. He popped the crystal into his reader and set the display for privacy. He quickly read

the message, then announced, "General Kratson, now you have
an opportunity to see how Force Recon responds to a live call
for assistance." He slid his reader over to Colonel Szilk.

Szilk read the message, then asked, "By your leave, sir?"

"Do it," Indrus answered. He told Commander Obannion
to go with Szilk.

Szilk popped the crystal from the reader and briskly left
the room, followed by the Force Recon commander.

Indrus looked at Kratson. "General, I have work to do. If you
wish, you may accompany me to observe. But," he finished
firmly, "stay out of my way, and don't interfere with my people." To Commodore Petrch, he added, "Commodore, you may
as well resume your interrupted duties." He strode out. The
chief referee closed his reader and excused himself, leaving
Kratson alone with his officers, a sour expression on his face.

"You may as well return to your duties, such as they are,"
Kratson said to Major General Olgah and Brigadier Generals
Lusey and Judite. "You, come with me," he said to Colonel
Evava.

The others stayed and stood at attention as Kratson stalked
out of the room. Evava waited until the other generals exited,
then hurried to catch up with Kratson.

```
          DIRECTORATE OF OPERATIONS
               HEADQUARTERS
          CONFEDERATION MARINE CORPS


***Most Urgent, Immediate Attention***Most
Urgent, Immediate Attention***

          ***Immediate Action Required***

TO: INDRUS, CG4FM, CAMBAS, HALFWAY
RE: SUPPORT OF ONGOING OPERATIONS, RAVENETTE

1. You are required to deploy all available
ForRec assets to support ongoing joint Marine/
```

Army operations in the armed conflict currently under way on Ravenette. The ForRec mission will be threefold:

A. Conduct reconnaissance missions behind hostile lines as required by ComNavForRav.

B. Conduct raids on hostile rear areas as required by ComNavForRav.

C. Conduct raids on targets of opportunity on hostile rear areas.

2. All available ForRec assets are to be deployed, to include ForRec assets currently on deployment to other missions, provided those assets can arrive at Ravenette in a timely manner and their redeployment from current missions will not unduly jeopardize the operations that they currently support. CG4FM discretion to be exercised in said redeployments.

> by order of
> Eggleston, LtGen
> for
> Aguinaldo, CMC

Most Urgent, Immediate AttentionMost Urgent, Immediate Attention***

Immediate Action Required

That was the order that Colonel Szilk showed Commander Obannion as soon as the two of them reached Fourth Fleet Marines Operations Center, the message that had allowed Lieutenant General Indrus to abruptly end the meeting with Lieutenant General Kratson.

"Start your preparations for deploying the people you have available," Szilk ordered Obannion as soon as the latter finished reading the orders. "I'll see which deployed squads can be redeployed." Then to a gunnery sergeant: "Gunny, get him transportation—now."

"Aye, aye, sir," Obannion replied. By the time he exited

the building, a landcar would be waiting to whisk him to his own headquarters.

Lieutenant General Kratson and Colonel Evava entered the OpCen immediately behind the Marines; Kratson tried to read the message over Obannion's shoulder. Szilk saw and glanced at Indrus, who gave a curt nod. When Obannion had finished reading the order, Szilk handed the reader to the army general.

A grimace flashed across Kratson's face when he read the orders. There was a real war on Ravenette, and one of his divisions was being wasted playing war games against Marines. "The Confederation forces on Ravenette need an army *division,* not a rump Force Recon company."

He meant to say it so softly only Evava could hear, but Indrus also heard him.

"General," Indrus said coldly, "you're right that the forces on Ravenette need more army divisions, and some are on their way. But Force Recon, properly utilized, is a force multiplier." He couldn't resist adding a dig: "You don't have to take my word for it, you can ask Major General Nikil what happened to his division when two Force Recon squads were added to the mix of Marines the Eighty-sixth Division is facing in its exercise."

Fourth Force Recon Company, Camp Howard, Halfway

More than half of the members of Fourth Force Recon Company on base at Camp Howard were in training away from the company area, so it was two hours before they were all brought back and could assemble behind the barracks. The two hours were by no means wasted time. Commander Obannion immediately put his entire staff to work preparing to move the company out.

When Obannion marched out of the barracks, his entire staff marched out behind him and took position to his rear when he took the company from First Sergeant Robeer Cottle.

Fourth Force Recon Company had more holes in its formation than would be expected in any similar-size unit formation. Most of those holes were because of the absence of elements on deployments, but two squads had just made it in from the field and hadn't had time to change out of their chameleons. Those Marines wore soft covers rather than helmets and had their gloves off, so at least their heads and hands were visible. First platoon was missing two of its eight squads, and fourth had four squads out. Third platoon was short an entire section, along with its platoon sergeant. Only second platoon was complete, but eight of its thirty-four Marines, including the platoon commander, were new, if not to Force Recon, at least to Fourth Force Recon Company. Moreover, not all of its men were fully recovered from wounds suffered in the platoon's recent deployment to the Ununified World of Atlas, though they were all well enough to deploy if necessary.

Of 170 Marines in the company, forty-three, including the corpsman who went with third platoon's first section, were absent on other duties; only 127 were on hand. And when the company departed, Obannion would have to leave behind a rump command element to handle matters in Camp Howard and deal with any currently deployed squads that returned before the rest of the company did.

Still, that left 120 members of the company available, and 120 Force Recon Marines could gather a tremendous amount of intelligence—and wreak unbelievable havoc in raids in the enemy's rear.

After looking over his company, Obannion addressed them.

"As you may know," he began, knowing full well that his Marines tried to keep current on events throughout Human Space so they could be as prepared as possible for deployments, "a coalition of twelve worlds is attempting to secede from the Confederation of Human Worlds. They have concentrated their forces on one of the twelve, a secondary Confederation-member world called Ravenette. All attempts by the Confederation to bring matters on Ravenette to a peaceful conclusion have been rejected by the Coalition, and hostilities have broken out.

"As of the most recent information I have, which could be

seriously out-of-date by now, one FIST and two Confederation Army divisions are on Ravenette, and more are on their way. The Confederation Navy has control of the space lanes around the planet. But the rebels have at least an entire field army, which has bottled up the Confederation forces on a peninsula on the main continent. Those forces are hard-pressed and are in danger of being overrun. They need the intelligence and the raiding capabilities that Fourth Force Recon Company can provide—and they need them last week.

"To that end, the entire company is deploying to Ravenette.

"When you are released from formation, liberty call will sound for twelve hours. That should be enough time for you to put your personal matters in order. When you report back for duty—I say again, in twelve hours—we will commence final preparations for the company to deploy. Within twenty-four hours of return to duty, the company will board the fast frigate *Admiral Stoloff* for transit to Ravenette.

"That is all I have for now." Obannion looked to First Sergeant Cottle. "Company Gunnery Sergeant, dismiss the company."

"Sir, aye, aye!" Cottle said sharply, and saluted.

Obannion returned the salute, about-faced, and marched back into the barracks. The staff followed him.

Cottle waited until Obannion and the staff were inside, then faced the company. "You yardbirds heard the man. You've got twelve hours to straighten out all your shit so it doesn't come apart while we're gone.

"COMP-ney, dis-MISSED! Twelve hours liberty call. NOW!"

Force Recon Marines prided themselves on their ability to deploy on only a few hours' notice, much faster than the two days it typically took a FIST to go from receipt of orders to liftoff to a waiting navy starship. All of the members of second platoon were back in the barracks within eight hours of being dismissed for liberty. Lieutenant Rollings and Gunnery Sergeant Lytle were waiting for them when they got back. Lytle assembled the platoon behind the barracks.

"While you were off in Havelock," Lytle snarled, "getting your ashes hauled and enjoying your last drunk for who knows how long, the lieutenant and I have been cloistered with the company staff drawing plans for this deployment. The lieutenant will brief you on them." He looked over his shoulder and nodded. Rollings had been standing just inside the rear door of the barracks watching. At Lytle's nod, he stepped out and marched toward the platoon.

" 'TOON, ten-HUT!" Lytle bellowed when Rollings came out. The Marines snapped to.

Rollings stepped in front of Lytle and the two exchanged salutes, then the lieutenant faced the platoon—*his* platoon. He'd been a platoon commander before, but that was in a FIST. And he'd been in Force Recon before—he couldn't become a Force Recon officer without that prior experience. His most recent duty was as the company's S2, intelligence officer, so he and the men who had been with second platoon prior to the platoon's last mission had at least a nodding acquaintance with each other before he was given command, and he knew their worth. So it was with pride that he looked over his platoon.

"At ease," he ordered after a brief moment. He waited a moment for the thirty-four Marines facing him to ease into relaxed positions, then briefed them. The briefing was far less detailed than he would have liked.

"A Confederation Army corps, reinforced by a Marine FIST, is under siege by a field army composed of units from a dozen rebellious worlds. The Confederation force on Ravenette is pinned on a peninsula, which means we will have no direct contact with friendly units once we are planetside.

"We will conduct reconnaissance, raids, sabotage"—he glanced at the sniper squad—"and, situation warranting, sniper operations against elements of the opposition field army. In short, we will be conducting the full range of Force Recon missions.

"The commander of Task Force 79, the navy forces in the campaign, is Rear Admiral Hoi Yueng. Fourth Force Recon will be operating under his orders." To prevent his Marines from wondering why they were going to be operating under command of the navy element rather than under the ground commander, as was standard operating procedure for Force Recon, he continued without break; Lieutenant General Indrus had decided he didn't want the Force Recon Marines to know about the prejudices of General Billie, not yet. "Admiral Hoi's task force has almost complete control of the space lanes, so the Coalition forces are having a lot of trouble reinforcing and resupplying their units planetside. Admiral Hoi will be coordinating our missions with Brigadier Theodosius Sturgeon, commander of the Marine forces on Ravenette.

"That's all I have at this time. Once we are aboard ship, study materials will be made available to you so you can bone up on Ravenette's terrain, climate, flora, fauna, and population, as well as the nature and capabilities of the enemy forces we will be facing. When I dismiss you, hit the squadbay and prepare to move out." Rollings abruptly stood at attention.

"Pla-TOON, aten-SHUN! Dis-MISSED!"

"Hey, did I hear him right?" Sergeant Bingh asked Staff Sergeant Fryman as they headed for the barracks. "We're going to be working for the squid in the sky instead of the doggie in the dirt? What gives?"

Fryman shrugged. "Damfino." He looked at Bingh and swung his glance around to see several other members of first section walking close and listening. "I'll see what I can find out, though."

Inside the barracks, Fryman went to the company office to see the sergeant major while the others headed for their quarters. Fryman was neither the only nor the first senior NCO who wanted to see the sergeant major.

Fourth Force Recon Company Office

Sergeant Major Periz took one look at all the curious and demanding faces in front of his desk and decided the company office was too crowded to deal with them. "Wait," he snarled as he rose to his feet and stepped into Commander Obannion's office.

"Sir, begging the commander's pardon, but I need you to get out of here for a few minutes and let me and my top NCOs have a little tête-à-tête in private."

Obannion turned to him with a look of surprise that quickly turned to one of understanding. "Ah, yes, Sergeant Major, I think we can manage that." He stood and walked around his desk to vacate his office. "Good afternoon, Marines," he said to the dozen gunnery sergeants and staff sergeants crowded around Periz's desk."

"Afternoon, sir," they said.

"Get in here," Periz snarled as soon as Obannion cleared the clot of senior NCOs. He went behind the desk and waited, glowering.

Obannion's office wasn't nearly big enough to hold a senior NCOs' meeting, but at least they had some privacy. The four gunnery sergeant platoon sergeant and eight staff sergeant section leaders made space, filling the area in front and on both sides of the desk.

"All right," Periz said as soon as the door was closed, "somebody surprise me and tell me you aren't going to ask the dumb question I know you're going to ask."

"No surprise, Sergeant Major," said Gunny Natilvash, the first platoon sergeant and senior enlisted man in the platoons. "We all want to know why we're reporting to the admiral instead of the general."

"Of all the goddamn dumb questions," Periz snarled. "Natilvash, you've been in this man's Marine Corps long enough to know the answers to questions like that." He shook his head sadly. "Maybe I should have a career counseler talk to you about the benefits of early retirement, you've got to be losing it."

Natilvash grinned. "You know better than that, Top. All I really need is the name."

Periz looked at the others; they were all nodding. "You got it. It's one General Jason Billie. Got promoted to four stars right before he shipped out to Ravenette. I've read his record, the man's got a chestful of medals. Every last one of them's an attaboy." Marines called personal medals awarded for

noncombat job performance "attaboys" and had no respect
for them. The Marines only awarded campaign medals for
those who went in harm's way, and decorations for personal
heroism under fire. "This is his first combat command."

A murmur went through the senior NCOs; they didn't understand how anybody could reach so high a rank without
extensive combat command experience. And for his first
combat command to be a corps in a major conflict was simply beyond their comprehension.

"You'd think a man like that would want all the help he
could get," Natilvash said.

"Anyone with brains would," Periz grunted. "But this guy's
got no use for Marines—and he thinks Force Recon is a bunch
of resource-wasting prima donnas."

The platoon and section sergeants had begun shaking their
heads at another army general who didn't understand how
valuable Marines could be in assisting his command, but
stopped and gaped at Periz when he described Billie's atti-
tude about Force Recon.

"So that's why we're reporting to the squid in the sky instead of the doggie in the dirt," Periz concluded. "Now, any
more dumb questions?"

Natilvash shook his head. "At least there's a good Marine
unit planetside. Thirty-fourth FIST is just about the best
there is."

"Got that right. Now, if there aren't any more dumb questions, we all have to get ready to move out—and the Skipper
needs his office back. Wait until we're in Beamspace before
you tell your people about Billie." Periz watched the twelve
file out and Commander Obannion returned.

"They wanted to know why?" Obannion asked.

Periz nodded. "I straightened them out. They won't tell
their Marines until Beamspace."

"Good."

Ensign Arvey Barnum, the company's S1 personnel officer, and First Sergeant Robeer Cottle were disappointed to

learn that they had to stay behind to pass squads returning from other deployments through to the campaign on Ravenette. Lieutenant General Indrus provided them with a junior supply sergeant and a senior clerk from his headquarters battalion.

Aboard the Fast Frigate CNSS <u>Admiral Stoloff</u>

A fast frigate is small as starships go. Fast frigates weren't designed for use as troop transports, though even back to the days of oceangoing warships they had sometimes been called upon to do exactly that. And when they are, they are very, very crowded. Crew are taken from their compartments and doubled up with other crew—hot-sheeting, in the ancient parlance—to make room for the troops being transported. Those troops are in turn double- or triple-billeted, two or three men assigned to sleep in shifts on the same bunks. A fast frigate's physical-fitness and recreation facilities are of a size to easily accommodate the starship's crew, but when those same facilities are required for the use of 120 Marines in addition to the crew, they can become congested almost beyond effective use.

To ease the congestion, Commander Stuard Alakbar, the *Admiral Stoloff*'s skipper, and Commander Obannion worked out a schedule that gave everybody aboard the starship reasonable access to the facilities. The Marines, sleeping in three shifts, had four hours per shift in the gym and two in the library and entertainment facilities. Two hours was just enough time to watch a trid in the ship's tiny theater. The rest of the time, the facilities belonged to the sailors, and the Marines were at mess or in their assigned compartments and adjacent passageways. That reduced the crew to half of their normal allotment of time in the gym and three-quarters of their recreation, but it was only for the few days the Marines would be aboard. Half of the allotted time in the gym was more than the sailors normally used anyway. And while the Marines of Fourth Force Recon Company used every minute of their alloted time in the gym, they took little advantage of their time in the recreational facilities. They were too busy maintaining their weapons and equipment, studying what they could find about their coming foes via the library hookups in the compartments assigned to them, and conducting limited training exercises in the passageways adjacent to their compartments.

All starships, regardless of type or class, whether military or civilian, travel through Beamspace at the same rate— slightly faster than six light-years per standard day. Fast frigates are so designated because of their speed in Space-3, and the *Admiral Stoloff* took little more than two days, standard, to reach jump point into Beamspace. Jump was somewhat problematic. There is a disorienting moment during transition between Space-3 and Beamspace when the universe seems to turn inside out, topsy-turvy, and every which way but up. At this time, everyone should—for safety sake— be strapped into a bunk, acceleration couch, or workstation. But with 120 or so extra bodies on board, there simply weren't enough bunks, acceleration couches, and workstations to hold everybody. The way the crew was berthed allowed every sailor to be properly strapped in. The Marines secured padding to the deck in their spaces and jury-rigged strapping to hold themselves in place during jump. It worked well enough that while there were a number of bruises and contusions, there were no broken bones or other serious injuries among them.

The Beamspace voyage took five days, at the end of which the Marines again had to fake their way through the jump back into Space-3. They'd learned enough the first time through that in this jump there were hardly any bruises or contusions at all. The *Admiral Stoloff* then needed another two days of deceleration to reach a high orbit around Ravenette.

Within an hour after the return to Space-3, Commander Obannion was on a secure link with Commander Bhati, Rear Admiral Hoi's N2, intelligence officer, as well as with Brigadier Sturgeon, commander of Thirty-fourth FIST.

Despite the Confederation Navy's having full control of the approaches to Ravenette, planetside mobile weapons systems had been effective in preventing the navy from maintaining a complete string-of-pearls surveillance satellite system. Therefore, once Sturgeon had given Obannion his initial orders, Commander Funshwa, Sturgeon's F2, had limited intelligence to give Obannion for the latter to use in making his plans.

Obannion wasn't greatly concerned about the lack of intelligence from the forces already planetside. After all, finding the enemy's positions, strength, and intentions was Force Recon's job. Even if Thirty-fourth FIST's F2 had been able to provide him with detailed intelligence, Obannion would have wanted to have his own squads confirm most of it, perhaps even all of it.

The first part of Obannion's plan was easy. The *Admiral Stoloff* carried one AstroGhost stealth shuttle, capable of carrying eight fully equipped Force Recon squads from orbit to planetside. He'd use it to drop eight of his squads behind Coalition lines to begin gathering intelligence. The hard part was deciding where to drop the squads. The drop points had to be in places where nobody was likely to spot the Astro-Ghost as it came in, yet close enough to possible enemy locations for the Marines to reach them in a timely manner. And they had to be situated in locations so related to each other that the AstroGhost could safely and quickly maneuver from one to the next.

The AstroGhost, with its thirty-two embarked Marines, the four squads of second platoon's first section and the four of fourth platoon's second section, launched while the *Admiral Stoloff* was still a half day out from orbit around Ravenette. On its second trip, the AstroGhost took a section from first platoon and the sniper squads from second and third platoons.

Commander Obannion transferred his command post to the CNSS *Kiowa,* the flagship of Task Force 79, as soon as the last of his squads launched.

CHAPTER
EIGHT

Arrival, Confederation Military Training World, Arsenault

The suborbital flight from Camp Alpha to Oceanside took about an hour. Before leaving Camp Alpha, Daly had changed into his dress reds so he could report in to OTC in the prescribed uniform. He looked splendid sitting next to his seatmate on the flight, a young man wearing an ugly gray uniform Daly had never seen before. "I see you are a Marine." The young man smiled, revealing a perfect set of white teeth. "I trained with the Confederation Marines and I am going to their Officer Training College," he added proudly, displaying a handful of colorful brochures describing Marine OTC.

"Jak Daly." He extended his hand. "I guess we're going to be classmates." Often, Confederation member worlds requested slots at the Marine OTC for their own army personnel.

"Manny Ubrik," the other responded. They shook. "I am a sergeant in the Soldenese Army. I was trained by a member of your Corps."

"Yeah? Maybe I know him. What were you trained in?"

"Force reconnaissance."

Daly couldn't restrain his astonishment. "*Force Recon?* Who trained you? Goddamn, *I'm* Force Recon!" It was not uncommon for military personnel of the Confederation armed forces to be detailed on training missions to the armed forces of member worlds. Force Recon was a popular request.

"Gunny Dubois. Do you know him? There was also a Corporal Renfew, as I recall."

"Bax Dubois! Bram Renfew! Goddamn! I know them both! Man, what a small world! Your name is Manny? Manny, my man, we have a lot to talk about! Boy, what a small world it is!"

Manny Ubrik smiled broadly.

"Can I see those brochures?" Daly asked. "You ever been to Arsenault, Manny?"

"No, we took our boot camp under a special program that kept us at home."

"Heh." Daly laughed, reading. "Listen to this stuff: 'At any given time, depending on the training cycle then under way, the Confederation's military training world, Arsenault'—that's 'Asshole' to anyone who's ever trained there," he added—"'has a population of approximately a million and a half. Of this number about two hundred thousand are military cadre'—lucky bastards!" he apostrophized—"'assigned to the various training centers and administrative headquarters required to operate the many schools that compose the training complex; a further two hundred thousand military personnel are trainees attending the various schools and courses; and the remainder are government civilian employees'—oh, those are the really lucky stiffs!—'contractors required to support the training activities, and the families of the cadre and civilians.' Listen to this stuff, Manny! Makes Asshole sound like a goddamn summer resort!

"'While life for the men and women undergoing basic infantry and naval training courses on Arsenault can be *very* hard, an experience to be remembered (and cherished as they grow older) the rest of their lives'—oh, the Virgin's wrinkled old buttocks! Gawd, I can't believe the government puts out such crap, Manny!" Daly laughed and shook his head in disbelief, continuing, "'The advanced courses are a lot less strenuous.' Yeah, I just *bet* they are! 'And for the permanent-party personnel and their civilian counterparts, life on Arsenault can actually be quite pleasant, so much so that many of the cadre request an extension of their four-year tours there.'

Manny, you'll have to excuse me, but I've got to go puke!"
Daly laughed.

But Daly read on in spite of himself. There was quite a bit
here he didn't know about Arsenault. It had only one port of
entry, Camp Alpha, in the northern hemisphere. He hadn't
known that. He had believed that cadre and civilians came in
through their own luxurious port of entry. Of course, when
he'd gone through Camp Alpha, he'd had no time to take in
the surroundings. From there incoming personnel proceeded
to their areas of assignment spread out all over the planet.
From his time there Daly knew that all recruits prayed for the
wonderful day when they would return to Camp Alpha to
leave the place, hopefully forever.

The Confederation armed forces operated several commissioning programs on Arsenault. In the northern hemisphere were the four-year naval and military academies that
were available to any citizen who could meet the rigorous entrance requirements. In various places around the world, the
army and navy also operated commissioning programs, similar to the Marine Officer Training College, which they referred to as officer "basic" schools. The army, for instance,
had schools for infantry officers, artillery officers, logistics
specialists, and so on. More advanced training for officers was
available on Arsenault also, or elsewhere, but the entire military education system, from basic recruit training to courses
for field-grade officers, was integrated into one program that
was run from the Heptagon back on Earth.

Marine OTC commissioned only infantry officers. Those
graduates designated for duty in other specialties—artillery,
aviation, ordnance, what have you—received that training
after commissioning.

"Hey, Manny, now we get to the good stuff, *Officer Training College*! Not that I don't know all this stuff, but for your
information: 'The Confederation Marine Corps OTC is located in Camp Upshur in the southern hemisphere, in the
tropics. The nearby liberty town, Oceanside, population ten
thousand, is right on the ocean.' Yeah, like we're gonna see
much of that! 'Oceanside boasts beautiful beaches that stretch

for kilometers north and south of the town, immaculate, affordable recreational facilities, well-run hotels and restaurants, and nearly perfect weather year-round. The town is run by Universal Catering and Recreation (UCR) under contract to the Confederation Ministry of War.' Man, maybe we can get jobs with them after we're discharged. Listen to this, Manny! 'UCR has had the contract to operate Oceanside's facilities for many years, and there have never been any complaints about the way they run it.' Hah! That only means they were always able to underbid everybody else competing against them when contract-renewal time came up, you can bet on that. I bet they're so good at contract renewal no one else even thinks it's worthwhile to bid against them anymore."

"What does it say about mess duty?"

"Aha! It's contracted out. UCR runs the messes at Upshur. Hey, man, they can't have us potential officers taking time out to pull pots and pans or dining room orderly, now can they?"

"I'm not used to civilians pulling KP for me," Ubrik sighed. "I'm beginning to think this OTC isn't such a bad deal after all."

Daly read between the lines. He realized that had Oceanside existed only on the business provided by the officer candidates at OTC, it could never have survived. Tourism was the main source of income for Oceanside's businesses. The permanent residents on Arsenault spent their vacations there, as did many Confederation government personnel from other worlds allowed to go there on special tourist visas. So equitable the climate at Oceanside—there was no "off season" there—so reasonable the fees, so excellent the services, even the Military Training Command held meetings, retreats, and seminars there, during the worst weather in the northern hemisphere, of course.

"Ah," Daly sighed at last, handing the brochures back, "tourists at Oceanside! Nubile young maidens! Well-preserved dowagers lousy with money and anxious to meet young gentlemen such as us!" When authorized liberty, the officer candidates at the OTC flocked to Oceanside as ascending souls to paradise, because Oceanside *was* a paradise.

Marine Officer Training College, Arsenault

Marine OTC was ten months long. Jak Daly's class was Session 39, the thirty-ninth OTC class to commence training on Arsenault since the college had been reorganized forty years before. There were 730 candidates in Daly's Session, divided into three battalions, A, B, and C. Since the Marines attending OTC had all had prior service in the Corps up to the level of the platoon, it was taken for granted they would have extensive knowledge of small-unit tactics. The goal of Marine OTC was to produce ensigns capable of eventually assuming company or battalion command. The motto of the college, emblazoned on a massive arch over the administration building's main entrance, was TAKE RESPONSIBILITY.

The college commander was a brigadier. Department heads were full colonels or commanders. Tactical officers, those who would be directly administering the courses, served in the grade of major or senior captain. All officer candidates were assigned to an administration battalion commanded by an officer in the rank of commander. This officer was responsible for all personnel and personal matters pertaining to the candidates, including the legal or medical procedures incident to dismissal from the college. To be dismissed for any reason was considered a profound setback to any Marine's career.

The dormitory provided was an excellent, state-of-the-art, self-contained building consisting of comfortable two-man rooms, study halls with complete online libraries, full recreational facilities, and two mess halls, both operating around the clock. For most of the Marines attending OTC, these were luxuries beyond compare. The classrooms were equally luxurious. The field training exercises, of which there were many, remained as they had been for the past five hundred years—rigorous. Once in the field on exercises, the candidates felt they'd somehow been transported back in time.

The first month of OTC was devoted to physical conditioning and refamiliarization with the basic duties of a Marine infantry private; fire-team, squad, platoon tactics, and weapons training. There was no liberty during that time, which was known as zero month, but afterward candidates were allowed liberty in Oceanside whenever they were in garrison; a candidate could go to town every night if he wanted, but woe unto he who fell behind in his class work. Written examinations were periodically given during the courses, and a final was administered at the end of each course, but a candidate's exam scores, while important to his class standing, were secondary to his demonstrated leadership skills, and this was finally determined by each candidate's performance in actual command of his battalion during a mock but realistic combat operation.

Female candidates trained alongside the men and were subject to the same physical demands as the men.

Introduction, Marine OTC

"Gentlemen," a tall, painfully thin tactical officer greeted Ubrik and Daly as they signed in to the student officer orderly room, "your first duty after quarters assignment will be to draw utilities and tactical gear plus a whole issue of other junk you'll need while you're here. You will wear *only* utility uniforms, I emphasize *only*, until your graduation parade. *If,* and I emphasize *if,* you go on liberty to Oceanside, you will wear your respective service dress uniform—dress reds for you, Marine." He nodded at Daly, who bristled. Of *course* he knew what his dress uniform was. The tac officer, a first lieutenant, was not much older than Daly, and it was obvious from the few service medals he wore on his chest that he hadn't been around the Corps as much as Daly had. But he was a tac officer, a little god to the officer candidates.

"Formations twice a day, gentlemen," the tac continued, "zero-six and nineteen hours, rain or shine. We march or *run,* I emphasize *run,* to every class. You will start each day with thirty minutes of physical training. PT is my job," he announced proudly. "You will be seeing a *lot* of me while you are here. My name is Lieutenant Stiltskein." It did not take long for the officer candidates to start calling him, behind his back, of course, Rumple. "Now hurry it up," Lieutenant Stiltskein continued. "There are plenty more of you to check in today. I will see you tomorrow at zero-six hours in the company street, ready for roll call and PT. Mess at zero-seven hours, first orientation at zero-eight. Now get a move on!"

Probably because they reported in together, the two were both assigned to the First Company of Bravo Battalion. Their company first sergeant, a real master gunnery sergeant, growled at them around a foul-smelling Clinton. He owned heavy, bushy eyebrows that met in the center of his forehead; he was totally bald and the top of his head showed numerous scars; his hairy fingers were as big as sausages; and thick, black hairs sprouted from his nostrils. He wore no campaign medals or decorations on his uniform. The plain brass nameplate on his desk announced only FIRST SERGEANT, and for all the time they were in OTC, none of the candidates ever used his last name, which someone learned later was Beedle. Inevitably, the candidates dubbed him Beetle, but of course *never* within his hearing. "You'll meet yer comp'ny commander when he's damn good and ready to meet you," the first sergeant announced. "Now, the officers round here call you birds 'gentlemen' and defer to you even when they're running your asses into the ground. But for me, you ain't even NCOs ennymore, yer 'in betweens,' and you ain't gettin' any deference from me until you put on your pips or whatever passes for an ensign's insignia where you come from. That is, *if* you make it. I can see now you two pussies droppin' out. And where do *you* come from?" He glared up at Ubrik.

"Solden, First Sergeant!" Ubrik replied.

"Never heard of it. You, Marine?" He cast his baleful gaze at Daly.

"I was in Force Recon, Top—"

"Aw *fuck*." The first sergeant imperiously waved Daly into

silence. "Go see the billeting NCO and get your room assignments. On the way out see my clerk and he'll download your personnel records and tell you where else you gotta go to complete check-in." He returned to the paperwork on his desk.

"First Sergeant—" Daly began.

"You ain't gone yet?" the top growled.

"Top, any chance Sergeant Ubrik and I can get the same room assignment? We sorta know each other," Daly added lamely.

The first sergeant glared up at Daly as if he were some form of disgusting insect. "You two are buddies *awreddy*?" he almost shouted. Then, shaking his massive head: "I don't give a fuck, if it's okay with the billeting sergeant. Just"—he glared balefully at the pair, shaking a massive forefinger at them—"don't let me catch you two lovebirds in the same bed together."

Orientation, Marine OTC

The orientation for new officer candidates was given in an auditorium large enough to accommodate them all. It lasted the entire day and consisted of overviews by members of the staff of the training they would receive. The introductory remarks were delivered by the commandant, a grizzled brigadier named Beemer. Beemer was short, with the physique of a long-distance runner. His remarks were brief and to the point.

"I'll have no Marine do anything I can't do myself," he began without preamble. "When you do your runs in the morning, I will be there with you. In the field, I will be there too. I'll be sitting in on your classes also. You will get to know this ugly face as well as your own." Nobody laughed.

"You are among the best in the Corps, that is why you are here. I know many of you have not carried a gun in some time. You may have come here from the staff or some special assignment. But you have performed those duties so well your commanders have recommended you for a commission.

"While I speak of the 'Corps' and 'Marines,' I know full

well that some of you are Confederation Army people and others represent the armed forces of Confederation Worlds, twenty of the former and ten of the latter. I want you to know that I consider you the same as my Marines, and when you get your commissions, you can be proud that you have made the grade and will be standing with the very best.

"Some of you will wash out. Our attrition rate is about ten percent. We will lose some of you through injuries or failure to live up to our physical or academic standards. We will tax your brainpower to the limit while you are here, but we emphasize physical fitness. A Marine officer *cannot* be out of shape, no matter what his duties! You set the example for every enlisted Marine, you will *always* be on parade.

"Liberty. After you have completed zero month and whenever we are not in the field, you are authorized liberty after you are dismissed by your instructors or tactical officers. Remember, though, you are each individually responsible for your grades and performance, and if you let liberty nights interfere with your progress as officer candidates, you and you alone will suffer the consequences.

"Fraternization. There will be some of that here. We can't deny human nature. But—and this is a very big but—there will be *none,* repeat, *none* while on duty or within the confines of Camp Upshur and the training areas, on or off duty. No 'public display of affection' by any candidate to any other candidate, cadre, staff, or civilian employee inside these gates. You get caught doing it and you're out, no appeal. Now, when you go on liberty, that's another matter. What happens on liberty stays on liberty. And when on liberty, we expect each of you to conduct yourselves as officers, not swabbies on a binge in from a six-month cruise. Enough said on that subject."

Beemer paused for a long moment, taking in the sea of faces staring back at him from the auditorium. "People, our forces are now deployed in a desperate battle on a place known as Ravenette. No Marine worth his salt wishes to be anywhere except with his comrades when they go in harm's way. But you are here and most of you will remain here for the next ten months, and I guarantee you will not have much time to think about events elsewhere. My staff and I are going to see to it that when you receive your commissions and rejoin the fleet, you are capable of leading your Marines into battle, winning the fight, and bringing them back alive."

The auditorium had gone totally silent, even the ventilation system seemed muted, the hundreds of candidates rooted to their seats, when suddenly, a staff sergeant sitting in the rear stood up and shouted, *"Urrahhhhhh!"* Instantly everyone was on his feet shouting *urrahhhhhh* until the rafters shook with the acclamation of four hundred years of esprit.

The brigadier let the roar sound out three times, and then he held up his hands for silence. "People!" he thundered. "I will see you tomorrow at six hours!" A slight smile crossed his face. He nodded at the candidates. "That is all."

CHAPTER
NINE

Planetfall, Ravenette

The AstroGhost with its thirty-two embarked Force Recon Marines plummeted toward an ocean on Ravenette's night side. The Marines all wore the version of chameleon uniforms issued specifically to Force Recon, which were even more effective at making their wearers invisible than those worn by infantry Marines and, additionally, had a seriously damping effect on the infrared signature of their wearers. Had they been visible, the thirty-two Marines would have looked bulky, as though they had been bred for life on a high-gravity planet. Part of their extra bulk was due to the packs they all wore on their backs, some packs larger than others. Pockets on the fronts and sides of their chameleons, from shoulder to knee, some on the outside, others on the inside, of their shirts were filled with gear and equipment, water and rations. The pockets and packs of most of the Marines did not carry much by way of weapons and ammunition, the mainstays of infantrymen. The Force Recon Marines were lightly armed; three out of four carried only a knife and a sidearm. In only two of the squads on the AstroGhost was each Marine carrying a blaster in addition to the knife.

The job of most of these Marines wasn't to fight, it was to gather intelligence. The thinking was, if they carried proper fighting weapons, they might decide to fight rather than silently slip away if they thought they were on the verge of discovery. But if armed only with defensive weapons, they'd be more likely to try harder to evade discovery and capture.

74

Six of the eight squads on this flight were there strictly to gather intelligence, and perhaps commit incidental acts of sabotage. Only two of the squads were there to fight if they found the right targets.

The AstroGhost's heavy refrigeration and trailing heat-bleeding filaments controlled its visible heat signature to such a degree that an observer would have dismissed its passage as just another minor meteorite's. When it was low enough, it used acrobatics and drogue chutes to arrest its plunge and went into nape-of-the-sea flight, headed for the west coast of North Continent. It dropped to subsonic speed before crossing the continent's horizon and commenced a jinking course as soon as it went feet-dry in order to avoid populated areas. The AstroGhost dropped the eight squads in as many spots, each over the horizon from populated areas inland from the Bataan Peninsula on Pohick Bay.

Planetside, Seventy-five Kilometers Northwest of the Bataan Peninsula

Second platoon's first squad got landed in a clearing on the reverse slope of a medium-size hill in a forest fifty kilometers to the rear of the closest known Coalition position, which was outside a town called Cranston, and two hundred meters from a road leading toward Ashburtonville, at the base of the peninsula. The AstroGhost's sensors hadn't picked up any sign of people in the area, but the four Marines quickly moved off the hillside at an angle toward the road—it was still possible that someone nearby had been in a sensor-shadow and invisible to the AstroGhost. They moved almost as silently as they did invisibly.

A hundred and fifty meters from the drop point and still more than a hundred meters from the road, Sergeant Wil Bingh called a halt and the squad went to cover, lying in an outfacing circle covering their entire perimeter. They waited fifteen minutes, with their ears turned all the way up and each of them rotating through his vision screens. They neither saw nor heard sign of people, land vehicles, or aircraft.

On Bingh's signal, they rose to their feet and removed the puddle jumpers from the chameleon cases on their backs. They rolled the cases up and stowed them in their packs, then donned the puddle jumpers—one-man backpack units capable of carrying one fully equipped combat Marine several hundred kilometers at low altitude; they had a range in excess of six hundred kilometers.

Bingh looked for a break in the forest canopy. When he found one, he jumped straight up through it a hundred meters to get a visual fix on the road. No traffic was in sight.

He dropped back down and raised his screens so his men could see his face. "Nothing's in sight," he said. "We're going to follow the road at low altitude for thirty-five klicks, then secure the puddle jumpers and go the rest of the way on foot. I'll pop up every klick to make sure we still have the road to ourselves. Now turn around." He lowered his ultraviolet screen and looked at his men's puddle jumpers. The UV tag on each of them was clearly visible. "All right. Now check me." He turned his back as his men turned to face him.

"Bright and clear," Corporal Gin Musica told him.

"Let's go."

They rose through the opening in the canopy until they were just above the treetops, then headed for the road. There, they dropped below treetop level and headed southeast, toward Cranston. The Twenty-third Ruspina Rangers were bivouacked at Cranston; first squad's mission was to gather intelligence on their numbers, armament, and morale.

The road through the trees didn't travel arrow-straight but rather wound along the landscape, which was why Bingh popped up every klick, to see what was around the next bend or two. He had to be careful where he jumped, as the canopy arched over the road from both sides, frequently completely roofing the roadway. The overhead was dense enough to give them almost complete concealment from the instruments on any enemy aircraft that might be flying surveillance in the area.

The squad covered about twenty kilometers before Bingh saw a landcar approaching. He signaled, and the squad darted fifty meters off the road, ducking below the lowest branches of the trees, and went to ground behind tree trunks. There was no need for concern; the landcar was civilian, carrying what looked like a family unit. Seven kilometers farther . . .

"Left!" Sergeant Bingh suddenly ordered into the squad circuit—the first word anyone in the squad had spoken over the radio since they'd made planetfall.

As one, the four Marines dropped from the three-meter height they'd been flying to less than a meter between their feet and the ground and swooped under the trees at the left side of the road. By the time they reached the deeper shadows, they all heard what Bingh had heard through his helmet's amplified aural pickups—the soft whoosh of many vehicles rapidly approaching from their rear.

Fifteen meters in—they didn't have time to go farther—Bingh ordered them to cut off the puddle jumpers' power and they dropped the last meter to the ground, then froze in place.

Bingh and Lance Corporal Stanis Wehrli were the only ones facing the road; Corporals Musica and Dana Pricer were looking deeper into the forest—they fell onto their faces so the UV strips on their puddle jumpers weren't visible from the road. None of the Marines spoke, none of them moved. That many vehicles, moving that rapidly along a little-used country road, could only be a military convoy. The Force Recon Marines couldn't talk over their helmet radios and they didn't dare move; they didn't know what kind of sensors the convoy might have active. The sensors the Marines didn't have to concern themselves with were visual and infrared; the Force Recon chameleon uniforms rendered them effectively invisible in those parts of the spectrum. This deep in their own rear areas, the approaching Coalition vehicles probably didn't have anything searching for enemy forces, but there was no need to take chances.

Bingh began recording. He counted: A staff car, bristling with assault guns, led the convoy. An open-sided six-tonne lorry, loaded with infantry, followed close behind. Then another infantry lorry, and another and another, until twenty of them had passed. Each of them appeared to have more than thirty soldiers crammed into it—an entire battalion. A battery of self-propelled artillery followed the lorries. A vehicle of a type Bingh didn't recognize brought up the rear of the convoy.

Bingh leaned close to Wehrli and touched helmets with him when the convoy disappeared from view. "Any idea what that thing was?" he asked.

"Not a clue," Wehrli answered. He sounded a bit awed by the Coalition vehicle.

The vehicle was about the size of a self-propelled artillery piece, but had protuberances on all sides, and what looked like a rack of antiaircraft rockets on top. Some of the protuberances were obviously barrels for projectile weapons, but the purposes of the rest were less obvious. Bingh suspected they were energy weapons of some sort, though they didn't look like any he had ever seen before.

Bingh turned about and looked for Musica and Pricer. Standing, he was able to spot the UV markers on their puddle jumpers. "On your feet," he said in the open. "Look at this," he told them when they stood, and transmitted an image of the last vehicle in the convoy.

"What the hell is that?" Musica asked after looking at the image on his heads-up display.

"I was hoping you could tell me. Pricer?"

"I never saw anything like it, either."

"Damn," Bingh muttered. Marine Force Recon was *supposed* to be up-to-date on all weapons and weapons systems in Human Space. Indeed, Force Recon Marines routinely oriented on weapons and weapons systems they might encounter on reconnaissance and raid missions, so they could use them if necessary. It was the first time Bingh had encountered a completely unfamiliar weapon system. What did the convoy have to do with the Twenty-third Ruspina Rangers? Was that weapon system somehow connected to them?

He wondered what other surprises his squad might encounter. He didn't like surprises; surprises could kill Marines.

"I'm going to uplink," he said out loud. "Stand alert." His men moved into an outward-facing triangle and lowered themselves to one knee. Bingh looked for the tallest tree in the immediate vicinity, stood under it, and used his puddle jumper to rise until the branches came too close together for him to continue comfortably. Then he grabbed hold and climbed.

The trunk and branches of the forest giant remained sturdy enough to support him until he was nearly at the canopy's top. He checked the timeline; the *Admiral Stoloff* should have reached orbit and been below the horizon on its second orbit, but should come into view in a little more than fifteen minutes. He used part of the time to prepare a message, including his squad's location and the recording he'd made of the convoy. He appended a carefully worded request that company headquarters downlink to him any data they had on the strange vehicle. A weapon system that he didn't recognize bothered him more than he wanted to admit.

When fifteen minutes had passed, he used his Universal Positionator Up-Downlink, Mark IV—UPUD—to scan the horizon. He found the *Admiral Stoloff* in a few minutes, locked on it, and sent his message in a half-second burst. Then he settled back to wait for a reply. It came sooner than he expected:

"Received and being analyzed. Continue mission."

Bingh stared at the reply for a long moment. "Being analyzed," it said. That meant that HQ didn't know what the thing was—it was going to be up to the squads on the ground to find out. He climbed back down to where he could use the puddle jumper and gave his men the news. They didn't like it any better than he did.

They continued cautiously along the road.

One Hundred Kilometers Due West of the Bataan Peninsula

Second platoon's third squad was inserted in a shallow valley one ridgeline away from a broad expanse of grain fields that was checkerboarded by farm roads. It was an area of minimal immediate military concern except for one detail—

sensor readings on board the heavy cruiser CNSS *Kiowa* indicated the presence of an underground complex on the far side of the wheat fields. Third squad's initial mission was to determine whether that subterranean complex was military or civilian.

Just like first squad, third squad scrambled away from its drop point as soon as it was on the ground, heading at an oblique angle up the ridgeline that separated it from the grain fields. The Marines moved more quickly and silently than first squad had—they weren't encumbered with puddle jumpers.

Two hundred meters from where they were dropped, they stopped and went prone in a circle, each Marine facing a different direction, their boots touching in the middle. They checked to make sure their ears were turned up all the way and rotated their screens through infrared, magnifier, and light-gatherer. Sergeant Him Kindy activated his motion detector and had it show on his heads-up display; Corporal Nomonon turned on his scent detector and checked that its alert would sound in his ear.

After a half hour of watching, listening, and sensing without detecting sign of anybody but themselves in the vicinity of their insertion point, Kindy signaled the squad to move out. Lance Corporal Hans Ellis led, followed by Kindy. Corporal Ryn Jaschke brought up the rear behind Nomonon. They continued on the same diagonal, pausing frequently to watch, listen, and sense for sign of anybody. Their movement was slow, each step deliberate, to avoid leaving prints, broken twigs, or bent leaves that could signal their passage to a tracker.

The ridge wasn't high, but their angle of climb was so shallow that it took close to two hours for them to reach the top, two kilometers from where they'd first waited after being inserted into the valley.

When they were still heads-down below the top of the ridgeline, Kindy stopped the squad and they went into the positions they'd hold, barring enemy action, for the next several hours. Kindy and Jaschke belly-crawled up the last few meters to where they could see across the grain fields. Ellis took a position five meters downslope and ahead of them, facing downslope and in the direction in which they'd moved. Nomonon was similarly positioned on the other side of Kindy and Jaschke, facing back and down.

The fields were more than ten kilometers wide. Machines trundled through them, fertilizing or weeding, Kindy didn't know which, but thought possibly both. Lorries moved purposely along the roads; they seemed to leave from an indistinct cluster of buildings and silos on the far side of the fields and return to it. None gave any appearance of interest in the ridgeline. The roads didn't appear to be paved, but they must somehow have been stabilized because the moving lorries didn't raise dust. Misters generated small fog banks over the growing crops, watering them.

The entrance to the suspected underground complex was thought to be on the far side of the fields, inside or adjacent to the cluster of buildings and silos. But at this distance, Kindy couldn't make out any detail, even with his four-power magnifier screen in place. From so far away, his infra screen couldn't give him any useful information either, not even when combined with the magnifier. Beyond the complex, the landscape was flat, covered with low-lying brush and occasional trees. Kindy suspected that the cultivated land had looked exactly like that before it was broken for farming.

Kindy made sure he was deep in the shadows of the bush he was snugged under and reached into an inside pocket of his shirt for his ocular. Carefully, slowly, so the movement wouldn't draw attention, he raised his helmet screens and lifted the ocular to his eyes. He adjusted it to thirty power and began examining the structures on the far side of the fields.

Numerous barns popped into clear view, as did three buildings that looked like processing plants. A long row of silos stood idle, waiting for the harvest. One sprawling building looked to be an administrative headquarters, another a dining hall capable of feeding more people than were visible in the fields and the complex. Two or three others might have been living quarters. People walked about casually; they all had destinations, but there was no sense of urgency in their movements. A few people rode in carts or small lorries. Like the walkers, they seemed in no hurry to get where they were going. The ground in the complex wasn't stabilized, so small dust clouds rose in the wakes of the carts and lorries. An athletic field with bleachers on one side lay at one end of the complex. There were other open areas within the confines of the complex.

The complex spread for about a kilometer and a half along the fields and several hundred meters beyond them. Fencing of some sort bordered the complex on the three sides away from the fields. Two gates with gatehouses were open in the far side. From the gates, roads ran arrow-straight at angles from each other into the distance. The gatehouses did not appear to be occupied. A roadway with no obvious reason for being ran around the outside of the fence.

While Kindy scanned the complex, his ocular recorded everything he looked at and stored the data on a crystal; the ridgetop was high enough for him to see the full shapes of the buildings. On command, the ocular could project an overhead view of what he saw to his HUD, or onto a flat surface for study by the squad.

After viewing and recording the built-up areas, Kindy turned his attention to the open areas. He hadn't seen a structure that looked like the entrance to the underground, though one of the barns might have hidden such. It was also possible that the entrance was camouflaged and in the open. He scanned the open areas even more intently than he had the built-up, paying particular attention to the pattern of road usage as shown by tracks in the dirt.

An hour of close study didn't reveal anything out of the ordinary that might indicate the presence of a camouflaged entrance to the underground, even when he displayed an overhead view on his HUD.

Kindy shifted his attention to the land to the left of the complex. Intense study revealed no roads or pathways there other than the few he had already noted. His examination of the land to the right was just as fruitless. So was the landscape beyond the complex.

He lowered the oculars and, after closing his chameleon screen, rested the chin of his helmet on his hands. Surveillance from the orbiting *Kiowa* had identified a probable underground complex here. Unless the AstroGhost had inserted his squad in the wrong location, there was no sign of such a complex from the ground.

The AstroGhost hadn't inserted third squad in the wrong place, Kindy knew that. The squad was here to determine whether the underground complex was military or civilian. Its entrance was concealed, which strongly indicated whatever was underground was military rather than civilian. But he had no proof of that. He needed proof.

Sergeant Kindy prepared a preliminary report to beam up to the *Kiowa* when Commander Obannion transferred his headquarters to Task Force 79's flagship.

CHAPTER
TEN

Five Hundred Kilometers Northwest
of the Bataan Peninsula, Ravenette

Fourth squad, and seventh squad from the second section, were inserted some distance from the other squads, farther out from Ashburtonville and the Bataan Peninsula. They were two of the eight squads on hunter-killer missions, tasked with locating and destroying the mobile antisatellite batteries the Coalition forces had on the ground. Ordinarily, antisatellite batteries were destroyed by navy starships from orbit. But the Coalition forces had come up with a new trick that defeated the best efforts of the blockading warships to locate and destroy the mobile units.

A mobile unit would move into an area that had a clean sight-line to a swatch of sky through which a satellite would move. There, the unit would emplace a single-pulse laser gun and roughly sight it in on the swatch of sky a satellite could cross. The mobile unit would then leave and activate the laser's target detection and sighting system from a safe distance. The laser gun was then on automatic and needed no further instructions before firing on a bird that passed near its aiming point. By the time a satellite was killed, the mobile unit that had emplaced it was off at a safe distance, setting another laser gun in place.

To make matters worse for the Confederation Navy, the laser gun detection systems were passive, so they gave off no radiation for the warships' Surveillance and Radar Divisions to detect. And no individual laser gun had to cover a large swath of sky, merely a few degrees, so they didn't have to be placed completely in the open, but could be hidden from most orbital view angles.

The only good things about the mobile antisatellite units, in the opinion of the Confederation forces, were that the laser guns were underpowered and couldn't reach the higher-orbiting warships—or damage them even if they could reach that far—and were too slow moving to track and fire on the Essays that ferried reinforcements to the Bataan Peninsula.

To Rear Admiral Hoi Yueng, commanding Task Force 79 in orbit around Ravenette, restoring real-time satellite surveillance to the Fleet Initial Strike Team, Thirty-fourth FIST, which was part of the defensive force on the Bataan Peninsula, was of vital importance in bringing the war to a timely and successful conclusion. Commander Walt Obannion agreed with him and was more than willing to devote a significant portion of Fourth Force Recon Company's assets to the mission of hunting and killing the mobile units.

Hoi and Obannion knew that the army forces that comprised the great majority of the besieged garrison would also use the data downloaded from the string-of-pearls once the navy was able to install one. Of course, the Marines also assumed the army would make good use of the intelligence the Force Recon squads developed.

Fourth squad was inserted in a clearing in a wooded area from which thirteen satellites had been killed. They already had puddle jumpers on their backs when they exited the AstroGhost: they knew an enemy unit might be close by so they wanted to get away from the drop point as quickly as possible. The four Marines scrambled out of the way of the AstroGhost's exhaust, quickly made sure the ultraviolet markers on their backs were activated, then jumped away from the AstroGhost, which was already moving off. They rose to treetop level and went at speed to get away from the insertion point before anybody might come to investigate. Sergeant D'Wayne Williams dropped a spyeye behind a fallen log before they left.

Five kilometers away, fifty meters downslope on the backside of a ridge overlooking a secondary road that ran northwest-southeast through a narrow valley between ridgelines, Sergeant Williams stopped the squad and they went to ground in a security wheel. The Marines lay prone, facing in different directions, booted feet touching in the middle. They kept their puddle jumpers on in case they had to move in a hurry. All four Marines turned their ears up. Corporal Harv Belinski activated his motion detector, and Lance Corporal Santiago Rudd his sniffer. Williams got out his UPUD, Mark IV, and locked Belinski and Rudd's sensors to it. He called up the map and centered its display on the squad's position. He had to make a small adjustment in the display's you-are-here—without a string-of-pearls, the UPUD's map was working on inertial and there was a slight drifting in the position it gave for their location. Lastly, Williams located and locked on the transmission from the spyeye at the insertion point.

They lay in place for half an hour, watching, listening, sensing. For all they heard, saw, and detected, they could have been the first humans ever to visit the area. There wasn't even any traffic noise from the road over the ridge.

Finally, Williams shifted position and tapped a coded signal on Belinski's shoulder. He waited until the signal made its way around the circle and came back to him from Lance Corporal Elin Skripska, then the four Marines rose to their feet and climbed the ridge on foot.

Again they went prone and burrowed into the undergrowth, quartering their surroundings. Williams faced north, with the northwest portion of the road in his field of view. Belinski faced east, his view included the southeast stretch of road. Rudd and Skripska covered south and west respectively. The forward slope of the ridge was lightly covered with bushes that never met each other, leaving wide swaths of bare, pebbly ground between them, though to the northwest the cover gradually became trees, and it thinned out to the southeast. The bushes gave way to a lower ground cover at the foot of the ridge.

After watching and listening for another half hour to ascertain that nobody was nearby, Williams and Belinski used their 4X magnifier screens to examine the road that ran below them two hundred meters away.

The road was paved with gravel. But the roadbed hadn't been graded well—or recently. Gravel was spattered to the sides of the road, and tire-wide patches were rubbed through the gravel to the underlying dirt.

Or maybe it's had a lot of use recently, Williams thought. He lowered his infra screen and looked at the road in infrared.

The road showed warmer than the ground to its sides. But he expected that; the gravel would naturally retain heat more than the green-covered ground. He wasn't looking to see if the roadway was warmer anyway; he examined it to see if it showed warmer lines that would indicate recent use. And there were lines. Faint, but present. Two pairs of lines. Neither pair ran straight down the middle of the road, each was offset slightly as though the driver was favoring one side of the road slightly over the other—if the tracks were going in opposite directions, it could mean one vehicle going and returning. He couldn't tell which was fresher from the ridgetop.

Williams moved to his side and touched helmets with Belinski. "Infra shows recent tracks," he murmured, his words carried from helmet to helmet by conduction. "I'm going down there to get a closer look. Tell Rudd and Skripska, and cover me."

"Roger," Belinski replied. He looked both ways along the road. No dust rose as far as he could see, the road seemed clear. He slid his infra into place and could barely make out Williams's shape as he carefully picked his way down the side of the ridge. Careful not to make noise—or lose sight of his squad leader—Belinski moved to the other two Marines and told them what Williams was doing.

Williams shrugged out of his puddle jumper and walked, erect, down the side of the ridge, stepping on the uphill side of the bushes whenever he could, placing his feet where footprints were least likely to take, or at least unlikely to be visible from the roadway. He crouched slightly as he crossed the

wide swale between the bottom of the ridge and the edge of
the road, head moving side to side, searching both directions
along the road for signs that someone might be approaching,
but mostly watching where he stepped. The swale flora was
scraggly, weedlike plants that somehow survived being pum-
meled by gravel thrown out by passing vehicles. Enough stems
and twigs were broken, enough leaves crushed or bruised from
the flung gravel, that it didn't matter if his boots broke a few
more. Provided he didn't leave a definable line of broken plant
life across the swale.

As though a casual passersby would notice, he thought.
But no need to take unnecessary chances.

What he mostly tried to avoid stepping on was the gravel
that lay loosely on the ground. Stepping on it could drive the
small, sharp-edged stones deep into the ground or turn stones
damp-side up, and that might be more easily noticeable than
broken or bruised flora. At first that was easy; the thrown
gravel was sparse. But it grew thicker the closer he came to
the roadbed, until the actual edge of the road was blurred,
distinguishable only if one was close enough to see the hard-
packed graded dirt beneath the gravel.

Williams didn't get close enough for his unaided eyes to
see the hard-packed graded dirt under the gravel on the
roadbed. He couldn't, unless he was willing to disturb the
scattered gravel on the verge. He used the infra screen to locate the lines that indicated recent use of the road, then raised
it and lowered his magnifier to examine the gravel along those
lines.

Yes, it was as he'd expected; the pattern of the disturbed
gravel showed one set of tires had gone in one direction, the
other in the opposite. This close, he could also distinguish
one set of tracks as slightly more recent than the other. It
helped that one inner line occasionally overlapped the corre-
sponding inner line in the other direction. The track that led
southeast was more recent. The gravel gave no detail of
tread, so even though both sets of tracks seemed to have been
made by tires of the same width, he couldn't tell whether

they were both made by the same type of tire, much less the same tires. Still . . .

The tracks went to—and returned from—the northwest. If it was the mobile unit that placed the satellite-killer lasers, that meant it had probably placed one somewhere to the northwest of his squad's current position, and not very far to the northwest. It could also mean that the mobile unit was somewhere to the southeast. Williams carefully turned and retraced his steps to the brush on the side of the ridge. There, he faced the road again, squatted, and thought about what the faint tire tracks had told him.

The squad's primary target was the mobile unit, not the laser guns—but if the tracks had been laid by the mobile unit his squad was hunting, it might have emplaced a fresh laser gun somewhere to the northwest, and fairly close. It had to be fairly close, because not much time had passed between the laying of the two tire tracks. And it was done within the past few hours, otherwise the tracks wouldn't still be visible in infrared. *If* both sets had been made by the same vehicle. It was likely the laser gun was closer than the mobile unit.

He made a decision. Taking out laser guns was a secondary mission. If the mobile unit had laid those tracks, the squad should be able to quickly locate the laser gun it had set, knock it out, and go after the mobile unit.

He climbed back up the ridge and gathered the squad into a tight circle. Touching helmets, he told his men what they were going to do.

Following a Road, Five Hundred Kilometers Northwest of the Bataan Peninsula

Corporal Belinski and Lance Corporals Rudd and Skripska flew nape-of-the-earth halfway down the reverse slope of the ridge, skimming the treetops, while Sergeant Williams flew closer to the ridge's top. Every two or three hundred meters, Williams hopped up to scan the road. At no place did he see the tracks spread apart as though two vehicles had passed each other, giving more credence to the idea they were made by the same vehicle going and returning. But returning from where? The walls of the narrow defile between the two ridges didn't seem to have a break as far as he could see to the north-west. Unless the thickening trees ahead concealed a break.

The infrared traces left by the vehicle were so faint, and fading with time, that Williams almost missed where they turned off the gravel road ten or so kilometers beyond where he'd begun following them. He broke radio silence for the length of two words, "On me," and shot up so his men could spot his puddle jumper with their infras, then dropped down to the ground to wait for them to join him.

In a moment the four Marines stood in a tight circle, touching helmets, as Williams told them what he had seen and what they were going to do about it. They acknowledged, and Rudd jumped across the defile, landing at the edge of the forest opposite, twenty meters to the left of where the tracks turned into an almost unseen break in the trees. Williams watched the UV marker on Rudd's back to follow his progress. Rudd turned all his sensors on at max and watched and listened. When after several minutes he hadn't heard nor seen sign of anybody in the trees before him, and none of his sensors indicated any sizable life-forms nearby, he removed a glove and raised his arm, letting his sleeve slide down, and waved his hand in a circle at shoulder height. Without looking to make sure the squad had gotten his signal, he lowered his sleeve and covered up again, disappearing from visual. Momentarily, soft thuds to his flanks told him the others had joined him.

Williams went from man to man, touching helmets. "Wait," he ordered Belinski and Skripska; to Rudd: "Drop your puddle jumper and come with me." Williams dropped his own, then oriented on the break where the vehicle had come and gone and paralleled it; Rudd followed the UV marker on his squad leader's back.

There was a break in the ridgeline, and an old, rutted road climbed slowly through the break. The trees grew taller there than on the ends of the ridges that bordered it, which was why Williams hadn't seen it earlier. The road hadn't seen regular use in years. Weeds covered much of it, and small, bushy plants, many crushed by the recent passage of a vehicle. Saplings that had taken root in the roadbed had been broken recently enough that some still leaked sap. The road twisted and turned, bypassing trees that had been old and large when the road was originally laid, skirting ancient boulders that had tumbled from the heights and were half-buried by later rock and dirt slides. The edge of the road had eroded and crumbled away in many places.

The two Marines didn't find where the road led or why it had been laid, but they did find what they were looking for, what Williams hoped for, half a kilometer along it, in a small clearing a short distance past the crown of the pass between the two ridge ends. On the far side of the clearing, just inside the trees, next to a boulder that loomed higher than it did, was a passively aimed, automatic-firing laser gun.

The two Marines froze in place, all senses and sensors on high. Just because the satellite-killing laser guns were automatic didn't mean there wasn't a crew nearby. Slowly, they lowered themselves to the ground. Williams faced the gun, Rudd the way they had come. Each was responsible for watching 180 degrees.

Williams reached into a side pocket of his pack and withdrew a minnie and its control box. The minnie was disguised as a bopaloo, a local rodentlike animal that looked like a cross between a kangaroo rat and a bipedal lizard. Williams sent the minnie scurrying around the left side of the clearing. He watched the minnie's progress on the control box's monitor as the minnie skittered under bushes, hopped over rocks, slithered between fallen branches and boulders. When the minnie reached the boulder that partially concealed the laser gun, Williams had it slink up to the gun's base and snuffle at it. Then he sent it hopping and bopping all around the installation, looking for sign or scent of people. The minnie found both visual and olfactory evidence of people all around the gun. But all signs led from and to the same place: where the vehicle that had made the tracks the squad was following had stopped.

Williams sent the minnie out in a wider search pattern, but it didn't find further sign of people. He signaled it to stay in place, then turned about to touch helmets with Rudd and tell him what the minnie had found—and what the two of them were going to do about it.

A quarter of a standard hour later, they had the gun and its tracking system rigged with explosives, a spyeye in place to watch the entire site, and a surface-to-orbit transmitter in place to alert the CNSS *Kiowa,* or any other starship in orbit around Ravenette, in the event of human activity after the laser gun was destroyed. Finally, Williams recorded a report of the finding and what they were doing, then located the *Kiowa* and sent the report to it via burst transmission. Moments later, he got confirmation of receipt. He set the timer for the explosives, then he and Rudd hurried back to the rest of the squad.

The four Marines were on the other side of the southern ridge, headed southeast at speed, when the timer set off the explosives and killed the satellite-killer laser gun.

CHAPTER
ELEVEN

Marine OTC, Arsenault

Everything about Commander Ben Venue, Deputy Director of Training, was "well rounded." He'd done just about everything a Marine could do from boot camp to embassy duty with a few wars in between, and he had the scars and medals to prove it. He was short, stocky, muscular; ham-fisted and hairy, except on his head. And he had a voice like a foghorn.

As soon as Brigadier Beemer had given his brief Welcome Aboard speech, Commander Ben Venue stepped to the podium.

"People," he told the assembled candidates, "all the time you've been in the Corps, and some of you have been in all day, you've heard that OTC is a goddamned 'finishing school,' a pussy-farted place where you learn 'which fork to use and how to hold your pinkie out while drinking tea from a china cup.' Well, I'm gonna tell ya something, my children, that is pure *bullshit*." He paused and looked at the hundreds of eager faces staring back at him. "Pure, unadulterated bullshit, people!" he thundered. "Let me tell you now, I've been shot at and missed, shit at and hit; I've humped my ass through jungles, deserts, city streets where every sumbitch on a rooftop had me in his sights, I've done it *all*, people, all." He tapped his left eye and his right leg. "These are the fruits of modern medical science, people. I've spent more time in the hospital recovering from wounds than many of you have in whorehouses on the fringes of Human Space, and I can tell from looking at you that's where most of you'll want to be in a few days hence, but *not here*." A nervous titter ran through the assembled candidates.

"You think I'm kidding? Okay." He shifted his weight and leaned on the podium, extending a stubby forefinger at his audience. "You want to know something? I don't have nightmares about the combat I've seen. I don't wake up screaming because of the phantom pains in my artificial leg, no-no-no, my babies, nope. I wake up in the middle of the night in pure terror because I've just dreamed *I was back in zero month at OTC!*" His words, amplified by the sound system, echoed through the huge auditorium.

Commander Venue stood there silently for a long time as if waiting for his words to sink in. "All right," he continued calmly, "relax. Today you're going to hear from all the department heads, and you'll get the full orientation on what we expect of you here at OTC. You'll be released early to go back to your quarters. My advice to you is to get a good night's rest, because at oh-dark-thirty tomorrow, zero month starts. Zero month, as many of you know, is intended to separate the wheat from the chaff and to remind all of you what it's like to be an infantryman in this Corps. Some of you, I know, have been through the mill and you're pretty tough customers already; others have had pretty soft duty since boot camp. Zero month will toughen the toughest among you. A lot of you won't make it, but remember this: if you don't make it, it's because your buddies let you down out there. *Pull together, people!*

"One final thing. Don't expect a break if you make it through zero month. After that is nine months of academic and practical exercises, and if you make it through all this shit, you'll be qualified to command Marines. 'Finishing school' my ass. You get through here and ain't nothing ever gonna seem impossible to you from then on."

He turned and stalked off the stage.

Manny Ubrik turned to Daly and said, "Whew! He must have been talking about *me* when he made that remark about some of us having soft duty! The hardest training I've had in

years was what Gunny Dubois gave us, back on Solden, and
that was a while back. Damn, Jak, I ain't lookin' forward to
this zero month malarkey!"

"Ah, Manny, relax! We'll make it through. We'll help each
other along. It'll be a *snap*!"

It wasn't.

Zero Month, Marine OTC

Zero month was divided into three phases. The first phase
took place on the OTC campus and at nearby training areas
and was designed first to assess, and then to develop, each
candidate's military skills and physical and mental endurance. The candidates ran everywhere. Sit-ups, pull-ups, chin-
ups tortured them even in their dreams, when they did dream,
which was seldom because they slept the dreamless coma of
the physically exhausted. When they weren't running obsta-
cle courses and enduring twenty-kilometer forced marches
with full kit, they practiced squad and platoon combat operations, land navigation, and patrol techniques. And, of course,
practical demonstration of marksmanship skills with all types
of infantry assault weapons.

No exception was made for gender. If the female candidates were able to keep up, they were kept on. But even Jak
Daly, who arrived in excellent physical condition, found
himself straining at times to keep up the murderous pace.
Partly that was because he spent a lot of his energy helping
other candidates, especially during the marches and patrols.
The most grateful recipient of this help was Manny Ubrik,
who honestly acknowledged he would not have made it without Daly at his side. Plenty of candidates did not make it.

Age was not a factor either. The oldest candidate was a
gunnery sergeant in his fifties, a scarred, implacably tough
Marine NCO who never fell behind in anything. He was in
the same company as Daly and Ubrik, but in another platoon, though all the candidates in the brigade got to know
him by reputation if not sight. So thoroughly noncommis-
sioned was this man, Gunnery Sergeant Folsom Braddocks,

that the tactical officers had difficulty remembering to call him "Candidate," the obligatory form of address for the budding officers in OTC, and often, to the suppressed grins of all within hearing, called him "Gunny." And even the foul-mouthed Lieutenant Stiltskein was afraid to address him as anything but "Candidate Braddocks." Rumor had it that he was sent to OTC to get rid of him because he was such a hard-shell and independent-minded Old Corps NCO.

The youngest candidate was a petite lance corporal of only twenty-five named Beverly Nasaw, who was assigned to the same platoon as Daly and Ubrik. On the range she fired a "possible," a perfect score, with the infantry blaster, only one of three Marines in the entire brigade who achieved that remarkable feat. Daly admired Beverly's modesty, endurance, fortitude, and can-do spirit; she was always ready to pitch in when someone needed help. During breaks and hurried meals the two fell into an easy camaraderie, and Jak used those occasions to try to persuade Beverly to volunteer for Force Reconnaissance duty. She'd make a great counterpoint to the Queen of Killers, the soulless Bella Dwan. Daly began looking forward to liberty, when maybe he could get to know Beverly better. He had started thinking she would turn into the kind of ensign he himself wanted to be.

And then there was the ubiquitous Lieutenant Stiltskein, "Rumple," as he was known at first; but by the end of the initial phase everyone was calling him by other, less printable, names. Lieutenant Rumple never seemed to tire and he was everywhere, screaming and cursing at the candidates even when they were performing the physical exercises properly. Compared to Rumple, not even the physically fit were fit; the man's endurance was phenomenal. The candidates came to hate Lieutenant Stiltskein, but at the same time they were in complete awe of the man. Everyone breathed a sigh of relief when they moved to the second phase of zero month and left Rumple behind at Main Side.

Phase two took place in a swamp forty kilometers from OTC. The candidates got there on foot. That phase was designed to test the candidates under conditions of extreme mental and physical stress through practical exercises in extended platoon-level patrol operations in an extremely hostile physical environment. Throughout they were subjected to constant harassment by "aggressor" forces laying ambushes, sniper attacks, and frequent nightly perimeter probes. Nobody got much sleep during that phase. And there was one fatality. A candidate drowned during an expedient stream-crossing exercise. After an attempt to recover the woman's body failed, the instructor asked Daly, who was acting platoon commander at the time, what to do next. It was Beverly who had disappeared into the fast-moving torrent. Without hesitation Daly responded, "Continue the mission, sir." Beverly's badly decomposed body was only recovered weeks later by a special graves registration team on loan to OTC from one of the army schools.

Phase three took place in the mountains. For that phase the candidates enjoyed the luxury of being airlifted into a mountain range about one hundred kilometers from Oceanside. Once there they practiced squad and platoon operations in a mountain environment, learning about knots, belays, anchor points, rope management, and the fundamentals of climbing and rappelling. During the following exercises they performed patrol missions requiring the use of their newfound mountaineering skills. When the phase was finished, they performed an extended, one-hundred-kilometer route march back to the OTC campus. For that event they were joined by the indestructible Lieutenant Rumple Stiltskein. That worthy, totally unfazed by the heat and the pace, ran up and down the company column, screaming imprecations at the foot-weary Marines. Several candidates admitted later they had actually contemplated landing a rifle butt on the back of the lieutenant's head. Suddenly Gunny Braddocks's powerful voice, from near the end of the column where the dust was thickest, began reciting an irreverent cadence ditty.

"Had a cook in Company C
"Sent him off to OTC.
"And all that fool [rest one count] learned to do
"Was [rest one count] boil water and burn the stew!"

Braddocks had a large repertoire of cadence calls and he went through them all. As they got more irreverent—and dirtier—and they spread through the column to the lead platoon, the weary candidates' feet seemed to move faster, their packs grew lighter, and their weapons hung easier off their sore shoulders.

By the time the march was over, several candidates in Daly's platoon swore they'd actually seen old Rumple smile.

CHAPTER
TWELVE

Lance Corporal Bella Dwan slowly shook her head. "Sniper teams work alone," she said when informed that one of the recon squads would be with her and Sergeant Ivo Gossner when they went planetside.

"Not this time, Lance Corporal," Gunny Lytle said. "You're being inserted into an area that may have a lot of unfriendlies in it. You need that squad for the extra firepower in case you get detected."

She showed him her teeth in a tight smile. "Gunny, do you have any idea how much easier it is to detect six people than it is to detect two?"

Something inside Lytle snapped. He'd come out of second platoon's raid on Atlas in a stasis bag; after that he wasn't taking guff from anybody. He took advantage of his greatly superior height to loom over Dwan and looked severely down into her pixie face—after the stasis bag, the hardness in her eyes no longer affected him. "Lance Corporal," he snarled, "I was snooping and pooping behind enemy lines while the best part of you was dribbling between your momma's ass cheeks. Disabuse yourself of the idea that you can teach me *anything* about movement behind enemy lines."

Dwan blinked, shocked at being spoken to so harshly. Before she could react, Gossner leaned close and whispered in her ear, "Be cool, Bella. Listen to the man. He was a sniper too. He knows his shit."

Dwan's jaw worked as she glared up at her platoon sergeant. Sure, she'd seen the sniper weapons badges on his dress reds, but that didn't mean anything. A lot of Force Recon Marines who had never been snipers had one or more of them. She shifted her eyes to Gossner's. He didn't flinch. Then she looked at Staff Sergeant Athon, the sniper squad leader. He met her gaze and nodded. She looked back at Lytle and closed her lips into a sweet smile—but the hardness didn't leave her eyes.

"We can lose them if we want," she said.

"Maybe," Lytle said. He didn't sound as if he believed it, but he backed away from Dwan and said to Gossner, "Second squad's providing security for you."

Gossner nodded. "Sergeant Kare's a good Marine, he's got a good squad." He looked to where first section's second squad stood waiting for the return of the AstroGhost. Those four Marines, like Dwan and himself, were in their chameleons, but with their helmets and gloves off for visibility. Sergeant Brigo Kare looked ready for anything. Corporals Anton Quinn and Rufus Kassel also looked ready. Only Lance Corporal Jadzi Ilon, looking at Dwan, displayed a hint of uncertainty. All four were carrying blasters; sidearms alone wouldn't provide enough security if they ran into trouble. Gossner himself was carrying his M111 fin-stabilized rifle— Dwan wasn't the only sniper in the team.

Minutes later, the AstroGhost returned from dropping off the first wave of Force Recon squads. While it refueled, all three sniper teams, each with a fully armed squad for security, along with three other squads going on independent missions, boarded. Refueling didn't take long, and soon the stealth shuttle was once again mimicking a meteorite as it plunged through Ravenette's atmosphere.

Two Days' Fast Flight West-South of Ravenette

The cutter *Hope's Folly,* out of Trinkatat, jumped out of Beamspace, cut all engines except for the few small motors necessary to maintain her life-support systems, and drifted toward Ravenette.

Lieutenant Commander Phopaw Irian, late a lieutenant in the Confederation Navy, was the cutter's captain. He sat in his station on the bridge, a position he'd keep until his ship reentered Beamspace more than a week standard hence on the other side of Ravenette. If she lived that long.

Hope's Folly hadn't been designed to carry cargo; she was meant for speedy interdiction of smugglers' starships in planetary space. Her name was meant to tell smugglers that it was folly for them to hope to get past her.

Lieutenant Commander Irian couldn't help but wonder if her name referred more to her current mission—for on this mission she carried cargo she wasn't designed for: two Essays, which, like *Hope's Folly* and her captain, were late of the Confederation Navy. Just as a third of the 120 soldiers berthed in the Essays for lack of space elsewhere on the cutter were late of the Confederation Army. The soldiers were confined to the Essays except for meals and head calls.

When Trinkatat had joined the secessionist Coalition, the government had seized *Hope's Folly,* the two Essays she now carried, and all other Confederation military craft, vehicles, weapons, and stores they could. That seizure was greatly aided by the significant number of Confederation military personnel, citizens of the twelve worlds that formed the Coalition, who switched sides to join the secession. Now Lieutenant Commander Irian was one who'd switched and was rewarded with a promotion and command of the cutter on which he'd served before capturing it for Trinkatat.

Irian had wondered more than once en route from Trinkatat to Ravenette why he'd volunteered for the mission.

The Confederation Navy controlled planetary space around Ravenette, including approaches to the planet. The Confederation could land reinforcements to its beleaguered garrison on the peninsula on Pohick Bay at will. The Coalition could land reinforcements only at great risk. Which was why *Hope's Folly* was carrying two Essays, and the Essays were filled with troops.

The plan was simple. Drift in as close as possible to Ravenette without being spotted by the cordoning task force. Fire main engines full thrust to pick up the greatest velocity as rapidly as possible. Skim the top of the atmosphere, breaking just enough to launch the Essays. Get the hell out of Dodge.

Others had done it, feeding needed reinforcements to the Coalition ground forces. Some of the starships that had made the run had even made it out alive. So, even though Irian sometimes wondered why he'd volunteered for the mission, he knew it wasn't really a suicide mission. Not always.

Over four days, *Hope's Folly* cut her distance to Ravenette in half before one of the Confederation starships in the cordon finally had an indication the drifting cutter might be something other than a large chunk of space debris. Irian watched the starship, a destroyer, turn her bow and fire her engines to break orbit on an intercept course. That was all he needed. He hit the panic button.

It was a literal button, which he'd had installed to issue a number of commands instantly: Horns whooped, sounding general quarters throughout *Hope's Folly;* Navigation put the cutter on an evasion course; Engineering fired the main engines; the soldiers in the Essays strapped in.

"Project courses," Irian ordered.

The main screen showed the locations of all known vessels around Ravenette. A limb of the planet's primary satellite, a fifth the diameter of Ravenette, was visible on the far side. Three traces appeared on the display: a line of fine dashes showed the course *Hope's Folly* had been on; a line of stronger dashes showed her current course, curving away from the original course; a third line of blinking dashes was the projected intercept course of the Confederation destroyer. That intercept path missed the cutter's current path.

Irian allowed himself a satisfied grunt. His starship was far enough away from the destroyer that it would be a couple of minutes before light traveled from her to the destroyer to tell the picket that *Hope's Folly* had come to life and changed course. Of course, it might also be a couple of minutes before light from the destroyer's current position reached out to let him know if she'd changed course.

Maneuvers at distances measured in light minutes were a

tricky cat-and-mouse game, but Irian had become skilled at it when *Hope's Folly* had been interdicting smugglers for the Confederation Navy.

Three minutes passed and the destroyer showed no sign of adjusting course or velocity to intercept *Hope's Folly*'s new course. Neither did any of the other starships in the cordon display any reaction to the cutter's presence.

"Navigation, set course to drop point," Irian ordered. Steering engines fired, and the cutter slowly changed vector to skim the planet's atmosphere. Twenty-five seconds later, the blinking dashed line of the destroyer's path began to shift, to intersect where *Hope's Folly* would have gone had Irian not ordered the latest maneuver. No other starships were responding as yet.

Irian repressed a sigh of relief; he didn't want the crew to know he'd been concerned. The cutter was fast, she could outrun a fast frigate in Space-3. The destroyer had waited too long to adjust to her first course change, she'd never catch up now. And neither would any of the other Confederation starships visible on that side of the globe. *Hope's Folly* carried enough defensive measures to deflect any missiles the blockading starships were likely to fire at her—unless they fired a large enough salvo to insure a hit on a heavy cruiser, and Irian couldn't believe the Confederation Navy would waste that much weaponry on a mere cutter. He settled back to wait.

The Top of Ravenette's Atmosphere

Hope's Folly plunged deeper into the planet's atmostpheric envelope than a troop carrier would. Like most starships and spaceships, she was built in orbit and would never make planet-fall, but she was designed to chase smugglers to where they'd have to surrender or break up. Which meant deeper into atmospheres than any but a few very specialized space-going craft were capable of. The launch of the two Essays went off without a hitch, and *Hope's Folly* went to full velocity, heading for sufficient distance from Ravenette's gravity well to jump into Beamspace—and right into a six-missile salvo fired by a light cruiser orbiting Ravenette's moon; the cruiser had been concealed from view by Ravenette until the cutter reached its side of the planet.

"Hard a port," Irian ordered as calmly as he could. "Fire forward flares. Forward guns, screening fire."

Hope's Folly lurched as her main engines, aided by thrusters on her starboard side, swiveled to turn her to port—headed back toward atmosphere. Muted *thup*s sounded as flares shot out of forward tubes. The cutter shook as the two rapid-fire guns in her bow sent out thousands of pellets in a steady stream.

Irian watched the main screen closely. Two of the approaching missiles were fooled and went off chasing the flares. One, then a second, were met by the pellets from the guns and erupted far enough away that they were no threat. The other two missiles continued to home on *Hope's Folly*. Like a flat rock skimming the surface of a pond, the cutter bounced when she hit the atmosphere. That jink, unintentional though it was, threw off the aim of one of the remaining missiles.

"Fire rear flares," Irian ordered. More muted *thup*s answered him. "Crash course starboard."

The starship screamed as her main engines twisted hard to change her course again, all the thrusters on her port side fired, and the braking thrusters in her bow swiveled to add their sideways thrust.

The last missile continued to close, but was no longer on a direct intersect course for the cutter. Then it began to adjust.

"Closing speed!" Irian ordered. The main engines fired straight to the rear, and the thrusters on the port and starboard sides, as well as those on top and bottom, swiveled backward.

The dotted lines on the display showed the cutter's course and that of the missile intersecting, the missile crossing behind the cutter. Then the missile began changing course again, once more shifting along *Hope's Folly*'s path, toward intercept.

"Aft guns, fire screen," Irian ordered. "Fire rear flares."

The rear guns turned to fire at the closing missile, and oxy-magnesium flares shot out and ignited almost immediately.

The missile seemed to pause indecisivly for a moment, then continued shifting to intercept the cutter. But the missile's line was crawling up *Hope's Folly*'s line more slowly than before. More flares shot out of the rear of the cutter; the missile ignored them. The aft guns fired another many-thousand pellet screen; and missed. The missile continued closing.

Then the flame from the missile's engine flared out, its fuel expended, and it exploded.

Hope's Folly lurched as fragments from the exploding missile hit her. Horns whooped throughout the cutter, and a voice commanded damage control and fire crews aft. On the bridge, Irian watched the image on the main display begin wobbling; he suspected one of the main thrusters had been hit. He didn't have to wait long to find out.

"Number two thruster's been hit," Engineering reported. "The thruster wall was penetrated and gases are venting through the break. Skipper, we have to reduce thrust, or the entire nozzle structure will be damaged beyond repair."

On the main display, Irian saw the previously hidden light cruiser on her flank accelerating in an attempt to close enough to fire another salvo. If he allowed *Hope's Folly* to slow down by reducing thrust, the cruiser would get close enough well before the cutter reached the sanctuary of jump point. As it was, her acceleration was so reduced by the loss of direct thrust that intercept was possible.

He couldn't allow the Confederation starship to capture or kill his ship.

"Negative on reducing thrust, Engineering," he said. "We need as much acceleration as we can manage if we're going to get out of here alive."

"It's possible that the damage to the nozzle could escalate and cause the entire engine to explode," Engineering replied. "If that happens, we get killed."

"If we don't keep accelerating, we *will* get killed," Irian said sharply. "Bridge out."

The captain of *Hope's Folly* continued to watch the oscillating image on the main display. The dotted line indicating the light cruiser's path slowly, ever so slowly, crept up the cutter's path toward intercept. Irian wondered who the warship's captain was; the cruiser was closing faster than anything that big should be able to. Then he more closely studied the actual path of his cutter. Thanks to the uncontrollable movements of thruster two, and the variable amounts of gases being vented through the breach, the path wasn't the straight line it should have been. Even though *Hope's Folly* wasn't accelerating as fast as she normally could, the wobble in her path should make intercept more difficult.

Irian looked at the time. Thirty hours to jump point. He projected the two paths thirty hours into the future. Yes, the light cruiser should begin falling behind before she closed enough to fire another salvo.

It was beginning to look as if it hadn't been a suicide mission after all.

CHAPTER
THIRTEEN

Liberty, Marine OTC, Arsenault

They were well into their third month at OTC before either Jak Daly or Manny Ubrik seriously considered taking some liberty in Oceanside. The training schedule for that week left seventh day free for most of the candidates—those not in remedial training or on some duty roster, neither of which applied to either Daly or Ubrik. So, pockets stuffed with recent withdrawals from the Navy Credit Union, at first light they waited for the liberty bus to Oceanside.

It was summer in that part of Arsenault, so the small crowd of candidates waiting for the bus outside the main gate to the OTC campus were dressed informally in ill-fitting clothing hastily purchased the day before from the Marine Corps Exchange store, loose shirts over shorts, feet stuffed into sandals or light shoes.

"These goddamn sandals are too big," Ubrik groused, loud enough for a buxom candidate standing nearby to hear.

"Well, look at this blouse," the woman complained. "I pulled it off the rack because I like the flower design, but see how it hangs on me like a general-purpose tent?"

She was from another battalion. The few female candidates left in the brigade by then were easily recognized by everyone, healthy men in their prime who'd had no female companionship for over two months. But this woman was extraordinary even in her loose-fitting blouse. "Ah, well," Daly said, "I think, er, you'd look pretty good even in a GP tent." Realizing that statement could be taken several different ways, most of them not complimentary, Daly's face reddened with embarrassment. "Er, I mean—"

"I know what you mean, Candidate." She grinned, holding out her hand. "My name is Felicia Longpine."

"I'm Jak Daly. This is my roomie, Manny Ubrik. Manny's from Solden, in the army, but he's an honorary Marine, one hundred percent!"

Ubrik bowed graciously and they shook hands all around. "I'm in the army too," Felicia announced, cocking her head, grinning widely, giving Daly a silent challenge. Felicia was about Daly's height, blond, muscular, and the loose-fitting blouse could not hide the well-developed endowments that inexorably drew men's eyes to her chest.

"Well, ah, you two were good enough to get into Marine OTC, so that means, I mean, *shit,* I'm *surrounded*!" They all laughed at Daly's feigned embarrassment. "That means," he continued, "that I guess I'll have to take you two"—he almost said "cunts"—"*guys* to breakfast!"

Oceanside was about five kilometers from the OTC campus. On the short ride into town the trio studied various brochures highlighting the recreational and dining facilities available in the resort town.

"The Four Seasons looks pretty good for breakfast," Felicia remarked. "It's on page three of the dining brochure." The other two turned to page three.

"Jeez," Daly exclaimed, "looks pretty classy. But what the heck, a roadside soup stand would be classy compared to anything back in Havelock."

Ubrik shrugged. "Let's go."

The Four Seasons restaurant *was* "classy." At that early hour the place was not crowded. The maître d' greeted them warmly and guided them to a sumptuously set table. "God," Felicia murmured as they were seated, "this stuff looks so fancy I think I'd be committing a sin just to touch any of the silverware."

"What's that music?" Daly asked. Muted classical music was playing in the background.

"Vivaldi," Ubrik responded at once, "*Juditha Triumphans,*

I think." Then, a look of embarrassment crossed his face as he noticed the expressions of almost shock on the faces of his companions. "Ah, that's the opening sinfonia. It's, um, I recognize the hunting horns, er, very distinctive opening sequence," he finished rapidly, and went back to studying the menu.

"You like that stuff?" Felicia asked.

"Um, well, it's based on the story of Judith, who cut off this general's head to save her people from his army."

Daly pretended to shudder. "She reminds me of Bella."

"Who's Bella?" Felicia asked, feigning suspicion.

"I'll tell you later, maybe."

Felicia narrowed her eyes at Daly, as if feigning jealousy, then turned back to Ubrik. "Well, jeez, you can't dance to that music."

Face turning red, Ubrik nodded. "Well, no," he went on rapidly, "but I like all kinds of music, you know?"

"Yeah, it does have a sort of very 'military' air about it, catchy," Daly interjected. He found himself a little confused at the coarseness of Felicia's language and Ubrik's evident embarrassment. "Old Manny, here, Felicia, he's a fucking— er, excuse me—I mean he's a regular genius," he went on quickly, covering his embarrassment with a weak grin. "He got all of old Mitzikawa's formulas down pat, first time through."

"You did?" Felicia asked, genuinely impressed. "That log support class of his was the worst crap I ever had to suffer through. I only got 70 on that exam where we had to figure out the time gaps between 'serial' formulas for a road march. Had to get some fucking coaching to pass that block of instruction."

Daly laughed. "Well, I only made a barely passing grade on that exam myself, and that was because Mannie here coached me through." He patted Ubrik's shoulder.

"I've always been good at mathematical stuff," Ubrik said, shrugging.

"Well, good for you!" Felicia exclaimed. "I admire anybody who can do things better than I can. Oh, Manny," she went on, leaning forward and placing a hand on his forearm, "I didn't mean to sound judgmental over your taste in music. You know what they say, 'Never judge a man by the music he likes, his dog, or his landcar.'"

Ubrik laughed. "That's a good philosophy of life."

A waitress came and took their orders. "Jak, where's this 'Havelock' place you mentioned?" Felicia asked.

"Oh, that's the liberty town just outside Camp Howard—that's part of Marine Corps Base Camp Basilone, on Halfway, my home station. Fourth Force Recon Company," he added.

"Force Recon?" Felicia nodded appreciatively. "Confederation Armed Forces Organization" was a class they'd all had, and Felicia knew just how Force Reconnaissance fit into the Marine Corps' mission.

"Yeah. Princeton Street in Havelock, Felicia, that's where we go on liberty to eat and drink." Daly looked around at the luxurious dining room that was slowly beginning to fill up. "Nothing like this place, though."

"I was reading in this brochure that UCR is famous just about everywhere for its food, hotel management, and recreational services. They run those theme parks on Havanagas now, you know, where you can live back in the Roman Empire and all that stuff. All their places got five-star ratings in *Honiger's Guide to Dining and Dancing in the Galaxy.*"

The waitress returned with a cart heaped with their breakfast order, and they fell to consuming it with gusto. "Boy, this is first-class chow, compared to the slop we get back at OTC, right?" Felicia asked around a mouthful of scrambled eggs. She snatched a strip of bacon from a tray and dropped it into her mouth like a baby bird receiving a worm from its mother.

Daly and Ubrik exchanged glances. "Ah, Felicia, just what is it you do, back in the army?" Ubrik asked.

"Me? Oh, I'm in fucking graves registration. That's a quartermaster MOS. I'll be a second john, er 'johnette,' if you prefer, in the QM Corps when I graduate. Remember that girl, I think she was in your battalion, Jak, the one who drowned during zero month? I've pulled many a body out of the water in my time, and let me tell you, they ain't pretty. Boys, you ever see a corpse that's been in the drink as long as that girl was, you'll flip your cookies from breakfast to midnight snacks. Anybody want that last sausage patty?" She speared it with her fork, plopped it on her plate, then cut it into four neat pieces, which she began popping into her mouth.

By the time both men shook their heads no they didn't want the sausage, it was already gone. "Hey"—she looked up at the pair—"I'm a woman. I can deal with stiffs, dead or alive." She laughed around a mouthful of sausage, pleased at her pun, and winked suggestively at Ubrik. His face reddened perceptibly.

"How'd you get sent to Marine OTC?" Daly asked Felicia. "Manny here, he was too smart for army OCS."

"They sent me here because I was too tough for army OCS," Felicia answered around a piece of sausage patty. "The army figured Marine OTC would take some of the rough edges off me."

"Has it?" Daly asked. "Doesn't look like it to me."

"Oh, sure! I used to piss standing up, now I have to do it sitting down."

Ubrik stiffened. "Oh, Christ," he whispered, and nodded toward the door.

Daly turned and looked in that direction. "Oh, boy, oh, boy," he whispered.

"What?" Felicia asked, looking questioningly at each man in turn. "What? You seen a ghost? I've seen them. I can handle them."

"No, *worse* than anything supernatural, Felicia, it's old Rumple Stiltskein, our PT officer." Daly groaned. "He's coming right over here!" he hissed.

"Are we supposed to come to attention when he gets here?" Felicia asked. When in the presence of OTC cadre, candidates were obligated to assume the position of attention, something that now came automatically to them, on campus, that is.

"No, no, we're off duty. Oh, boy, here he comes."

Lieutenant Stiltskein took a chair and sat down at their table. "May I join you?" he said cheerily. "Ah, looks like you gentlemen have enjoyed a hearty breakfast. Maybe tomorrow, to work it off, we'll run twenty klicks instead of the usual ten. I don't know this lady, do I?"

"No, sir, she's in another battalion."

"Well, I've seen you Miss . . . ?"

"Longpine, sir."

"Miss Longpine. Yes, I've seen you. Your PT officer is Lieutenant Wakefield, right?"

"Yessir."

"Um. Well, when you get your commission, Candidate Longpine, you stop by and see me. You'd make a good PT instructor. Maybe we can get you on loan from your gaining command."

"I don't think the army would let me go, sir."

"Army, huh? Well, nobody's perfect, Candidate Longpine. No reflection on you. Gentlemen," he addressed Daly and Ubrik, "you I know, very well, very well, I know you very well indeed. May I have a cup of your coffee?" he poured himself coffee from the carafe. "Have you people been keeping up with the news lately?" He looked at them over the rim of his cup.

"Ah, we haven't had much time for that, sir," Daly answered.

"Well, this just in: we're in a pretty desperate pickle in our war with the Coalition. And here we are, stuck in beautiful downtown Oceanside with all the feather merchants and their offspring. This session has, what, seven months left to graduation? The war'll be over by then, one way or the other. Guess none of us will meet the enemy on the Plains of Philippi, huh? Well, thanks for the coffee. Daly, Ubrik, see you tomorrow at oh-dark-thirty. Candidate Longpine, pleasure to meet you." He stood up to go. "Oh"—he put his credit card into the Billpayer device—"your hospitality is appreciated. Breakfast is on me."

"So what's wrong with him?" Felicia asked after Stiltskein had departed. "I sort of like the guy."

Daly only shrugged. "He beats your legs down into stumps," Ubrik volunteered. "But, damn, maybe there's actually a human being in there somewhere?"

"Where in the hell is this 'Plains of Whatever' he was talking about?" Felicia asked.

"Oh, that's a reference to Shakespeare's *Julius Caesar,*" Manny said. "Philippi was where Brutus was defeated by Mark Antony. Well, I mean it really happened, the Battle of Philippi. I never figured *him* for knowing the classics."

"We never figured *you* for knowing them! We got a real scholar among us, Jak." Felicia laughed and gave Daly a big wink.

They rented beach clothes and equipment and spent the day on the sparkling strand for which Oceanside was justly famous. That evening they had dinner in a restaurant that featured a dance band. "Come on, Manny," Felicia urged after dinner, "let's us hoof around the floor a little bit."

"Ah, I—"

"Whatsamatter, Manny, you got two left feet or something?"

"Well, it just is, I don't dance very well, Felicia. I'd step all over you and embarrass the both of us. Now Jak there, he's a ballroom dancer." He nodded desperately at Daly, hoping he'd take the bait.

"The hell I am!" But Daly was a little disappointed Felicia hadn't asked him first.

"I don't want to dance with Jak"—Felicia pretended to pout—"even if he is a devilishly handsome and virile Marine. I want to dance with *you*. I want to dance with a guy who's got some brains. Come on, Candidate Ubrik. We'll do the Mess, it's got real simple steps to it."

"The Mess? Never heard of it," Daly said.

"Yeah? You just stand in the middle of the floor and nothing moves but your bowels!" Felicia's laughter, fueled by several strong alcoholic after-dinner drinks, caused heads on the dance floor to turn in her direction. She covered her mouth in embarrassment. "Okay, Manny, sit here if you want to." She stood and grabbed Daly's hand. "Candidate Daly, show me your stuff."

Felicia proved to be a good dancer, so good she wound up leading Daly across the floor, which he didn't mind one bit. Her strong, hard, athletic young body pressed closely against his felt good. It'd been a long time. "Felicia," he whispered, "let's hit the beach afterward, watch the waves in the moonlight."

"You bet, Marine," she whispered back, "*if* you can rise to the occasion." They both laughed. "But what about Manny?" She nodded in the direction of their table.

Daly glanced back at the table. Ubrik was conversing with a pretty young woman. Daly smiled. "Manny's going to be out for the duration." They moved gracefully across the floor for a while, comfortable in each other's arms, then Daly chuckled and said, "Felicia, you remind me a little of someone back at Camp Howard," and he told her about Bella Dwan.

"'Queen of Killers,' eh?" Felicia murmured. "Sounds like the kind of woman I would like to meet. Does she also shit standing up?"

Daly couldn't help laughing. "Felicia, you don't have any soft edges at all, do you?"

"Yes, Candidate Daly, I do, but only the privileged few ever get to see them. But, Jak, remember this about your Bella. When she dies, she'll rot, just like anybody else."

Universal Catering and Recreation Inc. did not permit gambling, prostitution, or any activity at its resorts that wasn't appropriate for the entire family, but it also did not interfere with what people wanted to do in private. The pretty young woman Daly had seen talking to Ubrik introduced herself when they got back to the table as Julia, an off-duty waitress at one of Oceanside's exclusive nightclubs. She frankly admitted to being single and currently unattached. "I saw Manny sitting alone and thought he might like me to join him. I didn't know you were all together," she apologized.

"Hell, Julia," Felicia said, plopping herself down in her

chair and mock-wiping perspiration from her forehead, "I'm madly in love with my Marine here so you came at just the right time for Manny. Now we've got some *balance* to the evening." She grinned over at Daly. "Hey, Julia," she said as an idea suddenly came to her, "doesn't this place have a seamy side to it? I mean, Arsenault, military personnel all over the place, doesn't Oceanside have a 'strip'—you know, clip joints, all that?"

"You're on it now." Julia laughed, gesturing with her head at the sedate surroundings. "This is about as 'seamy' as it gets in Oceanside. But people still get it on, just not where everyone can see them." she smiled at Ubrik.

"Well," Ubrik said brightly, "shouldn't we be catching the bus back to OTC?"

"It's only twenty hours, Manny! Keep your socks on!" Felicia said. "I want to snuggle a bit with Jak here; besides, the last bus is at zero-one hours, and if we miss that one, they've got twenty-four-hour taxi service. We can sit here until first light if we want to and still be in time for roll call tomorrow."

"Yeah, if you stay sober," Ubrik muttered.

"Hey! Fuck you, GI!" Felicia said, loud enough so people at the nearby tables winced.

Oh, shit! Daly thought. There goes the evening. "Well, I think what Manny means, Felicia, is that our dear old Rumple Stiltskein gets up early in the mornings." Daly turned to Julia. "When we come in next time, how can we get in touch with you?"

She did not answer at once but stared coldly at Ubrik for a moment. "You can't, thank you very much," she answered, voice glacial. Throwing Felicia a killing look, she got up and stalked off.

The bus ride back to OTC was endured in stony silence.

"Muhammad's tits!" Daly raged when he and Ubrik were finally back in their room. "Why the hell did you have to piss Felicia off like that? She was ready to spend the night on the freaking beach with me. Damn! And that Julia? She was for you, Manny, any fool could've seen that. Damn! Damn! Damn!"

"I'm sorry, Jak, I-I'm really sorry," Ubrik stuttered. "I don't know what came over me! I just blurted that out! Besides, Felicia, she's such a-a—I don't know, *rough*. I guess— I guess if anybody had her job, they'd get rough around the edges too."

"Well, she is that," Daly admitted, calming down a bit. "But, Manny, you're a disaster with women. What are you, a misogynist or something like that? You don't like them? We could have had a foursome on the beach until you had to go and screw it all up."

"Jak . . . okay, I'll tell you." Ubrik looked up at Daly, eyes pleading. "Back home on Solden I've got someone, and I believe a promise is a promise, and when you promise yourself to someone you love, you've got to keep your word. A man who breaks his word to a loved one is—is not a gentleman."

Daly almost laughed. He shook his head. "Manny, you are a frigging piece of work, a literal throwback to Victorian times! But by golly, okay, buddy, I understand." He extended his hand and they shook. "I apologize, Manny. That girl of yours back on Solden is one lucky lady to have a guy like you. But I tell you what, old buddy mine, next time I get that Felicia Looonggggg-pine"—he drew out her name—"to go out on liberty with me, I'm going to give her some 'long pine,' you betcha!" He smashed a fist into his wardrobe door.

Ubrik laughed. "Go to it, buddy mine! But I guess I'll just stay back here in the old room and read my Shakespeare."

CHAPTER
FOURTEEN

The sniper teams didn't have specific targets, they were merely inserted near locations that might have targets worth taking out. A military staging area was such a location. Even if they didn't find a high-value target, it would only take a couple of hits from a sniper to begin eroding the morale of the troops being staged.

"Target," Lance Corporal Dwan murmured. "More targets!" They'd been in their initial security position, half a kilometer from their insertion point, for three-quarters of an hour, standard.

"Where?" Sergeant Gossner asked, looking around for an enemy patrol coming to look for them.

"Up there." Dwan slipped off her glove and pointed.

Gossner followed her pointing finger and saw the streaks of light left by two Essays making a combat assault planet-fall some distance away, probably right at the staging area. Surprised, Gossner wondered if Thirty-fourth FIST was making an assault on the staging area, but he only wondered briefly. Surely the Marines on the Bataan Peninsula would clear any offensive operations with Admiral Hoi's operations center, and the admiral wouldn't let them make an assault in an area where a Force Recon squad and sniper team were active without notifying the Marines already on the ground. Dwan was right, these had to be reinforcements for the Coalition troops in the staging area. Besides, the Marines would come with

117

more than two Essays—and they wouldn't land right in the middle of the staging area. He slowly shook his head. During the pre-insertion briefings on board the *Admiral Stoloff,* he'd studied the display showing the Confederation cordon around Ravenette. The captain of the starship that had brought these Essays had to be a brave man—or suicidal—to run that gauntlet. Gossner wondered how long the enemy starship survived after making its drop—and how many Essays were still in the starship's well deck when she died.

He shook that thought off, it didn't pay to dwell on enemy losses.

"Yeah, more targets," he murmured back. He burst-transmitted to the security squad, "Let's move out. I've got point." They'd checked their UV tags on the AstroGhost before they were inserted and again immediately after they assumed their initial security position, so he knew everyone would be able to follow him.

Second squad and the sniper team had been inserted into a nature preserve, a place where urban dwellers could come to observe and relax amid trees and other flora, or take tours to see wild animals in their natural habitats. According to the materials Gossner had studied while en route to Ravenette, and again after getting this assignment, some of the animals were predators big enough to take on a human being—and none of the animals had yet learned fear of man. In normal times, the park was thick with rangers, charged with keeping people from molesting the flora and fauna—or being molested by them. Neither Admiral Hoi's nor General Billie's intelligence sections knew whether the rangers were still patrolling the preserve. So the patrol had to be triply on the alert, watching not only for enemy soldiers, but for rangers and potentially dangerous animals as well.

Gossner knew this wasn't the first time he or Sergeant Kare had gone someplace where they'd had to be wary of the fauna; most Force Recon Marines had to deal with dangerous predators at one time or another. And Gossner himself had even gone where he'd had to be wary of carnivorus flora.

Because of the possibility of rangers in the area, they

couldn't use puddle jumpers, but had to walk the thirty kilometers to the staging area. Nobody knew how much time they had before the Coalition began its big push to overrun the forces pinned on Bataan, or when the troops in the staging area would begin to move out. That lack of knowledge lent an urgency to this patrol, so they couldn't go as slowly as Force Recon normally moved on the ground behind enemy lines. But they couldn't go so fast they would accidentally spook the local animals and thereby possibly alert any rangers or enemy troops in the preserve. That was why Gossner wanted to take point, he was sure he could lead the patrol fast enough to reach their objective before the troops there moved out, while avoiding disturbing the fauna. The animals might not have fear of man, but they'd likely run from men they sensed but couldn't see.

The nature preserve wasn't a totally natural landscape. It had been sculpted and planted to provide a wide variety of habitats. There were temperate and boreal forests, meadows, plains, a desert, and even small mountains. Creeks, rivers, ponds, and lakes watered it. Gossner led the way along interstices between the forests and the open areas—he calculated those were the places the Marines were least likely to encounter animals.

After a few hours of walking, he thought either his assumption was wrong or there were far more animals than he'd expect to find in such relatively small areas. Grazers wandered unconcerned between meadow and wood, from forest to savanna. Rodentlike animals darted or hopped underfoot, in and out of burrows in the grasses and between the roots of trees. Avians swooped to gobble insects in the open, then perched deep within the trees. At one point they passed less than fifty meters from a two-hundred-kilogram predator of a type they'd seen prowling under the trees; it was in the grass, dining on a grazer half its size. Catlike, the beast lifted its head and sniffed in their direction as they passed, then shook its massive shoulders and returned to its repast.

By nightfall they'd covered less than half the distance to the staging area. Gossner called a meal halt, then they set out again, using the light-gatherer screens on their helmets. They'd keep moving until they got where they were going.

Sunrise at Kampeer Aanval

As was his custom, Colonel Amptelik rose just as the sun peeked over the horizon. He didn't need an alarm to awaken, nor did his orderly ever have to rouse him. Wherever he slept, his bedchamber had an east-facing window, which he uncovered before retiring; the changing light of dawn invariably woke him. He made short work of his necessary ablutions in the *badkamer* attached to his chamber, then donned a royal-blue uniform with medals splayed densely across its left breast; it was the uniform he preferred to wear when he first met newly assigned troops. He hadn't yet been informed of the decision to give him command of the reinforced brigade being assembled at Kampeer Aanval, but he was certain such a decision had been made. Why else whould the Trinkatat General Staff assign one of its army's most decorated officers to the command of a troop assembly camp? And surely, that command would lead to a well-deserved promotion.

Ready to face the world less than half an hour after rising, he marched out of his chamber and through his office, with barely a nod at the staff seconds who were sleepily assembling to begin their day's work. Outside he marched to the officers' mess. His aide, still straightening his shirt, scampered to catch up to march a pace to Amptelik's left and rear.

At the mess, the aide darted ahead to open the door for his colonel. The mess major saw who opened the door and called the mess to attention. Only half of the available places were taken. Amptelik chose to believe the others weren't present because they were already working, rather than because they were still asleep or cleaning the night from their bodies. He nodded at the officers and seated himself in his place at the main table. Only when he was sitting did the mess major call out, "Seats!" and the officers resumed their places.

Almost immediately, stewards entered through two doors in the rear of the mess, pushing food-laden carts. The first steward through went directly to the colonel's table and, with the expected flourish, uncovered the lone salver on his cart. From it he served the colonel eggs, ham steak, sausage, fried potatoes, toast, and jam. He also poured a cup of real Trinka-tat coffee, made from the beans of trees long ago imported at great expense from the Brazil section of Earth. Amptelik didn't watch the serving; the steward knew exactly how much of each the colonel wanted on his bone-china plate. Instead, he looked at the other officers, who sat patiently waiting to be served, and mentally noted the names of the stragglers who entered the mess after his arrival.

"Your breakfast, sir," the steward said when he'd finished filling Amptelik's plate. He backed off, taking his cart with him. Around the room, the other stewards began to serve.

Amptelik sat with his back ramrod straight, cut his meats with precise slices of the steak knife set at his place. His hands moved with almost mechanical exactitude as he forked eggs, ham, sausage, potatoes, and jammed toast into his mouth in the order in which they'd been placed on his plate. After each round of foods, he took a measured sip of coffee from his cup. *His* cup, adorned on one side with the three gold and royal-blue lozenges of a colonel's insignia, and on the other with his name in gilt.

Colonel Amptelik ate methodically, neither leisurely nor in haste. When he forked the last morsel and patted his lips with the monogrammed napkin he lifted from his lap, the other officers also stopped eating and rose to their feet, to stand at attention when he stood.

"Gentlemen," Amptelik said curtly, and graced them with an equally curt bow. The others filed out after him; a few looked back longingly at the breakfasts they hadn't had time to finish.

Colonel Amptelik marched from the officers' mess and back to his headquarters, where his chief of staff handed him the list of men who'd arrived the previous afternoon.

Amptelik looked over the list, nodding occasionally when he saw a family name he recognized. "I will address them shortly," he said when he'd finished scanning the list. He didn't ask where the new men were. All new arrivals were billeted in the same place, whether they arrived from the hinterlands of Ravenette or via blockade runners from one of the other worlds of the Coalition.

He sat briefly at his desk, ignoring the bustle of the staff as they went about their duties in the large room. He preferred having his desk in the main room to having it in a private office; he believed the commander's immediate presence helped keep the staff focused on their duties. He made a tick or two on the training schedule that awaited his initials and riffled through the other top reports to see if there were orders for any of the assembling troops to be dispatched as replacements for other units. He smiled internally when there weren't. The lack of orders assigning him to command of the reinforced brigade didn't concern him; so long as none of the troops were being drawn away as replacements for other units, he was certain the expected orders would arrive shortly. A few more reports and schedules needed his initials or signature. He applied them.

Then he was ready to meet the new troops, an entire company's worth of fighters from his home world. He breathed deeply. These men would serve him well. Abruptly, he stood, grabbed his cap from where he'd set it when he'd reached his desk, and marched toward the exit. His aide scrambled to open the door so the colonel wouldn't have to break stride in marching out of the headquarters. Outside, he pivoted left, opposite the direction of the officers' mess, and marched down the middle of the street. A furlong away a barracks stood in front of a small parade ground. He could see men standing in formation on the parade ground as he neared the barracks.

On another post, Colonel Amptelik would go through the barracks, inspecting it on his way to the parade ground in its rear. But Kampeer Aanval was a temporary post, and so were nearly all of its buildings. This, the receiving barracks, had hastily been assembled out of second-rate materials and was never intended to last more than a year or so. Consequently its interior was dusty, floorboards loose, walls chipping, and tiles threatening to fall from its ceiling. At Kampeer Aanval, Amptelik chose to march around the receiving barracks.

He heard officers and sergeants barking the formation to attention before he appeared around the barracks' side and nodded approval—they'd been alerted to his approach, so the troops would be standing in proper soldierly fashion, as was only proper when a senior officer came upon them. He rounded the corner and there they were, 160 officers and men, all from his own home world.

Amptelik marched to the front center of the formation where a captain awaited him. The captain saluted; his arm quivered from the strength with which he threw his hand to his brow.

"Sir, we are the 142nd Company, Trinkatat Guards," the captain announced. "We are most happy to be here, to help the colonel drive the Confederation of Human Worlds into submission and for our freedom!"

Amptelik looked the captain up and down before returning his salute. He wouldn't say anything about the man's slovenly appearance just then. Between the cramped voyage from home and a night in the receiving barracks, it was perhaps understandable that his uniform was rumpled rather than properly pressed and creased. Still, the captain could have given a uniform to one of the enlisted men to clean for him. Amptelik contented himself with deciding not to shake hands after the salute.

"Captain," he acknowledged as he returned the salute. Then he turned to face the men of the 142nd Company of the Trinkatat Guards. The Guards were more a ceremonial than a combat unit, but they were generally well trained. He would find out soon enough if this company was.

Like their commander, the men were in rumpled uniforms. So were the lieutenants who stood in front of each platoon. Amptelik would have a word with the captain later about the men's appearance.

The colonel stood looking at the formation longer than he would normally have; he suddenly felt somewhat ill. Perhaps he needed to more thoroughly inspect the kitchen in the offi—

Outside the Staging Area, Four Hundred Kilometers Northwest of the Bataan Peninsula

The sniper patrol rounded a knoll more than a kilometer southwest of the staging area two hours before sunrise. They hadn't stopped, other than for five minutes each hour, since the previous evening's meal break. They'd encountered no one along the way, neither rangers nor army patrols, and with little difficulty had been able to avoid disturbing the animals. Sergeant Gossner stopped when he began to see lights shining in their objective.

He touched helmets with Sergeant Kare and Lance Corporal Dwan. "Wait here," he told them, and went on alone.

He stopped where he could see the entire breadth of the enemy camp. He wasn't surprised that the camp was lit overnight; it was far enough away from known Coalition forces that the camp commander had no need to order tight light-discipline. He was surprised, though, that the lights were so few. There were lights around the perimeter, but they didn't cover it completely; at least two-thirds of the perimeter was unlit. Inside the camp, he guessed that there were road lights only at street intersections; that would leave long stretches unlit, and there didn't appear to be any lights behind the barracks or other buildings.

The lack of lights in the camp didn't prevent Gossner from seeing into it; he used his helmet's light-gatherer screen to get a panoramic view, then a light filter on his ocular to see close up. Few sentries were posted, at least in the open— some could be in hidden locations, and Gossner saw a number of evident security cameras, some of which were pointed inside the camp. He used all of his sensors and light filters to examine the scrubby landscape between the knoll and the edge of the camp, but saw no sign of patrols. Invitingly open ground extended a quarter kilometer around the camp.

As the camp was four hundred kilometers from the nearest known Confederation forces, the camp commander obviously saw no need for outside security.

A menacing smile came onto Gossner's face; he and Dwan would soon teach the enemy commander otherwise. Anytime you go up against Confederation Marines, he thought, you have to be prepared to get hit anywhere—even in your most secure facilities.

Gossner had watched for less than fifteen minutes, but he'd seen enough. He rejoined the other Marines.

Gossner had Kare set his squad in a defensive covering position on the face of the knoll toward the staging area, high enough to see over the scrub vegetation, yet well below the skyline. Then he and Dwan moved toward the camp. Normally, Gossner would take hours to cover several hundred meters so close to an enemy base, perhaps not getting within maser range until after dark. But normally he'd expect more security than was evident here.

Close to the knoll, the scrub was nearly two meters tall, and the sniper team walked nearly upright for the first couple of hundred meters, then went crouched for two hundred more. He gave Dwan's shoulder a squeeze, it was up to her now—they were far too close for him to risk using his M111; the sound of its report would give away their position.

Dwan's nod and wicked smile went unseen inside her chameleoned helmet. She took the lead and soon lowered herself to hands and knees to stay below the top of the scrub. Gossner followed suit.

The sun broke the horizon shortly before Dwan began crawling, and it was fully up well before she and Gossner reached the edge of the cleared area. The two Marines settled, shoulder to shoulder, in the shadows to observe. Gossner activated his motion detector and his sniffer to give them warning if anybody approached from their sides or rear. They had watched for only a few minutes when Dwan touched helmets with Gossner.

"Juicy target!" she said, and eased into a firing position.

Dwan's "juicy target" was an officer in a royal-blue uniform with a cornucopia of medals splayed across his left chest. Other soldiers, probably officers, trailed out of the building the blue-uniformed officer had left. Gossner groped for Dwan's arm and held it down so she couldn't sight in; the officer was marching too rapidly for her to be able to hold her aim on him for the length of time needed to get a kill with a maser. He leaned close and said through helmet conduction, "He'll be back."

"But I want him now!" Dwan objected. But she didn't try to move her arm from his grip.

They saw a number of attractive targets as they watched, but Dwan wanted the one in the royal-blue uniform. Gossner agreed, he thought that one was either the camp commander or the commanding officer of a unit being assembled here. They could take out some of the other officers if that one didn't make a reappearance.

Throughout the camp, formations of soldiers engaged in physical exercises, while others ran along the streets or marched on a parade ground in the center of the camp. A group of soldiers, it looked like a platoon, held hand-to-hand combat training under the close eye of a sergeant, but that was the only combat training they saw. Another group, about a company, filed out of a barracks and fell into formation behind it.

Dwan poked Gossner with her elbow and leaned in to touch helmets. "He's back!"

"Wait for him," Gossner said. The royal-blue-uniformed officer was headed in the direction of the company that had just formed behind its barracks. When he reached the formation, he didn't look pleased with what he found.

Gossner smiled and squeezed Dwan's shoulder. She took aim and squeezed the trigger of her maser. A second later, the bemedaled officer in the royal-blue uniform crumpled to the ground. The officer he'd stood next to looked down at him for a moment before dropping to a knee to check him out. Then he looked up and shouted something Gossner couldn't hear. A few soldiers under the direction of a sergeant broke ranks and ran inside the barracks.

While Gossner watched that, Dwan looked for another target. "Gotcha," she murmured, and steadied her maser on a portly officer as far to her right as the first one had been to her left. Over the next several minutes, with Gossner spotting for her, she killed three more officers and got a probable.

"That's enough, let's go," Gossner finally said.

"No, it's not, I'm having fun!"

"Pretty soon they're going to figure out somebody's out here and come looking for us. Let's go."

"This is a big area, it'll take them a while to find us." But she lowered the maser from her shoulder and turned to lead the way out of their blind, back to the knoll.

Gossner looked at the marks they'd left on the ground and sighed silently. Well, there was always the possibility the marks wouldn't be found. And even if they were found, the simple fact that someone could get so close to the camp unseen, and kill five or six officers before anybody had any idea what was happening, would have an unnerving effect on the soldiers at the camp—particularly on the officers.

Three hours later, the sniper patrol was halfway to its extraction point, to be delivered to its next area of operation.

Base Dispensary, Kampeer Aanval

Lieutenant Colonel Nommertwee, the assistant base commander of Kampeer Aanval, stood between two rows of beds in the base dispensary's sick ward. Usually, most of the eighteen beds were occupied by junior soldiers, some sick, others malingering. At this time, however, all of them had been returned to their units, save for one laid up in traction from a training accident. Nommertwee brushed away the thought that this was another example of a grievance the worlds of the Coalition had against the Confederation: the Confederation had withheld the modern medical technology that would have let that injured soldier be repaired and returned to duty in a matter of no more than a week, instead of having to undergo months of healing and rehabilitation.

Grievances against the Coalition weren't Nommertwee's reason for visiting the sick ward. He was there because of the six sheet-covered bodies lying on as many beds at one end of the room.

The doctor, a young lieutenant, gestured for him to approach the first body and lifted the sheet from its head and shoulders when he did. Nommertwee looked impassively down at the face of Colonel Amptelik.

"What killed him?" he asked.

The doctor swung an arm at the other five bodies. "I'd say the same thing that killed them."

"And that was?" Nommertwee kept the impatience he felt out of his voice.

The doctor shook his head. "I have no idea, sir. None of them bear any marks, and so far as I have been able to learn, none of them complained about any malaise before they suddenly collapsed." Puzzlement furrowed his brow. "They all collapsed within a few minutes of each other," he said softly.

"You've examined them?"

The doctor nodded. "A surface exam. My next steps are to cut them open for autopsy and extract tissue samples for analysis."

"How long will that take?"

"I can complete most of the basic autopsies by the end of the day."

"You are a forensic pathologist?"

"No, but all military doctors in forward bases are required to have some training in forensic pathology. I have that training."

"All right. How long will the tests on the tissue samples take?"

The doctor shook his head again. "I don't know. They are more complex than my dispensary can handle. I'll have to send them to a pathology lab for analysis."

"That can take a while?"

"Yessir, it will."

A junior officer, the late Colonel Amptelik's aide, bustled into the sick ward and waited for Nommertwee to acknowledge him.

"Speak," Nommertwee said after a moment.

"Sir, I have completed my investigation of the movements of these officers for this morning."

"I doubt you'd be disturbing me if you hadn't," Nommertwee said. "What did you find?"

The aide swallowed and cleared his throat. "Sir, the only location the—the dead men had in common this morning was the officers' mess. They were all there for breakfast at the same time." He looked pale; he'd also been there.

Nommertwee turned back to the doctor. "Could it be food poisoning?"

The doctor arched his eyebrows. "Food poisoning usually has symptoms that build up over a short period of time. And if it was, the pathogen responsible should have affected more than just six officers." He shrugged. "But then, we *are* on a strange planet where there *could* be pathogens that act in such a manner."

"Check it out." Nommertwee glanced around at the six bodies. "And test for poisons, someone might have killed them deliberately." He turned to the aide. "I want the officers' mess closed until we find out what happened. And arrest everyone who was working there last night and this morning. I want them in the stockade where they can be questioned."

"Yessir!" The late colonel's aide scampered out of the sick ward.

"Doctor, I will leave you to your duties. Notify me immediately of anything you find."

"I'll do that, sir." The doctor watched Nommertwee's back as the man left and thought, I suspect whatever caused these deaths is beyond my abilities to discover.

CHAPTER
FIFTEEN

Logistics, Marine OTC, Arsenault

The academic standards required to graduate from OTC were strict. If any candidate fell below 75 on any written examination in any course, remedial coaching was required; to miss that mark twice meant going on probation; a third failure resulted in the candidate's immediate expulsion.

The most difficult course for Jak Daly was called "Logistical Support in the Company and Battalion Area of Operations." It was taught by a civilian, a Dr. Honsue Mitzikawa. Dr. Mitzikawa always dressed in a rumpled suit, squinted at the class as if he suffered from uncorrected nearsightedness, and spoke in a high, reedy voice that from the first moment of the class got on everyone's nerves. Plus, the subjects he taught were excruciatingly boring. They included, as he told them on that first day, but were not at all limited to, such arcane endeavors as rationing, water purification methods and procedures, transportation requirements, ammunition resupply—Daly looked forward to that—energy resourcing, and something Mitzikawa called "Hand Receipts and Statements of Charges: Conducting Inventories in a Hostile Environment."

But by the end of that first day of class, Daly had begun to form a somewhat more positive view of the skinny civilian instructor. At one point during Mitzikawa's introduction he asked Daly a question. Referring to his class roster and seating arrangement, he ran a bony finger down the chart and, as luck would have it, rested the digit right smack on Daly's name.

"Candidate Daly." Mitzikawa squinted in Daly's general direction. "Can you give us the formula for calculating the time gap in a convoy of two serials with two march units each with the gap between units as five minutes and the gap between serials as ten minutes? Quickly, quickly now, we're all waiting."

Daly thought quickly. "I don't know, sir."

"Don't call me 'sir,' Candidate Daly!" Mitzikawa screeched. "I work for a living!" Total silence enveloped the class as they stared back at Dr. Mitzikawa in unbelieving horror, as if he had just uttered an unforgivable blasphemy. Feigning utter amazement, he asked, "You never heard that expression before?" Sure, they'd all heard the expression before, but no one ever expected to hear it from the lips of a faculty member, in *Officer Training College*! Then someone laughed. "I learned that in the army," Mitzikawa admitted. "I was a professional private first-class. Then I got tired of hauling boxes and became an officer, a logistician, so I could *kick* the boxes instead. You've heard the expression, haven't you? 'Yesterday I could not even spell *logistician*. Today I are one'? Well, that's *me,* ladies and gentlemen! Then I got a real job: teaching at this charm school. Okay.

"Mr. Daly, we'll get back to figuring time gaps in convoys later in this course, and believe me, by the time we're done, you'll all be figuring them in your sleep—that is, when you aren't having nightmares of old Rumple Stiltskein making you do push-ups all over the grinder." He smiled, revealing crooked teeth, and the entire class burst into raucous laughter.

Mitzikawa stood grinning idiotically for a few seconds, then held up his hands for silence. "Keep it down, keep it down! If the commandant thinks you're actually *enjoying* this course, he'll have you all committed." Another big grin. "But, children, let me tell you at the beginning here, there are only four rules of military logistics that you should know. Know them and you can run any logistical operation. Are you ready? Write these down if you can't remember them.

"One. Fair Wear and Tear. You can write off almost anything due to FWT. Well, don't try it with a Dragon, but anything you can wear or carry can be turned in or junked due to Fair Wear and Tear. Got that?

"Two. Combat Loss. Ah"—he held up a bony forefinger—"*that's* how you write off a Dragon, an artillery tube, even your convoy of two serials, whatever in the hell they are!

"Three! Oh, you'll *love* this one, my children." Mitzikawa virtually beamed with pleasure. "RFM for short: Read the Fucking Manual! Yes! Nobody can remember all the crap he's going to learn in this course, but remember, *everything* is in the Marine Corps Orders, the manuals, the regulations, the instructions, the whatevers. You want distance, rate, and time calculations—are you listening Candidate Daly?—turn to Field Manual 55-15, SSIC 04000, 'Transportation Reference Data,' Chapter One, and voilà! There you have it!"

"But, Dr. Mitzikawa!" One of the students raised his hand. He'd been taking notes on his data pad and had just used it to access the library's online catalog. "That's an *army* publication!"

"What?" Mitzikawa came back to earth suddenly. He glared at the student and puffed out his cheeks. "Of *course* it's an army field manual, you cretin! The army figured all this business out years and years ago, back about the time Napoléon was hauling his guns around behind horses! The army *writes,* the Marine Corps *fights*! You don't expect the Navy Department to waste its money writing its own goddamned manuals when the army's already done that, do you?" He shook his head as if dealing with a recalcitrant idiot. "Silence in this classroom!" he shrieked. "Not one more syllable from anyone. We are now going to have a logistician's epiphany!"

Then Dr. Mitzikawa began to dance behind the podium, hyping himself up to reveal "Honsue's Fourth Secret of the Logistician's Code." He extended both arms over his head, revealing big sweat stains under his armpits. "Ah, ah, ah!" he intoned, as if he were reciting a mantra, looking at the ceiling, asking God Himself for guidance. "*Here it is!* Remember this rule, the Golden Rule of Box Kickers, and you can forget the other three! This rule is the definitive solution to any problem an S4 staff officer may encounter in a long career!" There now ensued a long, long pause as Mitzikawa stood there, arms raised, eyes closed tight, a beatific smile on his face. And then:

"FOURRRRRRR! When in doubt, *ASK YOUR SERGEANT*!" Dr. Honsue Mitzikawa shrieked. "Class dismissed!"

Later, as they were leaving class, Ubrik sidled up to Daly and asked, "Well, what do you think of this guy, Jak?"

Daly shrugged. "He's frigging crazy as a kwangduk on a hot mess kit, Manny. But what the hell, nobody's perfect."

Candidate Quarters, Marine OTC

Daly and Ubrik sat in their room going over the day's logistics class lesson, the dreaded distance, rate, and time calculations.

"Jak, let's take a break, go down to the gedunk, and get us some junk food, the kind of crap that'll make us into fat-assed staff officers," Ubrik said, laughing.

"Ah, I don't know, Manny. I've got to get this stuff figured out. Besides"—he shrugged—"I was just thinking about that lance corporal, you remember, Beverly Nasaw. For some reason all this, this"—he gestured at his computer screen, which was displaying chapter 1 of FM 55-15, "put me in mind of an early death."

Ubrik laughed. "Oh, Beverly, yes, yes, tragic accident." something in the way Ubrik spoke made Daly wince. He had the ridiculous impression that Ubrik, of all people, had been a bit jealous of Daly's budding relationship with the woman.

"I mean, Manny," Daly went on, "hell, I can sight in a maser rifle at a hundred meters in the dark! Do a forced march over the mountains with a whole army after my ass—"

"You don't have to tell me *that*," Ubrik responded with feeling. "Hadn't been for you, Jak, and I'd never have made it through zero month!" He patted his friend gently on the shoulder.

"But this stuff, Manny . . ." Daly gestured helplessly at his console.

"All right, Jak, here's how it's done. You have a column of two serials with two march units each and the gap between march units is five minutes and the gap between serials is ten minutes. Then: [(number of march units minus one) times march unit time gap] plus [(number of serials minus one) times (serial time gap minus march unit time gap)]. There it is, or expressed like this:

"Time gaps = $[(4-1) \times 5] + [(2-1) \times 5] = [3 \times 5] + [1 \times 5] = 15 + 5 = 20$ minutes!"

"But what the *hell* does it all mean?"

"Hey, Jak, who gives a damn? This isn't a course in teleology! This is the Marine Corps, we're only interested in getting from point A to point B so we can blow up point B! Remember the formulas! That's all you need to do to pass the exam. If this ever comes up again in real life, do what old Mitzikawa said, look it up or ask your S4 sergeant."

"Manny, you're a frigging genius when it comes to this stuff," Daly said.

"Naw, formulas just come naturally to me, Jak-O. All right, let's move on to calculating road space for a convoy of eighty-seven vehicles. You divide the number of vehicles by their density plus time gaps and time rate divided by sixty minutes. Density is 8.5 vehicles per kilometer; the rate is fifty kilometers in an hour; and the time gaps are equal to twenty, so:

"Road space $= \dfrac{87}{8.5} + \dfrac{20 \times 50}{60} = 10.2 + 16.7 = 26.9$ per klick . . ."

"Ah, the hell with it, Manny, let's go to the gedunk!"

Logistics, Marine OTC

On the final exam in transportation reference data, Daly scored an impressive 76. In fact, much to his amazement, he passed all the exams, even the pop quizzes used to surprise the students at the beginning of classes. Months later, just before graduation, Daly approached Dr. Mitzikawa, who had by then become almost a friend of the beleaguered candidates, and asked:

"Dr. Mitzikawa, on the first day of class you told us you'd be giving us a lecture on something you called 'Hand Receipts and Statements of Charges: Conducting Inventories in a Hostile Environment,' but we have never had this lecture and the course is almost over now."

Mitzikawa gave Daly a lopsided grin. "Jak, nobody ever fails my course. You and I both know half to three-quarters of the stuff I teach you in this course you will never need to use again. But the Marine Corps figures all its officers should be *exposed* to this material, so you have some idea of what the experts have to deal with. 'Hand Receipts and Statements of Charges'? Jak, were I to load you up with nonsense like that, they'd commit me! I just threw that in there to screw over your minds. Like I told you on the first day of class, Read the—"

"—Fucking Manual."

"Or?"

"Ask your sergeant."

"Candidate Daly, you ever read Hawthorne's *The Scarlet Letter*?"

"Can't say as I have, Doctor."

"Pity. Well, with those answers you just gave me, by the time this course is over, you may just have earned your own 'scarlet letter,' a great big 'A.'"

CHAPTER
SIXTEEN

Following a Road, Five Hundred Kilometers Northwest
of the Bataan Peninsula

Fourth squad flew close to the ridgeline, only a few meters
above the scrub that covered the slope, so they could quickly
drop into cover if they spotted traffic either on the ground or
in the air. Sergeant Williams kept an eye on the road, carefully looking for sign that the tracks the squad had been following for the past hour turned off or otherwise disappeared.
Every kilometer or so, the squad paused while Williams
dropped down to take a closer look. Every time he did, the
tracks shone a little brighter in infrared. The suspected laser-
emplacement vehicle had to be moving fairly fast, at least
seventy kilometers per hour; Williams thought they would
have caught up with it by now if it had been going fifty or
even sixty kpm.

Williams wondered about that; seventy kpm or faster
seemed too great a speed for a specialized military vehicle to
maintain for so long. Sure, a sturdy landcar could manage
one hundred kpm or even faster on a gravel road, even one as
poorly maintained as this one was. So could most military
vehicles. But the vehicle they were seeking carried passively
controlled laser guns, a relatively fragile cargo. Or had it emplaced its last gun and was heading back for another load?

"Dust cloud," Lance Corporal Rudd's voice interrupted
Williams's thoughts.

The squad leader didn't ask where; Rudd was on point and
mainly watching ahead. Williams looked that way. A few

kilometers to the front the road bent around a spur of the ridge it was following; a faint dust cloud rose above the spur. Williams accelerated to close with Rudd and signaled him to land. By the time Corporal Belinski and Lance Corporal Skripska caught up and began to drop to the ground, Williams had given Rudd new orders and the two of them were rising again, so Belinski and Skripska followed their leader without knowing what the change in plan was.

They figured it out soon enough. Alerted by Rudd's terse report, they'd looked forward and seen the dust cloud. Rudd was no longer paralleling the road, he was moving at an angle, climbing the ridge side, on a course to intercept the dust cloud on the other side of the spur.

The Marines increased speed and were only a couple of kilometers behind the dust cloud when Rudd topped the spur. He immediately dropped back behind the spur and landed. Belinski and Skripska joined him while Williams popped to the top to take a quick look for himself.

"Got him," Williams told his men when he joined them. "We're going to make a kill. The road bends back to the left up ahead. We're going ten klicks beyond the bend to set an ambush. I'm taking point. Let's go."

The four Marines took off at top speed, staying well below the top of the ridgeline so the puddle jumpers' exhausts couldn't be seen from the road.

When they were far enough ahead of the laser emplacer that it wouldn't notice their exhausts, Williams stopped the squad and hopped up to the top of the ridgeline to look for an ambush site. Half a kilometer ahead was a jumble of rocks on the side of the ridge that looked as if it could be dislodged by a small explosive charge to tumble onto the road. Other rocks on the slope could provide the squad with cover—thanks to their chameleons, he didn't concern himself with concealment.

To his left, back the way they'd come, he saw the dust cloud of the rapidly approaching vehicle.

Williams wasted no time getting his squad into position to the rear and sides of the rock jumble. As soon as they shucked their puddle jumpers, Rudd helped him emplace the explosives.

That done, Williams took his place to the left rear of the rocks; Rudd joined Belinski at the right rear. Williams would spring the ambush by setting off the charges. They waited for the vehicle to arrive.

And waited.

Williams had estimated that the vehicle was no more than five minutes away when he took his place with Skripska. After ten minutes he stood up to take a look. There was no dust cloud in sight. He got out his ocular and used it to scan the road and its sides. They were both empty of any traffic, moving or stopped.

"Saddle up," he tight-beamed to his men. "We have to backtrack and find out where he went." He strapped on his puddle jumper as he trotted to the rock jumble to retrieve the explosives.

A Hidden Track, Five Hundred Kilometers Northwest of the Bataan Peninsula

Six kilometers back, fourth squad found a narrow track in the trees to the north where the laser gun emplacement vehicle had turned off the road. Sergeant Williams silently swore; if he'd had somebody watching the road while the squad was getting into its ambush position, they would probably have seen the vehicle make the turn. But he hadn't and had lost ten or fifteen minutes on the satellite killer—perhaps long enough for the crew to set up another gun, perhaps long enough for the gun to find and kill another satellite. If the navy was still launching satellites . . .

Williams left his men on the ground at the entrance to the hidden track while he popped up to take a look, but the canopy was too thick for him to spot the way underneath it. From the brief look he'd taken of the track before he'd popped up, he knew it was too narrow and winding for the squad to traverse using their puddle jumpers at the speed they'd need to close the gap. So he needed to figure out where the vehicle might have gone. If they were setting up another gun, there had to be a clearing someplace.

He dropped back down to tell his men to wait while he went ahead for a quick recon. He rose to five hundred meters and flew a zigzag path over the forest. Five klicks in, he found the vehicle. Its crew looked to be setting up another gun at the edge of a small clearing. Taking time only to log the coordinates of the clearing, he spun about and headed back at top speed.

Sergeant Williams didn't hear the shout behind him as he took off.

Minutes later, the four Marines of fourth squad had dropped their puddle jumpers and were moving at route march through the woods twenty-five meters in from the track; at this point, speed was more important than silence. Fortunately, the canopy was dense enough that there was relatively little growth under the trees to impede rapid movement. Williams didn't know how long it would take the crew to set up the laser gun, or whether they'd leave the clearing as soon as they'd finished setting up. If the vehicle came back along the road before the squad reached the clearing, the Marines would hear them coming and could set up a hasty ambush. Otherwise, the Marines would hit them in the clearing, then destroy the laser gun and the emplacement vehicle. But if the crew got the gun set up and left via a different route before the Marines got there . . .

In that case, fourth squad would destroy the gun, retrieve their puddle jumpers, then try to find the vehicle again. With luck, they'd find and destroy it before they had to rendezvous with the AstroGhost to replace the rapidly decreasing fuel in their puddle jumpers.

Two hundred meters from the clearing, the Marines slowed down and spread out. They had to move silently if they wanted to catch their prey by surprise. Fifty meters from the clearing, they caught glimpses of it through the trees. They slowed even more, all senses alert, ready to respond with deadly force if they were somehow discovered.

Williams saw the emplacement vehicle but not the laser

gun. Ominously, neither could he see or hear any members of the crew. Where were they? Were they resting somewhere out of sight, or were they—

A sudden high-speed whine and bark splinters spraying off a tree trunk next to him answered his questions.

Williams dove to the ground and rolled away from the tree that had just been hit by a burst from a fléchette gun. He dropped his infra screen into place and looked for the red blotch that would tell him where the gun or the man firing it was. Before he found it, another fléchette gun sent a spray of deadly darts through the forest, as did several small arms. So far, none of the Marines had returned fire.

Williams toggled on the open-band squad circuit and ordered, "Count off!"

"Belinski, check" came the first reply.

"Rudd, I'm okay."

"Skripska. Where the hell are they?"

While the Marines were reporting in, Williams saw the glow of the second fléchette gun and swore—it was firing from a flexible mount on the armored front of the emplacement vehicle. They'd have to burn through the armor to get to the crew, and that would take enough time to give the soldiers outside plenty of opportunity to get to the Marines. So he decided on the next best thing.

Williams took careful aim with his blaster and fired three rapid plasma bolts at the stubby barrel of the fléchette gun. Without waiting to see the result of his fire, he rolled several meters to his right. And just in time—the other fléchette gun and at least two small arms tore up the ground where he'd just been. But he saw a target in the infrared and snapped off two quick bolts at it before rolling away again.

By then the other Marines had also found targets and were firing. Every time they did, they moved. They had to move, there was no way to shield the flame of a plasma bolt as it left a blaster and burned its way to its target. Even if the enemy soldiers couldn't see the Marines, their blaster fire would give away their positions.

A cut-off scream from somewhere around the clearing

told Williams that one of the enemy soldiers had been hit. He grinned grimly and looked for another target. There was one! He snapped two bolts at it and moved, rolling behind a tree. The remaining fléchette gun rat-a-tat-tatted the other side of the tree.

Damn, they know where I am! he thought. *How?*

Suddenly, the whirring of the gun stopped, and only two small arms continued firing at the Marines. Two of the Marines fired simultaneously. Williams saw their bolts converge, and one of the weapons went silent.

Then the other stopped shooting, and an oblong object flew from behind a boulder: a fléchette rifle.

"Don't shoot, I surrender," came a voice from behind the boulder. "I give up. Don't shoot!" A pair of raised hands appeared, and a soldier slowly stood with his empty hands held high above his head.

"Is there anybody else?" Williams shouted at the soldier.

"No, you killed everybody else," the soldier called back, his voice trembling.

"Belinski, keep him covered," Williams ordered, speaking in the clear so the surviving Coalition soldiers could hear him. "Rudd, Skripska, cover me. There's still somebody inside the vehicle. I'm going to get him out." The three Marines acknowledged the orders. The prisoner looked around nervously, shaken by not being able to see the people he heard calling back and forth.

Williams cautiously rose to a crouch. When nobody shot at him, he dashed to the emplacement vehicle. The barrel of the fléchette gun tracked him, but the plasma bolts he'd fired at it had caused the barrel to soften and bend. He clambered to the top of the vehicle and aimed his blaster at a hatch. "Throw out any weapons you have and come out with your hands up," he commanded.

"Come in and get me!" came the defiant response.

"I'm not going to do that," Williams replied flatly. "You can come out empty-handed and surrender, or you can die in that vehicle when we blow it. Your choice."

There was silence for a moment, then a hatch on the side

of the vehicle slowly swung open and a sidearm flew out, followed by a knife.

"Do you have any other weapons?" Williams demanded.

"No" was the sullen reply.

"Then show me your hands and come out."

A pair of hands appeared, followed by a gangly soldier, who climbed out to stand next to the vehicle, looking decidedly unhappy.

Williams didn't give the man time to think about what to do; instead, he jumped on his back, knocking him to the ground and pinning him. In seconds, he had the soldier's hands secured behind his back.

"You're a brave man," Williams told him as he stood. "It's a good thing you didn't stay stupid and get yourself killed." Then to the side: "Belinski, secure the other prisoner."

"Aye, aye, honcho."

A few minutes later, the two prisoners were secured to trees far enough apart that they couldn't talk privately, and the Marines had collected four bodies. Only then did Williams take stock of his men. Skripska was partly visible; fresh blood stained the side of his chameleons.

"How bad is it?" Williams asked as he opened Skripska's shirt to look at the wound.

"Doesn't hurt too much." Skripska grimaced when Williams probed the wound; three fléchettes had torn through the muscle over his ribs, but the bleeding had almost stopped. "I don't think any bones are cracked."

"We'll let a corpsman decide that when we get back aboard the AstroGhost." Williams affixed a patch of synth-skin over the wound. "In the meantime, I think you'll live."

"That's reassuring."

With Skripska's wound taken care of, Williams sent Belinski to question the soldier who had surrendered first, and Rudd and Skripska to fix explosives to the emplacement vehicle and the laser gun the crew had set up. The vehicle still had three laser guns in its cargo compartment. Williams himself questioned the prisoner from inside the vehicle.

"Do you know who we are?" Williams asked his prisoner.

He squatted and raised his helmet screens so the soldier could see his face.

"Yer Confederation scum," the man spat.

Williams shrugged his eyebrows. "I guess some would say that. Especially after we've kicked their asses. We're Marine Force Recon." He waited, but the prisoner didn't react to that information. Maybe he'd never heard of Force Recon. "You were ready for us," Williams said. "How'd you know we were coming?"

The prisoner smirked. "Sergeant Grotoks, he saw somethin' in the sky over yonder." He jerked his head to the south. "Said he thunk it were one a them puddle jumper thangs what the Confederation sometimes uses. He thunk mebbe it was a scout, and he'd bring back troops t' try an' take us out."

Williams silently cursed himself; evidently he'd been too careless when he reconned the clearing. But he didn't let the prisoner know that. Instead, he asked, "If you thought someone was coming, why did you wait? You had to know you'd be outnumbered."

The prisoner snorted. "We's from Embata, that's why. Embatans don't run. We been wanting t' fight, an' this laser-gun shit din give us no chance t' fight. So we got ready."

"So you fought, and we kicked your asses."

The prisoner shrugged; that they'd lost, that four of them were killed and the other two captured, mattered to him less than that they'd fought instead of running.

"You don't have infras," Williams said. "Even if you did, our infra signatures are damped down pretty far. Yet you seemed to know where we were. How'd you do that?"

The prisoner grinned. "Easy. Sergeant Grotoks thunk mebbe Marines would come, an' Marines sometimes wear invisible suits." He nodded at a part of Williams that he couldn't see. "So he put out motion detectors and gave us all monitors so's we'd know where you was."

Williams nodded to himself. Yes, motion detectors were more of a threat to Force Recon Marines than infras.

Rudd interuppted the interrogation. "We got them wired, honcho."

Williams rose from his squat. "All right," he said into the squad circuit, "let's saddle up. Hobble the prisoners so they can't run. When we're ready, Skripska has point. Me, the prisoners, Belinski, Rudd." He gave Belinski a look. Belinski nodded—if the prisoners tried to run, he'd kill them.

The explosives went off, destroying the emplacement vehicle and its laser guns before the Marines got back to their puddle jumpers. As soon as Williams got his puddle jumper on, he hopped up and transmitted the report he'd prepared to the *Kiowa,* where Commander Obannion had moved his headquarters. They lashed each prisoner between a pair of Marines and headed to meet the AstroGhost at their pickup point.

The prisoner who had been so surly and defiant after the fight wet his pants from fear during the flight.

CHAPTER
SEVENTEEN

One Hundred Kilometers Due West of the Bataan Peninsula

Sergeant Kindy decided to wait until dusk, then lead his squad across the fields to the building complex. While they waited, he set Corporal Nomonon and Lance Corporal Ellis to provide security to their flanks and rear and assigned Corporal Jaschke to take a census of the compound. He himself watched the compound, trying to discern any patterns of movement or activity that might give him a hint to the location of the entrance to the underground complex.

Jaschke got out his ocular and connected it to his comp, then began methodically looking at the people visible in the fields and the compound, focusing on each face. He wouldn't be able to get a complete record of everybody there, nor could the census tell what any of their positions were, but the census would give the Marines a minimum number of people present. At first, every face Jaschke focused on was new to his comp, so the numbers added up rapidly. But then he began recording faces a second and third time, and the count slowed down. This was also potentially valuable information, knowing which people moved around the most and where they came and went. Later, Jaschke would feed the data to Kindy, and Kindy might be able to see connections between the census data and his own observations.

When the sun was only a couple of diameters above the horizon, Kindy touched helmets with Jaschke and asked him for his data. By feel, they touched their comps together and

Jaschke initiated contact transmission. Seconds later Kindy had all the census data and began studying it.

Jaschke had been right about Kindy's being able to integrate the data with his own observations. Kindy quickly picked out three men from the data, men he'd particularly noticed while he was watching.

One was a young man, bare-headed, with a short haircut. Despite his civilian clothing, he looked every bit a junior enlisted man. He, more than anybody else in the compound, constantly went from place to place. According to Jaschke's data, he visited more places than anybody else in the compound. But no matter how many times he went out, or how many locations at which he stopped, he always returned to the same place—the building Kindy had tentatively identified as the headquarters building. Kindy thought he must be a runner.

The second man of note was older and grizzled. He wore a hat and held himself ramrod straight; his gait was nearly a march. Just like the younger man looked like a junior enlisted man, this one had the look of a senior sergeant. He didn't go out and about as often as the runner did, nor did he visit as many places. But whenever and wherever he went, he did so purposefully, and always returned to the headquarters building.

The third man who had caught Kindy's eye left the possible headquarters building the least and went to the fewest other locations—actually only three others, one of which seemed to be a mess hall. He looked to be intermediate in age between the sergeant and the private, and his gait was likewise between the sergeant's brisk march and the runner's more casual gait. The most distinctive thing about him was his clothing. Even though he was dressed in the same basic farmworker style as everybody else in the compound, his appeared to be of a finer cut and more meticulously cleaned. To Kindy's experienced eye, he looked like the senior officer of a small unit, a captain or perhaps a junior commander. Make that a major, Kindy thought—most of the armies of the Coalition forces had instituted the rank of major; majors normally held staff positions.

Kindy decided to think of the probable officer as a major. There was a joke he'd heard a couple of times: "The Confederation Marine Corps doesn't have majors because a major is an officer fit only for staff duty, and the Marines only have officers who are fit for command."

Of the other two locations the major visited, one looked to be his quarters. The other was a small, nondescript building that the sergeant and the runner also visited. That building had one odd feature—its roof bulged higher than one would expect of a building that took up so little ground. On reflection, Kindy thought the excess height could contain the workings of an elevator to the underground complex.

In all, the census had identified ninety-seven people in the compound, eighty-eight of whom were men. All but a few of those men—the ones operating equipment in the fields—had a clearly military air about them. Nobody wore a uniform, everybody was dressed as an agricultural worker, except for a few who were dressed in white, as though they were food service workers.

Ninety-seven people, eighty-eight of them men. Most of the men looked military. Kindy pondered the situation. Why would soldiers be going around their own compound in civilian clothes? Why would the military bury a complex underneath a farm?

The answer to the second question was obvious; the military complex was buried under the farm to hide it. But hide it from whom? Surely the Coalition wasn't expecting Force Recon, which was the Confederation's only military asset that could penetrate so deeply behind enemy lines. Didn't they realize how effective they'd been at preventing the Confederation Navy from launching its string-of-pearls? Or did they expect the navy to be able to search and analyze the entire landmass from the orbiting warships? That must be it— the Coalition didn't know the limits on the navy's surveillance abilities.

Kindy began to think about how the squad could get into the elevator building, if that's what the high-roofed, nondescript

structure was, and take the elevator down without anybody
noticing anything amiss.

The sun began sinking below the horizon and Kindy put
his squad in motion.

Kindy prepared another report and uploaded it the next
time the *Kiowa* was in range.

Inside a Farming Complex, One Hundred Kilometers Due West of the Bataan Peninsula

Sergeant Kindy started the squad moving when the bottom of the sun's disk kissed the horizon beyond the farm
building complex. They went single file at twenty-meter intervals, with Corporal Nomonon in the lead, followed by
Kindy. Corporal Jaschke brought up the rear, with Lance
Corporal Ellis between him and Kindy.

They took their time, there was no rush, they had eleven
hours standard to get in, find what they were looking for, and
get back out, before sunrise. Plenty of time. Besides, there
was still a good deal of activity inside the complex, and they
wouldn't want any of the locals bumping into a Marine because they couldn't see him.

Each of the Marines used most of his array of sensors during the movement across the fields. Nomonon had his ears
turned up, and his motion detector and sniffer on. He used his
light-gatherer screen to aid his vision. Kindy rotated through
his infra, light-gatherer, and magnifier screens, and sometimes
flicked on his UV finder. His ears were up and motion detector on. Ellis, the least experienced Marine in the squad, used
only his infra and his motion detector. His ears were halfway
up. Jaschke rotated between his infra and light-gatherer screens
and had his motion detector and sniffer on. Like the others,
his ears were turned up.

Third squad crossed the fields at a leisurely pace for anybody not a Force Recon Marine in hostile territory, but a fast
pace for them. It took three hours for them to move the ten
kilometers from their observation point to the building com-

plex, the last hour of which was spent crossing the last kilometer.

Fewer people were out and about by then. Those who were, mostly went back and forth between the barracks structures or between a barracks and the mess hall. The headquarters and the small building that was the squad's immediate objective were just about the only other buildings anybody went to. The grizzled sergeant was the most frequent visitor to the small building. Those two buildings were the only ones lit from inside—and the small building was only intermittently lit.

Kindy directed Nomonon to take a long route to the small building, passing by the headquarters and mess hall. He paused outside the heaquarters building and listened. All he heard was a low susurration of unhurried voices and the occasional ticking of office equipment. He stood a couple of meters away from a window and took a look inside. The only people he could see were the sergeant and two younger men. One of the young men looked like a company clerk, or duty NCO. The other, not quite as young, looked like a duty officer. Kindy wondered, if there is a duty officer and a duty NCO, where are the sentries? Except for the guard box at the far side of the complex, the Marines hadn't seen any evidence of sentries.

Whatever their function was, the three men in the room sat in relaxed conversation, evidently with no idea that an enemy reconnaissance patrol had them under close observation. The Marines then checked the building they had tentatively identified as a mess hall, which turned out to be a combination dining and recreation hall. Through different windows, they saw a dining room crammed with eight-man tables, a sparsely appointed weight room, two smallish rooms with tables at some of which men sat playing games, and a trid theater. Peals of laughter came out of that room, though Kindy didn't recognize the trid or any of the actors he saw.

In all, the headquarters and the mess hall presented scenes one might find on any military installation in time of peace— or far from any action during war.

Kindy directed Nomonon to proceed toward the shedlike building with the high roof.

The building was dark when the Marines reached it. Kindy had them settle themselves against the side of a nearby barn where they had a clear view of the entrance. Only a few minutes later, a light came on inside, then the door opened and the man Kindy called the major came out. The officer reached somewhere out of sight to the side of the door and the light went off. The door was open long enough for Kindy to see—nothing. The small building seemed to have only one room, and that room was empty.

Kindy didn't have enough information to go on yet, so the Marines continued to wait. He didn't think they'd have to wait long; during the hour the squad had spent crossing the last kilometer of fields, he observed that people came or went from the building at irregular but frequent intervals.

He was right. The next person came in less than ten minutes. A man walked up, opened the door, and reached inside. The light came on. Kindy was able to see past him to the far corner of the room where someone else was rising from below the floor. The elevator moved, if not silently, then at least quietly enough that Kindy couldn't hear it from where he stood, not even with his ears turned up halfway.

Now that he knew what he was looking at, Kindy saw runners set into the walls at the corner—he'd been right, the building held an elevator. The door closed and reopened a moment later to let a man out, presumably the one Kindy had seen rising.

Kindy gathered his men close and touched helmets to tell them what he'd seen and what they were going to do.

They waited three minutes, until nobody was visible nearby, then dashed to the building and inside. Kindy didn't grope to turn on the light; instead the Marines used their light-gatherer screens. The view through the light gatherer was eerie, and it could be unsettling to people not used to it. Everything was monochrome, and there wasn't a sharp perception of depth. But the Marines *were* used to it and had no trouble seeing where they were going or what they were doing.

The floor in the far corner of the room clearly showed the platform for the elevator, which was more than large enough for the four Marines to stand on together. A thin pillar at the platform's free corner helped support an overhead and anchored restraining chains that ran between it and the walls. An unobtrusive plate on one wall had two buttons, each marked with an arrow, one pointed up, the other down.

Kindy wondered at what he saw as an astonishing lack of security. Or was the security all below the surface? There was one surefire way to find out. He gathered his Marines on the floorplate and pushed the lower button. The elevator began to descend quietly.

As they dropped, he thought about what might meet them at the bottom of the shaft. How might a sentry, or even a passerby, react to the appearance of the apparantly empty elevator? Not with immediate violence, he was sure of that. Perhaps whoever was there would think the elevator was malfunctioning and put in a call for a service tech. Or think someone was playing a prank.

But what if the shaft bottomed in a locked room or locked cage? What if someone was waiting to get to the elevator and stepped onto the platform before the Marines had time to get off it?

Kindy decided to stop worrying and just be ready for anything.

The elevator seemed to drop down a featureless shaft for a long time; the walls of the shaft barely cleared the edges of the platform. But the drop didn't take all that long, really, nor was it a rapid descent. When the elevator eased to a stop, Kindy estimated they were no more than twenty meters below the surface.

No locked room, no locked cage, no sentry, met the elevator when it reached the bottom of the shaft. There wasn't even anybody casually passing by. The shaft ended at the intersection of two finished tunnels that looked more like hotel corridors than tunnels. Soft lights glowed from panels set at the tops of the walls.

The Marines quickly stepped off the platform; the platform rose as soon as they were all off. They listened for a long moment, but the elevator didn't come back down. Kindy looked at the walls and saw a plate with three buttons. Evidently the third one was used to call the elevator.

Kindy set his Marines to look down each of the four corridors. Kindy's was featureless until it ended fifty meters away in a door. Nomonon's had two doors on each side, then turned to the right forty meters away. Jaschke saw a ramp leading downward about twenty meters distant. Dim shapes were visible beyond the open door.

Ellis's tunnel ended in an open doorway through which came the sounds of air compressors. Kindy had him lead the way. Ellis and Nomonon walked along one wall, Kindy and Jaschke along the other. There was enough room between them for a large person to pass by without bumping into any of the Marines.

The Marines stopped at the entrance and Kindy and Ellis cautiously looked in and to the sides. The room was filled with armored personnel carriers.

Kindy signaled the others to wait and stepped into the room to estimate its size and contents. There were fourteen columns of APCs to either side of the doorway. He went to his right to make sure there were full columns beyond the rank he could see. There were. He then checked to the left and found the same.

There were twenty-eight columns of APCs that ran as far as Kindy could see into the dimly lit room. He used his range finder to check the length of the room, as well as the length of the APCs and the interval between, then calculated the total: enough armored personnel carriers in this one room to mount an entire heavy division. He looked at the overhead and wondered what held it up—he hadn't seen any pillars.

Kindy checked the time. They'd been inside the compound for more than an hour; there were seven hours left before sunrise and he wanted to be on the other side of the fields before sunup, and he wanted to reserve two or three hours for crossing the fields. Rather than examine the APC garage further, he had the squad backtrack to check out the downramp Jaschke had seen.

They froze halfway back to the intersection—the elevator was coming down and voices came from the shaft. Without needing orders, all four Marines lowered themselves to the floor and pressed against the wall.

The elevator reached bottom and two men stepped off; one was the "major," the other a slightly older man, also with a military bearing. They didn't look around, but turned straight toward the closed door at the end of the corridor Kindy had first looked down. Kindy eased silently to the intersection and watched the two. When they reached the door, the major placed his hand on the wall next to the door and the door slid open—there was an electric lock keyed to handprints, or some other biometric of the hand.

When the door closed behind the two, the Marines rose and continued to the downramp.

The ramp went down about ten meters deeper underground and ended in a cross corridor. A windowed door was at either end. Kindy sent Nomonon to one and went to the other himself. He decided immediately they weren't going through this door.

Kindy saw a large common room filled with soldiers in partial uniforms, going hither and yon, in and out of other spaces that opened into the common. He backed off. Nomonon reached the foot of the ramp at the same time he did. Nomonon had seen a similar setup on the other side of the door he'd looked through.

"Now we know where the soldiers are who go with the APCs," Kindy said, touching helmets.

"I saw another elevator over here," Nomonon told him.

"Show me."

This elevator wasn't directly below the one the Marines had taken from the surface, and it was much larger; Kindy thought it could easily accommodate twenty or more men at a time. It was set into an alcove, walled in on three sides, rather than in a corner like the other elevator, and no molding or other architectural device marked the edges of the al-

cove. That was why Kindy hadn't spotted it when he'd first
glanced in its direction—he had looked along the plane of
the wall, and there was nothing to catch his eye.

As Kindy looked up into the darkness of the shaft, the
platform started to descend. He moved his squad back onto
the ramp where they could go back up in a hurry and positioned himself at the entrance to the ramp so he could see
who came off the elevator. He heard low voices and a single
high-pitched laugh before the elevator reached bottom and a
dozen soldiers exited. They split into two groups and headed
to the doors at the ends of the corridor. They looked relaxed
and happy, as though they'd just done something enjoyable.

Kindy thought for a moment, figuring angles and distances. He decided that the large elevator's top end had to be
inside the mess hall, and that the soldiers were returning to
their quarters from watching the trid or playing games.

He wasn't going to learn more there, not without taking a
prisoner, but third squad had to get in and back out without
anybody in the complex realizing they'd had visitors. So taking a prisoner was out of the question.

He sent the squad back up the ramp. There were two corridors they hadn't checked yet. One was the corridor with the
door at the end, the one that had opened when the "major"
had placed his hand on the wall next to it. Kindy send Nomonon and Jaschke down the other corridor, which had doors
on both of its sides and turned at the end.

None of the doors was locked. The two corporals opened
each door and gave a quick look to what was inside before
moving on. They didn't take long studying what they found
around the corner at the end of the corridor, either. They rejoined Kindy in moments and touched helmets to report their
findings.

"The doors on the left are entrances to an armory," Nomonon
said.

"An *unlocked* armory?" Kindy asked.

Nomonon treated the question as rhetoric. "I saw thousands of small arms in locked racks. There were also large

strongboxes with padlocks. My guess is they hold ammunition."

"Enough small arms for a heavy division?" Kindy asked.

"Maybe enough for a regiment."

Kindy nodded to himself; that probably wasn't the only armory under the farming complex. He suspected the troop areas off the ramp the squad had gone down weren't the only troop areas, either.

"The right side had fuel drums," Jaschke reported, "probably for the APCs. There were also crates with markings that indicated they're ammo for the APCs' integral weaponry."

That rocked Kindy. What kind of fool would store ammunition and fuel in the same place? It wouldn't take much to cause a catastrophic explosion that might destroy the entire underground complex.

It was time to get out and report what they'd found. Kindy decided to request permission to come back and make an accident.

They had no way of knowing when the next person would want to use the elevator to the shed building, so they waited, one Marine in each of the corridors just a few meters from the elevator, for someone to come down. Someone did in just a couple of minutes—the grizzled sergeant.

The Marines dashed silently onto the platform as it began to rise. The sergeant must have felt something, because he turned and looked back quizzically, then shook his head and continued toward the palm-locked door.

CHAPTER
EIGHTEEN

Approaching Cranston from the West

Sergeant Wil Bingh popped up to see above the trees to beyond the next bend in the road, as he had regularly for forty kilometers. He hadn't seen any movement since the convoy with the odd weapons system had passed them an hour earlier. For the first time since then, he now saw something other than continuous forest. The treetops in the distance thinned, and the peaks of high roofs were visible through them; either the land hadn't been completely cleared when Cranston was established, or the citizens had gone on a tree-planting frenzy soon after moving in.

Bingh dropped back down and sent a burst transmission to first squad to halt and gather on him. He raised the screens on his helmet so they could see where he was.

"The town's up ahead," he told his men when they joined him. "It's got a lot of tree cover, so I couldn't see that convoy that passed us—or where the bivouac of the Twenty-third Ruspina Rangers is, either. We'll go deeper into the trees for the next five klicks, then drop our puddle jumpers and continue on foot. And from here on, we have to be particularly alert for enemy patrols.

"Any questions?"

They were all professionals, each of them with several successful missions to his credit, and they'd worked together for long enough to know what each of them would do. None of them had any questions about what they were going to do or how it would be accomplished.

"Let's do it." Bingh lowered his chameleon screen and vanished from view.

The four Marines headed away from the road, keeping track of each other by keeping the exhausts of the puddle jumpers, and the UV markers on their backs, in view. Their movement was slower than it had been when they were following the road; they had to weave among the tree trunks and stay under the spreading branches.

Nearly an hour later, Bingh stopped the squad while he popped up to take a look around. The ground gently rolled under the trees, but seen from above, the undulations of the treetops had no particular relation to the irregularities of the land below. Several kilometers to the east, Bingh could see the tops of some buildings poking through the tree cover, but he didn't dare go high enough to see down through the tree cover—while *he* was effectively invisible, someone sharp-eyed in the town might be able to spot the exhaust from the puddle jumper. He took a line-of-sight azimuth, fed it into his UPUD, then dropped back down and raised his helmet screens. The other Marines also exposed their faces.

"We're on foot from here," he told his men. "Unass your puddle jumpers. We'll secure them here."

In a couple of minutes they had the puddle jumpers bundled in a chameleon tarp with a line attached to it. Lance Corporal Wehrli took the end of the line and shimmied up a tree to a fork about six meters above the ground. He pulled the bundle up and used the line to tie it into the fork. While Wehrli was securing the puddle jumpers, Bingh marked the location of the tree on his UPUD.

"Wehrli, take point," Bingh ordered when the four of them were ready. "Then me and Musica. Pricer, rear point. That way." He removed a glove and pointed. "Move out." He closed his screens; so did the other three. Wehrli stepped out in the direction Bingh had pointed. They started off at a brisk walk and gradually slowed as they got closer to Cranston.

Just inside the Trees on the Outskirts of Cranston

Cranston was a town of some thirty thousand people, constructed entirely from local materials, mostly using hand tools and small power tools—it almost looked as though some massive time machine had lifted it whole from a mid-industrial-period culture and put it down there. The four Marines settled just inside the forest fringe at the edge of the town and observed.

After a time, Sergeant Bingh began wondering *why* the town was there. From his vantage he saw mostly close-packed housing, with a shopping district and some light industry. No heavy industry was visible from his position. Nor did there seem to be any major roads coming through. They hadn't passed through farmland on the way in, nor had he seen any clearings large enough for significant food growing. The nearest navigable river was more than twenty-five kilometers to the north. None of the materials he'd studied aboard the *Admiral Stoloff* had said there was anything worth mining near Cranston. None of the sensors the squad deployed picked up any of the chemical traces that would indicate the presence of industry—or several thousand soldiers with weapons and equipment.

So why *was* the town there?

And where was the Twenty-third Ruspina Rangers regiment? Or, for that matter, where was the convoy that had passed the squad on the road?

People walked about, or rode here and there on adult-size, muscle-powered versions of children's three-wheel toy vehicles. The only people who seemed to be in a hurry were children running from one playground to another.

After watching for a while longer, Bingh began to think Cranston might be a Potemkin village. He needed to get a closer look. He formulated a plan and passed it to his men.

Near dusk, people began ambling toward the houses and went inside—nearly all of the people were men. That might be reasonable if Cranston were an old-fashioned society where the men worked outside the home while women worked at home. But, Bingh reflected, with that many men outside, if most of them had a wife who worked at home, there should have been more children in evidence than he had seen. Lights began twinkling on in the houses, and lamps came to life one street at a time. The sensors that had failed to produce evidence of industry or a concentration of soldiers had also failed to pick up any indication of enemy sensors that might be capable of detecting the heavily chameleoned Force Recon Marines. Of course, the Marines' sensors couldn't detect passive sensors the Coalition forces might have watching.

Bingh stood; they had to take the risk. "We're going in now," he said.

Three Blocks inside the Cranston Town Limits

Sergeant Bingh wanted to go through backyards. The light-gathering screens in the Force Recon Marine helmets were better than those in the regular infantry helmets; they showed limited color instead of the infantry helmets' stark gray tones and allowed better depth perception. But there were too many white picket fences and hedges for him to be certain they could be as silent as he wanted. So he and Lance Corporal Wehrli walked as close to the fronts of houses on one side of the street as the fences and hedges allowed, while Corporals Musica and Pricer did the same on the opposite side of the street. They looked in windows as they went. What Bingh saw disturbed him; the furnishings and the way the people took their ease in living rooms, or sat around dining tables, looked to him like nothing so much as dioramas he'd seen in a cultural history museum—dioramas of middle-class American life in the middle of the twentieth century.

They had just crossed the inconspicuously labeled Fifteenth Street when Bingh received a burst transmission from Musica.

"I've got something you should take a look at, boss."

Bingh stopped and put a hand out to contact Wehrli and

guide him. Across the street, he saw a UV marker showing where one of the other two Marines stood next to the white picket fence in front of the house opposite; this house was smaller than most and was tucked tightly in between two others. He touched helmets with Wehrli to tell him they were joining the others, then crossed the street. When he reached the Marine whose marker he saw, he touched helmets and asked, "What do you have?"

It was Pricer. "Take a look where the side of the house meets the ground," he said.

Bingh looked and could hardly credit his eyes. "Where's Musica?" he asked.

"Taking a closer look."

Bingh kept looking. The masonry foundation of the house didn't look as if it went all the way down, but stopped two or three centimeters above the ground. The shadows under the edge of the foundation were deep, but he thought he could make out the regularities of the treads of a tracked vehicle. He looked into the window directly above. There wasn't enough space from the bottom of the foundation to the bottom of the window to fit a tracked vehicle. But—

He walked ten paces to one side, looking into the window all the way, then back ten paces in the opposite direction. The interior of the room beyond the window shifted, but not quite as smoothly as he expected it to. Could he be looking at a hologram image of a room?

A hand gripped Bingh's shoulder. It was Musica.

"That's the most fantastic bit of camouflage I've ever seen," Musica said when they touched helmets. "I got close and looked inside the window. It's only about thirty centimeters deep. Everything's foreshortened so when you walk past on the street and look in, it looks real no matter if you see straight in or at an angle. The whole thing is hiding a tracked vehicle of some sort."

"Then let's take a better look," Bingh said. He withdrew a minnie disguised as a local rodent and sent it scurrying under the house, then led the squad around the side of the house, where they hunkered down between it and the dense hedge that separated it from the house behind. Only then did he turn on the control box to direct the minnie in its search. He plugged the minnie's control box into his helmet so he could watch its movements on the heads-up display, eliminating the possibility of anyone's spotting the slight glow from the box's display.

He sent the minnie a climb-and-prowl order, and the small robot scampered about until it found a place where it could climb up a tread. The sides of the tracked vehicle sloped sharply, which left plenty of room for the false room inside the window next to it. On its top was a low-lying turret with a brace of barrels for some kind of energy gun, possibly lasers. It wasn't a tall vehicle; after allowing for the high ground clearance Bingh had seen when the minnie had searched for a way up, he thought the vehicle's crew must be recumbent when it was buttoned up. He suspected the crew could only be two men; three would probably be too crowded to be able to function well. Skittering all over the vehicle, the minnie found several shielded openings—one in the back, two in the front, and two in each side—that looked like viewports rather than gunports, and what looked like extensible arms on the front—arms with cutters on their ends. On impulse, he sent the minnie back to the ground and had it examine the vehicle's undercarriage. It looked to be solidly waterproof. He sent the minnie scampering back to the top to take another look at something he hadn't identified earlier. Seen in light of the vehicle's watertight bottom, he realized it had to be an extendable snorkle—this was an amphibious vehicle, probably submersible.

Satisfied that the minnie had completely inspected the vehicle, Bingh double-checked that he'd stored the data and sent the minnie looking elsewhere. It found two more of the slope-sided vehicles inside the house. Then he had it look for an opening to the house above. It found a ventilation tube with a joint that was loose enough for it to wiggle its way in. The robot's olfactory sensors picked up human scent from its left; Bingh sent it in that direction.

A grill opened into a low-ceilinged, windowless room a

few meters along the tube. Six men were in the room, sitting around a table, playing cards. The remnants of a meal were piled on a side table. Holstered sidearms hung on their belts from a rack near a door on the far side of the room. A military comm unit sat on the tabletop next to the elbow of the oldest man. Despite the military accoutrements, none of the men were in uniform. Still, they had to be the crews of the three amphibs under the house.

Bingh watched and listened for a few minutes, but the soldiers were talking in a dialect he could barely understand. He didn't think they were discussing anything about their unit or mission, and his squad needed to continue to recon the town. He set the minnie to continue observing and recording for two hours, then return on its own to a location on the outskirts of Cranston. That done, he touched helmets with his men.

"We need to take a closer look at these houses," he told them. "If this one's a blind, probably more of them are as well. Get your minnies ready." He gave them the rendezvous coordinates to feed into their spybots.

While his men prepared their minnies to go out on their own, Bingh readied his second minnie. He sent Musica and Pricer two blocks to the south and gave them instructions to have their minnies search the bases of houses in a two-block stretch east and west from there. As soon as they left, he led Wehrli two blocks north.

"Get the yellow one," Bingh ordered Wehrli when they'd gone two blocks. He sent his own minnie to scuttle around the foundation of a pastel blue house.

In less than two minutes, Wehrli touched helmets with Bingh. "Got a gap," he said.

"Show me," Bingh replied needlessly; from his command box he could tie into the transmissions from any of the squad's minnies without the Marine controlling it doing anything to assist him. He could even override the Marine and take direct control of the minnie if he wanted. But he didn't want to control Wehrli's minnie, he just wanted to see what it had found. He reduced the display from his own minnie to a corner of his HUD and locked onto Wehrli's minnie's transmission.

Bingh and Wehrli watched as the minnie squeezed through a slender gap between the base of the house and the ground. Inside, seeking in visual, infrared, and ultraviolet, the minnie found an excavated area, a sort of shallow cellar. Sitting in the cellar were two amphibious vehicles. These were much larger than the two-man amphibs they'd found in the first house they'd examined.

Bingh watched as Wehrli sent his minnie around a ledge that circled the outside edge of the cellar. The view would have caused vertigo in anyone not used to following the transmission from a minnie's searching in the dark—the robot's head moved constantly, looking up and to the sides, only occasionally looking where it was going.

The minnie's sideways glances as it skittered along the ledge quickly gave Bingh views of two of the sides of the nearer amphibious vehicle. Bingh recognized it; it was a modified Mark VII amphibious tractor, the kind called a Mudpuppy, manufactured on Carhart's World for that planet's own military. He'd heard a rumor that the Mudpuppy was available on the black market, but hadn't heard any confirmation of it. The Heptagon would be very interested in this piece of intelligence.

While Bingh was identifying the Mudpuppy, the minnie found a ramp at one end of the cellar; the ramp was wide enough to allow the amphibious vehicles to climb out.

Wehrli saw the significance of the ramp and immediately set the minnie to examining the wall next to it. The wall was false; it was a disguised door with tracks that allowed it to slide up and out of the way so the Mudpuppies could go in or out. He touched helmets with Bingh, and the squad leader agreed to let the minnie search for an entrance to the house above.

In the meanwhile, Bingh's minnie completed its search of the base of the pastel blue house without finding anything out of the ordinary. Bingh sent it on to check out the neighboring house.

It took Wehrli's minnie five minutes to find a way up into the interior of the house. It was a shell, except for shallow boxes in front of the windows, just like the boxes the Marines had found in the first house they'd examined. Bingh looked at the yellow house and saw a dimly lit room through its curtains, right where one of the boxes the minnie had found was.

In two out of two houses they'd entered, they'd found amphibious vehicles, and both had the eye-fooling setups. It looked as if the Twenty-third Ruspina Rangers were expecting a visit from Force Recon. Bingh wondered what they had in place to *catch* unwelcome visitors—he thought it was unlikely they would only have false fronts to fool the Marines.

Bingh hit the panic button on his control box to make the minnie stop transmitting and return to him *now,* then told Wehrli to do the same with his minnie. He switched the view on his HUD to pick up the transmissions from Musica's and Pricer's minnies and overrode their instructions, had them cease transmission, and return to their Marines.

"Let's go," he ordered Wehrli as soon as their minnies rejoined them. He turned on his scent sensor and turned his ears all the way up as he led the way south. He sent the two corporals a burst transmission: "Hold position, I'm on my way."

Bingh's skin was crawling by the time he and Wehrli reached the area where he'd dispatched Musica and Pricer, even though he hadn't detected any sign of pursuit. Or any other activity on the streets or in the yards. It took a few minutes for him to locate the UV marker on one of the Marines. He got everyone together and touched helmets.

"We found another false house," he said, "one of the first two we checked."

"Then we're four for six between us," Pricer said. "We found Mudpuppies in two houses."

Half of the houses the Marines had had their minnies examine were little more than false fronts, hiding amphibious vehicles. Bingh wasn't particularly surprised at finding amphibious vehicles; since the Coalition army hadn't been able to break through Bataan's main line of defense, it made sense for them to try a waterborne assault on the peninsula's flank. But why give the invasion craft such thorough camouflage? Sure, if the navy had been able to lay its string-of-pearls, intense camouflage would be necessary to hide the amphibs from orbital discovery and retain the element of surprise. But the navy *hadn't* been able to lay the string-of-pearls, thanks to the satellite killers. So the only reason Bingh could think of was the Twenty-third Ruspina Rangers were expecting someone to come on the ground. The Coalition commanders had to know the Confederation forces were completely boxed in, totally unable to get anybody out to recon, had to know that the only reconnaissance units capable of discovering them had to come from off-world. Surely with camouflage this intense, the Twenty-third Ruspina Rangers had some means of detecting the presence of snoops, even those as well chameleoned and infrared-cool as Force Recon.

"I think we're in a trap," Bingh told his men. "Time to leave. Everybody remember where the rally point is?"

They all did; where they'd left their puddle jumpers.

"Pricer, point. Me, Wehrli, Musica. Go."

Corporal Pricer led off at a faster speed than Force Recon normally moved this deep in enemy territory, not following the route the four Marines had taken to enter Cranston, but roughly paralleling it.

All four Marines listened and watched carefully, but neither saw nor heard any sign of a search or pursuit. Now that Bingh knew what to look for, he saw several more houses that appeared to have slight gaps between their foundations and the ground.

Almost half of this town must be false, Bingh thought.

They were soon out of Cranston and back into the forest. Bingh sent his men up trees to watch for pursuit, but none came during the hour they watched and waited. At last he had the squad return to the puddle jumpers, where he prepared a report and tight-beamed it up to the orbiting *Kiowa*.

The squad moved a klick to the south to await instructions.

CHAPTER
NINETEEN

By the time they were into their fourth month at Camp Upshur, the remaining officer candidates had begun to adjust to their daily routine quite well. That was when Jak Daly began to have a serious problem. He decided that he wanted to go back to the fleet, back to Force Reconnaissance.

Lieutenant Stiltskein's casual remark that there was a war going on while they were "stuck" back in OTC had got Daly thinking. He knew without anyone telling him that Fourth Force Recon Company would be involved in the war, and he began to feel his proper place was with them, not on Arsenault, studying battalion maneuvers in brigade operations and other esoteric matters far removed from the life-and-death struggle his buddies were engaged in. So each night Daly found a seat in the company dayroom to watch the worldwide news broadcast on the Military News Network, which kept the far-flung installations on Arsenault connected to the rest of Human Space. It made no difference that the news about the war was more than a week behind real-time events; for Jak Daly, the war on Ravenette was happening *right now.*

One night MNN showed recent footage of Marines in combat at Fort Seymour, successfully repulsing a massive attack by the Coalition forces. In passing, the commentator noted that Marine Force Reconnaissance units were operating behind enemy lines to develop intelligence and upset the enemy's logistical posture. That was all it took.

"Manny," Daly told Ubrik when he got back to their room, "tomorrow I'm going down to see the company commander and ask to be dismissed from OTC."

"What?"

"You heard me."

Ubrik sat up in bed. He'd been rereading Caesar's *de Bello Gallico* in preparation for a discussion on "great commanders" in their military history class the next day. "Family problems?"

"No."

Ubrik turned off his reader and swung his legs to the floor. "I could tell something was eating at you these last weeks, Jak. Why do you want to quit now? Muhammad's cavities, buddy, you're a cinch to graduate in the top ten percent of this class!"

Daly did not answer at once. "Manny, I want to go back to the fleet. I want in on this war on Ravenette." He shrugged. "I'm a Marine and I'm not going to sit here while my buddies are risking their lives on this goddamned Fort Seymour place, wherever in the hell that is."

"Jak, they'll *never* let you go, you know that."

"Well, I'm going to give it a try, old buddy."

"You're going to leave here before you even get into Felicia's drawers?" Manny grinned, trying to lighten the atmosphere. "That's not like you, Jak, to leave important business unfinished."

Daly perked up a bit. "How do you know I haven't? Mission accomplished, time to return to home station?"

"You bastard!" Ubrik laughed. They were both silent for a moment. "Well, Jak, I know you well enough now to know I can't talk you out of this foolishness. But, man, I'm going to miss you! I've never in my life felt as close to anyone as I do to you, Jak."

"Hey, I feel the same way about you, Manny. We've been through some shit together, haven't we?"

"You bet."

Neither man got much sleep that night.

Company Office, Marine OTC

"Get your ass the hell outta here, Candidate Daly, and don't bring this subject up again in my orderly room!" First Sergeant Beedle roared. His eyes flashed and his shaven head gleamed and the veins in his neck stood out, but Daly did not move.

"I request permission to see the company commander, Top," Daly repeated, staring at a space on the wall just above the top sergeant's head. In his hand Daly carried his formal letter of resignation from OTC. He leaned forward and placed it on Beedle's desk. "It is my right to see the company commander and request he forward this letter through channels, First Sergeant."

"Don't tell me what your 'rights' are, pissant!" Beedle roared as the hairs in his nostrils flared menacingly, but he took the letter. "Sit your ass down over there while I take this—this *letter* in to the CO's office. You can damn well wait there all day, for all I care." He snorted again, stood up, knocked once on the CO's door, and entered, closing the door behind him. Daly took a seat and grinned at the company clerk, a lance corporal who pretended to busy himself with office work.

From inside the CO's office that worthy roared, "Send that pissant little sonofabitch in here!"

That morning was the first time Daly could remember hearing anyone use the word *pissant*. He filed it away for future reference as a useful adjective and marched smartly into the CO's sanctum.

Office of the Commandant, Marine OTC

It took several days for Daly's letter of resignation to reach Brigadier Beemer's office. At each stage along the chain of command—battalion, brigade, Training Directorate—it was endorsed with a hearty "RECOMMEND DISAPPROVAL."

Duty uniform for all military personnel at Camp Upshur

was utilities, and that was what Daly was wearing—freshly cleaned and pressed, of course—the day he was ordered to report to Brigadier Beemer's office. He'd changed into a fresh set immediately after morning PT, which that particular morning, as luck would have it, consisted of a fifteen-kilometer jog under the baleful eye of the indestructible Lieutenant Stiltskein, the man whose casual remark had started Daly on his long and embarrassing odyssey to the commandant's office. Every step of the way up the chain of command each officer who had interviewed Daly had regarded him as someone halfway between a traitor and a madman, and they were not at all reluctant to let him know what they thought of his request.

Now he sat in the Spartan waiting room outside the commandant's office, anticipating the summons to his interview. People—officers and civilian staff—came and went while Daly sat patiently, regarding Brigadier Beemer's administrative NCO, a pretty sergeant, out of the corner of his eye. As each visitor passed through the waiting room, Daly imagined he looked at him as if he had leprosy. Time dragged on toward the lunch hour and still Daly sat there on a hard wooden bench. He tried to strike up a conversation with the sergeant, but she claimed she was busy. Actually, she was reading something on a vid display for most of the time Daly was there.

"Candidate Daly?" Daly jumped. His mind had been wandering. "You may report to the commandant now," the admin sergeant announced. "Report formally."

Daly stood and straightened his uniform blouse. "Sergeant, I've got more time reporting formally in this Corps than you have reading novels on duty time." He glared at the young woman and knocked once on the brigadier's door.

"Come."

Daly closed the door softly behind him and marched to within three paces of the brigadier's desk, where he came to attention. "Sir, Candidate Daly—"

Brigadier Beemer stood up and extended his hand. "Between two old salts like us we don't need that formality. Have a seat, Candidate." He waved Daly to some chairs around a small conference table. At first Daly thought he hadn't heard the brigadier correctly, but Beemer came around his desk, laid a hand on Daly's shoulder, and gently guided him to a chair. "Coffee?" he asked.

"Uh, yessir, thank you, sir." Daly was so astonished at this reception he would have drunk swamp water if the brigadier had offered him some. Daly felt a tiny prickle of satisfaction at the look of consternation on the snotty admin sergeant's face as she served them the coffee.

"Calling you 'Candidate' is so stilted and formal," the brigadier commented as he reached for the coffee carafe. "May I call you Jak?" he asked, pouring Daly's coffee for him. "Sugar, cream?"

The brigadier could have called him Jack Shit for all Daly cared, he was so utterly amazed at the commandant's informal, avuncular manner. The few times Daly had seen the brigadier at Camp Upshur he had appeared distant, "frosty," too far up the flagpole for a lowly officer candidate to be sitting like this, chatting and drinking coffee with him. "Yessir," Daly replied, then added, "I mean, you can call me Jak, sir, but, no thanks, I don't take cream or sugar."

"Aha, spoken like a Marine!" The brigadier, Daly noticed, *did* take sugar and cream. Beemer leaned back in his chair, crossed his legs, and balanced his coffee cup on a knee. "Jak, I've read your letter, and let me say I agree totally with your reasoning on wanting to leave here and go back to the fleet. I do." He nodded and sipped from his cup. "We're Marines, and when there's fighting to be done, that's where we belong. Jak, tell me a little bit about your family."

As Daly talked about his upbringing on New Cobh, the brigadier listened intently, nodding every now and then and smiling knowingly. "My dad whipped me too, when I was a boy, Jak, whaled the dickens out of me for breaking some windows in a neighbor's home." Beemer laughed at the memory. "Never broke another window in my life! Joined the Corps instead"—he winked—"really learned how to break things up!"

Daly laughed. He'd never before felt so relaxed and comfortable in the presence of a senior officer. Something about Brigadier Beemer, something he projected easily in the conversation, gave Daly the conviction that he really cared about him and that any enlisted man could talk to him and get a fair hearing. All the hours he'd been sitting in the anteroom waiting, all the harassment he'd gotten coming up the chain of command to reach that point, washed away in the first few minutes in the brigadier's presence.

The brigadier's office was as Spartan as the anteroom: his desk, the small conference suite, a few plaques and certificates hanging on the wall. One of the certificates made Daly's heart race faster. Across the top was embossed a midnight-blue ribbon speckled with silver stars, the unmistakable ribbon of the Confederation Medal of Heroism, the highest decoration for valor the Confederation could bestow. To meet a man who had one was the rarest of privileges because it was almost always awarded posthumously. Brigadier Beemer was one of those rare men. Almost as if reading Daly's thoughts, the brigadier said, "Jak, you and I, we've both been in the shit. I've seen your service record; four Bronze Stars with Gold Starburst devices, very prestigious decorations for valor. I've read with admiration the citations and, personally, I'd have recommended you for higher awards. You not only qualified Expert with the blaster, you made Sharpshooter with the maser, and Expert with the M111 sabot rifle. You probably can call cadence with the best of them in close-order drill too." Beemer smiled.

"Jak, I know what you've gone through to get up here today. All along the chain of command you've been told the only way to get out of OTC once you're accepted is to die, to be medically disqualified because of disease or injury, or to flunk out due to academic or disciplinary problems. You aren't the first candidate to make a request like this. All my people are expected to discourage such requests. But, Jak, I, of all the people in this college, do understand why you wish to be released and return to your unit, and I respect your reasons and I admire you for writing this letter." Carefully, he placed his coffee cup on the table and leaned toward Daly. "But I have to deny your request."

"May I ask why, sir?"

The brigadier smiled and leaned back in his chair. "I've been in this man's Marine Corps for sixty years, Jak. I once sat where you are now. Yes, I did. I'll tell you what that old colonel told me then. It's the men who served under you and the officers you served under who recommended you for commissioning. Oh, maybe not in so many words, but it was the confidence of the men under you *in you* as a leader, as much as what you did, that convinced your superiors to recommend you to attend OTC, and if you back out now, even for the best of motives, which you certainly have, you are not only letting them down, Jak, you're letting down the future generations of Marines who would be serving under you. I can't let you do that, Jak. Request denied. Return to your classes."

Daly knew he had taken his cause as far as it was going to go.

The brigadier stood and extended his hand and they shook. "I'll see you again, Candidate Daly." Daly stepped back two paces, came to attention, did an about-face, and marched out of the office.

On his way back to class Daly had to smile to himself. He'd just been given a snow job by one of the smoothest operators in the Corps, but the funny thing was, it had been one of the most satisfying experiences he'd ever had, far, far more satisfying, he knew, than getting into Candidate Felicia Longpine's drawers, which he had not yet been able to do. Now, though, he was going to have another chance, and like any good Marine, he fully intended to carry out his mission to a successful conclusion.

CHAPTER
TWENTY

**Three Hundred Kilometers Northwest
of the Bataan Peninsula, Ravenette**

After the sniper strike on the Kampeer Aanval staging area, first sniper team and second squad went out looking for more targets of opportunity. They went south on foot fifteen kilometers before donning their puddle jumpers and moving in a search pattern. Once they were in the air, it didn't take long for them to find a highway that showed evidence of military traffic.

This time, they were on a hunter-killer mission, not a sniper mission, so Sergeant Kare was in command; Sergeant Gossner readily agreed that he and Lance Corporal Dwan were along as extra blasters.

"I'm not carrying a blaster!" Dwan objected. Her meaning was clear; she was a sniper, she wanted a sniper mission.

"All right then, we're along as extra firepower," Gossner growled right back at her.

"Tell you what," Kare jumped in before Dwan could say more. "I'll let you take the first shot when we spring an ambush. You snipe the lead driver."

"Driver! I'm a *sniper,* I'm carrying a *maser,* I don't waste my shots on *drivers*!"

"We need the lead driver taken out first to block the road and jam up any vehicles behind it," Kare said reasonably.

"Do you have any idea how hard it is to hold aim on a target moving that fast?" she objected.

Kare nodded. "Yes, I do," he said, looking directly into her

eyes. "And I believe there's only one sniper in all of Human
Space good enough with a maser to be able to hold aim on a
target driving a military vehicle."

Dwan pursed her lips, glaring at him. He was playing on her
pride, using it to manipulate her—and she knew it. But her
pride insisted that she accept the challenge.

"If there's an officer next to the driver, can I shoot him?"

"After you shoot the driver, you can shoot the officer."

Dwan nodded curtly; an officer was a more proper target
for a sniper than a lousy driver—even if she had to shoot the
driver first.

"But you don't fire until I tell you to."

"WHAT!"

Gossner clamped a hand on Dwan's shoulder. "Sergeant
Kare's in command here, Lance Corporal," he said firmly.
"We do it his way."

Dwan glared at Gossner's offending hand, then turned her
glare to his eyes. He didn't flinch. She began to think maybe
she'd made a mistake when she'd jumped his bones after
making her kill on Atlas—Gossner was getting entirely too
familiar with her person and had lost some of his wariness of
her. But she had to agree, no matter how much she disliked
the idea, that Sergeant Kare was in command, so she'd do it
his way.

Dammit.

Overlooking a Bend in a Highway, Three Hundred Kilometers Northwest of Bataan

Sergeant Kare had selected an ambush site with the skill
of someone who had set many small-unit ambushes. While
looking for the ideal spot, he'd let two single lorries and a
five-vehicle convoy pass unmolested. That, of course, infuri-
ated Lance Corporal Bella Dwan; she didn't have the same
degree of patience in an ambush that she did as a sniper. Not
that she was all that patient about picking targets to snipe.

Finally, impatience got the better of her and she went to

Kare and touched helmets with him. "Why do you keep letting them go by? We could have taken any of them!"

"I want a bigger convoy, Lance Corporal," Kare snapped, "and I want to get everyone in it. Now get back with your team leader and stay alert."

Unseen inside her helmet, Dwan bit her lip. She shook herself with impatience, but the prospect of wiping out a bigger convoy made her back off. She rejoined Gossner and touched helmets with him.

"I talked Sergeant Kare into going after a big convoy," she told him. "We'll have lots of targets."

"Sure thing, Bella," Gossner said. "Sounds good." He could feel her jittering and knew how impatient she was for action, so he knew she hadn't talked Kare into anything, that wanting to hit a bigger convoy was the squad leader's idea. But he also knew that challanging Dwan on her claim would be the wrong thing to do.

The site Kare had picked was on a slight rise just outside a bend in the highway, where the Marines would be able to have both plunging and enfilading fire on the convoy he chose to ambush. The rise itself was wooded, and the ground had at one time been scoured by glacial rocks that had left deep gouges the Marines could use for cover. He carefully placed his people so that each of them had wide fields of fire between the trees, though the trees would keep any of them from having a clear shot at the full length of the ten-vehicle convoy he was hoping to catch. He set Dwan at the extreme left of his short line, where she was able to look almost straight down the highway. He positioned himself where he could watch the highway in both directions, control his Marines, and be able to signal each of them with a tight-beam transmission. He also assigned everybody two alternative positions. He didn't know how many soldiers would be in the convoy they ambushed, but there were only six Marines, and they would be severely outnumbered if the convoy they ambushed carried troops. If it did, his people would have to move, probably more than once, to avoid being overrun early in the fight.

The six Marines waited while several individual vehicles, a couple of pairs, and three small convoys passed by—all headed southeast, toward the besieged Confederation forces on the Bataan Peninsula. The Marines were alert but calm—except for Bella Dwan, whose jittering turned to twitches so violent she was making noise loud enough for Kare to hear from his position.

Kare tight-beamed to Gossner, "Can you calm her down? As much noise as she's making, if a convoy has ears pointed in our direction, she'll give us away."

"I'll give it a shot," Gossner tight-beamed back. He tight-beamed to Dwan, "Heads up, I'm joining you," and slithered to her position. He knew what would calm her down.

"Hey, Bella," he said when he touched helmets with her, "I know you're anxious to do this thing. The waiting's hard on all of us."

Dwan grunted something inarticulate.

"You've got a tricky shot coming up," Gossner continued. "Have you visualized it yet?"

Dwan snarled and jerked her helmet away. Gossner waited for a tense moment, then relaxed as he felt her helmet rejoin his.

"Visualize the shot," she said flat-voiced.

"That's right. Put your maser to your shoulder and sight it where you expect to see the cab of an approaching lorry." He felt her shift as she moved into firing position and put the butt of her maser into her shoulder "Picture it in your mind." Her jittering stopped, and he felt the growing regularity of her breathing. "Now lock in your aim. Picture the movement of the vehicle. Track the movement. Imagine squeezing the trigger." He felt her breathing stop. "Imagine holding your aim on the moving target." He felt her move slowly, smoothly, as the muzzle of her maser slowly tracked her imagined target.

"*Zap,* you're mine," she murmured. Then to Gossner: "Yeah, visualize. I can do this. No sweat."

"Good girl."

He smiled when she snarled at him, "I'm not a girl, I'm a Marine sniper."

"The *best* Marine sniper."

"Damn straight."

"I know you can do it, Bella. Now visualize your shot a couple more times. Keep yourself focused, and we'll get this done. We're all going to be proud of you today."

Three and a half hours after the Marines had settled into their ambush position, a convoy arrived that Sergeant Kare decided to take. A landcar with a mounted assault gun led, followed by another landcar in staff configuration. Eight lorries filled with soldiers and supplies followed them, and another landcar with a mounted assault gun brought up the rear. Best of all, the vehicles were tightly spaced.

Kare began snapping out orders. "Dwan, stand by for my signal. Kassel"—Corporal Kassel had the extreme right flank of the ambush—"on my signal, take out the rear gun. Gossner, work with Dwan to kill that lead gun." He instructed Corporal Quinn and Lance Corporal Ilon to fire into the first and second lorries when he set off the ambush.

The convoy approached rapidly, seventy or eighty kph, and reached the kill zone a few minutes after Kare tight-beamed his orders. Kare waited, judging velocity, range, and turn radius. When the lead vehicle was partway through the bend, he tight-beamed Dwan, *"Now!"*

Dwan had had the driver in her sights since the landcar was still half a kilometer distant. It was now less than a hundred meters away. She held her breath and gently squeezed the maser's trigger. The driver slumped at his controls and the landcar swerved, going into a high-speed skid. The convoy accordioned, each driver twisting his vehicle to one side or the other to avoid crashing into the vehicle to his front.

Kare shouted, *"Now!"* in the open so all his Marines could hear and fired his blaster at the driver of the staff car, sending it out of control.

In the lead vehicle, the gunner and assistant gunner were struggling to hold their places as the landcar skidded and threatened to roll over. It was a tough shot, but Gossner fired. The range was short. The bullet's fins didn't have time to stabilize before it bored through the gunner's chest.

The lead landcar was close enough that Dwan didn't have to track to hold her aiming point; she got a shot at the assistant gunner and was satisfied to see him release his grip on the roll bar and collapse.

With the assault gun out of the fight and the following staff car out of control, Gossner turned his attention to the first lorry. Its driver was struggling to bring it to a stop without hitting anything. A sergeant stood in the back of the lorry, holding on to the top of the cab, shouting orders at his soldiers to jump off the moving vehicle and start fighting back—orders some of them were attempting to obey.

Gossner fired at the sergeant, hitting him and a soldier standing close to him. Gossner turned his aim to the cab and fired six bolts into it, at least one of which must have hit the driver, because the lorry suddenly turned sharply and tipped over.

Corporal Kassel had more difficulty taking out the rear assault gun. The range was twice as far as it had been for Dwan and Gossner, and the last lorry partly obstructed his view. Still, he rained plasma at the assault gun's crew and took out both the gunner and driver, as well as two or three of the soldiers in the last lorry.

Lance Corporal Ilon began firing at the second lorry by shooting into its cab. He hit the driver or shook him up so much that he lost control and crashed into the lorry that had just tipped over. The tipped lorry was slammed forward and crushed several soldiers who had fallen out. Soldiers who were trying to climb over the lorry's sides were knocked from their feet; others, trying to clamber over the sides, were thrown to the ground. Ilon started shooting at them, taking a second to aim each of his shots.

Corporal Quinn fired a few bolts into the first lorry, but he saw how much damage Gossner was doing and shifted his fire to the third lorry. His shots into the cab didn't make it crash or tip over, but the lorry slewed sideways across the road, tumbling the soldiers in its rear and blocking the vehicles behind it.

A commanding voice roared from next to the staff car,

which had managed to come to a stop without tipping over. An officer with a voice amplifier had clambered out of it and was shouting orders to his men to dismount and get into assault formations by platoon.

"Mine," Dwan growled. She grinned as she took aim and dropped him. Then she started firing at anybody who looked as if he was trying to fight back.

"Shift positions!" Kare ordered. It was little more than a minute since Dwan had shot the driver of the lead landcar, and the soldiers from the lorries behind the one slewed across the highway were beginning to get organized, though their fire was sporadic and little of it was in the direction of the Marines. Crouched over, the six Marines raced fifty meters to their right and dropped into firing positions behind trees or in ripples in the ground.

"Let's light their fires," Sergeant Kare ordered on the squad circuit. "Hit the fuel cells!"

Everybody but Dwan opened fire on the lorries closest to the massing troops, aiming at their fuel cells. The hydrogen from a ruptured cell would normally dissipate too rapidly to ignite, but when struck by two or three rapid-succession plasma bolts the free hydrogen became growing balls of incandescence, incinerating the uniforms of the closest soldiers, and causing massive, horrifying burns.

Dwan's maser wouldn't ignite hydrogen, so she looked for the leaders. One man stood, angrily bawling out orders. She locked on him and squeezed the trigger. He collapsed midbawl. But Dwan thought he was probably a sergeant; she wanted an officer. She thought an officer wouldn't be standing up, loudly shouting out orders; more likely he'd be hunkered down behind cover, sending orders to sergeants to give to the troops. So she looked for someone hiding behind cover.

She incidentally shot two more sergeants before she spotted an officer. She knew he was an officer; not only was he using a body for cover, he was looking around and talking into a microphone held in front of his lips. Sunlight glittered off insignia on his collar. That was the clincher.

Dwan grinned evilly and sighted in on him. "You can

hide," she murmured as she steadied her aim, "but you can't escape the Queen of Killers." She squeezed the trigger, and the officer slumped, dead.

Dwan began searching for another officer, incidentally shooting sergeants and anybody else she saw shouting orders.

Once the other Marines had set the lorries nearest the mass of troops afire, they began firing into the troops; plasma bolts burned holes through bodies and heads, severed limbs, and cauterized the wounds as they went.

For a moment or two after the Marines shifted position, the fire from the convoy increased, but as the Marine fire reduced the number of soldiers firing back, and orders died with the officers and sergeants issuing them, the fire slackened and became less disciplined; fewer and fewer shots came near the Marines.

Suddenly, a soldier threw his fléchette rifle out in front of himself and, still prone, raised his empty hands.

"Don't shoot me!" he screamed. "I surrender! Don't shoot me!"

That set off a cascade of thrown rifles, raised hands, and shouts of "I surrender!"

One lone voice in the killing zone shouted the order to keep fighting. Some of the soldiers obeyed and began firing close to the Marines.

The Marines couldn't see the man shouting, but they could tell where he was—behind the hulk of a burned-out lorry. All four Marines armed with blasters began shooting at the undercarriage of that lorry and shifted aim until all of their fire converged on the underside of the engine block. In seconds the engine block began steaming, then droplets of molten steel began to drip from it, puddling on the ground. A tendril of molten metal slithered under the engine block toward the voice. There was a scream, and a man jumped up from behind the lorry.

Dwan fired. The screams stopped. He fell.

That was all it took for the few soldiers still fighting to throw out their weapons and surrender.

Sergeant Kare turned on his helmet's amplifier. "You are now prisoners of the Confederation Marine Corps," his amplified voice boomed. "Stand up, keep your hands high above your heads, and step toward the rear of the convoy, away from your weapons."

More than a hundred soldiers stood up, some staggering. But they did as Kare ordered. When they were far enough away from their weapons, he stopped them.

"Take off your boots," he ordered. They scrambled to obey. "Now strip to your underwear." They didn't obey this order as quickly, but when they did, it became evident why not—many of them weren't wearing undergarments and stood naked with their hands above their heads once they'd complied with the order.

Dwan turned on her amplifier and snickered at the naked soldiers. Some of the naked soldiers flushed at the sound of an obviously female snicker.

"Belay that, Lance Corporal," Kare tight-beamed to her.

Dwan snickered once more before turning off her amplifier.

"Now get in formation, four ranks," Kare said. While the prisoners shuffled into a ragged semblance of a parade-ground formation, Kare said on the squad circuit, "Gossner, take Kassel and Ilon, go down there, and check for wounded and mark any you find. Make sure no weapons are near them."

There were several wounded, mostly with severe leg wounds, though one man had had his arm nearly severed at the shoulder and was in shock. The Marines propped the wounded against dead bodies so they could easily be seen and threw all weapons they found as far out of reach as possible. Some of the prisoners saw the ripples of Marine movement in their recent battleground and gaped slack-jawed at them. Some of them had heard rumors that Confederation Marines were invisible men, but not all of them had believed that until then.

When Gossner, Kassel, and Ilon finished, they rejoined the others. Gossner reported on the squad circuit.

"Front rank, count off," Kare ordered with his amplified voice. When they reached twenty, Kare stopped them.

"All right, you've got ten wounded over there," Kare said. "You twenty, go and collect them. Bring them back and lay them in front of your formation."

Hesitantly at first, but then in a scramble when Kare barked *"Now!"* the twenty went to collect their wounded. When that was done, Kare said, "First five men in the second rank, break ranks and step to this side of the wounded." When they did, he ordered, "Come forward into the trees. Look on the ground. You'll find saplings and broken branches. Gather enough to use as litter poles. And make sure they're long enough!"

It took the five soldiers ten minutes to find enough saplings and poles that were at least one and three-quarter meters long. When they did, he sent them back to put the poles down near the wounded, then had them return to their positions in the formation.

"Third rank, count off," Kare boomed. He stopped them when they reached ten. "You ten, step forward. Make litters from those poles and your cast-off uniforms."

The Marines were surprised at how fast the prisoners obeyed that order; they must have had training in making field-expedient litters.

Once the litters had been assembled, Kare singled out the soldier who'd looked most competent in the making.

"You're in charge," he told the soldier. "Assign litter bearers and start your formation moving back the way you came. Do not stop to get dressed again. Do not stop to come back for your uniforms or weapons. We will kill any of you who disobey. Remember—you don't know how many of us there are, or how long we'll be watching you.

"Now *move!*"

As soon as the wounded were on litters and the prisoner formation was moving along the road, Kare said on the squad circuit, "And we don't know if they got a message off, or how soon a relief force might get here. So we're getting out of here." He told them where they were going, and they got.

CHAPTER
TWENTY-ONE

On the Beach, Oceanside, Arsenault

The three friends, Jak Daly, Felicia Longpine, and Manny Ubrik, had finished their breakfast at the Four Seasons and were discussing the latest news. They were now in their eighth month of OTC, had just finished their company-level command exercises, and were looking forward to battalion staff and command training and then graduation. They were in the best physical and mental condition of their lives, and to top it off, they were in Oceanside on the first day of a seventy-two-hour liberty pass.

Daly laughed suddenly. "Hey, you know that class Dr. Mitzikawa told us was in the lesson plan, 'Hand Receipts and Inventories in a Hostile Environment'? Remember, the first day of class?"

"Yeah, we had that block of instruction, didn't we?" Manny Ubrik looked bewildered. "Or maybe we will have it. Why do you bring it up now?"

"I don't remember it," Felicia said. "Most of that stuff went right out of my noodle as soon as I passed the exam on it."

"Well, we *didn't* have it." Daly leaned forward toward the others. "I asked Mitzikawa about it because I was curious. And you know what he told me? He said there was no course like that! He just threw it in to play a joke on us! Can you imagine that!" Daly laughed.

"The guy does have a great sense of humor," Ubrik said. "I found his classes some of the most, er, 'entertaining' of the course. He makes military logistics sound like fun."

A waitress came by and refilled their coffee cups.

"After eight months at Camp Upshur, I'm beginning, well, I don't know how to put this," Daly said, "but I'm beginning to feel, well, as though I like this place, the courses, the instructors, the tactical officers, hell, even the staff!"

"You would," Felicia remarked sourly, "since you have that 'special' relationship with the commandant." She knew now she'd hear the story again of Daly's interview with the brigadier, and it was getting a little old but she couldn't help ribbing Daly over it.

"Well"—Daly shrugged—"an outstanding Marine like me, you know?"

"I know what you mean," Ubrik interrupted hurriedly, to forestall another recital of Daly's interview. "We've grown into OTC and it's grown on us. The staff and instructors here have led us through eight months of hell and they've done a superb job. They've shown us what we're really made of. I've never felt better about myself in my whole life than I do now!"

"It *is* pretty amazing, if you consider how many really good people have dropped out since our class began. But, yeah, we're great," Felicia went on quickly. "Now, if you guys will get down off your Dragons for a moment, I've been thinking about what we're gonna do while we're here in Oceanside. First, I want to—"

"Good people," Daly echoed Felicia's comment, "some of them I considered better Marines than I'll ever be, but"—he shrugged—"you never know how the coin is going to flip on you. Well, today let's hit the beach, soak up some rays, enjoy that crystal clear water. And let's race each other out to the buoy today." The buoy floated about a kilometer off the beach, and on previous visits the trio had swum out there several times. Felicia had proved to be the best swimmer, but Daly was determined to beat her.

"Took the words right out of my mouth! Let's do some 'beachcombing' tonight." Felicia winked at Daly.

"Damn straight! We'll lie out there and admire the waves in the starlight." Daly winked at Ubrik.

"And tonight, while you lovebirds get sand in your Skivvies, I'm going to the Odeon and take in a live performance, have a few drinks if you guys are back by then, or hit the sack early." Ubrik grinned self-consciously but the other two had come to respect his cultivated tastes in the months they'd known him.

"You would." Daly grimaced, pretending disgust. "What's on?"

"Oh, they're performing Dean Shermer's version of *The Monkey's Paw* tonight. Shermer's a great playwright, I love all his stuff. His *Out of the Fire,* a wonderful retelling of the Faust legend, won a Gargoyle Award last year."

"Never heard of him," Felicia said, "but, Manny, you are a fine work of humanity." She laid her hand gently on Ubrik's arm. "If it weren't for that honey of yours back home"—she grinned at Daly—"I'd have you down there on the beach with me tonight instead of some oversexed jarhead who talks constantly about fire and maneuver, maximum effective ranges, and whose idea of romantic music is 'Prettiest girl I ever seen / Was takin' a shit in my latrine.' " They all laughed.

"And with you two spending the night on the beach, maybe our bungalow will be quiet enough that I can get a good night's sleep," Ubrik added archly.

"What do you hear from Solden anyway?" Daly asked, not envying Ubrik spending the night alone.

Ubrik shrugged. "All is well. They're anxious to have me back, of course, and Jodie is still waiting patiently."

"He gets a transgram a week from home," Daly said. "He reads them to himself for hours and won't let anybody else know what's in them. He's got them all tied up in a bundle, and when he dies, I'm going to open it up and read them."

Ubrik snorted. "A letter a week? Don't I wish. I'd show them to you, Jak, except you don't know how to read." Daly punched Ubrik lightly on his shoulder.

"Ah, Manny, you're a wonderful guy," Felicia sighed.

"Who's Jodie? Your mother?" Daly laughed; it was a private joke between them. "Only a mother could love an ugly duckling like you, Manny."

"You bastard!" Ubrik grinned and they did high fives all around. He had never enjoyed the company of anyone as much as he did that of his two companions.

Dawn on the Beach

The buoy's light blinked steadily on the gentle waves as the sky began to lighten. Daly stretched luxuriously. It was going to be another beautiful day at Oceanside. A thin line of clouds hung low on the horizon, which was already beginning to glow pink and red with the coming dawn. But otherwise the sky overhead was a vault of stars. Beautiful, Daly thought. He rolled over and laid a hand on Felicia's thigh. She was still asleep beside him. He wondered if he should wake her. A slight grumbling in his stomach told him breakfast would soon be in order. Goddamn, he thought, life is great! Then he felt a slight pang of guilt. There he was, having the time of his life in Oceanside, while his buddies were risking their lives on Ravenette. Well, what the Corps wanted of a man it got, and the Corps wanted him *here*.

He fumbled among his clothes and found his watch. It was half past 5 hours. The Four Seasons would be open in thirty minutes. He looked forward to washing up in the bathhouse and then walking up the boulevard with Felicia to the Four Seasons. Manny Ubrik was an early riser, maybe they'd meet him up there.

Suddenly the sound of the waves lapping gently on the beach was replaced with the strangest sucking, rushing noise as if vast quantities of water were flowing *away* from the beach! Then Daly noticed he couldn't see the flashing beacon of the buoy anymore. At first he thought it had automatically shut itself off due to the increasing light as dawn began to break over the ocean, but the beach lighting was still on; the shoreline behind him was still dark except for the streetlights of Oceanside, which gleamed brightly.

Mildly curious, he sat up to get a better look. *"Oh, holy shit!"* he exclaimed in amazement. He jumped to his feet. Before his eyes the water was rushing rapidly out to sea. The receding flow had lowered the buoy below eye level, but now that he was standing up, there was the blinking light, high and dry on the seabed, a full kilometer out from shore!

Daly grabbed Felicia and shook her. "Get up! Get up, god-dammit!" he yelled. He yanked her to her feet so hard he must have hurt her because she protested painfully, but he did not even notice. "*Run!* Run for the high ground!" Daly began pulling her up the beach.

"Wha—? Our things, Jak! We can't just leave—" Then she saw what Daly had seen and they began running for the street, running as hard as they'd ever run in their lives. "Head for that building!" Felicia screamed, and Daly veered toward a six-story structure about a hundred meters back from the beach. He didn't know at the time that it stood six stories high or what its purpose was, all he knew was that it was close by and it was *high*. Maybe even high enough.

Behind them, far out in the ocean, a gut-wrenching roar was growing louder with every passing second.

CHAPTER
TWENTY-TWO

Five Kilometers outside Cranston, Ravenette

First squad didn't have to wait long for orders to come back from Fourth Force Recon Company headquarters on the CNSS *Kiowa*. No more than fifteen minutes. The orders were brief and clear:

"In absence of pursuit or discovery, Charlie Mike."

Charlie Mike. Continue mission.

The squad moved back, closer to Cranston, and Sergeant Wil Bingh climbed a tree from which he could look over the town. It wasn't yet midnight, but it looked as if there were fewer lit windows now than there had been. Except for trying to find out how many amphibious vehicles were hidden in Potemkin houses, Bingh didn't see much value in doing a house-to-house survey of the town. Not that they had enough time to make such a search anyway. He thought it would be more productive to find the headquarters of the hidden unit.

He scanned the townscape with all of his optics, looking for anything that might be a headquarters building. All he could see were the public buildings normal for a town the size of Cranston. But which of them was the military most likely to use?

The public safety building was a possibility. It would have people coming and going at all hours; extra traffic might not be noticed by the hypothetical observer the amphibs were being hidden from. But that same hypothetical observer would probably be able to distinguish between the uniforms of the normal officials using the building and the soldiers—or the unusual number of civilians coming and going, if the soldiers weren't in uniform. Moreover, the military headquarters would interfere with the normal function of the public safety services.

A better bet, Bingh thought, would be a building that wasn't otherwise much in use. So what public building would have little use? Bingh smiled to himself; of course. This was where all the study Force Recon did on the local culture of their area of operations paid off. This was local summertime. Ravenette held to the pattern of the academic year that had been established back on Earth during the centuries when universal education was mandated, but civilization was still primarily agricultural. The children were needed to work in the fields during the summer, so school wasn't in session during that season.

Bingh called up the map of Cranston and displayed it on his HUD. He located the schoolhouse on the map and compared that with what he saw of the town. He fixed the school's location in his mind, then climbed back down the tree and told his men where they were going.

Moving through Cranston, Ravenette

Lance Corporal Stanis Wehrli took point going through Cranston to the schoolhouse. Bingh, as was his habit, followed him, followed in turn by Corporal Gin Musica. Corporal Dana Pricer brought up the rear of the short column. The squad didn't follow the same route it had entering or leaving Cranston the first time; aside from the tactical routine of never following the same route twice, Bingh wanted to gather as much intelligence as possible. While Wehrli primarily paid attention to where the squad was going, and Pricer to where they'd been, Bingh and Musica visually examined the houses they passed, looking for gaps between the foundation walls and the ground.

A surprisingly large percentage of the houses had gaps. Bingh estimated that if the houses with gaps were all occupied the same way as the few the squad had investigated were, there were easily enough amphibians in the town to ferry at least an infantry division.

Cranston wasn't densely built up; most houses had yards in the front, back, and sides. The schoolhouse was near the town center, almost two kilometers inside, adjacent to the main shopping district. Two taverns and a coffeehouse with sidewalk tables were open, but the rest of the shopping district was closed when first squad passed nearby.

The schoolhouse itself was dark except for what looked to be safety lights that showed dimly through a few windows. There were lights over the main entrance in the front, and one door on the left side. The Marines checked; neither the main rear entrance nor either of the doors on the right side were illuminated.

The Schoolhouse

Schoolhouse was perhaps not the best word to describe the building. When school was in session, more than a thousand children would fill its elementary classrooms. The building also housed a gymnasium; a theater that could hold not only the thousand children, but a large number of parents and other relatives; and there were faculty lounges and administrative offices. With ground space not being at a premium, the entire structure was on one level.

Unsurprisingly, the rear entrance and four side entrances were locked. There was a guard station in the lobby inside the main entrance, with two people at it. Neither was in uniform, but both appeared to be armed. Two closed doors led from the lobby deeper into the building.

Armed guards inside the main entrance to a schoolhouse in the middle of the night made it clear to the Marines that the building was more than merely an empty schoolhouse between academic sessions. The squad settled into the shadows of a nearby building where they could see into the lobby to observe. It wasn't long before they saw what they needed to know.

Three men approached the main entrance and stopped in front of it, facing inside. One of the lobby guards moved an arm and the Marines heard a low buzz. The door swung open, and the three men filed inside. The door closed right behind the last man. Once they were inside, the other guard moved an arm, and a door off the lobby opened. The guard remotely closed the door as soon as the men went through it.

The main entrance was locked and controlled by the guards in the lobby. So were the two doors leading deeper into the building. The outer door didn't close slowly enough for a chameleoned Marine to slip in unnoticed behind someone given entry by the guards.

They needed to find another way in. Bingh wondered if they should risk breaking a lock on a side door. Not if the doors were alarmed, which, considering the lengths to which someone had gone to conceal the amphibs and soldiers in Cranston, was probable.

At that moment, the other door in the lobby opened and two armed men came through it. A lobby guard let them out. They walked along the front of the school and turned at the corner. Bingh sent Musica to see where they went. Musica was back in little more than a minute and touched helmets with Bingh.

"They're checking the side doors," he reported.

So much for gaining entry that way.

Bingh looked at the building, not at the main entrance but at the façade. The lower meter and a half was masonry. Above that were alternating panels of glass and what looked like sheet metal, separated and held in place by metal risers. Above that a masonry cornice jutted out a few centimeters. If he remembered right, the building's sides were constructed the same way.

Bingh touched helmets with his men and gave instructions. The four Marines waited for the guards checking the doors to complete their circuit of the schoolhouse and reenter the building, then rose and headed for the side that didn't have any illuminated doors.

Five minutes later, they were on the schoolhouse's roof.

There were two access hatches, but both were locked from the inside. But those weren't the only ways into the building; there were also several vents into the air-circulation system.

Bingh prepared three minnies and sent them into the ducting. He would have preferred to take the squad inside the building, but none of the vents was large enough to admit a man. Even if any had been large enough, a man would have made too much noise in the ductwork.

Two of the minnies quickly found ways out of the ducting and into classrooms. Bingh checked their relative positions and was elated to find that one of them was near one of the roof hatches. He sent it to find the hatch and gave control of the other two minnies to Musica and Pricer.

While the first minnie searched for the hatch, Bingh followed the progress of the other two minnies. He almost salivated when the minnies found obvious military offices, and he hoped the minnie looking for the underside of the hatch would find its way to the hatch's locking mechanism; he wanted to take a *very* close look at those offices.

Then the minnie that was still in the ducting looked into an office, and what Bingh saw made him determined to get inside.

A map of Pohick Bay was hanging on the wall. The map had markings that looked like the plans for an amphibious operation against the north flank of the Bataan perimeter.

The hatch was above a folding ladder in an unlocked supply closet. The minnie was able to scramble up shelves all the way to the ceiling half a meter from the hatch. Bingh had it look all around for a way to get closer, but there wasn't any; the minnie was as close as it could get. Unless—

The folding ladder was hinged at the top at one end of the hatch opening, and springs held it close to the ceiling. Bingh examined the way the ladder folded and saw places the minnie could grasp to move along it—if it could get to the ladder. Minnies could jump, but they jumped like quadrupeds—they needed headspace for the arc of their jump or they'd simply arc downward. The arc needed to be higher for a standing jump than a running jump. There wasn't space for the minnie to get a running start, and there didn't look to be enough headroom for the minnie to make the distance before it dropped below the level of the bottom of the ladder.

He had to get inside the schoolhouse to get a better look at that map, but he couldn't risk having the minnie miss its jump and lay broken on the floor of the storage closet to be found by the Coalition. After a bit of thought, Bingh had the minnie drop down to the next shelf. Yes, the ladder was within the minnie's jumping range from the second shelf. Just barely, but it could do it. Bingh sent the command. The minnie gathered itself and jumped. Its forepaws caught on the ladder and it scrabbled onto it. Then it scooted to the hinged end. The hatch was secured with a simple throw bolt. There were no wires or touchplates indicating that the hatch was alarmed. *Good!* The bolt was properly aligned in its brackets and easily within the minnie's ability to throw.

"Got it!" Bingh exulted. He gathered his Marines and trotted to the now unlocked hatch—only to find when he began to lift it that it wouldn't swing open.

He had the minnie look more closely at the other end of the hatch. There was another throw bolt, positioned where the minnie hadn't been able to see it from the shelves. There was no way the minnie could reach that throw bolt from where it was.

Bingh jiggled the hatch and watched the far throw bolt. The bolt moved easily in its brackets. He jiggled it again, and the bolt seemed to move slightly. Again, and it definitely moved. But after that, no matter how he jiggled the hatch, the bolt wouldn't budge farther.

Bingh explained what was happening to his men and asked for suggestions. Wehrli asked exactly where the throw bolt was. When Bingh showed him, Wehrli smacked the corner of the hatch with the side of his fist. Bingh flinched at the sound of the thump, but realized it wasn't loud enough to attract the attention of anybody on the ground—and there wasn't anybody in the supply closet with the minnie.

The bolt jumped a centimeter. Wehrli hit the hatch again and the bolt jerked farther. And again—and the bolt was free.

They were in!

Operations Center, Schoolhouse

Sergeant Bingh took Lance Corporal Wehrli with him as security and left Corporals Musica and Pricer on the roof, monitoring the minnies.

"We need to find the One Shop," Bingh told them before

he and Wehrli lowered the ladder and disappeared into the schoolhouse.

The One Shop, the S1, the personnel department of the regiment. It would have the records of the division's personnel; how many there were and where they were. So far, first squad hadn't found any of the soldiers of the Twenty-third Ruspina Rangers, only the crews of the hidden amphibious vehicles. So while Bingh and Wehrli got all the intelligence they could from the operations office, Musica and Pricer would direct the minnies in a search for the personnel office.

Bingh sent the minnie out of the supply closet the same way it had entered—by squeezing under the door. The minnie looked both ways, and when it found the hallway empty, Bingh opened the door and he and Wehrli stepped out.

The only lighting in the hallways was from small signs showing the way to exits, but Bingh and Wehrli were able to see well enough with their light-gatherer screens. The only sounds were those of an empty building at night. Even with his ears turned all the way up, Bingh could barely hear the low *suss-suss-suss* of distant voices.

The school building was laid out in a quarter of squares; each square surrounded a courtyard. The main entry lobby was to the left of the supply closet. The operations center was in the cross-corridor that separated the two front squares from the two rear ones. Bingh sent the minnie scurrying to the right, to the intersecting corridor, to take a look. The way was clear there, as well. He and Wehrli followed the minnie, padding softly.

The minnie found the door to the operations center and stopped, snuffling all around the door. When its olfactory sensors didn't pick up anything indicating current occupation of the room beyond the door, only the scents of people who had passed by in the recent past, it sat up to signal the way was clear.

Bingh and Wehrli dashed to the door. Bingh tried it and found it was unlocked. He opened the door and turned his ears all the way up, listening for an alarm, or the sound of footsteps coming to investigate a door opening when it shouldn't. He didn't hear anything. He sent the minnie back to the central intersection to watch for anyone coming along, then he and Wehrli entered the room.

Most of the child-size desks the room would normally hold were gone, and those that remained were stacked in a corner. The teaching console had been moved to the middle of the room, and a dozen field desks were arrayed in two concentric circles around it. Bingh's eyes lit up at the two file cabinets standing out from the wall opposite the big wall map that had first caught his attention. There was a map case between the file cabinets.

He gave the big map a quick look, then had Wehrli record it while he turned his own attention to the file cabinets. Both were locked, but the map case wasn't. Three of the maps were of great interest to him; they showed greater detail of the large map on the wall—details for three different regimental assaults on the Pohick Bay flank of the Bataan Peninsula. This was far more than just the Twenty-third Ruspina Rangers. Now he *really* wanted to find the One Shop. He recorded the maps and put them back as he'd found them while Wehrli checked on the minnie.

He'd just closed the map case when Wehrli touched helmets with him.

"Somebody's coming from the rear of the building. Looks like security, checking the rooms."

Bingh turned his HUD on to see what the minnie saw. Two men wearing civilian clothes and goggles were walking the hall, opening doors and stepping inside classrooms. They only stayed in each room for a moment before coming out and proceeding to the next. One of them carried something in his hands. Bingh didn't recognize the apparatus, but knew it must be some sort of detector, just as he knew the goggles had to be night-vision goggles. He had no way of knowing what direction the security patrol would go when it reached the intersection, but he and Wehrli had to be well out of the way before the pair got there.

He recalled the minnie—couldn't leave it to be discov-

ered, even if it did look like a rodent—and had it follow him
and Wehrli to the nearer outside corridor.

This hallway passed between classrooms situated against
the outside wall of the building and others facing the court-
yards. Bingh left the minnie at the intersection, just poking
its head around the corner, while he and Wehrli withdrew a
few meters toward the front of the schoolhouse. His thinking
was, if the patrol turned this way, they'd more likely retrace
their steps to the middle intersection, or head toward the rear
of the building, than zigzag toward the front.

While they waited to see what the patrol did next, Bingh
scanned through the views from the other minnies. One of
them was stationary, peering through a grill in the ductwork.
Bingh knew that Musica and Pricer would have their two
minnies constantly on the move unless one of them found
something he needed to know, so he looked closely at what
the stationary minnie was viewing.

He saw a chart on the wall. The print was too small for the
minnie to resolve from its station in the ducting, but it looked
like a Table of Organization and Equipment for a large unit.

This had to be the S1!

Bingh checked the schematic. The classroom comman-
deered for the personnel department was in the corridor behind the main lobby in the front of the building. He swore;
that was probably the most dangerous part of the building for
the two Marines to penetrate. Still, even though access to the
schoolhouse was controlled, and a security patrol periodically checked all the rooms, it appeared that there weren't
any passive security devices in the hallways or classrooms.

Bingh touched helmets with Wehrli and told him about the
minnie's discovery and what they were going to do.

They dashed silently toward the front of the building.
Bingh kept the HUD of minnie one in a corner of his view.
When he saw the patrol turn to the far side of the school-
house, he summoned the minnie to join him and Wehrli.

At the end of the corridor, Bingh cautiously looked around
the corner and saw someone enter a room near the far end.
He overrode the control of minnie three and sent it through

the ducting to see what was happening in that room. He and Wehrli headed for the S1 while minnie three made its move. They were inside by the time the minnie reached its destination. Minnie one soon reached Bingh. He deactivated it and put it in a pocket.

G1, First Ravenette Naval Infantry Division, the Schoolhouse

The chart on the wall was indeed the TO/E of a large unit, the First Ravenette Naval Infantry Division, Reinforced. The primary reinforcing unit was the Twenty-third Ruspina Rangers.

A quick study of the TO/E chart revealed the division's strength was 18,548 soldiers, 23,619 including the reinforcing Twenty-third Ruspina Ranger Regiment.

This information meshed perfectly with the maps he'd copied in the operations center. Now, where were all those soldiers?

Bingh didn't dare turn on a computer. Even if they weren't password protected, the glow from a screen would be visible in the corridor outside and attract someone's attention. Even if someone came to investigate and didn't find him and Wehrli, this was an intelligence-gathering mission, they couldn't do anything to let the enemy know someone had been here. There weren't any papers lying about, or any unlocked file cabinets or desk drawers to open.

But there was another chart hanging behind the TO/E. And that one proved to be just as valuable; it gave the dispositions of each of the component units of the First Naval Infantry Division and its attached units.

Bingh recorded that chart along with the TO/E, then he and Wehrli got out of there. Five minutes later, all the minnies had been retrieved and first squad was descending the side of the schoolhouse. It was another hour, standard, before they were far enough away for Sergeant Bingh to safely transmit his report, complete with attached visuals of the maps and charts, to Commander Obannion on the *Kiowa*.

CHAPTER
TWENTY-THREE

In the navy's most recent attempt to lay a string-of-pearls, three of the satellites had been knocked out when they passed over an area south-southwest of the besieged Confederation forces on Bataan. The navy believed more laser guns were in the area, and likely one or more of the emplacement vehicles. Taking them out was a top priority for the navy. So, following its initial success, second platoon's fourth squad was one of four squads sent there to find and kill them.

Fourth squad's assigned area of operations was to the northeast of a village that served a large agricultural area. It didn't really matter to the success of their mission for the Marines to know the name of the village, but learning it was part of the Force Recon Marine's normal pre-mission: learning everything they could about the objective. The name of the village was Gilbert's Corners.

There were a couple of important things about Gilbert's Corners the Marines hadn't learned before being inserted to its northeast. One of them they found out almost as soon as they began patrolling.

Fourth squad was inserted near a road that led northeast of the village. They didn't follow the Gilbert's Corners road to its nether end to see just what, if anything, was there to justify its existence. But the Marines were surprised at the amount of traffic the road's well-worn surface indicated it had.

As they had on all of their previous hunts, the squad began

by examining the main road nearest the location from which a laser gun had killed a satellite. *Main road* was a grand term for the narrow, packed-dirt road that ran through a thin forest from the fields surrounding Gilbert's Corners to, well, nowhere in particular. The road was narrow enough that if two vehicles approached from opposite directions, one of them might have to back up to find a wide enough space between the bordering trees before the vehicles could pass each other.

As before, the Marines traveled via puddle jumper—the area they had to search was far too large to cover on foot. Sergeant Williams and Lance Corporal Skripska flew just above the road surface, looking for signs of a vehicle turning off the road, while Corporal Belinski flew a hundred meters ahead and a few meters above the trees, watching for traffic. Lance Corporal Rudd likewise flew above the trees a hundred meters behind Williams and Skripska, watching the rear for traffic from that direction.

Belinski was the first to see something. He dropped below treetop level and turned around, hovering. "Company coming," he said over the squad circuit. His transmission was narrow-beamed; the radio waves were directional in a narrow enough cone no one to his rear or sides could pick them up, unlike a tight-beam, which went to a point target.

Williams popped up and saw dust rising less than a kilometer to his front. He replied with a burst transmission to the squad: "In twenty meters, my right." He put action to words and weaved his way twenty meters into the trees on his right. Skripska came close behind, following the ultraviolet dot on Williams's back. A moment later, Belinski and Rudd reached them. Williams and Skripska already had their puddle jumpers off and hidden behind tree trunks to mask their infra signatures in case the approaching vehicles were using IR detectors. The infrared-damping chameleon sheets the Marines tucked around the puddle jumpers did more than the tree trunks to hide their signatures.

Seconds after arriving, Belinski and Rudd also had their puddle jumpers off and covered behind tree trunks.

The four Marines set into an ambush position, ready to fight if they had to.

Williams tight-beamed to Belinski, "What is it?"—hoping for one of the emplacement vehicles.

"Two landcars," Belinski tight-beamed back. "Personnel. No lasers I could see."

A small, open landcar zipped past at what Williams thought was a faster than safe speed for the road. In addition to the driver, there were four seated passengers—all of them armed soldiers. A sixth soldier stood in the back, clinging for balance to the mount of an assault gun. A second landcar, manned the same as the first, followed fifty meters behind.

Twelve armed soldiers in two landcars, going fast along a road to nowhere. Williams wondered whether he should have checked out the nether end of the road. He wondered if the rushing soldiers had anything to do with the insertion of his squad, if the AstroGhost had been spotted and the soldiers were going to search for them. Or were they somehow connected with the laser guns that were fourth squad's objective?

The soldiers on the two landcars raised too many questions to ignore. Williams decided to follow them and find out where they were in such a hurry to get to. He told his men; they quickly retrieved their puddle jumpers and took off, paralleling the road fifty meters from it. The dust cloud they could see from the landcars was heading away faster than they were following, but Williams didn't want to risk the soldiers spotting their exhausts, so he didn't try to catch up. So long as they could keep the dust cloud in sight, they were all right. If they lost it, then they could speed up.

They lost the cloud, but because it stopped and settled, not because it got out of sight. Williams maintained speed until the squad was three-quarters of a kilometer from where the landcars had stopped. There he signaled the squad to land; they'd go the rest of the way on foot.

Suddenly, they heard the vehicles accelerating back the way they'd come. The Marines raced to get the road in view and were in time to see the two landcars speed by with only their drivers and gunners—the passenger soldiers were gone.

"Let's find them," Williams ordered on the squad circuit. The Marines ran as fast as they could and still maintain silence to where the dust cloud had stopped.

The ground there clearly showed where the landcars had stopped and turned about. It also showed many footprints left by the dismounted soldiers as they stretched their legs, then organized themselves into patrol formation and moved off on foot.

Williams needed to know what those soldiers were doing. He considered caching the squad's puddle jumpers as they'd have to follow on foot to avoid detection, but decided against that; the Marines might not be able to come back that way. Besides, they might need to make a quick exit later on.

After checking all around to make sure no enemy soldiers were nearby, Williams raised his shields long enough to say, "Let's find out where they're going."

The squad moved out, following in the footsteps of the Coalition troops.

The Coalition squad didn't practice good noise discipline, and the Marines heard them well before they could see them. Williams, in second place in the squad's column, speeded up to catch Skripska on the point and told him to move to the flank, to close on the patrol from the side—he was beginning to think the soldiers were a security patrol, but security for what?

The sounds of the patrol grew louder and more distinct as the Marines gained on it: heavy footsteps, jangling gear, an occasional word.

Skripska was twenty meters to the left rear of the last man in the column when the leader sharply ordered, "Let's have some quiet here, men. If anybody's out here, they'll hear us coming."

That was met by some grumbling, but the occasional voices ceased, and the soldiers trod a bit more lightly and their gear jangled less.

They still make more noise than an entire Marine company, Williams thought.

Stepping lightly, the Marines paced the patrol for more

than half an hour before Williams decided the patrol wasn't going anywhere, that it was just patrolling an area. He stepped forward and touched helmets with Skripska.

"Break contact, left," he told him.

Skripska turned sharply left, away from the patrol. Belinski and Rudd followed the UV marker on Williams's back.

Ten minutes later, Williams decided they were far enough away to use their puddle jumpers and they lifted to treetop level.

Fourth squad could easily have wiped out the eight-man patrol, probably before the Coalition soldiers even had a chance to return a shot, but the squad was looking for satellite killers and their support structure. If the soldiers in that patrol were protecting a distribution center, which seemed possible, the enemy would be alerted when they didn't return when expected, and that could cause the Marines' mission to fail.

Of course, it was possible that the patrol was there for another reason. If it was, the Marines needed to find out what that reason was. A premature attack on Coalition forces could do more than jeopardize the squad's mission—it would alert the enemy to their presence and could get them killed.

Whatever the reason for the patrol, Sergeant Williams intended to find out before engaging any other foot patrols his squad encountered.

Fourth squad returned to the road they'd been following and resumed their investigation of it, looking for places where a vehicle might have turned off into the forest.

They found one a kilometer beyond the place where Belinski earlier saw the approaching vehicles.

Williams examined the tracks left by the wheeled vehicle that had turned into the trees at what looked like a game trail. The tread was familiar, and so was the tire spacing—exactly like those of the emplacement vehicles they'd previously found and destroyed. He signaled the squad; they would follow the trail on foot.

Twenty minutes into the forest they found a laser gun at the edge of a gap in the trees too small to call a clearing.

The Force Recon Marines tasked with destroying the laser guns and their vehicles had learned a great deal since they'd first found and killed one. Some of that was thanks to the engineers on the *Kiowa,* who were thrilled when one of the squads, instead of destroying a gun, had taken it to a pickup spot and loaded it aboard the AstroGhost to take to the starship.

One thing the engineers had figured out was how to rig a laser gun so that when it fired, it fed back on itself and committed suicide rather than killing its intended target. The engineers had gladly passed that information on to the Marines.

And Sergeant Williams applied that knowledge to this laser gun. The sabatoge could only be discovered by a detailed inspection of the gun, something the Marines didn't think was done, or at least not done very often.

Once the rigging was done, Williams directed the squad to continue following the emplacement vehicle's tracks. They found another gun a half hour later.

But before they could do anything to the laser, they had to go to cover because of the approach of a patrol.

The first patrol, the one they'd followed, had come from the northwest, then continued to the northeast when it was dropped off. This one came from the west.

The patrol's point man picked up his pace as he neared, then plopped down to sit against the laser gun's pedestal mount.

"Get away from that thing, dammit," a commanding voice ordered. "You don' wanna be sittin' there thet gun goes off. It'll flash-fry yer ass."

"Ah, gimme a break, Sarge," the soldier shot back. "Ain't no satellites come in two, three days now. This here gun ain't gonna fire while we takes us a break."

"Two, three days," the sergeant said, "tha's alla more reason thet gun's gonna go off anytime now. *Move!*"

"Ah, Sarge! Ah—" The soldier grumbled, but shoved himself to his feet and moved to a shady tree to sit under

"Take ten," the sergeant said, looking around at his men. It was a pointless order; he was the only man in the patrol who wasn't sitting down taking a break. He shook his head, muttering, and found a place for himself.

Unseen, thirty meters away from the sergeant, Williams slowly shook his head. He couldn't imagine leading a patrol and not establishing security when he called a rest break. But this sergeant hadn't. If nothing else, that told him the Coalition forces had no idea Marines were in the area. It also told him their discipline wasn't very good.

The soldiers looked hot, tired, and bored. At first they just sat listlessly, some drinking from canteens—at least one had already drunk all of his water and tried unsuccessfully to beg a drink from other soldiers.

Close to the end of the "ten" the patrol leader had called for, one of the soldiers called out, "Hey, Sarge, how come we gotta keep runnin' these here patrols. Ain't no Confedshon sojers here. They's all stuck inside that Bataan place."

The sergeant, looking as hot, tired, and bored as his men, slowly raised his head and looked at the questioner. "We keep runnin' these here patrols jist in case the Confedshon figgers out who's here an' decides ta do sumpin' about it. Tha's why. Now shut yer yap an' get on yer feet, we moving out agin."

The soldiers groaned, but got to their feet and shuffled off in a rough semblance of patrol order.

Williams's eyes widened. *In case the Coalition figures out who's here and decides to do something about it,* the sergeant had said. So who *was* here? And exactly where was *here*?

Williams thought about it while he rigged the laser gun to kill itself. Something big was in or somewhere near Gilbert's Corners, something bigger than laser satellite killers, something Commander Obannion needed to know about.

Williams had planned to continue following the tracks of the emplacement vehicle, hoping to eventually find it or its supply depot. But no longer. He checked his map. The squad was only a few kilometers from the edge of the cultivated area. He thought they'd learn something more important there than the location of another laser gun. He gathered the squad close and touched helmets to tell them what he was thinking.

When he finished, Skripska led off, and they reached the fields without seeing another patrol. Williams immediately sent his men up trees; they'd be able to see farther, perhaps even into the woods they'd been in; the canopy wasn't very dense.

Several Kilometers Northeast of Gilbert's Corners

Directly in front of the Marines lay a vast expanse of farmland. Sergeant Williams didn't recognize most of the crops he saw growing, since he had been raised in a city and his knowledge of the appearance of foodstuffs was primarily what they looked like when they were cooked and served. He did know what cornstalks looked like, though, so he knew what was growing in what he identified as cornfields. Here and there in the fields were small clusters of buildings. Examination with his ocular resolved them to farmhouses, barns, and other farm buildings. Farm machinery, some automated, some of which he could see humans directing, moved about the fields doing things incomprehensible to a city boy. Several kilometers away, across the fields, was the village of Gilbert's Corners.

Williams looked to his right. A few hundred meters away a low building that resembled an oversize shack lay where the road to nowhere emptied into the fields. A directional antenna on top of the building pointed at Gilbert's Corners; another antenna waved back and forth in a ninety-degree arc into the forest. Williams could just make out the nose of a vehicle on the building's far side; he suspected it was one of the landcars that had delivered the deep patrol fourth squad had followed earlier. He thought the building was likely a guard station, a barracks for the soldiers patrolling in the forest.

Williams looked to the west, but couldn't see much in that direction because the setting sun cast long, deep shadows on the fields.

Williams had his survey interrupted by a burst message

from Lance Corporal Rudd: "Lorry, two-zero-zero, klick and a half." Southwest, a kilometer and a half distant.

Williams looked and saw a military lorry filled with soldiers heading along a road through the fields. He watched as it turned left onto the crossroad that led to the low building at the edge of the trees. Using his ocular, Williams watched as about twenty soldiers jumped off the lorry and marched into the building; then an equal number came out and boarded the lorry. The second group of soldiers looked as tired as the first group looked fresh.

As soon as its new passengers were boarded, the lorry headed back the way it had come. Williams had to switch from his magnifier screen to his ocular to watch where it went.

Williams wished one of his men had a census module for his comp, but nobody had thought a squad hunting the satellite killers would have occasion to count troops, so no one had taken one. He would have liked to know whether the soldiers who just left were from one of the patrols his squad had seen or were a totally different group.

A few minutes later, he heard engines. Two landcars had started up on the far side of the building. He watched through the trees as they took off down the road, heading into the forest. Each landcar had several passengers in addition to the driver and gunner—another patrol going out. Moments later, he saw another patrol headed into the forest on foot.

Williams looked back at the lorry in time to see it turn to head into Gilbert's Corners. He took another look at the village through his ocular. There was a lot of new construction, and more was going up. His briefing materials had said Gilbert's Corners was a village with a population of not much more than a thousand people. The new construction could house and serve many times that population. And a good deal more than a thousand people were moving about in the village, and many of them were soldiers.

All thought of finding the satellite killers was pushed aside. Sergeant Williams and his Marines were going to find out who all those people in Gilbert's Corners were. But first they were going to take a closer look at the guard station. He waited until the swiveling antenna was pointed away, then sent his men a burst transmission, telling them to eat something and catch an hour's nap; they'd move out two hours after sundown.

CHAPTER
TWENTY-FOUR

En Route to Gilbert's Corners

No matter what their commanders thought, the soldiers on security duty northeast of Gilbert's Corners obviously didn't think there was a threat of Confederation ground action in the area—their light discipline was miserable. The task light that was on at the communications desk shone clearly through windows left half-shuttered to allow fresh air to circulate through the low building.

Not only that, but the commander of the guard station didn't bother to place sentries or listening posts outside the building. When Sergeant Williams looked through one of the windows, he saw that nobody was monitoring the sensor array, either.

The guard shack had five rooms—a command center with the comm equipment, the sensor monitors, and the guard commander's desk; a mess room with a kitchen on one side; a barracks room for two squads of soldiers, who just then were sleeping, playing cards, reading, or talking; a head/ shower room, which was unoccupied; and the guard commander's quarters, where the commander was sleeping.

Only one soldier was in the command center, sitting at the comm console, watching something on what looked like a personal trid unit. Williams wondered where the soldier who was supposed to be monitoring the sensor suite was—or whether the guard commander allowed it to go unwatched at night. Williams was surprised that no one was watching for the approach of somebody from Gilbert's Corners. A visitor

of the right rank could cause disciplinary action to be brought
against just about everybody at the guard station.

Considering how lax the security was, Williams decided
to enter the command center to get a look at the sensor monitors. Fourth squad hadn't seen any remote sensors during
their approach to the fields or to the guard station. He thought
it wise to know what kind of sensors were in place, and, if
possible, where they were.

Unlike the soldiers, the Marines had security out. Lance
Corporal Rudd was stationed at the front corner of the building, watching over the fields for anyone approaching from
that direction. Corporal Belinski and Lance Corporal Skripska watched the forest.

Williams found Belinski and touched helmets. "I'm going
inside," he told him.

"Be careful, boss," Belinski said.

"I always am."

"Not in this business you aren't."

Williams chuckled softly and squeezed Belinski's shoulder. They were both right; Force Recon Marines took risks
nobody else did—but they took them *carefully.*

The blackout curtain that was supposed to cover the window of the command center was pulled to the side, and one
of the shutters stood all the way open. The window was open
to allow air to flow through, but the screen was closed. Williams decided to check the doors before trying to enter through
a window. There were three doors: one into the far side of the
building into the barracks room, the others to the command
center, one on the forest side and the other on the field side.
The door facing the forest was closed.

After he looked at the other two doors, Williams decided
to check the forest side. He didn't want to enter through the
barracks. Even though he was effectively invisible, there was
too great a danger that one of the soldiers would make accidental contact with him or that something else would happen
to alert them to his presence. Nonetheless, the barracks door
was inviting, as it stood half-open to aid ventilation. On the

field side, the door to the command center was ajar, which Williams hadn't been able to see from the window.

Just a few meters away, Williams found Rudd and told him what he was doing.

The door was ajar, not open enough for him to simply slip through. Cautiously, he eased his hand into the opening and pushed the door a few centimeters wider. The soldier at the comm desk was far too engrossed in his trid to notice. Williams opened the door a little farther. Still, the duty soldier didn't notice. Another push and the door was open far enough for Williams to slip through.

A gust of wind caught the door and swung it fully open, banging it against the outer wall. The duty soldier started at the sound and twisted around.

"Who's there?" he said to the door.

Williams stood still in the shadows a meter from the door. Where he was, someone in the chameleons worn by infantry Marines would be totally invisible to anyone who didn't know he was there. The chameleons worn by Force Recon Marines were even more effective at conferring invisibility, so Williams had no worry that the soldier would see him, even now that he was alert. There was still the possibility of accidental discovery, though.

The soldier got to his feet and took a step toward the door. Belatedly, he remembered his weapon, a sidearm in a holster on a belt hanging on the wall next to the comm console. He reached for the weapon and took it in his hand, then went to the door.

"Who's there?" he asked again. He reached the door and placed the hand with the sidearm on the doorjamb to lean out. "Is anybody there?" he softly called out. When nobody answered, he shook his head and muttered something about the wind. He closed the door and made sure it was latched before he returned to his station. He replaced the weapon in its holster before he picked up the viewer and returned to his trid.

The now latched door didn't bother Williams. If that was

all the concern the duty soldier showed, Williams was confident that he could exit even through a locked door without raising an alarm.

He gave the soldier a couple of minutes to reimmerse himself in his trid, then eased his way to the sensor monitor station. What he saw there made him smile.

A bank of vid monitors showed views of patches of forest; a few showed the fields. Another bank displayed the results of infrared scans. Being effectively invisible, the Marines had little concern for vid monitoring, and their chameleons effectively damped their infrared signatures—they'd show up as faint traces only. There were no motion detectors. Where vids and infra detectors would miss the Marines, motion detectors could well pick them up. Schematics showing the layout of the vidcams and infra scanners lay on the desk.

Williams had the information he'd come for, it was time to leave. He had watched the comm man close and latch the door to the fields, so he checked the door to the forest, which he knew only was closed. The building used old, simple technology: a simple knob was set into the door next to the frame. He put his hand on it and twisted. The knob turned easily. Williams gently pulled the door in, slipped through, and drew it to behind him. The door made a slight click when it caught. The comm man looked up at the noise.

"What's going on here?" he asked the empty room. He jumped to his feet, reached the door in a couple of rapid steps, and flung it open. He stuck his head outside and looked all around. "All right, who's out there?" he demanded. "You're not being funny! I'm going to get the sergeant of the guard if you don't identify yourself. Now who's there?"

As Williams began to move to silence the comm man, the radio he was watching squawked.

"Now what?" the soldier muttered, turning to answer the call. He slammed the door behind him.

The radio call was a comm check. Williams stood at the open window and listened as the patrols reported in from the forest.

Muttering to himself and casting glares at the doors to the outside, the comm man picked up the trid viewer and returned to the evening's entertainment.

Williams shook his head at the sloppy discipline and lack of concern for security. He got Belinski from the front corner of the guard station; the two of them joined Rudd and Skripska and the four continued along the forest's edge to a point directly opposite Gilbert's Corners, where corn grew higher than a man, and started across. They reached the village without incident.

Outside Gilbert's Corners

The cornfields gave way to a half-kilometer-wide band of soya beans before they reached Gilbert's Corners. Sergeant Williams stopped the squad at the end of the towering cornstalks and took a hard look at the village. He quickly decided the three best words to describe the place were *extended construction site*. It was clear that Gilbert's Corners had recently far overrun its previous boundaries—on this side alone, new construction had eaten hundreds of meters into the fields. He briefly wondered how the loss of croplands was going to affect the local economy, but shrugged off the thought. The more important question was the *why* of the new construction. And why were all those soldiers someplace they obviously thought totally unimportant to the war effort?

It was about midnight local time, so it wasn't surprising that there was no construction activity, but people were out and about, and some lights were visible in the old village, which *was* unusual for a farming community. Williams drew his squad close and touched helmets.

"Rudd, come with me. I want to take a closer look at what's going on. Belinski, you and Skripska stay here. If you hear we're in trouble, get out of here and report to the Skipper." He touched Rudd's arm and the two of them slipped into the village.

Inside Gilbert's Corners

The ground in the newly built-up area closest to the northeast fields was gouged and scarred by construction vehicles. Buildings, low-roofed, blocky, and with no distinguishing characteristics, other than number signs next to their doors, had been put up in regimented rows along roads lit dimly by widely spaced lights. There was no evidence, at least in that area, that any landscaping was planned for the near future. Most of the buildings were about the right size to house an infantry platoon—provided they weren't encumbered with too many creature comforts. The lights were off in the buildings, but light-gatherer screens allowed Sergeant Williams and Lance Corporal Rudd to look in enough windows to confirm that the buildings actually were barracks. Williams made a quick count and estimated billeting for a reinforced battalion—fifteen or twenty barracks. Two other buildings, larger than the barracks, were a battalion headquarters and a mess hall. A couple of other buildings were smaller but windowless and more solidly built. Williams suspected they were armories or ammunition depots. A small motor pool was off to one side of the barracks area. During the time it took them to go through the barracks area, the two Marines spotted only one, two-man patrol.

Inward of the troop area was a modest parade ground, and beyond it a hundred-meter-wide stretch of forest undisturbed except for where several roads cut through it. Then came a stretch of better-constructed housing before the original village. There the ground had been sodded rather than left bare, with rows of young trees paralleling the roadsides; the streets were far better lit than in the troop area. Some of the houses still had internal lights burning. Families rather than soldiers were visible in them. Not many of the families in the lit houses seemed to have men present. Aside from the two-man patrol they'd seen in the barracks area, Williams and Rudd noticed that nobody was out and about on foot before they reached the original village, and few were in vehicles.

Three streets ran the length of the village; eight shorter streets crossed them. The only streetlamps were at intersections. The houses were mostly on the small side, all on lots much bigger, with wide side yards between the houses. Nearly all of them sat dark, as one would expect after midnight in a farming village. But two or three establishments on the central street were well lit. Williams and Rudd investigated; whoever was in those places must have something to do with the soldiers and all the recent construction.

The first lit place they came to was on the small side. The front half of the first floor was a bar with a few tables off to the side, and a door to another room in the back wall. About half of the places at the bar were occupied; a few people sat in twos and threes at some of the tables. Most of the patrons were men; the few women looked as rough and hard-used as the men. What little conversation went on was quiet, in tired voices. The people looked like construction workers. The bartender listlessly rubbed a rag along the bar top. Williams and Rudd slipped along the side of the building to look into the back room. Five men, who also looked like construction workers, sat around a table playing cards. They seemed as tired as the people in the front. Williams turned up his ears and listened, as he had outside the bar. In neither place did he hear anyone say anything of interest. Going all around the building, Williams couldn't see a way to reach the windows of the second floor that wouldn't make noise. It probably wasn't worth looking into anyway, the second-story windows were all dark. The two Marines returned to the street in front of the building. The next lights were three buildings farther along the way, on the opposite side of the street. They headed for the lights.

What had looked at a distance like two establishments side by side turned out to be one bar-restaurant, unexpectedly large for a village the size of Gilbert's Corners. It had been made by knocking archways through the common wall of two adjoining buildings. One half had a long bar running along the side, and a row of intimate tables along the other. The other half was a large dining room. The dining room was more than half-filled, and few spaces were open in the bar section. The crowd was more like what might be found in a good-size city following a theater performance—or in a village such as Gilbert's Corners on a Sixth Day night following harvest.

The people, again more men than women, looked as rough as the construction workers, though not hard-used. They were all dressed casually, but their clothes were of far better cut and quality. None of them looked any more tired than the hour would suggest. Two bartenders and three waitstaff bustled about, serving drinks and food, or clearing dishes from tables.

These were the people who had everything to do with the presence of the soldiers and the recent construction. Williams turned his ears up, but couldn't hear anything clearly from inside, merely the murmur of indistinct voices echoing at a distance. He couldn't make out anything even when he touched the window glass with his helmet—the place had some serious sound baffling. He used his optics to record as many of the faces as he could.

That done, Williams and Rudd headed out of Gilbert's Corners; the sergeant wanted his squad to be well back in the forest by daybreak. They were. Sergeant Williams prepared a report—including the scan of the faces in the large bar-restaurant—and tight-beamed it up to the *Kiowa* the next time she rose above the horizon.

It had been a long day and a longer night. Fourth squad hunkered down to rest while waiting for further orders—the discovery that something significant was going on in Gilbert's Corners was probably going to change their mission.

CHAPTER
TWENTY-FIVE

Oceanside, Arsenault

Far under the seabed a thousand kilometers from Ocean-side, two huge tectonic plates, perhaps as much as two hundred kilometers thick, suddenly shifted, thrusting one upward, displacing huge quantities of seawater. This happened twice within a space of ten minutes, the second quake being the greater of the two, about 9.0 on the scale used to measure such things. Both events created waves that raced toward land at up to nine hundred kilometers an hour in the open sea. The first wave to hit the beach at Oceanside was estimated to have reached a height of ten meters; it had slowed by then to a mere sixty kilometers per hour.

The building Jak Daly and Felicia Longpine picked as a refuge was a luxury hotel known as The Seaside. At that time of the morning the lobby was empty except for a uniformed night clerk who looked up, startled, as the pair came crashing through the front door. "Hey! You can't come in here like that!" the man shouted. "You didn't wash the sand off! It costs a lot to keep these carpets—"

"Run!" Daly yelled over his shoulder as they made for the stairs. "Tidal wave coming!" At that moment a huge roaring sound engulfed them. The night clerk bolted over the counter on one hand and made it to the bottom stair as water began rushing into the lobby behind him, destroying forever the expensive carpeting.

The Seaside was built with spacious verandas along both sides onto which the rooms exited. The verandas were de-

216

signed so that residents could sit on them during the day and enjoy the sights, spectacular views of the beaches on the side facing the sea or the town of Oceanside. Felicia was not even breathing hard when she stopped on the second floor, Daly and the clerk so close behind her they almost collided. "Are we high enough?" she asked. They were on the town side of the building and her question was answered immediately as a huge river of dirty water filled with debris swept down the street beneath them.

"Oh, keerist!" the clerk muttered.

People, dazed and sleepy but curious about the uproar, began emerging from their rooms, and soon the veranda was crowded with anxious observers. "Uh-oh," someone said, laughing, "I hope they don't charge us extra for this show."

"Can we get to the other side of the building from here?" Daly asked.

"Sure, but you have to go all the way to the end and around."

"Then let's go."

"Why?"

"In case there's a following wave, maybe bigger than this one. We ought to have time to get higher if we see it coming."

The clerk looked at the swirling water in the street below them. He could see smaller buildings collapsing under the water, and people all around them, realizing at last what was happening, began to panic. A woman started to scream. "But what about these people?" The clerk gestured toward the flooded streets and the collapsing buildings.

"We can't do anything for them right now and we sure won't be able to help anyone if we get washed away." Daly started threading his way through the crowd toward the opposite end of the building. Felicia and the clerk followed. By the time they reached the opposite side of the building, they were out of breath. The sun was beginning to rise, peeping, as if cautiously, afraid of what it might illuminate, but what they saw in the increasing light froze them with horror. *Another* wave was on the way, and although it was still out to sea, it looked much bigger than the first one.

"Omigawd," the clerk whispered.

"Goddamn, that thing's coming in fast!" Felicia laughed excitedly and grinned at Daly, who suddenly realized she was *enjoying* it all!

They stood at the end of the building, right by a stairwell. "Get higher!" Daly shouted, taking the stairs two at a time. They came out on the third floor, a good fifteen meters above the ground level. By then the second wave was just crashing over the beach, shoving before it the water from the first wave that had not yet had time to completely recede from the town.

An elderly couple stood at the railing, transfixed by the sight of the water rushing toward them. The door to their apartment stood open. Daly grabbed Felicia, pulled her inside, and shoved her into the bathroom. He was just returning to help the couple outside when the wave struck with a tremendous force. Daly thought he heard screams above the roar of the water, but he wasn't sure because the flow picked him up and slammed him into the opposite wall of the room, which filled instantly with filthy, swirling water up to his neck. Suddenly, as fast as it had come in, the water receded, dragging Daly helplessly with it across the floor toward the veranda. He stopped himself only by grabbing the doorjamb and holding tight. The wall on the veranda had disappeared.

Daly got to his feet and stumbled to the bathroom. Felicia lay there in a pool of dirty water, gasping for breath. He lifted her up and hugged her tightly to his chest. As they stood there, a sharp cracking, roaring noise enveloped them and the floor beneath them began to vibrate. The roaring grew in intensity, rising in volume as it seemed to approach them. They staggered outside onto what was left of the veranda. What Daly saw there froze him for an instant into helpless, animal terror.

The front part of the Seaside Hotel, its foundations undermined by the force of the water, was collapsing into the flood, each floor slowly, almost gracefully pancaking onto the one beneath it. The whole front of the building, like an enormous, disintegrating ice floe, slid in slow motion down into the water under a huge cloud of white dust. Daly could clearly see people, many people, among the debris disappearing along with furniture and huge chunks of masonry into the water that was beginning to flow back out to sea. All he could do was stand there and await his turn to tumble down into the water. But the collapse stopped suddenly about twenty meters from where the pair were standing.

The hotel clerk and the elderly couple that had been standing on the veranda when the wave hit had disappeared. A young man dressed only in a pair of shorts emerged from a nearby room, soaking wet, and stared at Daly, eyes wide, his mouth working soundlessly as if he couldn't get his breath. "Have you seen my girlfriend?" he finally managed to croak. The thick cloud of dust drifted back over them, coating them white, like bakers at the end of a long shift, making them cough and their eyes water. In an instant it passed on the wind.

At that point Felicia said, "Let's get the hell outta here!" Taking Daly by the hand, she stumbled back into the stairwell. Inside it was bedlam as dozens of people pushed and slipped down the stairs. Those near the bottom shrieked and screamed for those above to stop pushing because the first floor was still full of rushing water. Even so many fell into it and were swept out to sea with the receding flood. Daly and Felicia braced themselves against the railing and managed by physical force to stop the descent of desperate people from the upper floors in their mindless downward spiral. But they weren't sure for how long they could hold them, so strong was the instinct in everyone, even Daly and Felicia themselves, to *run*. In every mind was the unspoken dread of a *third* wave.

"Goddammit, get a grip on yourselves, you fucking animals!" a voice that sounded like God's bellowed down the stairwell from an upper floor. But it wasn't God, it was Gunnery Sergeant Folsom Braddocks.

Daly could never mistake Braddocks's voice for anyone else's. "Gunny! It's Jak Daly, down here!" he yelled.

Felicia laughed and shook her head in disbelief, a huge grin on her face. "Gunny," she sighed. Everyone at OTC knew Braddocks by then.

Braddocks shouldered his way through the crowd. He

would have been a ludicrous sight under normal circumstances as he was wearing only shorts and boondockers. A frightened young lady clung to his arm. "A guy can't have a goddamn weekend liberty without something fuckin' it all up on him," he groused. He stopped where Daly and Felicia clung to the railing, holding the crowd back. "Well"—he grinned at the pair—"we've got a job to do. Come on." He continued on down the stairwell, shouting, "You people, stand fast! We'll tell you when you can come all the way down." Daly had never heard a voice so commanding and penetrating, and it had the desired effect of calming the frightened survivors, who began clearing places to sit on the stairs as the two couples made their way down to the second floor. The young lady clinging to Gunny's arm never said a word, but it was clear she would *never* let go of his arm.

Gunny stood at the top of the stairs leading to the ground floor, surveying the turgid mess swirling through the first-floor level. "Oughta go down in a minute," he muttered, and the water immediately began to lower perceptibly. "Ah!" He dipped a foot into the liquid. "Go down, I say!" he grinned back at Daly, and the water lowered by several centimeters, and then suddenly, with a great sucking sound, it was almost all gone, leaving behind a dirty ankle-deep pool on the first floor.

"Now I know how Moses felt," Daly said, grinning. *They'd made it!* Well, not quite yet. The entire city of Oceanside had been reduced to jumbled wreckage. A few of the taller buildings, farther from the shore than the hotel, were still standing, but *everything* else was gone. Up to their knees in mud, they stood outside what was left of The Seaside Luxury Hotel and looked out over town all the way to the ridge on the far side, a view that would have been impossible before the waves hit. Some structures on the crest of the ridge still stood, but almost everything else between had been swept away.

"Did either of you bring your comm?" Braddocks asked. It was a rule that when candidates departed Camp Upshur, they were to take a handheld with them so that they could be contacted in an emergency.

Daly looked blankly at Felicia. she shook her head. "No, we left them on the goddamned beach!"

"Well, mine's up in my room and I'm not going back for it now!" Gunny replied. "Boy, we've only been here eight months and already we're thinking like ensigns, aren't we?"

"Well," Daly offered in justification, "wouldn't that have been a sight, us trying to raise the Upshur staff duty officer from the beach while twenty million cubic miles of seawater were rushing down on us?"

Braddocks laughed and thumped Daly on the back. "Daly, spoken like a true NCO! There's hope for you yet in this man's Marine Corps!"

Several of the survivors standing nearby did not know how to take this banter in the face of what had just happened to all of them. But they were civilians and did not understand the black sense of humor that kept combat veterans going in the face of the horrors they had to deal with in war.

Braddocks turned to the bedraggled group of survivors. "Listen up, folks, does anyone have a personal comm unit with them?" No one did, they had all fled their rooms in only the clothes they'd been wearing at the time.

"We have to get these people to that high ground." Gunny turned to Daly. "See that tall building over to your right? That's the UCR headquarters building. I don't see a single light on over there or anywhere else, so the power all over what's left of town must be out, but maybe they have something we can use to call for help. Daly, let's you and me get over there, see if anybody's organizing a rescue operation." Gunny turned to Felicia. "Girl, I don't know your name, but I've seen you around. Can you escort these people to that ridge and then get back to Upshur, get help? You'll probably have to make it on foot, but it's only five klicks or so, and you've been running three times that every goddamned morning for months. Can do?"

"Bet your ass, I can! My name is Felicia."

"Good girl, Felicia. Drop these people off there and get

back to Upshur. Tell them what happened here and that there'll be hundreds, maybe thousands of casualties. Muhammad's cavities, this whole town has been wiped out." The tension in Braddocks's voice was the only sign that he had himself been profoundly affected by what they'd just been through. He wiped his forehead and put his free arm around the shoulders of the young woman he was with. "Norma, ease up on that arm, would you? . . . Oh, this is Norma, excuse me for not making introductions earlier."

"Pleased, I'm sure," Norma said, extending a hand. It was ridiculous, Daly thought, there they were in the middle of a disaster area, death perhaps only minutes away if another wave was coming, performing the rituals of polite society. "I'll help you, Felicia," Norma said. They formed the hotel's other survivors into a group, about fifty of them, bedraggled, frightened, but calmer. They began to pick their way up the debris-clogged boulevard that led out of town. They had put about a hundred meters between themselves and what was left of The Seaside Luxury Hotel when even that collapsed with an earthshaking roar.

Aftermath, Oceanside

The trek to the ridge was a nightmare. Debris and bodies were everywhere, forcing Felicia to make many detours. Wading through the slop was exhausting. They tried to avoid looking at the corpses. Of them all, Felicia knew best that by the end of that day, certainly by the next, the unburied dead would become a serious health threat to the survivors.

She kept moving up and down the line of bedraggled refugees, encouraging and assisting those who were having trouble. Everyone understood that if another wave came and they were caught in the open, there'd be no hope for them. But with Norma's help and then the cooperation of the refugees themselves as they realized they were going to make it to safety, morale picked up and even the elderly among the group found they had reservoirs of endurance that they'd never before realized.

Several dozen others had crawled to the ridge before them. Many were injured, and all had lost family members and friends. Felicia knew many more would die behind them if help didn't come quickly.

But Felicia could not abandon her companions just yet. She made six more trips up and down the ridge, assisting other people she could see struggling vainly to make it to safety. She physically carried several elderly people who would not have made it on their own. When the physical exertion began to make itself felt at last, she rested briefly; she still had to make it back to Camp Upshur.

As she sat looking back over what had once been one of the most delightful spots in Human Space, Felicia realized for the first time the enormity of what had happened. "No more liberty here for a while," she muttered. Several people nearby looked up at her sharply, but she did not intend the remark as a joke, it was just all she could think to say in view of the enormous destruction they were witnesses to.

"Thank you, miss, for helping us get out of there," one woman said.

Felicia thanked the lady and explained that she was an officer candidate, as were her two companions, at Camp Upshur. "Young lady," an older gentleman who stood holding the woman's hand spoke up, "what's your name and the names of those two men you were with? My name is Sal Triassi, this is my wife, Ginny, and I'm on Minister Berentus's personal staff. What's your name and those of your friends, especially that guy with the leather lungs? I'll be goddamned sure the minister knows what you and those guys did for us this morning!"

"I have to leave you now. I have to make it back to Camp Upshur. There are Marines there. I'll get help. Will you people be okay until I can come back with help?"

"How are you going to get back there?" someone asked.

"I'm going to run."

"All the way?"

"Yes, just as fast as I can, it's only five kilometers. I can make that easily in twenty minutes, maybe less." But she wasn't sure she could really keep up that pace; the physical and mental strain of the last hours had taken its toll on her. The wild thumping of her heart had subsided after she had carried the last elderly survivor up the slope, but she'd have to run the five kilometers barefoot because the sandals she'd been wearing that morning had disappeared somewhere. She simply did not have the heart to ask any of the refugees to loan her their shoes. "I may find someone with a vehicle along the way and get a ride, but in the meantime my friends Gunny Braddocks and Jak Daly are down there at the UCR headquarters building, organizing a relief party, so you folks just sit tight here and they'll be with you shortly. I'll be back in an hour."

Felicia met no one along the road back to Camp Upshur. It took her close to thirty-five minutes to complete the run, and by the time she arrived at the main gate she was on her last reserves of energy. The soles of her feet were raw and bleeding. She stumbled into the guard shack just as the wild thumping in her chest turned into a massive jolt of pain, and before she could tell the MP on duty anything, she collapsed.

UCR Headquarters Building, Oceanside

The first two floors of the five-story UCR building had been washed out completely by the second wave. Because of the early hour, only a few employees were on duty at the time the disaster struck, and they had sufficient warning to seek safety on the upper floors. Fortunately, those few people, about a dozen, were security and fire personnel; unfortunately, all power systems were down. Because the climate was so equitable at Oceanside, with never any violent storms or other natural disasters, UCR had never bothered to install a backup system to supplement the town's power supply. But there was no panic among these personnel, only frustration because there was nothing they could do to help the survivors.

The two Marines walked into the UCR command center on the fourth floor. The room looked like a command center, with consoles and security monitors and communications equipment in place. But nothing appeared to be working. A small knot of people in uniform stood gathered about a window looking seaward at the devastation. "Just who are you two?" a burly, middle-aged man demanded of the two Marines. "We saw you coming," he added. "Tell us what you saw out there." He was wearing a big silver badge on his short-sleeve shirt and had the air of command about him. "These people"—he gestured to the men and women standing nearby—"are my night shift."

"My name is Folsom Braddocks and this is Jak Daly. We're from Camp Upshur."

"Yeah, I could tell by the way your hair is cut," the burly man said, and several others laughed nervously. "My name is Jacksen, I'm night supervisor for UCR operations here. We're gathering up what emergency gear and first-aid stuff we can so we can get to work. Will you help?"

"Damned straight," Daly replied at once, "but we think you should get out of here as quickly as possible. We just came from The Seaside and you probably saw what happened there. We were hoping you had some sort of communication with the outside world, so we could ask for help."

"We sent a runner back to Upshur on foot," Braddocks added, "but she won't be there for a while yet. Do you have anything here that'll reach Upshur or even Training Command?"

"No," a young woman answered. "My name is Anna Rice, I run the public service communications network. All we have that is working are these handheld two-way communicators we use to contact our police patrols and emergency crews but"—her voice broke—"but we haven't been able to—" She gave a helpless hand gesture.

"We know. You've seen what it's like out there. The streets are nearly impassable. Anyone who was outside when those waves hit—" Daly shook his head.

"Give us some of that gear," Gunny Braddocks demanded, "and we'll go with you."

"We don't have any heavy equipment and we'll need a

great deal of help to clear the debris, to get at any survivors and recover the bodies," Jacksen admitted. "All we can do is render first aid to those people on the ridge and hope that help is on the way."

"It is. But we'd better get out there quick," Daly said, glancing nervously over at Braddocks. He thought he had just felt a vibration in the floor beneath his feet. Braddocks nodded back at him. "Mr. Jacksen, we don't have much time. I think this building is going to fall."

They had been on the ridge for about twenty minutes when the UCR headquarters building finally collapsed.

A Ridgetop, above Oceanside

Hundreds of survivors gathered on the ridge above town. Many of them were seriously injured, and almost all of them were in some stage of shock. There were far too many for Jacksen and his small group of volunteers to help; within minutes their first-aid supplies were exhausted. All they could do afterward was comfort the injured with assurances that help was on the way.

"Are you military personnel?" a burly, middle-aged man asked at one point.

"Yes, sir," Jak answered.

"Do you know that young lady who was through here a while ago, then? She want to Camp Upshur to get help."

"Yes, sir," Braddocks responded, "Candidate Longpine. And who might you be, sir?"

"Sal Triassi, Ministry of War. You people have done a wonderful job today and I'm going to see to it everyone knows about it. If I could have your names . . . ?"

"Later, sir, when we get back to Camp Upshur and get everyone settled. Hell, Mr. Triassi, I'll buy you a beer in the goddamned canteen!"

"When will help get here? It's been a good two hours since Miss Longpine left. I gather it's not that far back to your installation."

Daly glanced at Braddocks. Well, yes, two hours, that wasn't unreasonable. But before either could answer, the unmistakable growl of laboring engines came to them distinctly from the direction of the road to Upshur. Daly smiled broadly, relief plainly written all over his face. "Sir, I am proud to announce that the Marines are about to land."

Aftermath, Oceanside

It was months before even an approximate count of the dead from the disaster at Oceanside could be computed. Of the 2,342 UCR employees in town on the morning of the disaster, 1,121 were confirmed dead; of the 121 OTC candidates in town that morning, only 4 survived. Even worse news for OTC, of the 40 staff members and their entire families in town that morning, only 6 people survived.

Of the 7,847 tourists determined to have been in Oceanside that fatal morning, 3,210 survived the disaster. So of 10,350 people in town that day, almost 6,000 died and only 2,671 bodies were recovered.

An extensive investigation into the disaster concluded there were many reasons why the death toll was so high. First, there was no warning system in place. If tsunamis had occurred in that part of Arsenault in the past, they had struck before the world was settled, and even though the military had been meticulous in its development of Arsenault as its training base, there had simply not been enough time or resources to devote to a comprehensive geological survey of the planet's crust.

The wave struck in the early morning, when almost everyone was still in bed. That contributed to the casualty toll because so many of the tourists and residents lived in bungalows and garden-style apartment buildings that were under two stories high: every structure in Oceanside was flooded to at least the level of the second floor.

The construction of the larger buildings was also called into question since so many of them collapsed. The entire town had been built on the sand and gravel of an ancient river delta, and the engineers who had built Oceanside took that into consideration when they designed the resort. That is why no buildings there were more than six floors in height. The most devastating of the structural failures was that of The Seaside Luxury Hotel. The only people in the hotel who survived, and over two hundred were known to be residing there when the waves hit, were those the Marines managed to evacuate.

UCR vowed to build a new Oceanside on the ruins of the old, a town bigger and better than the original, and the Arsenault Training Command moved quickly to install a tsunami warning system, but by the time Jak Daly was ready to return to Halfway, it had not yet been put in place.

Manny Ubrik's body was never found.

CHAPTER
TWENTY-SIX

Marine OTC, Arsenault

As soon as word of the Oceanside disaster reached Arsenault Training Command, a massive recovery operation was initiated. Since Camp Upshur personnel were first on the scene, they remained there until the relief forces could take over the rescue and recovery operations. Nevertheless, it was many days before the OTC personnel could be released from the exhausting and grisly duty of recovering bodies from the wreckage that had once been a tropical paradise.

Among the dead were many fellow candidates, OTC staff and cadre, and their families. That aspect of the tragedy left Brigadier Beemer with a hard decision to make, but Arsenault Training Command immediately concurred with it and duly forwarded his recommendation to the Heptagon, where it was kicked all the way up to the Assistant Minister of War for Personnel and Readiness and approved instantly, without comment.

It was Brigadier Beemer's decision to graduate the officer candidates of OTC Session 39 two months early.

Candidate Quarters, Marine OTC

"Did you know him well?" Lieutenant Stiltskein and Daly were inventorying Manny Ubrik's personal effects prior to shipping them home to his parents on Solden. This was Stiltskein's last official duty with Jak Daly's company. Brigadier Beemer had selected him to replace his adjutant, who'd died at Oceanside. Stiltskein's name had also come out on the captain's list; the new position called for an officer in that grade, and Stiltskein's promotion orders were expected any day.

"Yes, sir, he'd have made a good Marine officer."

"I agree," Stiltskein answered immediately, then added: "You don't have to call me 'sir,' anymore, Jak, and in my opinion you already *are* a good Marine officer." Stiltskein straightened up from bending over Ubrik's chest of drawers where he'd been sorting through his effects and faced Daly. "I've driven you candidates hard; that was my job, to push you to the limits of your physical abilities. As tired as you ever were when I was pushing you, that was nothing to the exhaustion you'd experience in actual infantry combat, you know that, Jak; you've been there. My name is Danny, by the way." He extended his right hand and they shook. He turned back to the inventory of Ubrik's things and straightened up with a packet of letters in his hand. "I didn't think people used these things anymore. List them. Let's see"—he counted the thin Docuseal packets—"ummm, sixteen personal letters addressed to Sergeant Manny Ubrik from a J. Lombok."

"That was his fiancée."

"Well, list them on the inventory and we'll ship them to his parents with the rest of his things."

"Uh, Danny, tell you what. I'm taking some delay-en-route after we graduate. I was going to stop by Solden and see Manny's parents." Daly shrugged. "He'd have done the same for me. Why not let me return these letters to his girl?"

Stiltskein hefted the packet and regarded Daly for a moment and shrugged. "What the hell. Okay." He tossed the packet to Daly.

"Uh, one more thing. Longpine, she's in the hospital up at Camp Alpha. The word is the brigadier's going to go up there and swear her in. Since you're now the brigadier's adjutant, how about asking if I can go along with him? Felicia and I, we went through some shit together down there, and I, well, I—" Now Daly shrugged.

Stiltskein grinned. "I'll speak to him about it, Jak. Sure. They say with a heart transplant she'll be okay and back on duty in no time." He smiled. "I knew that girl was a first-class runner. All right, let's finish up this business and then you come and have a beer with me."

Graduation, Marine OTC

With the recent events still fresh in everyone's mind and the sorrow many felt over the deaths of so many friends and comrades, the commissioning ceremony was a somber event. Murmured conversation filled the great hall as the candidates waited to be called to attention for the swearing-in ceremony. Candidate, momentarily to become Ensign, Daly sat silently, thinking of Manny Ubrik and Felicia Longpine. Well, at least Felicia would get her commission. Poor Manny—well, Manny Urbrik wasn't the first buddy Sergeant Jak Daly had lost.

Captain Stiltskein marched onto the stage and took his position to one side. The remaining principal staff officers and instructors filed on and took seats behind the podium. The auditorium fell into silence.

"Tennnn-HUT!" Captain Stiltskein bellowed as the brigadier walked out and took his place at the podium. As one, the candidates snapped to attention.

A tendril of perspiration trickled down the inside of his right armpit as Jak Daly's heart began to beat faster. He thought back on events that had led up to this moment: his adventures on the way to Arsenault; the people he'd met along the way; Manny Ubrik; the time and the pleasure with Felicia Longpine; the physical and mental tests they'd undergone together with their classmates; Oceanside and its aftermath. And in a few moments he'd be an ensign in the Confederation Marine Corps.

"We have lost many friends and comrades," the brigadier began, "so this otherwise happy occasion is marred by sadness, all the more devastating because it happened so suddenly. But, as Marine officers, we must steel ourselves to personal loss and human tragedy and continue our mission. Many of you, the combat veterans among you, know the truth of what I am saying, and you also understand that dealing with the loss of comrades does not get easier just because it may happen frequently. But one compensation you will have is that, after today, you will be privileged to lead the finest men and women the human race has ever produced.

"Adjutant, administer the oath."

Captain Stiltskein took the podium. "All raise your right hands. Repeat after me the Marine Oath of Office:

"'I do solemnly swear (or affirm) that I will support and defend the Confederation of Human Worlds against all enemies; that I will bear true faith and allegiance to the same; that I take this obligation freely, without any mental reservation or purpose of evasion; and that I will well and faithfully discharge the duties of the office on which I am about to enter. So help me God.'"

When the last syllable of the oath had echoed through the hall, Stiltskein stepped back from the podium and announced, "You are now ensigns in the Confederation Marine Corps or officers of equivalent rank in your respective military service. At ease and take your seats."

Brigadier Beemer returned to the podium. "Congratulations. We are done here. When you are dismissed, you will receive your commissions, travel orders, and travel vouchers and prepare for immediate return to your home stations. It has been a privilege serving with you. You have successfully completed the most rigorous schooling the Confederation can give you. Moreover, during a time of unanticipated crisis you rose to the challenge like Marine officers and thereby distinguished not only yourselves and this college but the Corps as well. I am very proud of you all."

En Route to Halfway, by Way of Solden

Daly had been a week en route to Solden when one night in his cabin he found himself hefting the package of letters he intended to give to Manny Ubrik's fiancée. He wondered for the umpteenth time what he would say to her. He wondered if he would keep his composure. He was turning the packet over in his hands when it fell to the deck with a thud.

The band holding the Docuseals together snapped and envelopes slid all over the compartment. When Daly gathered them up, he saw he was missing one. He found it way back under his bunk. He shook his head. It was amazing how things could bounce and slide away from you when you dropped them, almost as if they had a life of their own and were trying to escape.

The seal on that sixteenth envelope had broken and the letter inside had come out. Daly was not at all interested in reading it, but as he tried to insert it back into the envelope, he couldn't help glancing at the first paragraph. What he saw written there by J. Lombok made him catch his breath.

Manny Ubrik's lover was a man.

CHAPTER
TWENTY-SEVEN

Headquarters, Fourth Force Reconnaissance Company,
on Board the CNSS <u>Kiowa</u>

Commander Walt Obannion had just arrived in his office when Lieutenant Jimy Phipps knocked on his door. "Come!" Obannion said without looking up from the overnight reports on his console.

"Sir," Lieutenant Jimy Phipps, Fourth Force Recon Company's S2 intelligence officer, said as he entered. "We just got a very interesting report from fourth squad." He held up a crystal.

"Show me," Obannion said, reaching for the crystal. He popped it into his console and quickly read the report, then more quickly scanned the 2-D images that accompanied it. Sergeant Major Maurice Periz slipped past Phipps as Obannion inserted the crystal and read over his shoulder.

"Find out who those people are, Jimy," Obannion said, starting to remove the crystal to return it to Phipps.

"I made a copy, sir. Sergeant Benalshank's already on it."

Obannion nodded, then returned to the top of the report and read it more carefully. Periz started breathing heavily as he read over Obannion's shoulder.

"You thinking what I'm thinking?" the sergeant major asked.

"Quite possibly, Sergeant Major. Quite possibly." Obannion turned his head to look up at Periz. Unlike the sergeant major, he wasn't breathing heavily—but his eyes were shining. He turned back to Phipps. "Let me know the minute any one of these people is identified."

"Aye, aye, sir." As Phipps turned to leave Obannion's office, Sergeant Benalshank blocked him.

"Sir, I have preliminary IDs on four of the people in those images." Phipps grinned as Benalshank said, "Heb Cawman, chairman of the Committee on the Conduct of the War, leads the list. We've also identified J. Bubs Ignaughton, Duey Culvert, and Mort Hedgepath.

Obannion stared at Benalshank for a moment, then popped the crystal and stood. "Sergeant Major, that's from fourth squad," he said, striding out of his office. "Fifth squad is also in the area of Gilbert's Corners. Tell both of them to go to ground and await further orders. Mr. Phipps, ask Captain Qindall to contact Admiral Hoi and tell the admiral I would like to meet with him at his earliest convenience. I'm on my way to the bridge."

Obannion's comm buzzed when he was halfway to the bridge. He flipped it open. "Obannion."

"Sir." It was Captain Qindall, the company executive officer. "The admiral's compliments. He is in his CIC and will be pleased to see you at your earliest convenience."

"Thanks, XO. On my way."

Combat Information Center, Task Force 79, on Board the CNSS Kiowa

The fleet CIC, in one of the largest compartments on the heavy cruiser *Kiowa,* was dimly lit, mostly by console monitors, though red lights glowed dimly on the deck, indicating passage between console stations. Each station had an intent sailor sitting in front of it. Chief petty officers each oversaw several stations. Three officers backed up the chiefs. Rear Admiral Hoi Yueng, the commander of Task Force 79, which had broken the space defenses the Coalition had around Ravenette and landed the first wave of reinforcements for the beleaguered Confederation forces on the Bataan Peninsula, and since then had prevented the Coalition from feeding more than a few reinforcements to its own troops, sat at his command station in the center of the CIC.

Commander Obannion didn't enter the TF 79 CIC as silently as a Force Recon Marine could, nor did he enter it with the sharp footfalls of a Marine on parade—just loud enough for Admiral Hoi to hear him. Hoi didn't turn his head to see who'd entered his CIC, he merely raised a hand and crooked a finger.

"What do you have for me, Commander?" he asked as soon as Obannion reached him.

"Something that pleased me a great deal, sir," Obannion answered. "I think you'll like it too. If I may?" He made to insert the crystal in Hoi's console, and did so when the admiral nodded.

Hoi read the message, then began scanning the attached images. He stopped a few faces in.

"I know that face," he said. "Heb Cawman. Chairman of the Committee on the Conduct of the War." He resumed scanning the images. "Who else have you identified?"

"J. Bubs Ignaughton, Duey Culvert, and Mort Hedgepath so far, sir."

"So far?"

"Yessir. When we identified those four right off, I thought it was likely that the rest of them are in Gilbert's Corners as well. Especially considering that one of the four is chairman. My staff was continuing to attempt to identify the rest when I left my office."

Hoi nodded. "One of General Billie's infrequent reports said he believed the committee had moved out of Ashburton-ville. This is the first intelligence I've seen to verify that—or to indicate where the committee had gone to." He turned on his map and located Gilbert's Corners, then clicked on it. After studying the short column of data numbers that appeared next to the town for a few seconds, he said to one of the officers, "Tell Surveillance and Radar to get me whatever kind of real-time pictures they can of Gilbert's Corners." He gave the coordinates.

"Aye, aye, sir," the officer replied, then spoke into his comm.

"Not being able to string the pearls does make our job somewhat more difficult than it needs to be," Hoi commented. He raised his hand when Obannion started to say something and said, "But the way your hunter-killer teams have been performing, I expect that situation to vastly improve shortly."

"Thank you, sir."

Then they waited quietly for S and R to report back. Patience is a virtue for both navy commanders and Force Recon Marines, so having to wait for the report didn't bother either man.

Surveillance and Radar Division, CNSS <u>Kiowa</u>

SRA3 Nitzen looked at the coordinates, made a mental calculation, and snorted. "Why does the bridge want a picture of that patch of farmland?" he asked.

"It ain't the bridge wants it, Nitzen," growled Chief Blitzor. "It's the admiral wants it. When an admiral tells lowly techs like us he wants something, we says, 'Aye, aye, sir,' and we gives it to him. Now get to work and make some pictures—the admiral wants them *now*."

"Aye, aye, Chief," Nitzen said, shaking his head. "At this range, though, I sure hope he isn't expecting real pretty pictures with tons of detailed analysis."

Chief Blitzor turned his head to Lieutenant Dondor, the assistant division commander, who had given him the request from the admiral's CIC.

"He wants pictures, not analysis," Dondor told Blitzor.

"You heard that?" Blitzor said to Nitzen.

"Yep." Nitzen was already bent to his work, trying to focus the S and R cameras and radar on the coordinates of Gilbert's Corners, barely still visible near the horizon. With the planet rotating in one direction and the *Kiowa* orbiting it in the opposite, Nitzen didn't have much time to acquire images, and what he did get wasn't very detailed. "Now what?" he asked when he had what he could get.

Blitzor turned to Dondor; the officer hadn't told him what to do with the pictures.

"Transfer them to my console," Dondor said. When he got the images, he transmitted them to the TF CIC.

Combat Information Center, Task Force 79

"That was fast," Commander Obannion said, surprised at the shortness of the wait.

"Gilbert's Corners was nearing the limb when I requested these images," Rear Admiral Hoi said dryly. "It's probably all they had time to get before the next orbit, or unless they got the data from another ship. Now let me see what we've got here." He peered closely at the visual, infrared, and radar images that slide-showed on his monitor, then called up the Gilbert's Corners data again. He nodded sharply, then swiveled the monitor so Obannion could get a better look. "Gilbert's Corners has a population of little more than a thousand. Tell me, does that look like a village that size?"

Obannion leaned closer to take a good look. The visual images didn't tell him much. It was just dawn at Gilbert's Corners; the structures were silhouettes, obscured by long shadows. But the infrared and radar told him quite a bit. "Sir, that looks more like a growing town than a small village."

"Uh-huh. I do suspect your people on the ground have found what my people above the sky couldn't have discovered without a good deal of work and luck, even if we had the string-of-pearls in place. Just goes to show the value of Force Recon."

No matter what that doggie thinks, Obannion thought, though he wouldn't say that in front of the admiral. Out loud, he said, "Force Recon, sir, we go where no one else can."

Hoi leaned back in his chair for a moment, thinking, then sat erect. "General Billie is in overall command of this campaign, albeit he has little direct control of what my task force does. The proper thing to do is for me to download this data to him and request direction. I will, of course, recommend a course of action. Two of them, as a matter of fact.

"My primary recommendation will be that he detach elements of sufficient size from the garrison on Bataan to stage a strike against Gilbert's Corners with the objective of neutralizing, capturing if possible but definitely neutralizing, the

Committee on the Conduct of the War." He again paused to think, and shook his head. "Given who he is and how he thinks, I doubt he will consent to detaching any part of his force for such a strike. Since he won't, I will alternatively recommend a raid conducted by Force Recon. If nothing else, we can throw a scare into them." He looked into a distance only he could see for a moment, then looked at Obannion. "In any raid, there will be casualties. If we have to fight in the village, we run the risk of civilian casualties. In the past the Coalition has made considerable political capital from inadvertent civilian casualties. To the greatest extent possible, we have to avoid civilian casualties."

Obannion nodded.

"However, I think the members of the Committee on the Conduct of the War are legitimate military targets. If any of them gets killed, so be it. Try not to kill them, though; the Confederation can make better political capital out of captured committee members than dead ones."

"I understand and fully concur, Admiral," Obannion said.

"Commander, begin drawing plans for such a raid."

"Aye, aye, sir."

Hoi turned back to his console and replaced the images of Gilbert's Corners with a schematic of the warships in orbit around Ravenette. Obannion took that as a dismissal and left the CIC.

Headquarters, Fourth Recon Company

The entire staff of Fourth Force Recon Company, minus Ensign Barnum and First Sergeant Cottle, who were still at Camp Howard on Halfway, assembled in Commander Obannion's office. It was a tight fit for the six of them, especially after Sergeant Major Periz closed the hatch to the outer office.

"I suspect it's possible that one or two of you haven't yet heard about the latest report from second platoon's fourth squad, so I'll let Lieutenant Phipps brief you on it," Commander Obannion began, with a nod at his S2 officer. "At this point, he should have more information than I do. Mr. Phipps, if you will."

"Yessir," Phipps said, and stood a little taller; in Barnum's absence, he was the company's most junior officer. "Yesterday, local time, second platoon's fourth squad was on a hunter-killer mission a hundred and fifty kilometers southwest of Ashburtonville, searching for satellite-killers and their emplacement vehicles, when they discovered the area was heavily patrolled by Coalition infantry. Second platoon's fifth squad also encountered numerous foot patrols in a nearby patrol area. Sergeant Williams decided to find out why the area was being aggressively patrolled, as the patrols could interfere with his squad's primary mission. Fourth squad's hunter-killer area was adjacent to a small farming village called Gilbert's Corners—as was fifth squad's. Sergeant Williams made a cursory examination from a distance and noted extensive recent construction, and what appeared to be housing for far more than the thousand or so people known to be resident in the village. So he led one other Marine into the village to investigate. They discovered newly constructed barracks sufficient to house a reinforced battalion, as well as numerous single-family dwellings. Inside the original village, they found a bar-restaurant that was open and busy despite the late hour—by then it was past midnight, a most unusual time for such an establishment in a farming community to be open and busy. Sergeant Williams thought the patrons of the establishment didn't look like farmers, so he took 2-D images of them and attached the images to his report."

Phipps paused long enough to grin. "We have identified some of the people in those images—at least eight of the eleven members of the Coalition's Committee on the Conduct of the War are in Gilbert's Corners."

"Thank you, Mr. Phipps," Obannion said before the S2 could continue. At some point, he realized, he'd have to give his intelligence officer a primer on briefings—that was a bit too stilted. "You did indeed know something I didn't. Please inform Admiral Hoi and give him the names of every member of the committee you've identified. You can give the names to his aide. Return here as soon as you've done that."

"Aye, aye, sir." Phipps squeezed past Periz, who again closed the door behind him. Everybody breathed a little easier with one fewer body in the commander's office.

"Now," Obannion continued, "Admiral Hoi is sending a report on that discovery to General Billie planetside. With recommendations. He wants his primary recommendation to be for the general to detach a sufficient force to attack Gilbert's Corners with the objective of killing or capturing the committee members present there. He doubts—and, for what it's worth, I concur—that General Billie will want to detach anybody for that mission. So in addition to the assault by elements of his command with Force Recon in a supporting role, Admiral Hoi is recommending a raid on Gilbert's Corners conducted by us." Obannion paused while the sergeant major opened the door to let Lieutenant Phipps back in. "So, I want you to start planning for three missions. One, an unsupported Force Recon raid on Gilbert's Corners using all company personnel, those planetside who can reach the objective in a timely manner, and those who are available in orbit. Two, a platoon-size Force Recon raid on Gilbert's Corners. Three, Force Recon operations in support of a regiment-size army assault on Gilbert's Corners. In each case, the unsupported raids and the operations in support of a larger action, civilian casualties are to be avoided to the greatest extent possible. If the opportunity arises, members of the committee are to be captured, though their capture is not the primary objective of the raids. The primary objective is to sow as much confusion and fear as possible.

"Questions?"

"How much time do we have?" Captain Wainwright, the S3 operations officer, asked.

"Your guess is as good as mine, but I'd say a minimum of two days, maximum one week. Anybody else?"

"Can we kill the members of the committee?" Captain Qindall asked.

Obannion looked at his executive officer and realized that

he was giving voice to a question he thought the others were reluctant to ask. "Admiral Hoi assures me that the members of the Committee on the Conduct of the War are legitimate military targets. However, killing them is low priority and to be avoided if reasonably possible. Anybody else?" When nobody else had any questions, he said, "Let's do this thing."

Sergeant Major Periz opened the door and stepped out of the way of officers anxious to get to work.

CHAPTER
TWENTY-EIGHT

Office of the G2, Bataan Peninsula, Ravenette

Colonel Wilson "Wumwum" Wyllyums, even in the best of times, cut a most unmilitary figure. But, after weeks in the fortress on Bataan, he looked worse than ever. His uniform, always disheveled, was hanging off him like an old maid's washing on the line; three days' growth of beard darkened his jawline; unruly tufts of hair stood up on his head like crabgrass in a badly mown lawn. But under that hair worked one of the most brilliant minds in the Confederation army on Ravenette.

Colonel Wyllyums reread the message from Rear Admiral Hoi on his screen. So Force Recon had been out in the boonies again? Privately, Colonel Wyllyums loved FR operations. Nothing like the human eyeball to find out what the enemy was up to. The admiral was making a suggestion that could be critical. "This could turn the tide in our favor," he muttered. He wondered why nobody had thought of this before. Well, that was obvious enough: nobody on General Jason Billie's staff was paid enough to think of such things. Absently, he reached over and shook out another cigarette from the ever-present pack at his elbow. Yes, yes, yes, he thought as he lit the Capricorn and sucked the smoke deep into his lungs. Tiny tobacco embers cascaded down the front of his uniform. He brushed them off automatically; he considered the little holes they burned in his clothing as just the occupational hazards of a heavy smoker. They only came to his attention when they burst into flames.

Colonel Wyllyums squinted against the harsh cloud of smoke wreathing his head and leaned back in his seat. The decoded, highly classified message he was reading had been addressed, as staff protocol required, to the G3, the operations shop, with info to the deputy commander, the chief of staff, and the G2, which was Wyllyums. It was a list of operations Fleet was proposing for its Force Recon elements behind the Coalition's lines. These messages were routinely furnished to the ground-force commander for his approval, after staff recommendations, and once approved, further disseminated within the army so that the commanders would know if friendly troops would be operating in areas of interest to them. The G2 and G3 staff forwarded their recommendations to the chief of staff, who in turn referred them to General Billie or sometimes, on his own authority, either approved or denied them. The deputy commander, General Cazombi, was included as a courtesy only. The chief of staff could approve these missions on his own because General Billie had confidence in his judgment, and like Billie, Major General Sorca had intense disdain for Force Reconnaissance—or anything Marine. Those recommendations that did make it in to Billie were almost always disapproved.

Colonel Wyllyums had been elevated to the job of General Billie's chief of intelligence because at the time no one else had been available. He had learned it was safer to stay as much out of Billie's sight as possible, so he usually delegated the daily intelligence briefings to a subordinate. But now he had to beard the lion. He applied his digital signature to the message to indicate he had read it. That distinctive signature, scrawled in haste, had given him his nickname, Wumwums, because that's what it looked like.

He sucked on his Capricorn. How to get in to see the commander? Proper military protocol required that he take his concerns up with the chief of staff, but Wyllyums knew what Sorca's reaction would be. Nope. Cazombi the Zombie, Billie's deputy, that was the guy to take this to. General Cazombi was respected throughout the army and he had the guts to take this in to Billie and argue the recommendation's considerable merits. Not that that would do any good, but Wyllyums had to give it a try. He reached for his console, then hesitated. If Cazombi took this to Billie, he'd want Wyllyums to come along with him. Unconsciously he brushed the ashes off his tunic. Did he want another ass-chewing from Billie?

Suddenly a series of heavy blasts shook the walls of Wyllyums's cubbyhole office. *Incoming* artillery. That made up his mind. He punched the console.

Office of the Deputy Commander, Coalition Forces, Ravenette

"How long has this thing been in the system?" General Cazombi asked. He answered his own question, glancing at the date-time group on the message. "Not that long," he muttered, reading it once more. He rubbed his jaw with one hand. "Ummm, Balca might not have read it yet," he mused. "If I haven't read it until now, I know he hasn't."

"Sir, if we let Admiral Hoi act on this intelligence, it could be critical to our breakout plan. I don't think we have any choice except to argue this with General Billie."

Cazombi smiled. "Well, you can damned well bet that Billie won't detach any of his force to carry out this mission. So if it's going to be carried off, the Marines will have to do it, and you know how our supreme commander feels about Marines." Cazombi leaned back in his chair. "Jeez, Willie, you ready to risk another dressing down from Billie? You think this is *that* important?"

"That I do, sir, that I do."

"Sergeant," Cazombi called to his enlisted aide, "get the G3, have him meet me here ASAP." He punched General Sorca's number into his console. "Balca. Alistair. I'm bringing G2 and G3 over and we're going in to see the commander. I'll brief you when I get there."

Colonel Wyllyums reached for the cigarette pack he always carried in a breast pocket. "Uh-uh, Willie, don't light up just yet"—Cazombi waved a hand—"you know how Billie hates cigarette smoke."

"Uh, yes, sir. But he smokes those damned cigars—"

The G3, Brigadier General Thayer, arrived.

"Sy, we're going up to see Billie," Cazombi said. "Have you read the traffic from Task Force 79 yet?"

"Not yet, sir," the brigadier answered, "I usually leave that stuff to last." He took the proffered message and glanced at it. Wyllyums had ticked off the paragraph on the printout. Thayer shook his head. "He'll never approve something like this, sir, especially never release any of his ground forces for a mission like this."

Cazombi scratched his nose. "I know. But Willie here thinks this is a great opportunity and so do I. What do you say, Sy?"

Thayer ran a bony hand through his thinning hair. Like Colonel Wyllyums, he'd been appointed by Billie as operations officer, because no one else was available. Billie's method of running an army was to make all the decisions himself, so Thayer's job had devolved into ensuring Billie's orders on troop dispositions and tactics were passed on to the unit commanders, not recommending or even commenting on them. "Well, it has possibilities, sir. If you're willing to go into the lion's den to argue them, I'll go with you."

Willie stood up and grinned. "Once more into the breach, dear friends! Once more!"

Office of the Supreme Commander, Coalition Forces, Ravenette

"Wyllyums, why is it you *always* look like a damned bag of rags whenever I see you?" General Billie thundered when the three officers with General Sorca bringing up the rear filed into his tiny cubicle.

"The slimies ate my dress uniform, sir."

"Goddammit, Colonel, don't smart-mouth me!" Billie slammed his fist on his desk. "You're a goddamned field-grade officer on my staff, goddammit, and I expect you to set an example for everyone else. I know, I know, shortage of water and all that, but, Colonel, an officer is *always* on parade. At least you could tuck that damned tunic in." He glared at the officers. "What the hell brings you all in here like this? Balca, your job is to shortstop traffic out there, so I, so I can—*concentrate* on important matters." He glared at Sorca.

"Yessir, but General Cazombi has something he thinks is important and I couldn't—"

"Well, Alistair, what is it then? You had to bring Wyllyums and Thayer with you? Afraid to face me alone, are you?" Billie laughed.

"Sir, here's a printout of a message from Admiral Hoi Yueng recommending some Force Recon missions. I've highlighted the one I'd like to talk to you about. Most of these missions are the usual snoop-and-poop stuff, but Marine Force Recon—"

"Not *them* again!" Billie muttered.

"—has spotted something at Gilbert's Corners the admiral thinks is highly significant." He handed Billie the flimsy sheet.

"I know all about Gilbert's Corners."

"Well, sir, I guess that was something we forgot to pass on to Admiral Hoi," Cazombi said.

Billie ignored the comment. "Goddamned smartest thing old Lyons did, getting those meddling politicos as far away from him as he could. I'd bring them all back here if I could, really gum up his works." He took the sheet. "Hoi Yueng," he muttered, "goddamned space-going squid, sits up there on the *Kiowa* on his fat ass, scratching his Buddha head," Billie grumbled, glancing at the paragraph. "NO, goddammit it, *NO!* Absolutely not! Jesus H. Hertzog, Alistair, you know better than to endorse a proposal like this! I will *NEVER* authorize an attack against civilians, *NEVER!*" Billie's face had turned brick red. "And, dammit, who the hell does Hoi think he is, recommending that *I* detach troops from *my* command to conduct this wild-goose chase?"

"Sir"—it was Colonel Wyllyums—"if I may? We know that the Coalition government is less than united in their views on how to prosecute this war. Our intercepts of their diplomatic messages spell that out very clearly. In fact, I'd go so far as to say it's the personalities of Summers and Lyons that are holding the whole thing together. Every one of those politicians thinks he knows better than Lyons how to fight this war."

"So?" Billie glared back at the colonel. "I know all about that. So what? This war's going to be won right here"—he jabbed his desk with a forefinger—"when we break out. Dammit, men, I have six full divisions crammed into this shithole or hanging loose in orbit, champing at the bit for me to let 'em go, and we're almost ready to do that! I'm going to split Lyons's army in two and defeat it in detail. So what good is a goddamned Force Reconnaissance raid on Gilbert's Corners?"

"Sir," General Cazombi said, "those politicians out there are a fractious bunch of quibblers and cowards. Now, if the Marines—Marines, sir, not our troops—can put the fear of God into them, shake them up, hit them in the guts with a raid, maybe even capture or kill a few of them"—he spread his hands—"they'll shit a brick—"

"You don't need to use expressions like that with me, General."

"Sorry, sir. We think that's all they'd need to force General Lyons to detach significant number of *his* troops to protect the place from further raids, weaken *his* forces. There's a division a few klicks away from Gilbert's Corners, sitting on its hands, another at Phelps. They constitute an important reserve. Once you mount your breakout, those troops are available to plug holes in Lyons's line. We need to ensure they are kept where they are. This raid will do that."

Billie shifted his position. "It's straight-leg infantry that's going to win this war, gentlemen! You're not Marines, you should know that! All this behind-the-lines stuff, it's mere grandstanding, a bunch of prima donnas out there taking very little risk and bragging about how damned brave they are. Typical Marine publicity stunts! And who are these Force Recon boys anyway? Company-grade officers, junior officers, and *enlisted people*! You expect me to divert any of my forces on the recommendation of these nobodies? Not a field-grade among them?" He snapped the flimsy with his fingers. "Ambushes, raids, sniping, *murder,* gentlemen, pure and simple, and I won't put up with it! Not on my watch! Not in my war!" He crumpled up the flimsy sheet and tossed it onto the floor. "That's what I think of this bullshit! Now you all get the hell out of here and don't bother me again!"

There was not enough room in the tiny office for a proper salute, so the four officers filed out unceremoniously. "Balca! You stay here for a while." Sorca remained standing. "Have a seat." Billie angrily bit the end off a Clinton and lit it up. Significantly, he did not offer one to his chief of staff. Billie blew a thick cloud of smoke and leaned back. "Balca, this is the kind of shit I've been working against ever since I took command of this army, and I'm getting really fucking *sick* of it. I want you to get rid of Cazombi—"

Sorca made as if to protest.

"I know, I know, he outranks you, Balca. So what? You're a devious plotter, a good staff man, find something to get him out of my hair. Come up with something and I'll use it to send him off, send him off on a wild-bopaloo chase somewhere." Billie grinned and blew more smoke.

A light went on in Sorca's head and he grinned in his own turn. He reached down and retrieved the crumpled flimsy, spread it out on his knee. "Sir, that makes me think—"

"Bad sign, Balca, you're not paid enough to think. That's my job." Billie chuckled.

"Well, sir, this raid, now—"

"Yessssss? I sense something coming on."

"Well, I'd have disapproved it without hesitation, but Cazombi, he barged in here—"

"I know, I know. The man's a zealot, Balca, one of those highly principled fellows who does not understand the need for expediency in military affairs. He's like all do-gooders, he gets in the way. Myself, I don't give a slimie's ass about killing civilians, they're all goddamned traitors anyway, and we'll hang them when we get them, but this proposed raid won't have one iota of effect on the outcome of the war, I assure you. What are you thinking, man?"

Balca cleared his throat. "Well, sir, this proposal is clearly an attack against civilians. It will not go unremarked in our own government circles. What would the Confederation Congress think, their forces attacking the representatives of another democratically elected government? Lyons has to face this so-called Committee on the Conduct of the War? You wait until word gets out about this raid and our own politicians will have you over the coals. Unless—"

"Unless what, Balca?" Billie squinted at his chief of staff through the tobacco smoke.

"Here's what I suggest, sir. You've got Admiral Hoi making this recommendation, that's in the record. You've got Cazombi and your G2 and your G3 recommending you approve it. You argued forcefully against it. We're all witnesses to that. Now you have Cazombi write up his own recommendation and submit it to you. You'll have him on the record then. You approve it—with strong reservations and restrictions—and you warn him verbally that if there are any repercussions, he's on his own. You stress the necessity of limiting civilian casualties. That's an impossibility in an operation like this, but you stress that in writing. Then let the Marines go in there. You know how they operate, they'll shoot the place up. It's heavily defended. It won't be a walkover. There'll be casualties, hopefully some of the politicians. Summers's government will protest vigorously, and Chang-Sturdevant will have to answer to her own party for what happened. You come out looking good and maybe even get Cazombi, Hoi, that whole crowd recalled."

Billie leaned back and regarded Balca through a cloud of cigar smoke. He studied the Clinton carefully for a moment, turning it in his fingers. "Balca," he said at last, "you're a freaking devil, anyone ever tell you that? But"—he held up a forefinger—"you're *my* devil." He shoved the cigar humidor at his chief of staff. "Have a Clinton, old buddy, you've earned one."

On the Line, Charlie Company, Bataan Peninsula, Ravenette

"Life has sure improved a lot around here," Platoon Sergeant Rags Mesola sighed, squeezing the last juice out of a ration packet. Since reinforcements had started arriving on Bataan, real field rations had become more plentiful.

"I dunno," Corporal Happy Hannover said from where he sat in a corner of Charlie Company's bunker, "I was sorta gettin' used to slimies."

Second Lieutenant Herb Carman shook his head as he spooned more "mystery meat" out of his own ration pack. "You guys'd bitch if you had your balls in a vise."

"Well, El Tee, from where I sit seems you've managed to gain about a kilo on that stuff you're eatin' there, so life *must* be good for ol' Charlie Company at last," Mesola said, laughing.

Hannover burped contentedly. "Delicious," he murmured, then: "What's the Word, El Tee?" Carman had just returned from the daily battalion situation briefing.

"Can't say, Hap, Ultra Secret. If I was to tell ya, I'd have to kill ya."

"Come on, Herb, we're goin' on the line in a few minutes, we'll miss Captain Walker's company brief and have to wait for the latrine rumors to circulate. When the hell we are gonna break out of this shithole?"

"Okay, Rags, but this can't go no farther than you and Hap, understand?" The other two nodded and sidled closer to where Carman sat. He ran a hand across the stubble of his beard and leaned close to the other two. "We're gonna surrender," he whispered.

"Lieutenant—" Mesola frowned.

"Look, guys, it's 'All Quiet on the Western Front,' same as yesterday and the day before. Everybody knows the Big Man's gonna stage a breakout, but he ain't tellin' us cannon fodder. Soon, Colonel Epperly's been saying." Colonel Epperly was the battalion commander. "Anyway, you all know General Billie's got six full divisions crammed in here and waiting in orbit to be landed, so the Big Push can't be that far off. So relax, guys, relax."

"Shit," Hannover muttered.

"Herb, what the heck would you do if you were in charge of this jug fuck?"

"Me, Rags? Hell, first thing I'd do is fire General Billie and give the army to General Cazombi."

"Amen to that," Hannover said with feeling.

"And then?" Mesola prodded.

"And then I'd do what any dumb-assed infantryman'd do. I'd peel off a couple of those divisions and the Marines and do a landing behind enemy lines, catch them between us, and squeeze their nuts real hard."

"Yer sayin' our supreme commander is not a 'dumb-assed infantryman'?"

"Not even that. That damned dugout rat is gonna fuck this war up, Herb." Mesola cursed and got to his feet, gathering up his gear.

"Let's get off this topic, men, it's not good for the morale of the enlisted swine, of which you two are prime examples. Get your guys together, Rags, and relieve second platoon. I'll be around to your positions as soon as it gets dark, so keep alert. If I catch you guys jerkin' off out there again—"

" 'Jerkoff,' Herb, that's a good description of our supreme commander." With that, Sergeant Mesola stalked off to rally third platoon for another sleepless night in the company's fighting positions.

Office of the Deputy Commander, Coalition Forces, Ravenette

"Read that one passage back to me, Wilson." General Cazombi sat with Colonel Wyllyums and Brigadier General Thayer, going over the recommendation General Billie had asked Cazombi to make about the proposed raid on Gilbert's Corners.

" '. . . and disrupt to a considerable extent the Coalition government's decision-making procedure,' " Colonel Wyllyums read. "Sir, I'd substitute *process* for *procedure*."

"Very well." Cazombi made the change. They'd been at the editorial process for about an hour by then. "I think that does it. Do you gents agree we've laid it all out?" He reached for the Send key.

"One thing, sir," Brigadier General Thayer said. "Please put in as the last paragraph, 'Brigadier General Sy Thayer, Assistant Chief of Staff, Operations, concurs in this evaluation.' "

" 'And,' " Wyllyums added, " 'Colonel Wilson Wyllyums, ACofS, Intelligence.' "

"You guys understand Billie's having me do this so if anything goes wrong he can hang my ass? Do you two want to swing with me?"

"We understand. Fully, sir," Colonel Wyllyums replied, nodding at Thayer, who inclined his own head in silent agreement.

"General, I put my reputation behind Admiral Hoi's recommendation. You've stated here that he should be advised that civilian casualties be kept at a minimum, what any reasonable commander would advise, but it does not tie the Marines' hands. And I also fully concur that if successful, this raid'll upset the Coalition's government and subject Lyons to pressure to redeploy valuable troop strength, which would give us an invaluable strategic advantage when Billie mounts his breakout. Lyons should've removed the whole shebang to one of the other Coalition worlds where it'd be out of harm's way."

"He waited too long," Colonel Wyllyums added. "By the time the move took place, Task Force 79 was in the area and he risked losing the entire government before it could escape planetary orbit. I think we're beginning to see that the infallible Davis Lyons has some chinks in his armor."

"Yeah, and one of them might just be our redoubtable Admiral Hoi Yueng and those Marines," Cazombi chuckled. He added the paragraph. "Well, here goes." He sent the message, saying, "Past the lips, over the gums, look out, asshole, here it comes!"

CHAPTER
TWENTY-NINE

Office of the G2, Confederation Army HQ, Bataan, Ravenette

Colonel Wilson Wyllyums sat with his feet up on his rickety field table, a Capricorn hanging out of one side of his mouth, contemplating his chances for promotion to brigadier general. They were zero, he reflected, and sighed. He'd retire a colonel, not because he wasn't effective in his field, he was a top-notch intelligence officer, but because he just wasn't a spit-and-polish soldier. Just then his tunic was hanging open and he was smoking. General Billie had issued specific directives there'd be *no* smoking in the Bataan fortress and officers and NCOs would be in the *proper* uniform at *all* times.

The no-smoking edict Wyllyums could understand. With so many men crammed into the fortress, the air was bad enough without tobacco smoke to foul the depleted oxygen supply. But General Billie smoked. He smoked foul-smelling Clintons. "Bastard," Wyllyums muttered, thinking about that, as he did every time he lit a cigarette. " 'Do as I say, not as I do,' " he said aloud. "Rotten bastard," he said again, inhaling deeply on his Capricorn.

The Hot Button on his console bleeped suddenly. The Hot Button was his direct line to General Billie's office. Wyllyums cursed but continued smoking his cigarette. Each staff officer had such a line. If it bleeped more than two times before someone answered, the senior officer in that section would get an ass-chewing from General Billie. Wyllyums let the instrument bleep four times before he reached for it.

"Wyllyums? I need you, front and center!" a voice demanded.

Rage suddenly overcame Colonel Wilson Wyllyums's caution and sense of self-preservation. It was the imperious tone of the voice on the other end of the communications system that did it. He was sick of it. "Who the *fuck* is this?" he shouted back.

The line was silent for all of six seconds. "This is General Billie" came the very slow, very deliberate answer.

"Oh, I'm *sorry*, sir! *Sorry*. I didn't recognize your voice, sir," Wyllyums protested, grinning, feigning abject obedience and deep embarrassment, twirling his cigarette between his fingers. Good thing they didn't have vid hookup.

Another long pause, then: "Please visit me as soon as possible, Colonel." The line went dead.

"Yes, Master," Wyllyums replied. He really didn't care if it was dead or not. He shifted his feet to the floor. Well, what did the supreme commander want this time? Wyllyums knew he was in for another chewing out, for not answering the stupid line immediately, for insubordination, for being sloppy, for—for who knew what. But one curious thing: Billie had not roared at him as he usually did when issuing a summons.

Tunic unbuttoned, jaw unshaved, Colonel Wilson Wyllyums walked out of his tiny, smoke-filled cubicle. "Sergeant Craiggie," he told his grizzled master sergeant, "I am off to see General Jeans of the Horse Marines." That was his favorite sobriquet for General Billie, based on an old, old barrack ballad poking fun at useless officers.

"Very good, sir," the sergeant replied, drawing himself to attention behind his desk while surreptitiously shoving the half-full bottle of Old Snort back into a drawer.

"If I am whores de combat, Sergeant," Colonel Wyllyums said with dignified gravity, mimicking the First General Order. "Kindly take charge of this post and all government property in view."

Sergeant Craiggie began to wonder if the colonel had been into his own supply of bourbon that morning. "Thy will be done, sir," he replied, using his most gravelly Old NCO Voice.

Wyllyums and Craiggie had been together for years, on and off, and such banter was a ritual with them. "Oh"—Wyllyums made an airy gesture with one hand as he minced out of the tiny office—"don't call me *sir. Master* will do just fine."

Supreme Commander's Office, Confederation Army HQ, Ravenette

"Ah, Wilson! Do have a seat," General Billie greeted Colonel Wyllyums. The colonel stood there, mouth almost hanging open in astonishment. "Have a Clinton, Colonel?" Billie shoved the humidor across his desk.

"Uh, thank you, sir, but, no, thank you." Wilson could not believe what was happening. Where was the ass-chewing he had expected—deserved, in fact?

Billie lit his own cigar. "Wilson, I've called you in here to get your opinion on something." He leaned back and exhaled a blue cloud of smoke.

My opinion? Wilson thought. Now *that* was something new.

"But first, some good news." Billie grinned. "I'm recommending you for the Legion of Merit. The adjutant general is cutting the orders even as we speak."

What? Wyllyums sat bolt upright. Had he heard that right? "Ah, well, s-sir, that's a great h-honor," he stuttered. What's going on here? he wondered. What does this guy want me to do? What's the catch?

"Yes, Wilson, you deserve a decoration. For the way you discovered that seaborne invasion scheme the Coalition pulled on us a while ago—"

"But, sir, it was the—"

"And the job you've done finding and eliminating those antisatellite laser batteries. Excellent work, Colonel!"

Wyllyums could not believe what he was hearing. It was the Marine Force Recon that had discovered the seaborne attack force, and if it hadn't been for Brigadier Sturgeon of Thirty-fourth FIST disobeying Billie's orders to shift to the main line of defense, it would have succeeded. Wyllyums re-membered distinctly General Billic's rage against the Marine when he disobeyed Billie's direct order and deployed his force to repel the attack. And it was Marine Force Reconnaissance that had been taking out the satellite-killer lasers. All Wyl-lyums did was track their progress in those operations and keep the army commanders informed of what they'd been doing.

"Good work, Wilson, I repeat. And a decoration is inade-quate recognition for what you've done here." Billie handed Wyllyums a crystal. "Pop this into your reader when you get back to your office. You'll like what's on it."

Wilson regarded the crystal suspiciously. "Sir, I-I—"

"It's your Officer Efficiency Report, Colonel, and in it I recommend your immediate promotion to the rank of briga-dier general. I have the authority to grant you a temporary, field promotion as brevet rank and those orders are being prepared. As of now you are a brigadier general. The next drone to Earth will carry my request that the President for-ward my recommendation to the Senate, and I assure you, they will approve it. Of course, until your promotion is con-firmed, you'll have the rank and privileges of your new grade but not the pay. But"—Billie laughed—"not much you can spend your pay on around here, is there?" He handed Wyl-lyums a pair of silver stars. "Wear them proudly, General."

Wyllyums, utterly speechless, could only stare at the stars in his hand.

"Sure you won't join me in a Clinton, General?" Billie grinned and offered the humidor again. This time Wyllyums took the cigar and Billie lit it for him.

"Sir, I-I—don't know what to say, except, thank you! I'll try my best to live up to your expectations." Wyllyums felt like a swine saying that, but he meant it. *Brigadier general,* just like *that*! And he thought he was going to receive the mother of all ass-chewings this morning!

"Now, Wilson, there's something I want you to do for me."

"Yessir?"

"You endorsed that recommendation by General Cazombi

that Admiral Hoi be authorized to mount a raid on Gilbert's Corners."

"Yessir, I did. And you approved it, sir, which I think was very wise—"

"Yes. Well, the admiral has been able to launch a partial string-of-pearls, so we now have some satellite surveillance capability, uh, thanks to your work knocking out those laser guns, Wilson. So. I need you to do two things. First, request Admiral Hoi give us his latest SOP data on the Gilbert's Corners area, and then I want you to take this"—Billie handed Wyllyums another crystal—"memo for the record, sign it, and put it into your system."

"And what does it say, sir?"

"Well, Colonel, er, *General,* hah, hah, takes some getting used to, don't it? Did me too, when I made my first star. Ah, it comments on General Cazombi's recommendation. Your private comments, Wilson, not for me, just for the record, you understand. I want you to keep this between us, of course. The rest of the staff does not need to know about your private reservations. In the MFR you endorse Cazombi's plan, naturally, but you also have reservations about casualties and you mention how reluctantly I approved the plan, my own concerns about harm to civilians being paramount. Read it. It's all in there. Then sign it. Can you do that for me, Wilson?"

"Oh, er, yessir! Certainly. At once." So that was the old fox's reason for calling me up here, showering me with a decoration, a promotion, this stinking cigar, Wilson thought. Billie was hedging his bet on the raid's outcome. He was asking Wyllyums to request the surveillance, to make it look routine, so nobody would know that Billie was having second thoughts about its success. And no matter how the attack on Gilbert's went, old Billie would come out smelling like a rose. And to make sure, he would have the satellite surveillance beforehand, to make his own assessment of the raid's chances of success. But if, as Billie hoped, the raid went wrong and axes fell, he, Wyllyums, with this MFR in the system, would keep his promotion. All he had to do was—was betray Cazombi and the Marines.

Intelligence Division, Confederation Army HQ, Bataan

At first Sergeant Craiggie did not notice the two silver stars on Brigadier General Wyllyums's tunic, but when he did, he jumped up from his desk. "What in the—?"

"Never thought you'd see them, eh, Craiggie? Well, neither did I, Sarge, neither did I."

"Sir, what—how—?"

General Wyllyums reached absently for the packet of Capricorns he kept in a tunic pocket, shook one out, and Sergeant Craiggie leaned forward to light it for him. "What did I have to do to get it? Well, I have to eat shit, Sergeant. By the way, I've just come from personnel. Now that I'm a flag officer I'm authorized a sergeant major on my staff. I put your name in. I'll have the orders to you in a few minutes. Congratulations."

"I guess we should have some of this, then," Craiggie produced his bottle of bourbon.

"Yes, Sergeant Major, we should, we should. I need something to wash down the nine yards of shit I am about to swallow."

"Ah, sir," Craiggie said philosophically, "everyone's gotta eat some sometime or another. There's two kind of people in this army, those, like you and me, who do it because we got to, and then there's those who do it because they like the taste."

"Sergeant Major, that's the problem. I think I'm beginning to like the taste."

Only at that moment did Sergeant Major Craiggie notice that General Wyllyums's tunic was buttoned up tightly.

CHAPTER
THIRTY

Commander Obannion and his staff met again in his office the next afternoon, but not before Obannion received a message from Rear Admiral Hoi:

"1. It's as I expected, Commander. General Billie has declined to mount an assault on Gilbert's Corners. He has, however, authorized a raid by Force Recon. The raid has the endorsement of Lieutenant General Cazombi, Brigadier General Thayer, and Colonel Wyllyums, who are respectively Billie's deputy commander, G3, and G2. Show me your plans as soon as they are ready.

"2. My congratulations to your hunter-killer teams. Thanks to their efforts, enough of the Coalition laser guns have been destroyed that the starships of Task Force 79 were able to launch the string-of-pearls during the third watch, and most of the string is still in orbit."

"Gentlemen," Obannion said, "I have just heard from the admiral. First item of business, the navy is now able to sustain a nearly complete string-of-pearls. The Admiral offers his congratulations to Force Recon for making that possible."

The small office reverberated with cheers and the thumps of backs being slapped.

"Get it out of your systems now," Obannion said loudly enough to be heard over the congratulations being shouted back and forth, "because now we have very serious business to conduct.

"As we expected, General Billie has declined to mount an assault on Gilbert's Corners. However, he is authorizing Force Recon to mount a raid. So, Captain Wainwright," Obannion said with a nod, "if you can brief us on whatever plans you have for a Force Recon raid . . ." He gestured for Wainwright to begin.

"Before I begin, sir," Wainwright said, "I think we need to hear from Captain Gonzalez about transportation, as that has had considerable bearing on my planning."

Obannion made a gesture for the logistics officer to speak.

"Thank you, sir, Captain Wainwright," Gonzalez began. "The first thing I did was ascertain just what transportation is available to mass the company, or just a platoon, within striking distance of Gilbert's Corners. I believe everybody knows that we have been exclusively using the *Admiral Stoloff*'s Astro-Ghost to move our squads to and from planetside, and to change their positions planetside. It turns out that the *Admiral Stoloff* has the only AstroGhost in all of Task Force 79." He paused to let that sink in. "The *Kiowa* herself has more than sufficient Essays to land the entire company in one wave." He paused again, then turned to Wainwright. "Do you want me to continue, or would you rather pick it up here yourself?"

"I'll take it," Wainwright said. "Sir, to beat the obvious, if we make planetfall via Essay, there is little chance the Coalition will not detect our landing. The only way to avoid putting the garrison at Gilbert's Corners—not to mention the members of the Committee on the Conduct of the War—on notice of our arrival is to make planetfall at a considerable distance, perhaps as far as a thousand kilometers, from Gilbert's Corners. If we do that, we then have the problem of moving the company into strike position. Over that distance, it's unlikely that vehicles could reach the vicinity of the objective without being discovered. Which leaves puddle jumpers for transit. And puddle jumpers simply don't have sufficient range to go that far; the company would have to rendezvous with the AstroGhost three times to replace the puddle jumpers. Also, even though our Marines are effectively invisible in their chameleons, the exhaust from the puddle jumpers isn't, so there is a high risk of discovery if we attempt to move the entire company that distance via puddle jumper.

"Alternately, we could have the Essays make planetfall in different locations, dispersing the company from the beginning, thereby reducing the chances of detection during movement to the objective. But, since the AstroGhost would have to make several widely spaced stops on each of its puddle jumper resupply runs, that resupply would take longer, further delaying rendezvous at the objective and increasing our chance of discovery.

"Another option is to have the AstroGhost assemble the company in waves, which would be time-consuming."

As soon as he'd heard Captain Gonzalez say there was only one AstroGhost available in the entire TF79, Obannion knew all the problems in landing the company that Wainwright had brought up. He'd let his operations officer run through them in the hope that he'd come up with a solution to the problems, or an objection to which he saw a solution. That didn't happen.

"Does anybody have a solution?" Obannion asked. When nobody did, he slapped his palms on his desk and stood. "All right, then, focus on a one-platoon raid. Captain Qindall, contact the squads in the vicinity of Gilbert's Corners and instruct them to gather intelligence on the entire perimeter. I want them to focus first on patrols, secondly on lines of defense—and I'm particularly interested in the area west to south. I'm going to inform the admiral."

Command Information Center, Task Force 79, on Board the Kiowa

"Why am I not surprised, Commander?" Rear Admiral Hoi Yueng said when Commander Obannion told him a company-size raid wasn't feasible. "My apologies, I should have realized that you needed AstroGhosts to make your planetfall and that the Task Force only has one. Is there anything you can do?"

"Sir, I've got my staff working on an operation plan for a single-platoon raid," Obannion replied.

"Hmm. Well, I believe one Force Recon platoon, inserted surreptitiously near its objective, can do as much damage as an army battalion landing team, and do it in less time and with fewer unnecessary casualties." Hoi looked at Obannion for confirmation. When the Force Recon commander agreed with a thank-you, Hoi said, "So go get them."

"Aye, aye, sir."

Headquarters, Fourth Force Reconnaissance Company

Captain Qindall followed Commander Obannion into his office. "Got some good news, Walt," he said when he'd closed the hatch behind himself.

"Give it to me, Stu, I could use some."

"Two more squads were close enough to Gilbert's Corners to join in the recon by sundown, local time. Three others can get there by tomorrow afternoon local—if the AstroGhost can rendezvous to replace their puddle jumpers. I've arranged for the replacement."

"Which squads?"

"Seventh squad from first platoon and third from fourth platoon are on their way to help with the recon. I've given the go-ahead to sixth squad, first platoon, and fifth and eighth squads from third platoon. All are moving to meet the Astro-Ghost."

"How long have they been planetside?"

"They can use the head on the AstroGhost," Qindall said with a grin. Force Recon Marines took the adage "Leave nothing, not even footprints" seriously—they not only brought all their trash back with them, they held their bowels for the days of a mission.

Obannion took a deep breath. "Thanks, that is good news—

we'll be able to use more than just one platoon; if we land an entire platoon, we'll have three whole sections for the raid."

"Suggestion?"

"You don't have to ask permission to make a suggestion, Stu, you know that."

"Use second platoon."

"They conducted the company's last platoon raid; shouldn't we use somebody else for the main force?" Obannion knew the answer to that question, but he wanted to know if his XO had other reasons—pro or con.

Qindall snorted. "Second's the only full platoon we have. All the others have squads either still out on other missions or en route here after returning to Camp Howard from other missions. The AstroGhost can easily take the three squads we have aboard and pick up the other three when it makes planetfall. Besides, most of the intelligence we have on the Gilbert's Corners defenses will come from second platoon."

"Do you think Lieutenant Rollings is ready to run a platoon raid, much less a platoon and a half?"

"Come on, Walt. He's as ready as any of the other platoon commanders, even if he is the newest of them. The only officers in the company who have experience with platoon-size raids are you and me. Unless you want to go yourself . . . ?"

Obannion smiled. "I'd like to, you know that. And so would you. But we can't, we have to use one of the other officers." He leaned back for a moment, staring at the ceiling, then sat straight again. "What do you think about Pter? He's drawing the OpPlan."

Qindall laughed. "That would certainly inspire him to make the best plan he could—as if he wouldn't anyway."

Obannion nodded. "Get Pter and Kady in here. Morrie too."

Ten minutes later, Captain Qindall was back with Captain Wainwright, Lieutenant Rollings, and Sergeant Major Periz.

"We have a slight change of plans, gentlemen," Obannion told them as soon as Periz closed the office door behind himself. "We're using second platoon for the raid, reinforced by first and sixth squads from first platoon, fifth and eighth from third, and third squad from fourth platoon, one squad more than a platoon and a half. Captain Wainwright, would you like to go planetside and run this operation, with Lieutenant Rollings as your number one?"

Wainwright's face split in a grin. "Damn, and here I'd thought I'd never again be allowed planetside on an operation. Thank you, sir." He reached out and shook hands with Rollings, who also beamed at the opportunity to go planetside on a raid. "It's like getting to be a sergeant again!"

"Except that you'll have fifty-six Marines and a corpsman under your command, instead of just three Marines."

"Sir, when you think you've been relegated to a desk for life, you take what you can get." That drew a laugh from Obannion, Qindall, and Periz.

"If I may, sir," Wainwright said when the laughter died. "I'd like to bring Lieutenant Rollings into the planning. And let me have"—he paused to think of which squads he had—"Staff Sergeant Keen as the third section leader—his section is the only one that has more than one squad designated for this mission."

"You've got him. Does Doc Natron meet with your approval?"

"He's a damn good corpsman, I'll be glad to have him aboard."

"All right. XO, inform Staff Sergeant Keen and Doc Natron—and their respective chains of command. Now, does anybody have anything to add?"

"I do, sir," Wainwright said. "The squads reconning Gilbert's Corners report that the heaviest patrolling is to the northeast and east of the village. It appears that they're providing a screen to detect an attack from Bataan, or an amphibious operation from the coast to the east. Their patrolling is lightest on the west side."

Obannion nodded sharply. "I had a feeling that would be their thinking. Pter, I want the OpPlan on my desk when I come in tomorrow morning. Take the latest intelligence from the squads reconning the objective into consideration and plan to hit it from the west."

"Aye, aye, sir. By your leave?"

"Go and do it."

Periz opened the door for Wainwright and Rollings to leave. Wainwright was filling the junior officer in on the plans before they made it out of the office.

Periz made sure nobody was near the door before he closed it. "Sir," he said, "do you think it's wise to send your S3 planetside to run an operation like this?"

"Do you think he can't do the job?" Obannion asked seriously, surprised by the question.

"Not at all. I think he'll do an outstanding job. It's just that he's the S3. If he becomes a casualty, we'll have to slot someone else into that position."

"Petr knows the OpPlan better than anybody else. And it doesn't matter who's in command planetside. If the commander becomes a casualty, just as with any other Marine, somebody else will have to be slotted into his position. That's the way war works, Sergeant Major."

"Thought that's what you'd say. Just wanted to make sure."

"My conscience," Obannion said ruefully.

"I've been called worse."

Obannion dismissed the obvious: that if Wainwright as the commander of the raiding party was replaceable, so would he or Qindall be replaceable.

The plan was waiting for Commander Obannion when he arrived in his office the next morning. His staff, bleary-eyed from having spent the night working on it, filed into his office behind him. The company commander had one question before he examined the plan:

"Ten of the fourteen squads in this mission are already planetside. How will they be briefed?"

"Sir, if you'll be so good as to put on your helmet," Captain Wainwright said, "I can demonstrate at the same time I brief you on the plan."

Obannion reached behind himself to an apparently empty stretch of wall and plucked his chameleoned helmet from the peg on which it hung. He put it on and strapped on his comp, which he pulled from another stretch of seemingly empty wall.

The other members of the staff were already wearing their comps and carrying their helmets. When Obannion's head disappeared, they donned their helmets. The office now looked as if it were inhabited by six headless men, one of whom began tickling his own solar plexus.

Nobody spoke, nobody had to say a word. Captain Wainwright's fingers danced over his comp, tight-beaming the operation's plan to Commander Obannion. Words scrolled across Obannion's heads-up display, describing the objective of the raid, the company elements involved, everything that was known about the enemy forces in place, known defensive works, the topography of the terrain in which the Marines would be operating, the layout of the village and its newly constructed suburbs, and the likely numbers and locations of reinforcements available to the enemy. Passwords and countersigns were given, along with rally points, the extraction point, who would have what weapons, the chain of command, and one by one, each squad's mission in the raid. The words were accompanied by maps whenever and wherever the visuals were useful. And a timeline accompanied everything. The briefing took half an hour.

"The squads planetside will get a somewhat abbreviated version of that," Wainwright said when the briefing was over.

"Two assault guns and sufficient blasters for everybody planetside who is only carrying a sidearm are already stowed aboard the AstroGhost," Captain Gonzalez said.

"We are ready to launch on your command, sir," Wainwright finished.

"Gentlemen," Obannion said, "you have done an outstanding job. I will take this to the admiral, and as soon as it has his approval, it's a go. Now get some sleep—especially the two of you who are making planetfall."

Commander Obannion didn't give Rear Admiral Hoi the full treatment that he'd gotten, but rather a shorter verbal briefing. The admiral approved the raid as planned.

On the AstroGhost, En Route Planetside

The AstroGhost wasn't crowded, not even with the additional squad added at almost the last minute. Four squads, three section leaders, one platoon sergeant, a corpsman, and two officers were just 75 percent of an AstroGhost's combat assault landing capacity—the vehicle was rated for a whole platoon plus corpsmen. It still wouldn't quite be at that level when it picked up the three squads from second platoon that were already planetside.

The Force Recon Marines were tough men, the toughest men in the toughest military organization in Human Space. None of them screamed when the AstroGhost hit the "high speed on a bad road" of their powered straight-down plunge. Most of them yawned to equalize pressure in their inner ears; the most experienced yawned in their sleep. The plan said the raid was only supposed to last twelve hours from planetfall to pickup. But all of them, including Captain Wainwright, knew what happened to plans once the shooting started. None of them had full confidence that the pickup would be on schedule; they were all prepared to spend several days planetside. If they did, it wouldn't be because the plan was faulty, or because they didn't do their jobs right, or because the AstroGhost broke down—well, maybe because the AstroGhost malfunctioned. It was because that's the way war is, things always happened that nobody could anticipate. So some of them slept during the "high-speed ride on a bad road."

Planetside, Thirty-five Kilometers West of Gilbert's Corners

It took two hours from the time the AstroGhost first touched down to rendezvous with the first of the three squads it was picking up until it reached the assembly point, where the other seven squads were waiting, thirty kilometers west of Gilbert's Corners. The stealth shuttle stuck around long enough to allow all the planetside Marines to make quick head calls, then took off to await its pickup call.

The seven squads that had arrived in the AstroGhost had already been briefed on the raid. Captain Wainwright had Gunny Lytle establish them in a defensive perimeter around the waiting squads, which he drew close to brief on the raid. Then they had a bit of time to wait and rest; it was late afternoon, and they were going to strike during the middle of the night. The reinforced platoon moved out at dusk, using puddle jumpers to cut the distance to their objective to ten kilometers. The squads moved independently to avoid too large a group together and cut down on the chance of being spotted. Each squad secured its puddle jumpers in a location where they could be found again, then continued its movement to the objective on foot.

CHAPTER
THIRTY-ONE

Coalition Army Headquarters, Ashburtonville, Ravenette

General Lyons had two reasons to evacuate Ashburtonville to a location remote from the seat of the war. The first was to spare its citizens and the Coalition government from the inevitable harm that would come to them if they remained close to the fighting.

The other reason, and one he came to think more important than the first, was to get the Coalition Congress out of his hair so he could fight the war the way he wanted. He quickly realized he was wrong. The rambunctious, meddling politicians who represented the worlds of the Coalition were not about to give their military commander the free hand he needed to prosecute the war against the Confederation of Human Worlds. Not if they could help it. The Committee on the Conduct of the War bombarded General Lyons with requests to appear before them and answer their questions. He had been able to avoid most of these peremptory summonses with the help of Preston Summers, the President of the Coalition and a Lyons supporter, using the justification that the actual conduct of the war was more important than debating it with a committee.

"I should have evacuated the whole bunch of them to Trinkatat," he remarked bitterly to an aide. Trinkatat was the most remote world in the Coalition. But inevitably he had to appear.

Gilbert's Corners, the new seat of government on Ravenette, lay about 150 kilometers south-southwest of Ashburtonville in what had been a farming region. Two hundred years earlier the place had been a mere crossroads with an inn for weary travelers and a general store, both owned by Amos Gilbert, an enterprising businessman who believed in the future of the region. When Amos died, killed in a drunken brawl at the inn, his wife, Jezebel, inherited the properties, and with wisdom and foresight, she encouraged the growth of a small settlement at the crossroads, which in time blossomed into the modest city known as Gilbert's Corners. Over the years nobody had thought seriously about changing the community's name to something more cosmopolitan. The people on Ravenette, in fact most of the people in the Coalition, just did not think that way. Calling the place Gilbert's Corners was good enough for them.

General Lyons had easily obtained the approval of the Coalition Congress to move the government to Gilbert's Corners. The place was remote enough from the war to offer security for the politicians, and it boasted an urban infrastructure that could support the Coalition's government, such as it was, and make life comfortable for its members.

"Gen'rel"—Preston Summers's voice sounded hollow and distant as he spoke to General Lyons over the secure communications net—"you gotta show up this time. I can't stave these fellas off anymore." He was referring to the Committee on the Conduct of the War, which Lyons had again refused to appear before.

"Mr. President, we are at a crucial stage of the campaign. I can't just leave my headquarters here in the hands of a subordinate. That would be military insanity. I can point out to you a dozen examples of how that lost wars in the past. Can't I get away with submitting a written response?"

"I know, Gen'rel, I know, that's worked up till now, but this time they mean business and they want you before them in person. I can't hold this Coalition together without their support in the Congress, that's the truth, pure and simple. The guys on that committee are key members of their worlds' delegations. They take themselves very seriously, and they are fully capable of gettin' into a snit and just backing out, concluding a separate peace with the Confederation, and leaving you and me holdin' the bag on this war. Believe me, they're as liable to do something like that as crack a bottle of Old Snort. Keepin' this Coalition together is a bitch of a job, Gen'rel, when I got all these independent souls tryin' to tell me how to run this government and each damned one of 'em so sensitive about his 'honor' he'd cut his own nose off if he thought he'd been disrespected. You *gotta* take the chance and come on down here, and you *gotta* leave today. Davis," he said, reverting to the general's first name, "you just *have* to come."

Lyons was silent for a moment. "Getting there will be half the fun," he said sarcastically.

"I know. The Confederation's got reconnaissance patrols roamin' all around behind your lines. I read yer reports, even if those fools don't. Take a powerful escort, Gen'ral, and barrel ass right on down here. You got air cover, don't you? Air superiority?"

"Sometimes we do and sometimes we don't."

"Well, come the safest and fastest way you kin. That's up to you."

Both men were well aware that Marine Force Recon teams were active between Ashburtonville and Gilbert's Corners, in fact had only recently destroyed a battery of mobile anti-satellite guns without being detected, apparently operating with impunity behind the lines.

"Ever heard of Admiral Yamamoto?" Lyons asked.

"He in charge of their fleet?" Summers thought Lyons was referring to a Confederation naval officer.

"No, he lived a long time ago. He was a brilliant naval tactician back on Earth in the days when navies fought in the oceans. Well, the enemy broke his code and knew he was flying somewhere so they ambushed him."

"Oh, Judas's nuts, Davis, do you really think they might ambush you on the way?" There was genuine concern in Summers's voice. If the enemy got General Lyons, it would really be all over for the Coalition.

"There's always that chance. I'm not sure just how secure

this comm system we're using is, Preston, so just tell the committee I'll be there when I get there and they can damned well sit on their hands until I arrive. Have them send me their agenda so I can be prepared for their questions." He toggled off the system.

"And how are you going to get down there?" his aide, a colonel from Lannoy named Rene Raggel, asked. Raggel was an experienced infantry officer who'd seen his share of combat. The men from Lannoy were known to be rough characters, but Lyons had picked him as his aide-de-camp because he was a solid, no-nonsense officer who anticipated problems before they became problems.

"How are *we* going to get down there, Rene. You're comin' with me. I dunno." Lyons leaned back and put his arms behind his head. "Any horses left around here? We'll dress up as farmers. That way nobody'd ever suspect us."

Raggel smiled. "They haven't had horses here in over a hundred years, sir. But you're right, you don't want to attract attention either from satellite or aerial observation and certainly not from their ground recon teams. The bastards are all over back there. First, let's send out sweeps, patrols in random directions to divert their attention and keep their recon teams' heads down. Let's dress up as civilians, take a private car, and use the south road. It's lightly traveled. It'll take us three, maybe four hours to get to Gilbert's Corners, but that route does not seem to be under very close surveillance."

"Took the words right out of my mouth." Lyons straightened up and fished in a cargo pocket. He took out a Davidoff and stuck it between his teeth. It was an expensive chew, but he'd come to like the cigars ever since Preston Summers had given him a box from his private supply. Lyons seldom lit the cigars, preferring to chew on them. Chewing relaxed him and allowed him to think. Since he cut them down when the ends got too soggy, each cigar would last several days. "I don't like to smoke," he said to Raggel, "but you know, it's funny. Here we are in a combat zone, we could get killed any moment, and I'm worried about the effects of cigar smoke?" He shook his head and laughed. "Well, soon's the committee's agenda arrives, get Admiral Porter and my deputy in here and run it by us, and then we'll get ready for our trip. If they expect me to leave today, they can get screwed. We'll leave tomorrow at dusk, those assholes like to do their business at night."

"I can tell you two items on the agenda already, sir." Lyons nodded that Raggel should continue. "One's going to be putting that damned Seventh Independent MP Battalion on coast watch between here and Phelps. They're gonna see that as a prime landing zone for seaborne forces. They'll want to know why you haven't reinforced them with troops from the Fourth Division at Phelps. And, those guys in that battalion have been making end runs, complaining about their mission directly to their rep from Lannoy, so be prepared for him to spring that on you."

"Yep. Continue."

"And the other will be an explanation why you mounted that seaborne attack against Bataan and why it failed so miserably." Lyons could tell from Raggel's tone of voice that he didn't understand the reasons behind that maneuver himself.

"Bet you're right, Rene. We'll see. Okay, then we pull out at dusk tomorrow. Line up a tactical vehicle and be doggone sure the stealth and night vision suites are in perfect working order. I'll drive the first leg. We'll wear battle-dress uniform. I don't mind doing an end run to get to Gilbert's Corners, but I'll be damned if I'm going to go in disguise."

Gilbert's Corners, Ravenette

Colonel Raggel slowly relaxed his grip on the steering levers. His hands came away wet with perspiration. He had tried not to show it but the drive down to Gilbert's Corners from Ashburtonville had been the most frightening trip of his life. Every moment he expected either to be ambushed or attacked by enemy aircraft. But they'd made it unscathed. He let out his breath.

"Good driving, Rene." General Lyons laughed and patted his aide on the shoulder, which was soaked through with sweat. "Little warm for this time of the year, ain't it, Rene?" He grinned.

Gilbert's Corners was awash in civilian traffic, even at that late hour, both foot and vehicle. People swarmed everywhere like ants whose nest had been disturbed. But the once sleepy little village was now the seat of the Coalition government, and all the rushing about was just the organized confusion of a multiplanetary government in action.

"I want to pay a courtesy call on the garrison commander, Rene, a Colonel Osper, I think. Can you find his HQ in this mess?" Lyons gestured at the surging traffic.

"But, sir, the committee is waiting—"

"Let them wait. I'm only down here 'cause President Summers asked me to come, otherwise I'd just ignore these nattering nabobs. Come on, let's go."

Colonel Osper's staff was both delighted and panicked when the commanding general suddenly appeared among them. A sharp-eyed sergeant had called everyone to rigid attention at Lyons's entrance. They were delighted because they were hard at work when he walked through the command-post door in the school building, and staff officers loved to be seen by the brass when working; panicked because they had not expected him. Lyons had not informed the local commander he was coming in case his communications weren't secure. But there he was, an unlit Davidoff clasped between his teeth.

"Colonel, good to see you." Lyons stuck out his hand before the colonel even had time to salute. "Everyone at ease, back to work. Come on, give me the twenty-five-credit dog and pony show. I've got a meeting to attend and can't stay very long."

Colonel Osper, a heavyset, older officer with a fringe of gray hair surrounding his gleaming pate, offered General Lyons and his aide chairs. "Coffee, sir?"

"Don't mind if I do. We had a long trip down here, Colonel. Tell me what you've done to secure this town against enemy attack."

Colonel Osper called up a schematic overlay on his briefer's screen. "Sir, Gilbert's Corners proper covers four square kilometers. Its peacetime population is about eight hundred. That has swelled to eighteen thousand with the entire government now situated here. We've had to put up a regular tent city to accommodate all the civilians, but we are building temporary structures—mostly barracks and housing for the government leaders and the officers—here, here, and here." He pointed to several areas on the screen. "The engineers and technicians have done wonders creating the infrastructure we need here. I have to compliment—"

Lyons raised a hand. "Sorry, Colonel, but cut to the quick. What kind of security do you have set up?"

"Sir, I have a reinforced infantry battalion of 1,265 men as of this morning. Almost all of those men are under arms. I've set up a system of aggressive foot patrols, day and night, around the entire town but concentrating on the northeast and the east." He glanced at Lyons. "Any attack is most likely to come from the sea, so my patrols are concentrated in that direction. The patrols are backed up by quick-reaction forces. The patrolling is supplemented by anti-intrusion devices—infrared scanners, video monitoring of the most likely approach routes, that kind of stuff. But we are not relying totally on technology, sir. It's men and not machines that'll attack us here."

"Good, good. Most of the time that equipment either doesn't work or can be defeated. How about reinforcements if you come under attack by a really big force?"

"Sir, the Ninth Division has put two regiments at my disposal twelve kilometers to the southeast, at Grenoble's Shop. If the enemy tries a vertical envelopment or an overland end run on us here, I'm confident we'll know about it in plenty of time to meet the threat. The Ninth Division has the whole array of heavy weapons at its disposal, and I have a strong network of integrated fire-support weapons if needed." The colonel pointed to numerous locations on the overlay that indicated fortified weapons positions.

"They won't come in force, Colonel. They'll come in small units and their mission will be to penetrate your defenses and disrupt life here at Gilbert's Corners. Colonel

Osper, I can't overemphasize this: all we need now is for
these namby-pamby politicians to get a scare thrown into
them and they'll be screaming for massive reinforcements
here to protect their sacred behinds. I can't have that. I cannot afford to draw off any troops from the front to protect
these people. You and the Ninth Division have *got* to secure
this area." He stood up. "I've got to go to that meeting. Pass
on my compliments to your officers and men, Colonel.
You're doing a fine job here."

Outside, Colonel Raggel shook his head. "Are they doing
such a fine job, sir?"

General Lyons paused before getting into the car. "They're
doing the best they can, Rene, but this damned place is a
juicy target for the enemy. They'll hit here, you can bet on it."
He shrugged. "But come on, drive me over to this, this con-
fabulation of meddling idiots, and let's get the farce over
with."

The Committee on the Conduct of the War,
Gilbert's Corners, Ravenette

The Committee on the Conduct of the War had established
itself in the restored tavern that had once served the farmers
coming to buy supplies at Gilbert's Corners. They had set up
their hearing in an old taproom. When the weather was
damp, the place still smelled of stale beer. For most of the
members of the committee—there were eleven of them, one
from each world of the Coalition except Ravenette—the lin-
gering odor of stale beer and old wooden floors reminded
them of home. The floor, made of native wood more than two
hundred years ago, actually creaked when walked across.

"How was yer trip down here, Gen'rel?" Chairman Heb
Cawman asked after Lyons had seated himself before the
long table at which the committee perched. He was a perpetu-
ally angry man from Embata whose florid complexion and
bulbous nose matched his evil disposition.

"Tolerable, Mr. Chairman, tolerable." Actually, it had been
terrible. The road had been sabotaged about seventy-five

kilometers from Ashburtonville, forcing them to backtrack and go cross-country to avoid the huge crater blocking the way. If anyone in Lyons's command knew about the sabotage, they hadn't reported it to headquarters, and that really made the general angry, but he was not about to tell the committee that.

Cawman suddenly fell into a sneezing fit. He bellowed *arrr-hummmm* like a fighter bomber revving its turbines, reached for a huge handkerchief, and began blowing his nose, *hooonnnkkk,* so loudly Lyons imagined the floorboards creaking; the committee members sitting to either side of Cawman leaned discreetly away from him. Finally, tears streaming down his face, which had turned brick red with the effort, he gasped, gesturing with the handkerchief, "You come by yerself? I don't see no horse handlers, Gen'rel."

"I brought my aide-de-camp, Colonel Raggel," he hefted a briefcase, "and various reports and graphics that detail the answers to the questions this committee has—"

"I know Rene!" the committee member from Lannoy shouted. "He's the mos' constipated man I ever did see! Sips his whiskey like a woman." Lyons took an instant dislike to the man, who looked as if he'd been dead for ten years but refused to admit it.

Lyons ignored the man. It was obvious he'd already been into his own whiskey supply. "Sir," Lyons addressed Cawman with an air of gravity and deference he did not feel, "I am ready to answer the committee's questions."

"Why ain't you increased security around here?" the member from Ruspina shouted. "We got only a battalion of infantry and they spend most of their time on their asses in the taverns."

Lyons felt like responding that his troops were only following the example set by the congressmen on the committee, but he restrained himself. "Sir, those are combat veterans and they are commanded by a fine officer. I did not assign a larger security detail because I cannot afford to diminish my strength at Fort Seymour. The troops assigned here conduct aggressive patrolling supplemented by a considerable array of anti-intrusion devices. No substantial body of enemy troops can get within striking distance of this place without being detected."

"What about a small body, then?" one of the members asked.

"Yes, enemy reconnaissance elements may already have been in this area, gentlemen. We cannot deny small, well-trained recon detachments access to any area, no matter how well guarded. But their efforts cannot affect the strategic balance of forces in this war, and I hasten to advise you that we have the preponderance of that balance."

"Jesus!" someone else muttered. "They could come in here in the night and slit all our throats! Why in hell didn't you and Summers move us to another planet?"

Lyons almost said he wished he had evacuated Congress off-world. "That would've made it difficult, no, impossible, for the members of this government to remain in my chain of command. I could not have attended this committee's meetings," he added archly.

"I bet that jist broke yer heart, Gen'rel," Cawman grunted. "Okay, we are now formally in session." He glanced down the table. "I'll start the questioning." He cleared his throat, wiped his dripping nose, took a sip of brown liquid from a glass at his elbow, shuddered, and made a display of shuffling some crystals before popping one into a reader. "You lost a lot of men and equipment on that seaborne attack against this Billie fella and his troops on Pohick Bay. We need to know why." He glared indignantly at Lyons.

"I screwed up, gentlemen." That frank and completely unexpected admission froze the committee members into a dead silence; they stared back at Lyons blankly, completely at a loss for words—for a change. Lyons continued, "That was a totally ill-advised attack, and I regret I let myself be persuaded by the incomplete intelligence available to me beforehand and let it go ahead. The chances for success seemed valid at the time." He shrugged. "But unknown to us, the area had recently been reinforced by Confederation Marines, who put considerable backbone into General Billie's defenses in that sector. If they had not been present, we would've broken through."

"Um," Cawman muttered, glancing again at his colleagues. This kind of forthright response was not expected. It wasn't appreciated either. Cawman did not like anyone getting the upper hand on him. "Now, we move on to the defense of the coast between Phelps and Ashburtonville. Gen'rel, you got only an MP battalion—"

"The Seventh Independent MPs!" the representative from Lannoy shouted, half rising out of his seat. "They are sturdy fellows, tough customers!"

"Ah, thank you, thank you." Cawman motioned for the man to sit back down. "We appreciate that those boys are tough, but, Gen'rel, no mere battalion of military police could stop a serious seaborne invasion along that coastline. An' once the enemy got a foothold there, he'd be behind you. What in the hell were you thinking when you put such a small force in there?"

"Gentlemen," Lyons addressed the entire committee, "that is a very rugged stretch of coast. The cliffs there approach in some places one hundred meters in height. The area where the Seventh MPs have been assigned can be reinforced quickly by elements of the Fourth Division at Phelps, and should an attack along that coast develop into a forced landing of troops in strength, I can and will divert major forces from the siege of Fort Seymour to repel it. Besides, that battalion is heavily armed." If they haven't traded their weapons away for whiskey, he wanted to add, but did not.

"Th' *hell* you kin!" someone shouted.

Cawman called for order. "This is a deliberatin' body," he intoned, "an' the members will maintain their decor while it is in session." He took another sip from his glass, which Lyons judged to be whiskey. The room was redolent with the aroma of fine sour-mash bourbon. But it was clear to Lyons that Cawman agreed with the comment.

"I can and I will," Lyons responded firmly. "We are at a crucial moment in the campaign, gentlemen. I am about to squeeze General Billie's nuts in a vise." He chided himself for falling into vulgar language, but he realized the only way to get through to these men was by coming down to their level and using language they could understand.

"Those MPs," J. Bubs Ignaughton, the representative from Lannoy, interjected, "they been communicatin' with me, an' they ain't happy, Gen'rel, with that assignment you gave 'em. They say they should be guarding POWs, not walking up and down on the seashore. What you got to say to that?"

It was getting late and Lyons was beginning to lose his patience with the committee, but he restrained himself. "Congressman, processing and guarding prisoners of war is a mission assigned to military police, I grant you that, but so is security. The POWs we have interned at Cogglesville are being guarded by a reserve MP battalion from Mylex. In coordination with General Sneed, the Fourth Division commander, I determined that the best mission for the Seventh MPs was guarding that beach. Besides, they do have a prisoner of war compound."

"Gen'rel, that is the purest *bull*-shit I ever heard," Ignaughton interrupted. "They got themsevs a few pris'ners, but that ain't no proper POW camp there." The man had a narrow, heavily lined face that terminated in a wispy white beard; his blue eyes were watery orbs that kept blinking as if he was allergic to something in the air, and from where Lyons was sitting, he could clearly see the man's filthy hands, nails yellow and chipped, fingers flexing in rage like a blackbird's claws grasping for carrion.

That was it for General Davis Lyons. "Sir, with respect, the Seventh Independent Military Police Battalion is the most useless collection of downright criminals ever to disgrace a military uniform. If I had my way, I'd take every one of them, put *them* behind the barbed wire at Cogglesville, and let the POWs go. Those POWs are real soldiers; your MPs belong with the slimies, crawling around in the gutter. Since I can't send them back to the latrine where they came from, I put them on the coast where they can be a trip wire if the enemy invades there, where they can play a useful military role for a change, maybe actually get shot at for once, and where once and for all they can get what they deserve."

J. Bubs Ignaughton jerked bolt upright in his chair and squawked like a blackbird with its tail in a trap.

Chairman Cawman gasped in genuine horror at what Lyons had just said and was about to slam a fist down on the table preparatory to delivering a devastating rebuke when the unmistakable hissing and cracking of small-arms fire commenced from outside in the direction of the newly constructed barracks, quickly rising to a deafening crescendo. The muzzle flashes reflected brilliantly off the windows. From outside the taproom men shouted and heavy footfalls pounded throughout the building. Cawman's eyes bulged in terror and his face turned paper-white; the members of the committee sat, their mouths open, frozen in fear.

Lyons grinned and said laconically, "Mr. Chairman, we are, apparently, under attack." Calmly he retrieved his briefcase and stood up. "I presume this session is now closed? Gentlemen"—he bowed before the congressmen—"you are now experiencing firsthand what my soldiers face every day. I hope it helps you understand what war is all about." He looked at Cawman directly but included all the committee members in what he said next: "If you ever again presume to call me before this congregation of fools to question my decisions as a military commander, or if any of you on this committee dare to recommend to your home-world governments withdrawal from this war, I will have *real* military police arrest you and see that you are publicly castrated. Good night." He stuck a Davidoff in a corner of his mouth, made another mock bow, and walked out.

On the Streets of Gilbert's Corners

Chaos reigned in the streets outside the tavern. Colonel Raggel met General Lyons as he came through the door. "Sir, you've got to get over to Colonel Osper's CP, you'll be safe there!"

"Listen." General Lyons held up his hand. "Rene, this is

not a major assault. Can you hear that? It's infantry weapons, an assault gun or two, blasters, no artillery, no air. Hell, this has all the hallmarks of a Force Recon mission! They got here using those damned hoppers, I bet. No, this is only a raid. It's concentrated in the northeast part of the town. I'm not going into Osper's CP. He's got his hands full without any VIPs hanging around."

A civilian, eyes bulging, ran up to them. "What should I do?" the man screamed.

"Bend over, grab your ankles, and kiss your ass good-bye," General Lyons answered. The man stared at him in un-comprehending horror, then ran off down the street screaming something about "everyone's dying!"

Raggel shook his head. "You shouldn't upset civilians like that, sir," he chuckled.

"Fuck him. I am entirely fed up with civilians." Lyons thought of his own dead son and all the men under his command who had already died in the war. He was secretly de-lighted the government at Gilbert's Corners was under attack.

"What if they know you're here, sir?" Colonel Raggel's voice was tense with anxiety, not for himself but for his commander. "Why else would they raid down here?"

"No, I doubt they know I'm here, Rene," Lyons re-sponded, but in the back of his mind he remembered his ear-lier offhand remark about the ambush of Admiral Yamamoto. "This"—he nodded at the confusion all around them—"is just too big and too juicy a target for the enemy to ignore. As soon as they've put the fear of Beelzebub into everyone, they'll withdraw to their rally point and be evacuated. Colonel Osper and his boys can deal with this situation. Come on, let's get into the car. I'm not fighting, I'm not hid-ing, I'm just getting my ass out of Dodge."

Once inside the landcar, Raggel called up a map of the area on his display screen. "Give me 1:24,000," General Lyons asked. "Okay, most of the fighting seems to be con-centrated around this barracks complex to the northeast, so we ain't going that way. The Ninth Division is at Grenoble's Shop, right? That's down this road here. There's sure to be an ambush laid along that road to stop reinforcements. So, looks like this road here, that leads in a south-southwesterly direction, is the route we're taking to get out of here. I'm not going this way"—he pointed to the west—"because I bet their rally point is in that direction. Now let's see where this road of mine goes." He toggled to the next map quadrant. "See? It connects eventually with another road that leads back in the direction of Ashburtonville and"—he increased the scale to 1:50,000—"aha! connects with the road we took to get here in the first place!" He slapped Colonel Raggel on the shoulder. "Let's get rolling!"

It proved to be one of the longest rides of General Davis Lyons's life, but they met no one the entire way back to Ashburtonville.

CHAPTER
THIRTY-TWO

Gilbert's Corners, Ravenette

It was late when the Marines filtered into, through, and around Gilbert's Corners—late enough that the bars and restaurants had finally closed and everybody had gone to whatever place they called home around there that wasn't home to most of them.

Second platoon's eight squads slipped silently, invisibly, through the village of Gilbert's Corners and the new housing complex to its northeast. The Marines avoided the few houses where their patrols had found dogs. The platoon stopped in the trees between the houses and the barracks area. Two of them faced the new housing while the other two spread wide behind them and faced the housing. Fourth platoon's third squad—joined by that platoon's seventh squad, the last-minute addition to the raid—had almost the farthest to go to get into position. The squad carried one of the two assault guns assigned to the assault force. Those two squads also had arguably the most dangerous part of the operation: they went south, where they would set off the raid by taking the barracks area under fire. Sergeant Timony of third squad welcomed the four extra blasters of seventh squad to his part of the raid; the eight Marines, armed with an assault gun and seven blasters, could wreak havoc on the unprepared troops in the barracks. And, in the coming fight, eight Marines had a far better chance of survival than four. The squads that had to go the farthest were first and sixth of first platoon, which set up blocking positions in the fields between third and seventh squads and the patrolled forest. Fifth and eighth squads of third platoon, with Staff Sergeant Keen and the second assault gun, were the raiding force's reaction force, to the south and west of the two squads that would set off the raid, available to go wherever they were needed.

Wainwright had his command group, which consisted of himself, first section's Staff Sergeant Fryman, and Hospitalman Second Class Natron, in the middle of second platoon, twenty meters behind second platoon's seventh squad. As a safety measure, to avoid the possibility of everyone in the command group's being taken out at once, Wainwright had Lieutenant Rollings form a Bravo command group, consisting of himself, platoon sergeant Gunny Lytle, and second-section leader Staff Sergeant Morgan. Bravo was two hundred meters to Wainwright's left, behind first squad.

Captain Wainwright's comp had a direct feed from the string-of-pearls, and he fed it into his HUD so he had a real-time view of the area in infrared. Each squad leader carried a marker that was visible only from above—visible to the satellites. Wainwright watched the progress of the squads as they moved into position. He alternated watching the movement of the squads with examining a larger view of the area, one that showed the forest to the northeast. The forest was speckled with tiny dots, each indicating a man-size animal. Deciding which of the speckles were Coalition patrols was easy—they were the five groups of eight or ten specks that moved in columns. When all his squads were in place, Wainwright sent a burst message to the nearest satellite, which tight-beamed it to the marked squad leaders—a communications tactic that almost guaranteed the Coalition couldn't intercept the transmissions:

"Everybody's in place. Stand by for three-four's signal."

Sergeant Timony passed the word to his Marines on the short-range squad circuit: "Look for the sentries." The eight Marines peered into the barracks area through their light-gatherer screens. The barracks area suddenly popped into clear view on Timony's HUD.

The view was monochrome, white-on-gray with black undertones. Shadows were filled out with easily discernible shapes and identifiable forms. The only thing was, everything was equally distinct—the distance to something couldn't be determined unless something else of known height or bulk was next to it. But that wouldn't matter to a Marine firing a blaster; the blasters were line-of-sight weapons, and their aiming point never had to be adjusted for range.

Timony watched for the two sentries who held fire watch in the barracks area. When both came into sight, he and one of the other Marines would shoot them to set off the blaster fire that would ignite the wooden barracks and engulf the barracks area from two directions. Timony waited patiently, as was the nature of most Force Recon Marines. His wait wasn't long; the first sentry came into view short moments after the message from Captain Wainwright.

"Alert," Timony relayed through the string-of-pearls, the signal to the other Marines that the sentries were in sight and to get ready to open fire.

The sentry walked at the pace of a bored man marking time until his shift was over. His path took him along the center of a road between two rows of barracks. When he reached the near end, he turned to his left, heading for the next road over. Before he reached it, the other sentry came into view and turned right. The two sentries were going to meet briefly before resuming their tedious night duty.

But they never met. On Sergeant Timony's command, he and one of his Marines aimed and squeezed the firing levers of their blasters.

The double *crack-sizzle* of two blasters shattered the night's quiet, and the two sentries slammed into the wall of the barracks, each with a hole burned through his chest.

Captain Wainwright's command *"Fire!"* was redundant; the Marines of the eight squads aiming at the barracks opened fire as soon as they heard the initial shots.

Timony and two of his Marines joined fire at the base of the wall of the barracks behind the two dead sentries, where wood met the ferrocrete foundation. The plasma bolts burned through the wall, charring the wood; their combined heat set small flames licking about the hole they'd made. The bolts flew at an angle slightly above level and seared into the wood of the barracks floor from underneath, charring it and starting small fires. The four Marines shifted their fire, again concentrating on one spot. Then shifted again. Smoke from the burning wall and floor began percolating into the barracks rooms.

Seventh squad aimed at the wall of the next barracks and began a small fire at the bottom of its wall. They fired again and once more before raising their fire from the base of the wall and shooting independently through the walls, into the barracks rooms at an elevation calculated to hit standing or crouching men.

The assault gun sprayed slowly, side to side, along the wall of the barracks to the left until the wood suddenly whooshed into flame.

Along the main line, the west side, the squads fired at barracks.

"Keep your shots low!" Sergeant Bingh shouted to his Marines as he fired his first bolt at the bottom of the wood of a barracks wall. Three more bolts slammed into the wall in nearly the same place as his men fired at the spot. As soon as flames were licking up the wall, he had his men shift their fire higher, shooting blindly into the barracks rooms.

Less than a minute after the first shot, the streets between the barracks were filling with soldiers, most of them clad only in underwear. Only some of the soldiers from the now burning barracks had thought to grab their weapons in their mad dashes to get away from the fires. Many of the unarmed soldiers heard the blaster fire and ran deeper into the barracks area to get away from it; some were so panicked they simply ran away from the flames, some toward the firing Marines.

"Let them go!" Bingh shouted when Lance Corporal Wehrli sent a bolt through an unarmed soldier sprinting toward them. "Only shoot the armed ones!" Bingh looked into the interior of the barracks area and saw a man wearing an unbuttoned shirt, waving a sidearm as he shouted orders in an attempt to gain control over the panicked soldiers. Bingh shot him.

The flames in the nearby barracks were growing and crackling as the resin in the green wood used for the structures began expanding and exploding. But commanding voices were rising above the noise of the fires as sergeants went about organizing soldiers and getting ammunition to distribute among them. Some of the soldiers began returning fire in the direction of the Marines.

"Fire and move!" Bingh ordered. He snapped off a shot and rolled a few meters to the side. The Marines were invisible, but their plasma bolts flashed brilliant lines of fire that gave away their positions. Someone within the barracks had seen Bingh's bolt and sent an accurate stream of fléchettes to the place he'd fired from. Bingh saw the glowing lines from several recently fired fléchette rifles on his infra. He sent a bolt into the red blob behind one of the lines and rolled in the opposite direction from before—just before another stream of fléchettes spattered into the space he'd vacated.

Damn, but he's good, Bingh thought. He scooted back, into a slight hollow, and fired at another red blob, then ducked low with his head turned to the side. Almost immediately, a stream of fléchettes shot by, missing him by centimeters. It was enough for him to catch in infrared the direction the fire came from. Three times, the shooter had fired at the position Bingh had fired from, so the sergeant doubted the soldier was still aiming at his current position. He raised himself enough to see beyond the hollow and looked in the direction the fléchettes had come from.

There! He saw the moving trace of a fired rifle looking for another target—the line didn't move far, the shooter was waiting for him to fire again. The soldier was in a good position, behind a stack of construction material, with only his rifle and part of his head and right shoulder exposed to Bingh's view. The Marine took aim and saw the line of the barrel suddenly shift toward his position! He rushed his shot and ducked back down, just in time to be missed by the fléchettes that came from the shooter.

He must have infra! Bingh thought, and wondered how he

knew how to spot the faint infrared signature of a Force Recon Marine.

Bingh popped up again for a quick look. He saw his shot had hit the construction materials rather than the soldier; but the strike had been close enough to make the man duck back. Bingh aimed at the corner of the materials and waited for his quarry to expose himself again—for all the soldier knew, the bolt that had almost hit him had been a random shot. At least, that's what the Marine hoped.

The fléchette rifle snaked around the corner of the pile and Bingh took up the slack on his firing lever. Then the soldier's head and shoulder popped up behind the rifle, and Bingh sent a bolt of plasma into the shooter's head.

Then Bingh had to duck down again as several soldiers fired at the source of his bolt. He felt a ripping along the seat of his trousers and swore—he'd been hit.

Sergeant Kindy wasn't happy about third squad having to face the housing complex; he doubted there would be any trouble from that direction and thought third squad would do more good firing into the barracks. Sure, the officers and senior non-commissioned officers lived in the housing area, but the troops were in the barracks, and that was where the fighting would be. The officers and senior NCOs would be fools to attempt an assault on the rear of the Marine line; such an attack would have them heading straight into the fire from their own soldiers. Still, orders were orders, so he kept watch into the housing complex.

Kindy jerked at an unexpected *crack-sizzle* twenty meters to his left where Corporal Jaschke was. He looked where the plasma bolt from Jaschke's blaster went and saw an armed man flip backward.

I guess some of them are fools, he thought. Then his light gatherer showed him a man hunkered down behind a bush, speaking into a comm.

"People are coming our way," Kindy said into his short-range squad circuit as he took aim on the talker. He fired a bolt and moved. When he looked again, the man he'd shot had crumpled behind the bush.

Grazing fire started coming at the covering Marines from within the housing complex. The fire wasn't heavy, there weren't enough officers and senior NCOs to bring heavy fire along a front as wide as the housing complex. Unfortunately, that also meant they were scattered and hard for the Marines in the two-squad screen to spot.

"Don't fire unless you've got a target," Kindy ordered his men. "Keep moving, that'll give you a better chance to locate a target." He followed his own instructions, and before long he spotted someone looking through a tube. Kindy didn't know what the tube was, but knew it had to be some kind of imaging device. He aimed at the back of the tube, where it met the man's face, and squeezed off a bolt—he wanted to both destroy the device and kill the officer. He rolled as soon as he fired. He found the officer—he had to be an officer to have special equipment like that viewer—and saw the man was down, unmoving. The tube was flung aside, but Kindy couldn't tell if it was damaged.

He looked for another target as he listened to the occasional *crack-sizzles* of blaster fire from the two screening squads.

Three minutes into the battle, Sergeant Williams had mixed feelings about it. On the one hand, he felt that firing the barracks with soldiers in them was simple slaughter. On the other, those men were soldiers of the Coalition and as such were the enemy; in combat a Marine's job is to kill the enemy and keep killing them until there aren't any left or the survivors quit fighting.

His feelings didn't stay mixed for long. The Coalition sergeants from the barracks started getting the troops organized and fighting back. Then it was shoot and move, shoot and move, and make sure his men were doing the same.

Crack-sizzle! Roll. "Belinski!"

"Shooting and moving," Corporal Belinski answered.

Crack-sizzle! Roll. "Rudd!"

"Shooting and moving," Lance Corporal Rudd answered.

Crack-sizzle! Roll. "Skripska!"

"Shooting and moving," Lance Corporal Skripska reported.

Crack-sizzle! Move. Make sure his men were doing the same. Repeat.

The Coalition soldiers were building up a base of fire despite the casualties they were suffering. Some of them were even returning fire at individual Marines. Here and there within the barracks area, sergeants had squads advancing by fire and maneuver, threatening to gain a position from where they could jump up and charge their attackers. But the burning barracks between them and the Marines slowed their advance—it was simply too hot for them to advance far enough.

Captain Wainwright split his time between looking over the battleground through his light-gatherer and infra screens, and studying the string-of-pearls view of it. He gradually quit using his infra screen because the fire was so hot he could no longer make out the heat signatures of the soldiers. He switched the satellite view to a larger area and saw that the columned dots of the patrols to the northeast had stopped moving. At least they aren't coming in, he thought. There were nearly as many soldiers patrolling the forest as he had Marines in the fight. If a courier was going to alert the Ninth Division to the assault, the defenders were even less prepared for action than he'd thought. If not . . . either way, he didn't have to worry about it.

He suddenly got a report from one of the squad leaders that required immediate action.

On the northernmost end of the Marine line, Sergeant Kare saw soldiers sprinting out of the barracks area, toward his left.

"Kassel," he shouted, "can you see where they're going?"

Crack-sizzle! Move.

"It looks like they're grouping," Corporal Kassel reported. He sighted in on one of the soldiers gathering seventy-five meters to his left front, fired, then rolled. Fléchette fire pelted the ground around what had been his position.

"How many are there?" Kare asked.

"Can't tell. At least a platoon." Kassel took another shot and changed position.

Kare swore; more soldiers were running through the barracks in the direction of his flank.

"Quinn, maintain fire into the barracks area," he ordered. "Ilon, shift to the flank." Kare moved himself, to help Kassel with the soldiers grouping to flank the Marines. He flipped back and forth between his light-gatherer and infra screens, attempting to get an idea of how many Coalition soldiers were there, and swore again. He toggled the platoon command circuit and reported to Lieutenant Rollings.

"We've got a reinforced platoon, maybe more, seventy-five meters to our left," Kare told second platoon's commander. "More are joining them. I believe they're massing to roll up our flank."

"What are you doing about it?" Rollings asked, as he toggled his comm to patch Captain Wainwright into the conversation.

"Three of us are firing at them, but more of them are coming." Kare looked to his right front. "Looks like another platoon is headed out to join them."

"That'll make half a company?" Rollings asked.

"That's affirmative. Maybe more." Kare fired and rolled again.

"Do what you can to keep them from advancing. I'll get back to you." Rollings toggled off the platoon command circuit and spoke to Wainwright. "How much of that did you get, sir?"

"We're about to be flanked by half a company or more?"

"That's about it."

"Time to commit the reaction force." Wainwright zeroed his satellite feed to the north of the burning barracks. They were hard to spot in the glow from the burning buildings, but he could make out a mass of dots indicating a large number of soldiers a short distance from the Marines' left flank. He toggled the task force command circuit and relayed the satellite view to Staff Sergeant Keen. "Reaction force," he said, "the enemy is massing to hit our left flank. Two-two needs help. Get there ASAP." Then he toggled the all-hands circuit. "Heads up. The reaction force is passing behind the main line at speed. Don't anybody shoot them."

Before Wainwright was finished giving the orders, Keen and his two squads were running north; it was five hundred meters, but they didn't have time to pace themselves.

Still more troops were gathering to attack the Marines' flank. Sergeant Kare quickly assessed the situation and decided on a change of tactics.

"Quinn, Ilon, try to pin down the people running to the north." Kare fired at a group of soldiers running to join the reinforced platoon. When he came out of his roll, he saw that they were down and some were returning fire. Using his light-gatherer screen to see, he sighted in on one of the shooters. By the time he fired, he saw bolts from two other blasters hit targets in the pinned group.

"They're coming!" Corporal Kassel shouted.

Kare looked and swore—forty or fifty soldiers were on their feet, racing toward his position, firing as they came. He fired three times in rapid succession, moving his aiming point with each shot, before he changed position. Between him and Kassel, they knocked down four of the charging soldiers. Kare fired three more shots and moved. Fewer soldiers were charging them now, but they were still coming and had cut the distance in half. He fired again.

Kare couldn't see it, but Corporal Quinn and Lance Corporal Ilon were keeping the reinforcing group from joining the assault. But while second squad was dealing with the flanking movement, other soldiers were moving forward, between the burning buildings, holding their fire as they were getting into place to strike the end of the Marine line from the front. The only Marines in position to see their maneuver were too busy dealing with the flanking movement to notice them.

The steady, rapid fire from Kare and Kassel was taking a toll on the flanking assault. The Coalition soldiers didn't break, or even slow down, but they saw their comrades dropping at their sides and heard the screams of soldiers with cauterized holes burned through their limbs and trunks. The attacking soldiers were nearing panic, and their fire became erratic, their fléchettes frequently going into the sky or into the dirt bare meters in front of them.

Still, more than thirty of them reached the four Marines who'd been struggling to beat them back.

The Marines couldn't shoot, not at that range—there was too great a chance of hitting each other in the mêlée. And their main advantage was their invisibility, the fire from their bolts would tell the enemy where they were.

Sergeant Kare lunged to his feet and slammed the butt of his blaster into the nearest face. The struck soldier fell back, screaming, and Kare jumped away and spun, plunging the hot muzzle of his blaster into the stomach of another soldier, then butt-stroking him on his way down.

Corporal Quinn left his blaster on the ground and drew his fighting knife. A backhand slash ripped out the throat of a Coalition soldier. Quinn left the man gurgling through his open throat and turned in time to duck under a rifle butt swing by another soldier. He came up under the man's rifle and thrust his blade upward, through the soldier's solar plexus and into his heart. Quinn jumped back before much of the spurting blood could get on his chameleons.

Corporal Kassel held his blaster in one hand like a short lance and his fighting knife in the other. He flicked the knife at a head and took that soldier out of the fight with a face torn open and an eye sliced through. Kassel lunged forward, thrusting the muzzle of his blaster into the throat of another foe, crushing his larynx. Kassel twisted away, looking for another opponent.

Lance Corporal Ilon used his blaster as a club, swinging it back and forth as he waded into a knot of milling soldiers. He knocked three of them down before the others closed on him. Ilon dropped to the ground, curled into a ball, and, invisible, rolled away.

Freed from the fire that had kept them pinned to the ground, the two dozen or more soldiers who'd been trying to join the flanking unit to make its assault rose up and charged to join in the hand-to-hand combat.

Kare paused after hitting yet another soldier in the upper

arm with a horizontal butt stroke to see if the man needed to be hit again to take him out of the fight. That pause was all a barreling body needed to slam into him and bear him to the ground. Kare twisted, to break away or to fight with his hands, but the soldier was yelling for help, and another body plummeted onto the Marine.

Quinn's knife was all too visible—and so was the blood that splattered his chameleons. Soldiers holding their fléchette rifles as clubs or thrusting lances closed in on him from all sides.

A lucky swing with the butt of a rifle caught Kassel between the shoulder blades and knocked him to the ground, wheezing for air.

A groping hand connected with Ilon's shoulder, followed by an arm that wrapped around his chest and a shrill shout of "I've got one of them!"

Everybody in the mêlée was abruptly jolted by the far-too-close buzz-saw sizzle of an assault gun—the reaction force had arrived, and the gun was spraying the two dozen reinforcements. Seven other Marines, huffing and grunting from their run, leapt into the fight with swinging blasters and fighting knives. Coalition soldiers, stunned by the unexpected whine of the assault gun from just a few meters away, began collapsing to the ground.

Not all of them fell because they were hit by the fighting Marines; a couple dropped prone and wrapped their arms around their heads. "Don't kill me!" they screamed. "I surrender!"

The Coalition reinforcements, raked by the assault gun fire, buckled and collapsed. The few who lived through the rain of plasma fire dropped their weapons and crawled away.

Staff Sergeant Keen looked toward the barracks and saw more soldiers breaking out to join the fight. He turned the assault gun on them, and they fell back, dead, dying, or fleeing.

The fight was over in another moment. Most of the hundred or more soldiers who had attacked the Marine flank were dead. Eleven surrendered.

CHAPTER
THIRTY-THREE

Exfiltration from Gilbert's Corners, Ravenette

The flight of the survivors from the failed assault against the Marines' left flank acted as a catalyst. The soldiers to their left saw them running, saw the wounded and dead men lying to their right and left, and joined in the flight. Then the soldiers to *their* left did the same, and the next soldiers, and the next after them, in ripples, until everybody in the barracks area who was able to run or hobble toward the fields, away from the Marines, was on the move.

"Let them go," Captain Wainwright ordered on the all-hands circuit. "Sections, report." While he waited for the section leaders to get casualty information from the squad leaders and report back, he checked his satellite feed to see where the forest patrols were and made a preliminary report to Force Recon headquarters on board the CNSS *Kiowa*. He was in turn given news.

"Commence withdrawal as soon as possible. Elements of the Ninth Division have left their base and are en route your position."

"Third section," Staff Sergeant Keen was the first to report in, but he was only reporting for the reaction force, "no casualties."

"Second section," Staff Sergeant Morgan reported, "no casualties."

"Blocking section, no action, no casualties," Sergeant G'Knome reported for the two squads in the fields.

"South section, no casualties," Sergeant Timony reported;

he sounded astonished that no counterattack had been launched against the two squads he'd led on the south of the barracks area.

It took Staff Sergeant Fryman the longest to report in. "First section, no Kilo India Alpha, four Whiskey India Alpha. All mobile."

"You all have your exfiltration routes," Wainwright said. "Go. First section, hold your positions, the corpsman is on his way to you."

Doc Natron had begun moving as soon as he heard Fryman say "no Kilo . . ." because that told him there were wounded Marines in first section.

The first casualty he found was Sergeant Bingh. Three fléchettes had ripped across his left buttock, peeling off a two-square-centimeter patch of skin and gouging the muscle underneath. The wound was already bandaged. Natron reached to undo the bandage to check the wound.

"You don't want to see what's under there, Doc," Corporal Musica said with a grin. "It's not as ugly as it was before it got hit, but Bingh's still got to have the ugliest ass I've ever seen."

"I'm a corpsman," Natron said, ripping the bandage off. "I've seen uglier than you can imagine." He looked at the wound as he pulled some synthskin out of his medkit. "But you're right, that's a damn ugly ass." He quickly applied the synthskin and a fresh dressing. "I'm not going to give you anything for the pain," he told Bingh. "That scratch isn't bad enough to seriously impede your ability to get out of here, but if you don't feel any pain, you run too great a risk of aggravating the injury."

He patted Bingh on the shoulder and stood. "Gotta go!" He was off to tend to the other casualties.

All three of the other wounded Marines were in second squad. Lance Corporal Ilon had a fierce bite on his right forearm that he'd suffered when the Coalition soldiers piled on him. Natron gave the wound a disinfectant, injected an antibiotic, then dressed the wound.

"You need to give that arm a rest and jerk off with your other hand until that heals," he told the Marine.

Sergeant Kare had a broken arm. Natron splinted the arm. "You heard what I told Ilon? You don't have any choice in the matter.

"Where are you hit?" he asked Corporal Quinn, whose chameleons were heavily blood-spattered.

Quinn shook his head. "None of that's mine. I don't get a wound stripe this time."

"I'd hate to see the other guys," Natron said with a shake of his head.

"Look around, you'll see them," Quinn said, and waved a hand at the dead and wounded Coalition soldiers slumped around the squad.

"You said four WIA," Natro said to Fryman. "I've only seen three."

"It's Kassel."

Corporal Kassel was standing, but now that Natron looked at him, he saw the reconman looked a bit queasy.

"What's the matter?" the corpsman asked.

"My back." Kassel sounded as if he was in pain.

"Where?" Natron began probing Kassel's back.

"A bit to the left." Kassel gasped when Natron's fingers probed in the right place.

"Here?"

"There."

Natron gently felt the area that Kassel said hurt. "It feels like you've got a couple of cracked ribs. There's not a lot I can do about that here. Take off your shirt."

Kassel's torso became fully visible as he gingerly peeled off his shirt. His back was bruised where it hurt.

"There's not a lot I can do for broken ribs in the field," Natron said as he rooted through his medkit. "Stand erect."

Kassel winced when Natron applied tape over the injured area.

"That'll help stabilize the bones," Natron said when he'd finished taping the ribs. "You can put your shirt back on. I'll give you something for the pain. Not enough to knock it out,

I don't want you to cause yourself any more injury, but enough to dull the pain so you can move without too much discomfort."

In another moment Natron reported to Captain Wainwright that the wounded were ready to move. He requested and was granted permission to travel with the injured Marines of second squad.

Second platoon's second squad's exfiltration route took it north of Gilbert's Corners; fourth squad's went south of the village. Captain Wainwright had Lieutenant Rollings and Bravo command group go with fourth squad. He took his own command group, minus the corpsman, with first squad through Gilbert's Corners. Even though it was no more than a secondary objective and he didn't have time to search for anybody, he still hoped to capture a member of the Committee on the Conduct of the War. Third squad took a different route through the village, while the reaction force separated into its squads, each of which took a different route around Gilbert's Corners.

Inside Gilbert's Corners

Kory Dillard, a farmer who sometimes supplemented the family's larder by hunting game birds, was wakened by the sounds of battle at some not-too-great distance. The distance was great enough, though, that he concluded it had nothing to do with him, and he rolled over and spooned his wife, who made a faint moan in her sleep. Dillard didn't want to wake her and take the spooning to the next step, he wanted to go back to sleep, which was why he draped his arm over hers instead of cupping her breast. But before he dropped off again, his night was further disturbed, by shouts. The shouts were much closer then the shots, they were in the streets close to his home. So he groaned, gently disengaged himself from his wife, and eased out from under the sheet that was all the covering he and his wife needed for night comfort. He slept naked, so he took a few seconds to pull on a pair of trousers before padding barefoot out of the bedroom to look out the living room windows. What he saw shocked him to full wakefulness.

The streetlamps were out, which told him the time was past midnight—with everybody abed at a decent hour, the village fathers saw no need to keep streetlamps burning all night and turned them off soon after the last of the bars and restaurants was supposed to close. Despite the lack of streetlamps, Dillard could see what was going on; a red glow in the sky to the northeast cast enough light for him to see by. And what he saw was people milling about or running back into their homes. Most of the people were village farmers or shopkeepers in various states of undress, but some were soldiers—like the villagers, in varying states of dress.

Two of the soldiers were yelling—one at the other soldiers, apparently attempting to get them into some kind of military formation, the other at the villagers. When Dillard listened, he could make out that second soldier's words over the din of shouts from most everybody else—he was telling the villagers to wake their neighbors and grab whatever weapons they had to repel an invasion.

An invasion! "Goddamn!" Dillard swore. He'd known no good would come of having that damned committee move into Gilbert's Corners. Soon enough the Beelzebub minions of the Confederation of Human Worlds were bound to find out and come after them. And so they had. Muttering under his breath, Dillard went back to the bedroom to pull on a shirt and boots. He grabbed his birding gun and a box of shells from the closet.

"Wazza madda, 'oney," his wife asked as he dressed.

"Nothin' fer you to worry yer little hay-ed about, honey," he answered. "Now you jist get yersef back ta sleep." Dressed, he got his bird gun from the closet and went outside. He didn't hear his wife get out of bed behind him.

Outside, Dillard recognized the soldier who was yelling at the villagers to wake their neighbors and get their guns; he was some kind of officer, maybe the general in charge of the soldiers here. Something like that, anyhow. Unlike the other soldiers, he was mostly in uniform, even had those ivy leaves, or whatever they were, on his shirt collars. Dillard could also see that the red glow in the sky was from a growing fire, probably at the soldier-housing buildings that had taken part of the cornfields. He heard the sounds of fighting from that direction, and it was a lot louder than he'd realized before he came out.

"What the hell's goin' on, Gen'l?" Dillard demanded.

"It's 'Colonel,'" Colonel Osper snapped when he turned from a yapping man Dillard recognized as one of the tutti-frutti big shots who'd moved to Gilbert's Corners. "The Confederation has launched a major attack, what do you think that's all about?" Osper waved a hand in the direction of the burning barracks.

Dillard cocked his head and listened for a second. "Don't sound lak no major attack now, Gen'l."

"That's because they whupped our troops and is comin' here now!" the tutti-frutti shrieked.

"Shut yer yap," Osper snapped at the tutti-frutti. "Either get yerself a weapon and get ready to fight, or get the hell out'n my way!" He looked back at Dillard. "That don't look like much of a gun you got there, but it'll do. You got people in another part of town, go get them and their weapons. We need 'em all to hold until our reinforcements arrive."

Osper turned his back on Dillard and the still yapping member of the Committee on the Conduct of the War and marched to the ragged formation of officers and senior noncoms that had been assembled by his executive officer. He grimaced when he saw how many of them weren't armed, and how many of the others had only sidearms.

"I want you to start pulling these here civilians into fire teams and squads," he barked. "I figure we only has a few minutes before them Confederations are here, so find yersefs some fighting positions with cover. Now *do* it!"

Dillard thought he knew what that meant, and he didn't want to get organized into no damn fire team or squad, whatever they was. So he made off like he was going to get relatives and friends from another part of Gilbert's Corners. He didn't, though. He'd seen near everybody he knew what had a gun, so's there weren't nobody else for him to find. If he had to fight them Confederations, he'd fight 'em his *own* way!

As soon as Dillard was out of sight of the soldier boys on his street, he began wending his way toward the north edge of the village. One thing he knew from bird hunting is you comes at your game from a direction it doesn't expect—and you hides when you get there and let *it* come to *you*.

The Widder Throgmorton lived on the edge of the village and had a root cellar where she kept the tubers and vegetables she dug up from her kitchen garden. The entry hole to the root cellar faced northeast, the direction from where the Confederation soldiers would come. That's where Dillard headed himself; he figured that root cellar would make a mighty fine blind. But before he took up his position, he thunk he otter let the Widder Throgmorton know he was there, and that mebbe she should get into a good hidey-hole her ownself before the shootin' started. So's he knocked on her door.

"Who's there?" came her quavery voice.

"It's Kory Dillard, Widder Throgmorton."

The Widder Throgmorton opened the door just a crack to see if it was truly Kory Dillard. "What do you want, comin' round in the middle of the night like this?" she demanded. Despite her name and her quavery voice, the Widder Throgmorton weren't no old granny-lady, nossir! She was a mighty fine-looking lady of forty-five.

"What, didn't you hear all that shootin' down by the soldier area? The Confederation's comin'. They done whupped ass on the soldier boys and they's coming here next. I'm goan get in yer root cellar and fight 'em from there. Thought you should know and find yersef a hidey-hole."

The Widder Throgmorton gave him a searching look, but saw only truth in his face. "Give me a minute to get decent, and I'll join you in the root cellar. It's the best hidey-hole I got." She glanced at his bird gun. "That all you got to fight with?"

Dillard shrugged.

"I still got my husband's deer rifle, I'll bring it; it's better for shootin' Confederations than a bird gun is." She disappeared into the darkness of her house.

Dillard shook his head. The woman was right about his bird gun; a deer rifle would be a whole lot better for shooting men. He went around the side to the root cellar and stood next to its entry hole. True to her word, the Widder Throgmorton joined him in a minute, dressed in what looked to be her late husband's hunting clothes. Had to have been his, the way it all bagged and hung off her frame. She thrust the deer rifle into his hands. He juggled a moment until he had a firm grip on both weapons.

"I'll go in first," she said. "Then you hand the guns in to me and follow after." The root cellar was almost totally underground; a seventy-centimeter-tall mound was the only thing above the surface. The entry hole was right at the base of the mound. She unlatched the door and moved it aside, then sat on the ground with her legs inside the hole and slid inside. Once in, she twisted around and held out her hands. "Gimme the bird gun first," she ordered. When Dillard gave it to her, she slid it down the hole by her side and reached back up for the deer rifle, then completely disappeared down the hole.

Dillard followed. The tunnel down into the root cellar ended on a step less than two meters down; it was just the perfect length for him to stand on the step and have only enough of himself exposed to aim. He stepped down into the cellar proper just as the Widder Throgmorton lit a lamp. The lamp gave off a faint red glow, just enough for him to make out her shape and the shapes of mounded tubers and vegetables. From the looks of the edges of one mound, he suspected she'd been pilfering in the cornfield. The root cellar was a tight fit; he found he had to crouch, which put him face-to-face with the fine-looking Widder Throgmorton, and he instantly understood why so many men in the village come sniffing around her. But all that sniffing didn't do them no good; they was all married, and she weren't having no truck with married men. So it wouldn't do no good for him to take advantage of the closeness.

She handed him the rifle and said, "Scoot."

He twisted around and slid up the hole until he could climb onto the step. He noticed she turned the light off before he got in position. Good, light would give him away when the Confederation soldiers came. He looked in the direction of the fires and saw the damnedest thing he *ever* seen!

There was some shapes, man-sized and man-shaped, moving away from the fire. The damnedest thing about them was, the one farthest away, what was right on the edge of the fire glow, was there he is, there he ain't. It were like he disappeared when he wasn't in front of the fire. And when he was, it was like seeing his shadow instead of him. The same with the other four who were between Dillard and the fire; they looked like shadows rather than the men what threw the shadows.

Shadows or men, they had to be Confederation soldiers. Dillard put the deer rifle to his shoulder, drew a bead on the nearest shadow, and squeezed the trigger. The crack and buck of the rifle caught him by surprise, just like it should when the trigger is being squeezed right. He brought the muzzle back in line and looked side to side through its sights. Men or shadows, he didn't see anybody. He didn't know if he'd hit the one he'd aimed at or not, but . . .

"Where'd that shot come from?" Sergeant Kare asked on his radio's squad circuit.

"I think it was almost directly to my front," Corporal Quinn said. "I was looking into the village, but I caught the muzzle flash in my peripheral vision."

"Kassel, Ilon, did either of you see it?" Kare slid his infra into place while he asked the question and looked along the line directly ahead of Quinn.

"Negative," Ilon replied. "I was checking our rear."

"Kassel? Speak up." Kare's infra vision spotted something. "I see him. Seventy-five meters. Looks like he's in a hole. Kassel, where are you? I'm going to fire on him. Ilon, when you see where my bolt goes, put another one in the same place. Quinn, watch for anybody else." Aiming with a broken arm was difficult, but Kare managed. He aimed at the image of a man's head—and arms holding a just-fired weapon—and squeezed his blaster's firing lever. There was a double *crack-sizzle* as Ilon's bolt followed his by a split second. Kare squeezed off three more rapid-fire bolts in case someone else was in the hole with the shooter.

"Where's Kassel? Ilon, check for him."

A moment later Ilon reported, "He's hit. It's a through-and-through in the belly."

"I'm on my way," Doc Natron said. "Show me."

Ilon raised a bared arm. Natron saw the arm and sprinted to it. It was two long minutes before the corpsman reported to Kare.

"I've got the bleeding stopped," Natron said, "but he's hit too badly for me to deal with here. I have to put him in a stasis bag—we have to carry him out of here."

"Shit! All right, get him ready to be moved. Quinn, come with me, let's check out the shooter." Along the way, Kare gave a report to Lieutenant Rollings.

"One of the reaction squads should be near you," Rollings said. "I'll ask the boss to divert it to help you." Then he broke the connection to call Captain Wainwright.

Kare and Quinn found a body slumped in the entry hole to what looked like a root cellar. Quinn grabbed the rifle that had fallen from the body's hands and tossed it away.

"A civilian!" Kare exclaimed when he looked at the body through his light gatherer.

"How the hell did he see Kassel?" Quinn mused. "That wasn't just a blind shot."

Kare put that question aside for a moment in favor of something more immediate. "Is anybody else in there?" he shouted down the hole. He got a moan in reply.

"I'm hurt," a female voice said.

"Sorry to hear that, ma'am. Anybody else with you?"

"No, just me and Kory, and he's dead—you kilt him." The voice ended in a whimper.

"Kory, that's the man up here?"

"Yes. I'm hurt bad."

"I'm sorry about that, ma'am, but he shouldn't have shot

at us. We would have left him and you alone if he hadn't shot at us. Now you wait right where you are, and I'm sure somebody will come and help you in a bit."

"Can you pull Kory out of the way? Mebbe I can crawl up and find help myself if you do."

"Can't do that, ma'am. I don't know you're hurt. If I move him, you might come up and shoot us in the back. Can't have that. Now you just be patient." Kare signaled Quinn, and they headed toward the group around Kassel.

Kare stopped after a few meters and let Quinn go on ahead. He raised his shields and looked at the corporal in visual light. What he saw made him swear; Quinn showed up as a shadow against the light from the burning barracks. "I should have thought of that," he muttered: chameleons pick up the color and visual texture of whatever is nearest, not what is behind. Quinn's chameleons were the color and texture of the ground cover he was walking on and stood out sharply against the fire. When the squad moved on, he'd have to endeavor to keep them from being silhouetted by the fire.

"Down!" Kare shouted; he spun and dropped at a thumping and scrabbling to his rear. There was a loud bang, and he felt something hit his splinted arm and his side at the same time he saw a muzzle flash. He didn't pause to wonder what hit him or to check it out; he pointed his blaster where the muzzle flash had come from and squeezed the firing lever three times in rapid succession. A voice was cut off in mid-scream.

"Cover me," Kare ordered Quinn. He jumped up into a low crouch and ran toward where he'd fired.

It was the root cellar. The man's body was out of sight. In its place was a woman, her dead face contorted in rage and surprise.

"Dammit, woman, why'd you do that?" Kare shouted. "If you and your husband had stayed in that hole and let us go by, you'd both be alive and well." He drew back a foot to kick her, but put it back down. She was dead, her stupidity didn't merit further punishment.

Doc Natron had Kassel in a stasis bag by the time Kare

and Quinn reached them. The corpsman quickly checked out Kare's new wounds. All they needed immediately was a daub of antiseptic and a patch of synthskin.

"You were hit by tiny pellets," Natron said. "A surgeon can easily pluck them out when we get back aboard the *Kiowa*."

"Show us where you are," Sergeant Hemrich's voice suddenly came over the radio—third platoon's fifth squad was on its way to help.

"Here we are," Kare said. He lifted a bared arm.

"I've got you." In a moment, Hemrich and his three Marines were there. They quickly rigged a litter and lifted Kassel onto it. Quinn and two of Hemrich's men carried the litter past the sounds of a firefight raging inside Gilbert's Corners.

Kare made sure they were far enough away from the village that nobody inside it could see them silhouetted against the fire. As they went, he heard voices from their left rear; someone had discovered the two civilians he'd killed.

CHAPTER
THIRTY-FOUR

Gilbert's Corners, Ravenette

Colonel Manuel Osper looked at Lieutenant Colonel Jay Scroggins, his executive officer, and his battalion sergeant major, Cliff Talus. Unlike many of the other officers and senior noncoms he'd just sent to organize the locals into a militia, both had managed to pull on full uniforms and pistol belts. Scroggins's uniform was sloppily pulled together, but Talus looked ready for the parade ground. The sergeant major had also managed to snag a fléchette rifle and pouches of reloads for it. He also had a radio.

"What do you hear from the troops?" Osper asked Talus.

"Not a damn thing," Talus said sourly. "Nobody thunk to get on the horn and report."

"Did you try all the frequencies?"

Talus gave him the kind of look a question that stupid deserved.

"I had to ask," Osper apologized. "What about the patrols?"

"I been in contact with all of 'em. They didn't see nuttin'. I tole 'em to sit tight where they was."

Osper nodded, that was really all the patrols could do without running the risk of being wiped out in detail. He looked toward the burning barracks, now visible mostly as brightness in the sky; the buildings and houses of Gilbert's Corners, the officer and senior-noncom housing area, and the intervening trees blocked most of his direct view of the barracks area. He wondered *how* the Coalition forces who'd attacked had managed to get there undetected by the patrols or any of the security devices he'd had installed. Perhaps General Lyons had been right, that it was a small raiding party, not a major assault force, and they had infiltrated in small groups.

Where *was* General Lyons for that matter?

If this was a raiding party rather than a full-scale assault . . .

They attacked the barracks from this side. That meant that they could still be between Gilbert's Corners and the burning barracks area! We can still beat them!

Osper looked around to see if the locals were yet being organized. Yes, a few small groups were being led by his own people. "Over here," he yelled. "On me!"

Quickly, a group of about a hundred soldiers and armed civilians were gathered in front of the colonel.

"I want you to divide into five twenty-man platoons." Colonel Osper pointed at a major. "You're in command of first platoon. Take them down Center Street. You"—he pointed at another major—"are second platoon. Take them down East Street." He gave command of the other platoons to three captains and sent one down West Street and the other two along the edges of the village—Gilbert's Corners three streets along its main axis were unimaginatively named. "Kill anybody you see in a Confederation military uniform."

"Wait jist a minute there, Colonel!"

Osper looked and saw Heb Cawman, the chairman of the Committee on the Conduct of the War, the very man who'd just a few minutes earlier been whining and crying about how the Confederation forces had just whupped the Coalition defenders.

"Mr. Cawman," Osper said, "what do you want?"

"Ya can't kill 'em all. Ya gotta take a pris'ner."

"All right then, you go with first platoon. Your job will be to pick out a prisoner and take charge of him. Now everybody get *moving*!"

Cawman blanched and took a step back when Osper told him to go with first platoon, but a sergeant grabbed his arm and pulled him along with the platoon.

Entering the Village of Gilbert's Corners

Through his infra screen, Captain Wainwright saw that Sergeant Bingh was favoring his right leg, but the limp wasn't pronounced and he didn't think it would hold the squad leader back. Bingh had said as much when the captain had asked him about it. But Wainwright didn't linger on Bingh's injury, he mostly watched ahead, looking for some indication that a member of the Committee on the Conduct of the War might be in his way. He *really* wanted to capture one if he could without jeopardizing any of his people.

But what he saw was a mass of men coming down the middle of the street. From their dress, most of the men were armed civilians, but three men who were herding them along and trying to instill some order and discipline were definitely soldiers.

Before Captain Wainwright could alert the other squads, Sergeant Kindy reported a group of armed civilians led by four soldiers coming along the street toward him.

"First and third squads," Wainwright ordered, "get between the houses and let them pass. We don't need to leave a lot of dead civilians behind us."

Bingh and Kindy acknowledged the order; Wainwright and Staff Sergeant Fryman followed first squad into the side yard of a house. They had barely settled in before they heard the shot of a projectile rifle, followed by several blaster shots, to the north, where second squad was bypassing Gilbert's Corners. Then silence. It sounded as if someone had taken a shot at the Marines, and the Marines had responded with greater violence than whoever had shot at them wanted to deal with. Wainwright decided to wait for a report.

The people on the street froze and listened, looking to their left. When nothing more happened for a moment, the soldiers began moving them forward again. Kindy reported the people in the street ahead of him had stopped but were moving again.

There was another single projectile shot and multiple

blaster shots from the same direction, and the people in the street scattered for cover; some of them ran away.

"They's whuppin' us!" a civilian shrilled. "We's gotta git out of here while we kin!" He tried to run, but one of the soldiers had a firm grip on his arm and he couldn't get away.

That looked odd, so Wainwright turned up his ears in case someone said something that would explain it. Someone did.

"Now, now, Mistah Cawman, you heard the colonel. It's up to you to capture one a them Confederations. You cain't do thet if'n you runs away."

Cawman! Was that really the chairman of the Committee on the Conduct of the War? Wainwright used both his magnifier and light-gatherer screens to get a better look at the man's face. Yes, except for the panicky expression, he looked just like the images of the chairman that Wainwright had seen.

Captain Wainwright suddenly felt less reluctant about civilian casualties; Heb Cawman was too valuable a prize to let a few civilians stand in the way of his capture.

"Three-two," Wainwright radioed. "Move through the yards toward my position. Stay across the street from me. We have a chance to catch a big fish. Over."

"Roger," Kindy came back. "I have your position. We are moving now."

The soldiers in Wainwright's view pulled their remaining civilians together and resumed their advance down the street.

Advancing down Center Street

The major that Colonel Osper had turned into a platoon commander was named Belvadeer. He muttered subvocally as he led his makeshift platoon of—of *civilians*—along Center Street. He had great respect for Colonel Osper, but what was the man thinking? There was no possible way an undisciplined rabble could take on a regular military force the size that must have struck the reinforced battalion and do anything but get slaughtered. And then to send that *nincompoop*

Cawman along! It would be bad enough if Cawman were willing and gung ho about capturing a Confederation soldier, but the man was whining and crying the whole way and would have run off long ago if someone weren't physically dragging him along. This was purely *insane*!

But maybe the colonel had a sound reason for what he was doing. If so, Belvadeer wished he'd have told at least his "platoon" commanders what it was. Belvadeer was certain the other officers leading the rabble felt the same as he did. But, dammit, a colonel was a colonel, and a major was a major, and when a colonel said *do,* a major *did.* He just hoped he could spot the Confederation forces that were probably— most likely, almost positively—in front of him before they spotted him. If he did, he might just survive the battle.

Major Belvadeer's "platoon" was just crossing Fifth Street when something happened behind him that nearly made him lose control of his bowels.

The Snatch, Gilbert's Corners

Captain Wainwright touched helmets with Staff Sergeant Fryman and Sergeant Bingh and told them what he was going to do. He finished with "Watch my UV marker. Bingh, when it looks like I'm close enough, take out the soldier holding him. Fryman, have both squads give me covering fire if the civilians decide to fight."

Wainwright lay low while the gaggle of armed civilians shuffled past, then silently rose to his feet and padded into the street behind them. Moving as fast as he could without making noise, he shuffled up behind the still-complaining Cawman. He was only a meter behind him when a blaster bolt flamed past and struck the soldier holding Cawman's arm between the shoulder blades. Wainwright lunged forward and wrapped his arms around Cawman, flung the man over his hip, and spun about to run back to first squad.

Gunfire erupted behind him and was immediately answered by blaster fire from the two Marine squads. He felt the impact of a bullet that hit Cawman; Cawman's shocked scream came half a second later. Wainwright was almost back at the squad when he felt the impact of the bullet that hit him high on the left side of his back. He collapsed next to Bingh, dropping Cawman. Cawman screamed in agony.

The civilians were firing in all directions, including over the nearby houses. The two remaining soldiers were yelling at them, trying to get them to concentrate their fire on the Marines' fire, but they were panicked by the plasma bolts tearing through their mass and wouldn't pay attention. When a bolt hit one of the soldiers, some of the civilians dropped their weapons and began crawling, scrabbling to get out of the killing zone. A couple threw away their rifles and screamed, "Don't shoot me! Don't shoot!"

In a moment it was over; Fryman was able to turn his attention to the two casualties lying next to him. "Bingh, check out Cawman," he ordered as he began to examine Wainwright. The captain's wound was bad, so maybe it was fortunate that he was unconscious. The bullet that had hit him wasn't powerful enough to go all the way through and was still in there someplace. At least he was only bleeding from one place—at least only one place on the outside; Fryman had no way of knowing whether he also had serious internal bleeding.

Fryman contacted Doc Natron. Natron told him to pack the wound and said he'd try to infiltrate to their position with a stasis bag. Fryman had talked to Natron on the command circuit so Lieutenant Rollings could hear—that was faster than making a separate report.

Lieutenant Rollings radioed to stand tight, he was on his way with fourth squad.

Only after he'd packed Wainwright's wound and talked to Rollings did Fryman turn his attention to Cawman.

"He just got winged," Bingh said, and lashed Cawman's hands behind his back.

"The way he's crying, it sounds like his guts have been ripped out."

Bingh grunted.

East Street, Gilbert's Corners

"Wha' the hell is thet!" someone shouted when the firing broke out on Center Street.

"Damfino," someone else shouted.

The major commanding the East Street "platoon" swore out loud. He didn't have any communications, so he couldn't talk to Major Belvadeer to find out if he needed help. He stood in indecision about what to do. If Confederation troops were on Center Street and had attacked Belvadeer's group, they might also be coming along East Street—even though no matter how hard he looked, he couldn't see anybody down the length of the street.

Some of the civilians made the decision for him.

"We gotta git over there, give 'em some hep!" someone yelled. That started the whole mob running toward Center Street.

When they got there, they were shocked by the number of bodies lying in the street. The hunters among them were surprised there wasn't any blood on the street; they didn't know that the plasma bolts fired by the Marines cauterized wounds as they made them so there was usually no bleeding.

Lieutenant Rollings and fourth squad reached East Street right after the "platoon" of locals moved off it; they heard the locals running along the cross street to their right.

"Let's go!" Rollings ordered, and ran faster between the houses. He spotted the UV markers on the backs of the Marines of third squad and alerted them to his approach. When he got there, he dropped to one knee next to Sergeant Kindy.

"Where are they?" Rollings asked.

"First squad's directly across from us," Sergeant Kindy answered.

Using his infra screen, Rollings was able to make out the faint heat signatures of Staff Sergeant Fryman and first squad. He looked to his right, where the group from East Street was milling about, and sprinted across to first squad after telling fourth squad to stay with third. Gunny Lytle went with him.

"How is he?" he asked as soon as he got there.

"Pretty bad, I think," Fryman said. He described the wound again.

Rollings radioed Doc Natron and asked where he was.

"I'm only about a hundred meters from you. But there are armed people between us, and they're moving in your direction."

"Is anybody with you?"

"Corporal Quinn."

"Get out of the line of fire. If they're coming toward us, we're probably going to have to fight."

"Will do. We'll swing around to your left, try to bypass those civilians."

"Roger." Rollings looked back to the civilians who were now checking the bodies in the street and heard someone out of sight on the side street yelling at them to move, telling them the street was a killing zone. The civilians looked up and around uncertainly, but four soldiers who were among them took the voice at its word and sprinted toward it. That set off the others, and they ran after the soldiers and out of sight. Rollings then looked west and saw a group of armed men led by two soldiers less than thirty meters away—easing toward the Marines' position. He looked toward Captain Wainwright and thought quickly. The captain was in no condition to be moved; he'd likely die if he was. That meant they had to stay in place until Doc Natron arrived and was able to put him in a stasis bag. Which meant they were going to have to fight. He estimated there were twenty men, close to it anyway, coming toward them. He had six Marines with him here. Gunny Lytle, Staff Sergeant Morgan, and two squads were across the street. If these seventeen Marines couldn't break twenty men, mostly civilians, they needed to turn in their Eagle, Globe, and Starstreams.

"Gunny, Fryman, and first squad," he said into the first section circuit, "you're group one. Third and fourth squads are group two.

"Group one, on my command, engage the armed men to our west." Rollings gave the Marines with him a few seconds to get into position, then ordered, *"Fire!"*

Five blasters and two hand-blasters blazed into the approaching men, and nine of them fell immediately. The others screamed and scattered for cover. Not all of them made it.

"Cease fire!" Rollings ordered when the last of the men was out of sight. He heard the sound of people running, crashing through hedges and fences. Another sound drew his attention to the south. When he looked, he saw men advancing toward his position. But these weren't walking in the open, they were flitting from concealment to cover, staying out of sight as much as possible.

Assembly Point, Gilbert's Corners

More armed civilians poured in, led by officers and non-coms, beginning almost immediately after Colonel Osper sent off his first five "platoons." Soon he had close to two hundred men. He had to restrain the first arrivals from following Major Belvadeer down Center Street, they were so anxious not to miss the action. But as more men arrived and saw others mustering, they were more willing to stand in place and wait for orders.

Colonel Osper was huddling with Lieutenant Colonel Scroggins and Sergeant Major Talus, working out a plan to use the people they had as a reaction force, when the first firing opened up on Center Street.

When Osper and Scroggins turned to look toward the fighting, Talus turned to the gathered men and roared in his best sergeant major's voice for them to hold in place. When the civilians, who just wanted to help their neighbors, stopped and gaped at him with the fear his voice elicited, he glared, then nodded in satisfaction and turned his back on them.

Colonel Osper was struck by a sudden thought. "Is it true," he asked Talus, "thet the Confederation Marines have some kind of invisibility suit?"

Talus, who had served an enlistment in the Confederation

Army before going home to Cabala and joining the planetary army there, nodded. "Yes, sir. They calls 'em chameleons."

"*Damn!* That's how they were able to get past our patrols and visual detector system. Thet's Confederation Marines we's fightin', not the damn army."

Talus gave Osper another of *those* looks. After spending an enlistment in the Confederation Army, he knew how much more capable it was than the Cabala Army.

"How many of 'em do you think there is?" Osper asked nobody in particular.

Talus gave him another look, but turned his gaze toward the dying firefight without saying, "How the hell should I know?"—which was on his tongue. Instead, he said, "From what I seen down there, and what I heard t' the west, I'd say a platoon."

Osper looked at him in disbelief. "One platoon couldn't have done all thet to the barracks area."

Talus shrugged. "This is mebbe a blocking force, t' keep reinforcements from coming from the village." He turned back to the impatient armed men, who were now being held back by the officers and noncoms among them, and gave them a glare that swept from one side to the other. They backed off and settled down.

"A blocking force," Osper murmured, "that makes sense." He thought for a few more seconds, then turned to face his irregular company.

"Listen up, men!" he shouted loudly enough for all of them to hear. "This is what we's gonna do."

Marine Defense, Gilbert's Corners

"You sure shook them up," Doc Natron said when he reached the group guarding Captain Wainwright. He gave the wounded raid commander a quick examination. "You're sure there's no exit wound?" he asked as he searched for one.

"If there is one, I couldn't find it," Staff Sergeant Fryman answered.

"Well, neither can I. A couple of you, give me a hand getting him into a stasis bag." Corporal Musica and Lance Corporal Wehrli helped lift Wainwright into the bag, which Natron closed and activated. "He should be all right now until we get him back to the *Kiowa.*" He looked at Heb Cawman, who had stopped whining. "Now what about that one?"

Cawman looked up, his eyes rolling in terror. The Marines were talking on their short-range radios, so he couldn't hear them, but he could tell they were all around him.

"He just got winged," Sergeant Bingh said, "he can walk on his own."

Cawman whimpered, but looked up when Bingh nudged him with his foot.

"We can go now," Natron said.

"Right," Rollings said. "First squad, you carry the captain. Fryman, lead the way." He called for Gunny Lytle to bring the other two squads over. The lieutenant grabbed the prisoner and yanked him to his feet. "You're coming with me," he snarled through his speaker.

"Aye, aye," Fryman said, and headed deeper between the houses, heading toward West Street. He looked around the back corner of the house when he reached it and stopped. "Company's coming," he said into the command circuit. "Snooping and pooping, like the ones on the street."

"How close are they?" Rollings asked. "Can we get across before they reach us?"

"If everybody's here and we run, yeah."

"Then move out at the double."

The Marines ran on the balls of their feet, to keep the noise down. But eighteen men are going to make some noise, especially if one of them is reluctant, and Heb Cawman was most decidedly reluctant.

"I hear 'em!" somebody yelled from twenty meters away, and fired a wild shot down the backyards.

"Don' shoot! It's me, Heb Cawman! Don' shoot or y'all'll hit me!"

That brought a fusillade of fire down the way, but the Marines were already between the houses fronting on West Street and running faster.

Gunny Lytle caught up with Rollings and Cawman. "I've got him," he said through his speaker so Cawman could hear, and gripped the chairman's arm in a grip far tighter than Rollings's. "Mr. Cawman," he snarled close to his ear, "one more peep out of you and I'm going to break your arm." He squeezed tighter. Cawman yelped, but cut it off when Lytle increased the pressure even more. "And then I'll gag you so tight you'll think you're suffocating."

"I-I'll be quiet!" Cawman squeaked.

Fryman stopped again at the front corner of the house the Marines were passing. "More of them coming," he radioed, "and they're right here."

One of the passing armed men suddenly stopped and looked to his right, between the houses where the chameleoned Marines were. He didn't hear or see anything out of place, but something felt *wrong* about the side yards. He twisted to point his shotgun into the yards and jerked the trigger.

Fryman shot him.

Fourth squad, by then right behind Fryman, opened up on the passing men, flaming holes through many of them. The others ran, ignoring commands to get down and fire between the houses. A few flung wild shots behind themselves as they ran.

"Let's go," Rollings ordered. "Move!" The Marines sprinted across the street, chased by gunfire from Center Street.

"Third squad," Rollings ordered, "put a few rounds into them."

Third squad went prone, facing back the way they'd come, and fired into the men they saw moving between the houses from Center Street. When the men from Center Street stopped shooting, and nobody else was entering the side yards, third squad got up and sprinted after the other Marines.

Two minutes later, all the Marines were out of Gilbert's Corners and headed generally southwest. Continuing gunfire in Gilbert's Corners receded behind them.

Once they were a few hundred meters south of the village and there was no sign of pursuit, Rollings had third squad head for its puddle jumpers on its own. He stayed with first

squad and had fourth squad join them for security—and to
trade off carrying the stasis bag—until they reached first
squad's cached puddle jumpers. Within hours of the Battle of
Gilbert's Corners, all of the Marines had their puddle jumpers
and were assembled at the pickup point where the Astro-
Ghost was to take them up to the *Kiowa*.

Heb Cawman had been carried slung between Corporals
Nomonon and Jaschke. With Gunny Lytle's firm grip off his
bruised arm, he felt free to scream the entire time he was airborne.

CHAPTER
THIRTY-FIVE

"That kwangduk-eating gristle between Muhammad's pointy teeth," Commander Walt Obannion muttered. He had just read the latest orders he'd received from the Confederation forces planetside. Then he looked at the routing again and saw the orders had indeed come through Rear Admiral Hoi's hands and realized that if the admiral had had the same immediate reaction to them that he did, these orders wouldn't have reached him. He double-checked the duty roster, then hit the office comm.

"Sergeant Major, kindly get Captain Qindall, Captain Gonzalez, Gunner Jaqua, and Lieutenant Rollings. I need to see all of you."

Force Recon's area on the CNSS Kiowa was necessarily small, so it only took three minutes for the officers Obannion had called for to precede Sergeant Major Periz into the commander's office. Obannion waited until the sergeant major closed the door behind himself before speaking.

"His supreme commanderness planetside has ordered—*ordered!*—a ground recon of possible landing beaches along the shore a hundred klicks north of Bataan, east of where second platoon found the amphibious division in Cranston. In an area controlled by the Seventh Independent Military Police Battalion from Lannoy."

That was not the way a commanding officer would normally speak about a general in front of his staff, but the disrespect the Force Recon Marines had for General Billie was profound. Particularly after the way he had credited his own staff with taking out the satellite-killer laser system, a mission accomplished by Force Recon at the direction of Admiral Hoi. And Billie had credited his staff with developing the intelligence that had allowed the ground forces to successfully defend against the Coalition's amphibious assault— intelligence that Billie had offhandedly rejected when it was given to him. Most recent was Billie's less than enthusiastic endorsement of the highly successful Force Recon raid on Gilbert's Corners, an endorsement that had clearly been designed to shift blame to someone else had the raid failed.

And Gilbert's Corners had cost Obannion the services of an excellent operations chief.

This Marine commander was going to say whatever he bloody well pleased about General Billie, to anybody he bloody well pleased—but he was circumspect enough to keep his bloody-well-speaking behind bloody-well-closed doors.

"Look at this." Obannion shoved the orders at Warrant Officer Jaqua, the company's training chief, who, as the number two man in the Operations Shop, was the acting S3.

Jaqua read the orders, including the routing and endorsements. Captains Qindall and Gonzalez squeezed in to read over his shoulder. When they were through, Jaqua looked at Obannion, who nodded, and passed the orders to Periz, who read them with Rollings.

"Meat and potatoes," Periz said with a shrug when he and the second platoon commander finished reading the orders. He said it as a reminder for his boss that orders like this were what they should be getting from the ground forces commander. Running recon missions for large army units was a primary mission for Force Recon.

"He's kind of late to the party, though," Obannion said, not very mollified. Then he took a deep breath to get full control of himself and gestured for Periz to give the orders back to Jaqua. "How long?"

The gunner glanced at Rollings and considered what assets were immediately available. He knew Obannion wanted to give the mission to second platoon—that was why Rollings was at the meeting. "How many squads do you want on this mission?" That detail was totally absent from the orders.

A corner of Obannion's mouth briefly curled in a grimace, but he had already decided. "Two squads. Take them from first section."

Jaqua took a couple of seconds to think, then looked at Rollings. "This time tomorrow?" When Rollings nodded, Jaqua looked at Obannion and more firmly repeated, "This time tomorrow."

"Then make it so," Obannion said in dismissal.

The others filed out, with Jaqua and Rollings already discussing plans for the recon mission. Obannion was certain he heard Jaqua whisper "Cakewalk" to the lieutenant.

Sergeant Bingh was fully recovered from the flesh wound he'd received at Gilbert's Corners, and Sergeant Kare and Lance Corporal Ilon were almost as fully healed, but Corporal Kassel was still in the ship's surgery. Gunner Jaqua and Lieutenant Rollings had no trouble agreeing that third and fourth squads, which had suffered no casualties in Gilbert's Corners, would run the mission. Jaqua, who was a betting man, offered odds that those were the exact squads Commander Obannion had in mind. Rollings wisely refused to take the odds.

Planetfall, One Hundred Kilometers North of the Bataan Peninsula, Ravenette

The AstroGhost was less than half-filled—all it had in its bay were two Sea Squirts; eight Marines were secured in webbing along the bulkheads near the Sea Squirts. The AstroGhost settled almost gently when it hit the water, which splashed barely higher than the shuttle's dorsal side, and it only rocked once or twice before it stabilized. Thirty seconds after it touched down, the Marines were out of their webbing and unstrapping the Sea Squirts. The Sea Squirts were in place at the rear ramp before the crew chief made his way aft to open the ramp.

"Let's do this thing," Sergeant Kindy said to the crew chief.

"Better you than me, jarhead." In a moment the crew chief had the back of the AstroGhost open to the night air. "Break a leg," he said to the Marines as they shoved the submersible vehicles into the water and jumped after them.

Kindy gave the crew chief a thumbs-up, then shouted, "Gung ho!" and took his leap into the ocean.

With the speed and economy of movement born of well-rehearsed actions, the Marines gained their stations in the Sea Squirts and headed shoreward at a depth of five meters. They had almost reached their cruising speed of twenty-five knots by the time the crew chief had the rear hatch of the Astro-Ghost closed again. By the time the shuttle lifted off the surface of the water, the Sea Squirts were far enough away that the Marines couldn't feel the AstroGhost's departure.

Blue Beach, One Hundred Kilometers North of Bataan

An hour after leaving the AstroGhost, Sergeant Kindy signaled Sergeant Williams, and the two squad leaders slowed the Sea Squirts and started to rise slowly. The angle of ascent was less than the angle at which the ocean bottom rose toward the land; once the bottom got within three meters of the Sea Squirts, the submersibles maintained position midway between it and the surface, until the water was barely deep enough to keep them covered without touching bottom. Then Kindy signaled Williams again, and they brought the Sea Squirts to a full stop.

Kindy detached the rebreather from his helmet and slithered backward, out of his tube, and drifted up until his head broke surface. He took his UPUD and aimed the pickup at the path of the string-of-pearls. In a moment he had an infrared view of the narrow beach to his front, and the cliff tops behind it. No sentries' heat signatures were detected. Kindy scanned the beach and the cliff tops with the UPUD's motion detector and again got a negative read. He resubmerged and signaled the two squads to prepare to land.

The Marines quickly took their gear from the storage tubes of the Sea Squirts, and the squad leaders, who'd piloted the vehicles, gave the Sea Squirts the command to hide. The Sea Squirts backed away and headed for a jumble of submerged rocks, where they would settle on the bottom and await the command to rendezvous for pickup.

The Marines headed for shore, paddling underwater, never exposing anything more than their heads, and then only long enough to take a breath. When the water was shallow enough that they could hold themselves with their fingertips on the bottom and their heads at the surface, they stopped while Kindy again used the UPUD to check for heat signatures and motion. Both were negative.

"Hit the beach!" Kindy ordered.

The eight Marines surged to their feet and sprinted out of the water to stand with their backs against the face of the cliffs. If anybody had been close enough to observe, that person would have been very curious to see eight man-sized and -shaped splotches of dripping water against the cliff. But the Seventh Independent MPs didn't have anybody on the beach. Which didn't really make that much difference to this part of the mission, because if there had been anybody there to see, the Marines would have had to kill them.

After a minute, Kindy and Williams touched helmets to confer privately for a moment, then Williams led fourth squad north to recon possible landing beaches. Kindy gave them a couple of minutes to get away, then got out a minnie and attached a line-box to it. He put the minnie on the cliff face and gave it a nudge. The recon robot began scrabbling up the fifty-meter-high cliff, playing out a lightweight line as it climbed. Kindy held the end of the line lightly in his fingers. The Marines' uniforms had dripped dry by the time the minnie reached the top of the cliff.

The minnie quickly gained the cliff top, then skittered about, sending visual, infrared, and amplified views of the landscape to the waiting squad leader. When Kindy was satisfied that no local was likely to stumble upon the minnie or what it was doing anytime soon, he attached another lightweight line to the thin one he held and sent a command to the minnie. The minnie skittered to a convenient boulder and secured itself to it. Then the line-box reeled the line up, dragging the thicker line with it. After the first several meters of the second line reached the top, the squad leader twisted it *just so,* and its top end frayed, reaching out to the ground all around, and anchored itself like a clinging vine. Kindy attached a climbing grip to the line and, holding the grip, half climbed and half was pulled to the cliff top. As soon as he disappeared over the top, Corporal Jaschke attached another climbing grip, then followed. Lance Corporal Ellis came next, and Corporal Nomonon brought up the rear.

Up the Beach

The cliffs gradually lowered, petering out to nothing five hundred meters north of where the two Force Recon squads had come ashore. There the beach was wide, gravelly, and firm, rising gently from the waterline to a broad sward. Several hundred meters out, a reef below the surface slowed the ocean's waves and gentled them for the final leg of their journey to the shore. A spindly forest began fifty meters inland from the beach.

Sergeant Williams had constantly checked both the infrared satellite feed from his UPUD and the UPUD's motion detector during fourth squad's movement along the declining cliffs to the beach. Neither had given him any indication of the presence of anybody other than the two Marine squads in the cliff-top camp a short distance south of their landing point. Now he checked more carefully, including not only the UPUD's scent detector but the screens on his helmet as well. He also had his Marines examine their surroundings with all the resources they carried. None of them detected anything larger than a prowling animal the height and length of a midsized dog. There weren't even any emanations of the kind that would give away the presence of electronic detection devices.

Strange, very strange, Williams thought. Surely the Seventh Independent MPs were supposed to be guarding this beach. Why didn't they have any detectable sentries or, at least, sensors?

"Listen up," Williams said on the short-range radio. "Belinski, Skripska, watch the land. Rudd, with me. We're going to check for amphib traps."

Corporal Belinski and Lance Corporal Skripska took positions at the high edge of the gravelly beach, while Sergeant Williams and Lance Corporal Rudd lay down and bellied their way into the surf and under the lapping waves. An hour later, Williams and Rudd were back without having found a single trap all the way out to the reef. Williams had even checked the reef itself for traps on its top, and a short distance seaward of it, without finding any traps.

Curiouser and curiouser, Williams thought. It's almost as if the Coalition is inviting an amphibious landing here.

Belinski and Skripska could only report, "All quiet."

Williams took his squad into the spindly forest to see what they could find there—if there *was* anything to be found.

Atop the Cliffs, with the Seventh Independent Military Police Battalion

Sergeant Kindy split third squad in two for its infiltration of the Seventh MP's camp; Corporals Nomonon and Jaschke took the half closer to the cliffs, Lance Corporal Ellis went with Kindy to examine the area deeper inland.

The camp was obviously temporary, in spite of its having buildings rather than tents. It had all the hallmarks of hasty construction—the structures weren't aligned in proper military manner; not all the walls were plumb; there were occasional gaps between roofs and walls; the roads were unevenly graded, oiled rather than paved; the street lighting was irregular. Maintenance was spotty at best. A door hung ajar on a barracks. Cracked and broken windows hadn't been repaired. Some streetlights were out. And litter marred the grounds.

The only buildings that seemed to be properly maintained were the clubs, one each for enlisted, noncoms, and officers. Sounds of poorly played music and drunken merriment cascaded out of all three clubs, which complemented the sounds of drunken merriment and drunken fights from the barracks. Drunk soldiers in disheveled uniforms staggered through the streets between clubs and barracks. Even the two helmeted soldiers Kindy saw, evidently on fire watch, took furtive nips from covered bottles and wavered when walking.

Sergeant Kindy shook his head; he'd never seen a military station in such shoddy condition, not even an overnight bivouac. Nor had he seen such undisciplined soldiers in a war zone. The only good thing about the Seventh MPs was the almost total lack of weapons visible among the soldiers on the streets. The only exception were half-meter-long sticks carried by the fire watch. It was clear that some of the soldiers who were fighting would have been killed if firearms had been at hand.

There was a fenced area at the inland side of the camp, and Kindy wanted to find out what was in it. Several things made the fenced area of interest: it was the only fenced area the Marines saw in the camp; the fencing was antipersonnel razor wire; and it appeared to be electrified. Was that to keep people out, or to keep them in? More, the buildings seemed to have been reinforced after their construction. Curiously, while the grounds within the fenced area were brightly lit, the buildings themselves were dark, with the exception of one. No sounds of revelry came from any of the buildings. Lastly, there were two guard towers, on opposing corners. When third squad got close enough, Kindy could see that both were occupied—and the weapons of the guards were pointed *into* the area rather than away from it.

In all, the fenced area looked like a prison stockade. So who was being held prisoner?

Kindy decided to approach the stockade from inland and led Nomonon into the forest that had been cut away to a distance of seventy-five meters from the fringes of the camp. When they were on the side of the stockade away from the main camp, the two Force Recon Marines crossed the clear-cut to see if they could find a way through the fence. Considering the overall state of the camp, Kindy thought it was more than fifty-fifty that there was an unobstructed way in, no matter that the stockade's construction and maintenance appeared better than anything else but the clubs'. Kindy and Nomonon used all their sensors on their way across the clear-cut, but found no intrusion detectors other than visible-light cameras. Kindy had to shake his head in wonder.

The guards may have had their weapons pointed inboard, but up close it was obvious they weren't paying much attention to whomever they were supposed to be guarding, which failure Kindy felt fit fully within what he had seen in the rest of the camp. So he wasn't at all surprised to learn that the most direct route into the stockade, the gate in the campside fence, was not only unlocked, but open far enough for him and Nomonon to slip through.

There were five buildings in the stockade. The two largest were open-bay barracks, the open windows of which were protected by bars. Kindy and Nomonon looked through the windows with their light-gatherer screens. Sleeping men lay on rows of cots in the bays, and clothing that had seen better days was folded on lockers at the feet of the cots. Some of the clothing might once have been Confederation Army uniforms. The rest were a motley array of civilian garb. One of the two barracks was divided into two open bays, and one of its bays held women. Together, the barracks held more than a hundred prisoners, a quarter of whom were women.

The smallest building was a sanitation facility, with toilets, showers, and laundry equipment.

Another building, larger than the sanitation facility, was an office. Someone, evidently the sergeant of the guard, sat nodding at a desk in the sole lit room. Four other soldiers slumped asleep on chairs in the room. The rest of the office building was dark and unoccupied.

The final building, larger than the office, smaller than the barracks, had what were probably interrogation rooms. Two chairs faced each other in those rooms. One of the chairs was festooned with restraining straps and had light fixtures aimed at it; dark spots on the walls and floors of the rooms may have been blood—but colors didn't make it through the light gatherers, so Kindy and Nomonon couldn't tell for sure. Two of the rooms had metal tables with gutters running around them. Here again, dark spots on the walls and floors may have been blood. The final room had a rumpled bed that looked as though its linen hadn't been changed in some time.

Kindy had seen enough. It was time to leave anyway. Third squad rendezvoused at the cliff top; fourth squad was already at the base of the cliff. Kindy retrieved his minnie and was the last man down. When he reached the foot of the cliff, he twisted the rope *just so.* The rope's tendrils gave up their grip on the ground atop the cliff, and a single jerk was enough to pull it back down; Kindy coiled it as it fell. The Marines entered the water, recalled the Sea Squirts, and headed out to sea to be picked up by the AstroGhost and returned to orbit.

Debriefing, aboard the CNSS Kiowa

After all eight Marines individually described in detail what they had found, the two squad leaders gave their overall impressions to Commander Obannion and his staff. Rear Admiral Hoi's intelligence chief sat in on the debriefing. Sergeant Williams, as the junior squad leader on the mission, went first.

"I've never seen such an unprotected beach near a military facility," Williams said. "I believe an entire army regimental landing team could land there before anybody in the Seventh MPs realized anybody was that close to them. If a FIST went in, they could reach the camp before that MP battalion had a hint it was there."

Kindy expanded on the last part of Williams's analysis. "From what we saw, discipline is so lax—and security so nonexistent—that nobody in that camp would realize they were being attacked until they were taken prisoner."

Kindy had a final point he wanted to emphasize. "I am

David Sherman & Dan Cragg

certain that the prisoners are tortured. Given the state of the bed in the interrogation building, I believe they rape the women prisoners as well." He settled back in his chair and grimaced. "Personally, I'd prefer killing them to taking them prisoner." He shook his head. "Maybe not all of them participate in the torture and rapes."

CHAPTER
THIRTY-SIX

Headquarters, Coalition Army, Ravenette

The ragged little man stood quietly just inside the entrance to General Lyons's command post. He had talked his way past the sentries by telling them he had an important piece of intelligence for the general. But once inside the bustling nerve center of the Coalition's army, he seemed to lose the power of speech. At first no one noticed him there. Several times he made as if to speak to a passing officer or noncom, but each time he lapsed back into embarrassed silence.

The CP was in turmoil, which was one reason nobody noticed the visitor at first. Organized confusion is the normal state of affairs in a CP during a battle, but that day the frenzy was at its highest level because General Lyons was marshaling his troops for an all-out assault on the Confederation's besieged garrison at Fort Seymour. So when the civilian intruder was finally noticed, eyebrows were raised.

At last a burly sergeant carrying a toolbox on his way to fix a malfunction in someone's communications console stopped and asked the man, clearly a civilian who did not belong in the command post, "Who in the hell are *you*?"

"Tatnall Toombs," the little man answered, his voice cracking on the last syllable, "and I have information of importance to General Lyons." He cleared his throat nervously.

"Yeah? Why ain't you bein' escorted, Mr. Tumbs?" The sergeant, like all sergeants throughout time, sensed a breach of discipline. He was, of course, outraged.

"*Toombs,* sir," the little man corrected timidly, "and I have a message for the general." The sergeant regarded the little man carefully. He was dressed in rags; his hair was stringy, unkempt, and offensively unwashed; he had not shaved in days; and his fingernails were *filthy*. The sergeant's first thought was, What could this bum possibly have to tell General Lyons? But then he noticed Tatnall Toombs's eyes: they were the brightest blue and clear and they did not waver. The sergeant had seen such men before, recruits who outwardly feared military discipline but who refused to be broken by it. Often such men turned into excellent soldiers. This ragman seemed to have that quality—he was here, wasn't he, where clearly he did not belong and did not want to be, but here he was nevertheless. Certainly he had *something* going for him to get inside the well-guarded CP without a military police escort.

"Major?" the sergeant hailed a passing staff officer. The major took Mr. Toombs to his lieutenant colonel, who in turn took him to a full colonel, who took him to a brigadier general and thence to a major general. The latter officer, a man who hated red tape, after listening to what Mr. Toombs had to say, jumped channels immediately and took him to see General Davis Lyons.

Office of General Lyons, Coalition Army Headquarters

When the order had come to evacuate Ashburtonville in advance of its becoming a battleground, some residents refused to leave, stubborn people, attached to their homes, who simply refused to desert them, homes they owned, homes where generations of their families had lived and died, homes that defined what kind of people they were.

Such a man was Tatnall "Tat" Toombs. He'd sent his family away but he refused to evacuate. His house was a sturdy affair in an affluent suburb some distance from Pohick Bay and Fort Seymour, sufficiently removed from the scene of action that it had only been partially destroyed during bombardments by the Confederation ships in orbit around the planet.

The modern structure, in the cantilevered Archadian style, actually rested on two homes that had previously occupied

the site. They had been built by ancestors of the Toombs
family. The first, built during the planet's early settlement,
had burned; the second had been built over the ruins of the
original building; and the home Toombs lived in had been
extensively renovated by succeeding members of his family.
The advantage it had over the other properties in the neighborhood was a deep double basement. In this basement, Tat
Toombs took up housekeeping after he'd seen his family
safely off to a more remote region of Ravenette, where they'd
be safe from the fighting.

The lower basement was dry and snug because the neighborhood was high enough above the water table and Pohick Bay
that it was not subject to seepage. Its drainage was so good it
did not flood even during the rainy season. During the first
Confederation bombardment the roof had been blown off the
house, leaving the rest of it open to the weather, but that did
not affect Tat Toombs, safe in the basement surrounded by
his family heirlooms and a stockpile of food and drink
hastily collected when the first evacuation order had been issued. He could always rebuild the upper story.

But life in Ashburtonville was far from pleasant for those
who remained behind. At first the army had orders to forcibly
evacuate all civilians from the city, but as the tempo of the
fighting increased, the military's attention turned elsewhere.
And those few civilians remaining in the city soon learned to
move with caution when they left the safety of their hiding
places.

Day and night the furtive residents hunkered down in the
ruins, buffeted by the constant ripping and roaring of heavy
weapons, the *thump-thump-thump* of projectile guns firing
massive barrages followed by earthshaking detonations, the
dreadful *riiiiiip-CRASH* of high-energy weapons, the screech-
ing of low-flying aircraft that forced men in their burrows to
cover their ears, and the intermittent crescendo of thousands
of small arms firing during the infantry assaults that seethed
back and forth over the no-man's-land between Fort Seymour and the redoubts on Bataan.

The ruined city was blanketed under a choking and continual pall from the smoke of the fires that never went out mingled with the dust kicked up by the constant bombardments; blackbirds and slimies swarmed everywhere, the constant companions of the miserable humans crouching terrified beneath the debris. While the human sense of smell can be dulled rather quickly, no one who stayed behind in the city—and that included the tens of thousands of soldiers—ever got the stench of death and decay out of his nostrils. It pervaded everything, clothes, food, equipment. When it rained, the dreadful miasma sank deep into the ground assuring that it would endure long after the fighting was over.

Whole streets had been reduced to rubble and were impassable; others were lined with the façades of ruined buildings, some with roofs gone, walls collapsed revealing the rooms inside, all unsafe for habitation. Occasionally a partially destroyed building would finally collapse with a roar in a vast cloud of dust. Still, desperate scavengers ventured into the upper floors of buildings in their never-ending search for food, supplies, and valuables. No one would ever know how many were trapped in the collapsing ruins.

Finding food was the first and constant priority for every living creature left in Ashburtonville. Scavenging soon became a full-time occupation for them. Men learned to move under the cover of darkness or right after an orbital bombardment, when increased volumes of fire and smoke obscured them from the troops hunkered by the thousands in defensive positions. Occasionally the troops would share their rations with the locals, although that was strictly against orders. When small groups of scavengers searching for food would meet by chance in a deserted store, violent confrontations broke out as they struggled for possession of whatever scraps had been overlooked by the slimies. Tat Toombs avoided that by scavenging alone.

In peacetime Tat Toombs had been a district supervisor for the City of Ashburtonville. He'd also been a prominent member of the Ravenette Liberation Party (RLP), the most vocal and influential of several secessionist political parties on

Ravenette. The RLP had been foremost in opposition to continued membership in the Confederation of Human Worlds and agitated for secession even before the disaster at Fort Seymour that had resulted in the deaths of so many Ravenites. Tat Toombs knew something about that incident since he had participated in the planning for the demonstration that had ended so violently.

So Tat Toombs took his life in his hands and went out into the ruined city one day, not to scavenge, but to redeem his honor.

"Mr. Toombs, is it?" General Lyons asked as the little man was ushered into his presence. He gestured toward a camp chair. Almost reluctantly, Toombs took it. "My ADC informs me you have information of importance, sir. Will it help in the coming battle?"

"Uh, no, sir. But it is information you need to know."

"Mr. Toombs, I'm very busy. But you have five minutes. Incidentally, how did you get in here to see me like this?"

Toombs shrugged. "I jist asked."

Lyons nodded. "I'll just see about that," he said darkly. "Well, Mr. Toombs, what is it you have for me? Ah, one thing before you begin." He held up a forefinger. "I'm afraid I cannot let you out of here for a while." Lyons smiled apologetically. "You see, we're about ready for the big push, and with enemy patrols swarming all over the rear, I can't take a chance one of them might nab you, get you to tell them about what you may have seen or heard while you were here. So until the assault is well under way, I'll have to keep you here under"— he shrugged—" 'house arrest,' let's say. You do understand, don't you?" Lyons regarded the disheveled little man carefully. He looked as if he could use a rest, even an army meal, such as they were.

"Yes, sir." Toombs nodded. "That's all right, General. That's perfectly all right."

"Proceed, then."

"Well, sir"—Toombs shifted in his chair—"you see, I was

a district supervisor for the city and also I was an officer in the RLP. You know who they were?"

"Yes, I do. Mr. Toombs—"

"Call me Tat, sir."

"Tat, then. I'm really not interested in your political affiliation." Lyons smiled, but from the way he said this, Toombs sensed General Lyons did not think much of the RLP.

"Well," Tat sighed, and took a breath, "that demonstration at Fort Seymour, where all those people got killed? It was a setup. The RLP set it up, sent those folks in against the Confederation's soldiers. Provocateurs were secretly infiltrated into the crowd. It was they who fired the first shot, got them soldiers to shoot back. We wanted something to hold against the Confederation, something so nasty everyone out here'd want to secede, we needed a 'cause,' we needed a massacre, an' by God, I guess that's just what we got."

Lyons was silent for a moment. "There were rumors—Mr. Toombs, Tat, how do you know this?"

"Because I was in on it."

"You—?"

Toombs nodded and hung his head. "I was in on it. Oh, at the time I thought, what the heck, a few busted eggs, a few folks hurt, but if that's the price we gotta pay for an independence omelet, that's the price. I never thought"—he waved a hand vaguely—"I never thought it'd lead to *this*." He nodded his head to take in the command post, the armies, the vast war now engulfing his world. "I never thought . . . ," he whispered, then was silent for a long moment. Then he looked up at General Lyons, his bright blue eyes flashing. "I know who set it up, I know their names. Some of 'em is high up in the Coalition government. I'll give you the names, and when the time comes, I'll stand up and swear what I know is the truth." He paused, catching his breath. "I jist thought you needed to know that, sir. Me, I'm sick to death of what's happened and I jist can't live with it anymore without tellin' somebody. I figured you was the one to tell."

"Well," Lyons said, "well, well, well. Hmmmm. This sure

changes things." He was silent for a moment, taking in what Toombs had just confessed. Then he came around his desk, got down on one knee, and laid a hand on Toombs's knee. *"Who were they?"*

Without hesitating Toombs handed over a crystal. "I recorded the meetings, General. It's all on there. You'll recognize some of those folks, they came in from off-world for the meetin's. That's how far-reachin' the plot was." Lyons returned to his desk and viewed the crystal in silence for a few minutes. *"Was Preston Summers in on this?"*

"No, sir. The plan was to keep certain politicians in the dark, so they'd support the secessionist movement. Summers'd never have gone along with it."

"The Virgin's bloody hangnails," Lyons sighed at last. "Are you willing to add your testimony to what's on this crystal, Mr. Toombs?"

"I'll swear to it, General."

General Lyons arose and strode to the heavy curtain that served as a door to his office, leaned outside, and yelled, "Colonel Raggel, front and center!"

"Yessir."

"Rene, this is Tat Toombs, my *very important* guest. Will you put him up down here for a while? Make him comfortable. See that nothing happens to him? When you have him situated, get the judge advocate to take a statement from Mr. Toombs, will you? He has something very important to tell him. Tell the provost marshal to see me in here when that's done, would you?" Lyons put a hand gently on Toombs's shoulder. "Tat, you did the right thing by coming in here with your story. I promise I'll do something about it." He grinned broadly. Only that morning he'd promised the chairman of the Committee on the Conduct of the War he'd be arrested if he tried to oppose him any further. "Well, you bastard," he muttered, "your time has come." He turned to Colonel Raggel. "Rene, after you get Tat here squared away, set up a secure line to the commanding officer of the Seventh Independent Military Police Battalion. I have a mission for him."

The Taproom Headquarters of the Committee on the Conduct of the War, Gilbert's Corners

The members of the Committee on the Conduct of the War had been badly shaken by the previous night's attack, so badly none had as yet remembered to complain about General Lyons's threats. They had remained in the old taproom throughout the day and were still there in the early evening, deep into their cups and feeling no more pain.

The door opened suddenly and an officer stepped in. "Which one of you is Heb Cawman?" he asked.

"He ain't here," said one. "Ain't seen him since last night."

"Then who's in charge?"

The committee members looked at each other uncertainly for a moment, then one volunteered, "Guess I am."

"And you are?" the officer asked.

"Duey Culvert." Noticing the officer's red face, he said, "Come on, Colonel, siddown 'n' have a drink with us!" The other members of the committee, equally soused, laughed and banged their cups on the table.

"I am Lieutenant Colonel Delbert Cogswell, commander of the Seventh Independent Military Police Battalion," the officer said, "and I am here to arrest you, sir."

Culvert laughed and the delegate from Lannoy staggered to his feet and shouted, "I know you, Delbert, you old bastard! Stop kiddin' around an' siddown." He slumped back into his chair.

"I am not kidding. Are any of you here the following?" He read off several names. Two members acknowledged that they were present. "That's all right, I'll just arrest you all and we can sort out the innocent and the guilty later."

"Thass how they do it in the Seventh MPs!" the delegate from Lannoy giggled.

"On whose authority, Colonel?" Culvert blustered. He was beginning to realize the MP was serious.

"On General Davis Lyons's authority, sir."

"Hell, he ain't got no authority over *us*," Culvert blustered.

"He does over me, sir, and my orders are to arrest you."

"On what fucking charges?" Culvert shouted.

"Treason, murder, starting a war," Cogswell said. He signaled with one arm. A squad of MPs filed into the room. "These men will secure you as my prisoners and transport you to the POW compound at Cogglesville, where you will be held until formal charges can be drawn up and your trials convened."

"Like hell I will!" Culvert screamed.

Cogswell stepped to the table and slammed his billy club down with a bang, making the glasses and bottles rattle. "Listen, you slimy bastard, you get yer ass over there or I'm rammin' this club so far up your behind your tonsils'll get bruised."

EPILOGUE

Colonel Delbert Cogswell rubbed his hands together enthusiastically and chortled, "Sarn Majer, we'll have us the goldangest beer bust anybody here or back on Lannoy's ever seen!" Among his own, he chose to speak the vernacular of his home planet, a place where "book learnin'" was actively frowned upon. He laughed and slapped his thigh. "Sarn Majer, you shoulda seen those old boys! They was drunk as bopaloos when we picked 'em up and puked all over on the way to the POW camp! Funniest damned thing I ever saw. Made 'em clean up their mess when we got there." He laughed again. "Personal orders of General Lyons. He called me personally and gave me that mission, Sarn Majer, by God!" The call from Lyons had been the first time anyone in command had bothered to recognize his existence.

The colonel was beside himself with joy and satisfaction. He had been given a mission by General Lyons himself, personally directed to arrest the members of the Committee on the Conduct of the War. Well, not *all* of them, but what the hell, innocent people are always gathered up in sweeps. The commandant of the camp at Cogglesville would sort the innocent from the guilty in good time. "Went off without a hitch, without a *hitch*! Got 'em all, Sarn Majer, got 'em all. Ah, you shoulda been there! The boys did well, very well."

"Well, you din't ask me along, Colonel."

"Ah? Hum, well, er, Sarn Majer, I needed to leave *some-*

342

body behind who could, er"—he waved vaguely—"make decisions, keep things running. You know. Anyways, back to the beer party. The boys done well yesterday and we're gonna reward everyone. We are gonna get some kinda drunk tonight."

Krampus Steiner, the Seventh Independent MP Battalion sergeant major, regarded his commanding officer quizzically out of one eye. Steiner was not known for joviality. Of all the men in the battalion he'd be the first in line to beat somebody up, but never drunk, always sober. He loved *controlled* violence, and the one thing that annoyed him most about his battalion was the spontaneity of the carnage its men unleashed. That is why the Seventh MPs had the nickname Vigilante Battalion, and it was one of the reasons they'd been consigned to coast watch duty, to keep them away from civilization and out of the way of the truly effective military units that were fighting the war. Isolated as they were, the men had fallen to fighting among themselves, and Steiner did not like that. "You get the boys liquored up, Colonel, 'n' they'll be at each other's throats like wild dogs," he warned.

Cogswell made a dismissive gesture and grunted, "Aw, the boys need to blow off some steam, Sarn Majer! You know how they is. Damn, git on board here, will ya?"

"Colonel"—Steiner decided to change the subject—"we might have some real information with them two prisoners Lieutenant Keesey's got down there in First Company. We oughta be extractin' that intelligence—"

"You mean the two beachcombers who washed up the other day? Naw, Sarn Majer, they's a couple of bums. Let Keesey play around with 'em for a while before we turn 'em over to Division. Or maybe not. After Keesey gets through with 'em, won't be too much left," Cogswell chuckled good-naturedly. "Be good training for Keesey," he added, "string out the interrogation process, maybe really git somethin' outta them two. But who gives a shit?" He shrugged.

Steiner came back to the prospective party. "You know, Colonel, once word of this party gits out, the division commander's liable to relieve the both of us?"

"Huh?" Cogswell's mind was on the imminent arrival of

the girls and booze. "Relieve us? Why? 'Dereliction of duty'? Hah! They put us away out here to git rid of us, Sarn Majer, this ain't no majer vulnerability, this damned coastline. Otherwise they'd have put some real combat outfit here to watch out fer the enemy. Anyways, I don't give a damn. Let the old fancy pants relieve me! This is a bullshit war anyway. Besides"— he thumped his chest—"I got a personal relationship with General Lyons, after what we did for him yesterday."

"Well, sir, we need to detail a couple of platoons to coast watch tonight—"

"Forget it, Sarn Majer! I declare a training holiday for the battalion! No staff duty officer, no staff duty NCO either. Jus' let the men enjoy themselves fer one night. They can go back to this bullshit coast watchin' when they sober up, whenever that might be. An' if division tries to get in touch with us tonight, put 'em on hold." Cogswell laughed.

Steiner gave up. What the hell, he thought, life on the coast is a crashing bore, no chance of any action, the boys may as well enjoy themselves. But he would return to the command post and harass his clerks some more. He knew from experience that once the colonel got an idea fixed between his ears it was a waste of breath trying to change it. He thanked the colonel for his time, stepped back one pace, saluted smartly, about-faced, and marched out of Colonel Cogswell's tent. On his way back to the CP, he noticed a long line of heavily escorted lorries pulling into camp. As each vehicle came to a stop in a swirl of dust, men crowded around and began to unload crates and boxes under the direction of the battalion supply officer; the battalion medical officer escorted a crowd of young women to his aid station. From where he stood watching, Steiner could tell the women were the kind who needed medical attention. Well, by nightfall there wouldn't be a man in the battalion, Colonel Cogswell included, who'd give a damn. With that thought in mind he had to laugh out loud.

Seventh Independent MP Camp

In the deluge of alcohol and clouds of thule that had engulfed the men of the Seventh Independent Military Police
Battalion since sundown, they had lost track of time, but no
one really cared. Dawn would soon arrive, and when it did,
the men would be just as inebriated as they had been at midnight. Best of all, they would still be at it by sundown, those
who could still lift an arm by then. "Boy, it sure is drunk out
tonight!" men exclaimed, pounding each other on the shoulders in alcoholic bonhomie.

Colonel Cogswell, a disheveled girl from town on one
arm, had dropped in at the Fourth Company's tent to pay his
respects to the company commander and his first sergeant.
He had been both booed and cheered good-naturedly by the
men as he rolled unsteadily through the tent flaps. With a casual gesture involving the middle finger of one hand, he rendered a bilious acknowledgment to the greetings that sent
everyone into peals of laughter. "Mighty fine war we got ourselves into, eh?" he exclaimed to the vast amusement of the
men. Someone handed him a schooner of ale, half of which
ran down the front of the colonel's uniform as he tried to
drink and talk at the same time. That was probably a good
thing because the ale washed off the flecks of vomit clinging
there from his visit to the Third Company's soirée, where one
of the enlisted men had thrown up on him. His only comment
at the time had been "Aw, shit happens."

The girl on his arm was so drunk she virtually floated along
by his side. "Lissen!" she shrilled, interrupting Colonel Cogswell in midsentence and popping an olive into her mouth.
"You can hear it splash as it hits my stomach!" The men
roared their approval. She had informed Colonel Cogswell
that her name was Blossom, which he graciously acknowledged fit her very well. To a sober man, Blossom was nothing to look at; but drunk as they all were, despite her huge
hips, pendulous dugs, scraggly locks of indeterminate hue,
and the gaps between the stumps of her teeth, the men saw

her as something akin to Botticelli's Venus rising demurely from the sea. Of course, some of them would probably have thought the same of her sober. The Seventh Independent Military Police Battalion was the best thing that had ever happened to Blossom.

A corporal—the company's orderly-room clerk and the only woman in the battalion—had been arguing with the first sergeant all night about which had, at any time in their lives, done the most outrageous thing while under the influence. By the time of Colonel Cogswell's grand entrance they had both recited an extensive litany of stupid pranks, each one trying to top the other. Toward the end each had found it necessary to be slightly inventive in their tales.

"Awrrrriiight!" the first sergeant bellowed at last. "We are gonna end this right now! Corporal Puella Queege, you are a bullshit artist, plain an' simple, and I'm a-gonna prove it. Colonel, you be the judge here." The first sergeant held up his arms and called for silence. When he had it at last, he stood on a chair and addressed the men who could still stand. "I bet Corporal Queege here one hunnert credits she won't eat what's under this cover on this here tray!" All evening the first sergeant had jealously guarded a tray on the table behind him. It was covered with a large linen napkin. Dark brown stains had crept through the fabric during the evening, and despite many inquiries, the top sergeant had vehemently refused to let anyone see what was under the cover. "I got sumptin' here for a special purpose," he kept telling everyone. With a dramatic flare, he pulled off the napkin.

"What in the name of Holy Hepzibah are those?" Colonel Cogswell exclaimed.

"These," the first sergeant exclaimed, "are half a dozen baked baby slimies covered in chocolate!"

A collective scream of horror escaped from the crowd. Everyone hastily stepped back from the table. Blossom was so unsteady on her feet that she fell over backward, but all eyes were on the six tiny lumps on the tray, and nobody, not even the battalion commander, noticed Blossom's sudden descent. There she remained the rest of the evening. She was in good company, however; several men lay there who'd passed out earlier.

"I baked 'em myself," the first sergeant announced with pride. "Now, here's the deal: Queege here, she's gotta eat all six of these babies in five minutes flat. Then drink a full liter of beer 'n' keep it *all* down for another five minutes to win this here hunnert credits."

"Oh my, oh my, oh my," Colonel Cogswell chuckled facetiously, "for a *thousand* credits I might do that myself!"

"It ain't for the money, sir," the first sergeant replied, "but the glory 'n' honor of puttin' her big mouth where her big mouth is, sorta, so to speak. Whaddya say, Queege old squeegee? Put up or fuckin' shut up. That's the deal, an' here's the credits." He slammed a bill on the bar.

Corporal Queege regarded the six little lumps on the tray. Well, they were only, say, a mouthful each. Six mouthfuls of slimie? Hell, she thought, anybody could choke that down in five minutes, and a liter of beer afterward. By her calculations, she'd already consumed several liters of beer. She bent forward and studied the lumps. Yep, they were slimies, all right. She could make out their little heads, the bulging eyes and the tiny cilia all over them that looked like hair, the reptilian snouts, the rows of sharp little teeth, the squamous hides covered with little nodules, the various appendages and the long, ratlike tails. Everyone knew the troops under siege at Fort Seymour had been reduced to eating the things, and the ones they ate were *adults*. These looked to be almost newborns. And they were covered with chocolate? She reached out a finger experimentally and tasted the sludgy brown coatings.

"Not so fast, Queege!" the first sergeant shouted. "No tasting!"

"Yep, that's chocolate!" Queege exclaimed, a huge smile slowly creeping over her face. If Corporal Puella Queege could win the contest, she would be assured lasting fame in the Seventh MP Battalion, fame and respect that would find its way far beyond that desolate camp on Ravenette. Once the story got out, she could go into any bar back home and drink for free just on the basis of her courageous deed. All she'd ever wanted to be was a woman who was just one of the boys. "Yer on, Top!" she shouted. She matched the first sergeant's bet with a wad of crumpled bills. Men in the crowd quickly made side bets. The wagers ran in favor of the first sergeant. Everyone knew the company clerk was a blowhard. They also knew there was a lot more between her and the first sergeant than duty rosters and morning reports, which is why none had ever attempted to put the make on her, as pretty, in a manly way, as she was. In their drunken stupor they saw the contest as a unique lovers' quarrel.

"I shall observe the gustatory proceedings," Colonel Cogswell pronounced with drunken gravity, swaying slightly, "and judge the contest fairly and squarely." He bent close to observe Queege better.

"I need a fork!" she said. Someone handed her one. She took up her position before the table, flexed her shoulders, took a deep breath, and dug into the first slimie. The creature's body crackled distinctly as the fork cut through the chocolate into its insides. Slowly Puella raised the mess to her mouth. Tendrils of blue-gray intestine dangled obscenely from the mess. She closed her eyes, popped the meat into her mouth, and swallowed. A long soulful sigh, a collective gasp of awe, escaped from the onlookers. Someone placed a full schooner of ale on the table beside the tray.

"Thirty seconds!" the first sergeant shouted. "You jist gettin' started, girl!"

The first slimie went down easily. Puella swallowed the material quickly, to avoid tasting it. The next one, at one minute, was a little more difficult. She couldn't help looking at the four left on the tray. She'd have to hurry! She got number three down in fifteen seconds. A strange purple juice mixed with chocolate dribbled down her chin, but Puella paid it no attention. Numbers four and five each disappeared in ten seconds flat, but on number six, she had trouble. It was the *taste;* it was finally penetrating her senses. She realized with horror that the first sergeant had not baked the slimies after all, only covered them with a thin layer of chocolate!

She was eating *raw* slimie! She fought desperately to keep
down what she'd eaten. As from a vast distance she was aware
of someone's counting, like the referee at a prizefight giving
the count to the man on the canvas.

"Twenty-five, twenty-four . . . ," the first sergeant counted.
Good God, had that much time slipped by? Twenty-four, no,
twenty-three seconds of the five minutes left?

Puella grabbed the remaining slimie in one hand and
stuffed it directly into her mouth and forced it down with a
huge spasm of effort.

"I declare the corporal the winnah!" Colonel Cogswell announced, holding up one of Puella's dangling arms.

"Not so fast! She's gotta drink this liter of ale an' keep it
all down five minutes!" the first sergeant reminded everyone.

"Okay, okay," Puella gasped, wiping the viscous juices
from her chin. She grabbed the stein, put it to her lips, and
began to drink. She drank slowly, steadily, so as not to spill
any of the beer.

As each mouthful went down, the crowd stamped its feet
and shouted, "Down! Down! Down! . . ." Finally, victori-
ously, Puella held the stein bottoms-up and let out a satisfied
burp.

"Goddammit, girl, keep it down for *five minutes.*" The first
sergeant was getting desperate now that his clerk was so
close to winning the bet. "Tasted good, eh?" he goaded her,
and pretended to vomit. "Yer stomach is bulgin' like a woman
nine months pregnant, Queege old squeegee, looks bad, looks
bad. How y'feelin'? Ready to toss yer cookies?"

"Four more minutes, Corporal," Colonel Cogswell announced.

Puella's stomach really did feel bloated. She burped again.
A terrible smell escaped through her mouth, so bad she
waved the fumes away with a hand.

"A mouth fart! A mouth fart!" the first sergeant yelled.

Puella fought to keep the mess down. It felt, good God, as
if the stuff was *moving around* down there! She swallowed
hard. Another burp escaped her stomach. She began to perspire. *"Three more minutes!"*

At last the ordeal was over. "I now declare the corporal the winnah!" Colonel Cogswell announced, putting a hand on Puella's sweat-soaked shoulder. He couldn't help regarding her with a bit of anxiety because she did not look well. Cautiously, he stepped back a pace. Puella gave him a sickly grin and leaned over the bar, scooped up her winnings, and held the crumpled bills on high.

Men bellowed curses and cheers. Someone stepped out of the crowd and began pounding Puella on the back. That was all it took. Puella reeled over to the first sergeant. "You lyin' sonofabitch!" she screamed, and emptied the entire contents of her stomach down the front of his uniform.

Interrogation Center

But one officer of the Seventh Independent Military Police Battalion was not participating in the festivities that evening. He was Lieutenant Keesey, commanding First Company, and he had serious business to attend to.

Keesey's "business" was Charlette Odinloc, who lay stripped and tied to a table in a storage room hastily converted into an interrogation chamber. "Well," he hissed, running a clammy hand along her rib cage, "I don't really keer if you tell me the truth 'cause what I'm about to do to you is find out the truth my own way, and this will hurt you a lot more than it'll hurt me." He smirked and stroked her silently for a moment. "On second thought, maybe you'll enjoy what's comin', honey. Most wimmen do. Laugh at me, willya?" he said, referring to their first encounter as he unbuckled his trousers. "Well, this time the last laugh's—"

Someone kicked the door open with a crash. Keesey whirled. "Goddamn drunks!" he screamed, but no one was there. The wind, he thought. But there was no wind that night. His heart began to race as the first tendrils of fear crept into his stomach.

"Freeze, asshole! You are now my prisoner," a voice said out of thin air.

Charlette let out a shout of joy. She knew what chameleons were. *The Marines had landed!*

Want to learn how the troubles first began on Ravenette?
Then check out this riveting excerpt from

FLASHFIRE

by David Sherman and Dan Cragg

Now available from Del Rey Books.

A small, black object arced out from the crowd, described a graceful parabola, and burst into greasy orange flame in the middle of the street. "Steady, men, steady," the lieutenant murmured from behind the thin line of infantrymen facing the mob. To his men he appeared calm and in control; in reality his legs were about to give way on him.

"Shee-it!" one of the infantrymen exclaimed, grasping his lexan shield more tightly and glancing nervously over his shoulder at the sergeant of the guard, who shook his head silently, gesturing that the man should watch the crowd and not him. The troops had only just been called out to face the unexpected mob of irate citizens. Already the area between the Fort Seymour main gate and the demonstrators, a very short stretch of about one hundred meters, was littered with debris that had been thrown at the soldiers. Now a firebomb! Things were getting serious. That firebomb belied the innocuous messages on the signs carried by the demonstrators, GIVE US INDEPENDENCE!, NO TAXES TO THE CONFEDERATION!, CHANG-STURDEVANT DICTATOR!, and others.

Lieutenant Jacob Ios of Alfa Company, 2nd Battalion, 1st Brigade, 3rd Provisional Infantry Division, Confederation Army, was pulling his first tour of duty as officer of the guard at the Fort Seymour depot. Neither he nor his men had received civil-disturbance training, and the only equipment they had for that job were the lexan body shields they were using to protect themselves against thrown objects. Fortunately, none of the crowd's missiles had yet reached them. He wished that Major General Cazombi's recommendation to keep the contractor guard force—all men recruited on Ravenette—responsible for the installation's security, had been followed, but he'd been overridden by General Sorca, the tactical commander with overall authority for security. Still, Ios couldn't help wondering what Cazombi had done to get himself stuck at Fort Seymour.

The sergeant of the guard interrupted his musings. "El Tee, should I have the men unsling their arms?" he whispered.

"Not yet." Ios made a quick estimate of the crowd's size and his stomach plummeted right into his boots. There had to be at least three hundred people in it; his guard force was outnumbered ten-to-one.

"If they start coming at us, Lieutenant, we won't be able to stop them," the sergeant whispered. Surreptitiously, he unfastened the retaining strap on his sidearm holster. As if confirming the sergeant's fears, several men in the crowd ran forward a few paces and tossed more firebombs. They exploded harmlessly in the street but much closer to the soldiers than the last one.

"Confederation soldiers! Go home! We do not want you here! Confederation out!" a woman with a bullhorn began chanting shrilly. Ios couldn't see the woman. That was ominous, someone leading the mob from behind.

"That's okay with me!" One of the soldiers grinned and several of his buddies laughed nervously. More and more people in the crowd took up the chant, *"Confederation out!"* until the slogan swelled to a roar. People banged clubs and iron pipes on the pavement as they chanted, beating a steady *Whang! Whang! Whang!* A chunk of paving sailed out from the mob and skittered across the roadway, coming to rest against the knee-high stone wall that flanked the main entrance to Fort Seymour. That wall was the only shelter the soldiers would have if the mob charged them; the iron gates across the entrance, which had never before been closed, were chained shut and two tactical vehicles were drawn up tight behind them in the event the mob tried to break through.

"Climate Six, this is Post One, over," Ios muttered into the command net, trying very hard to keep his voice even as he spoke. Climate Six was the Fort Seymour staff duty officer's call sign.

"Post One, this is Climate Six, over."

"We need immediate reinforcement, over," Ios said, his voice tensing as more bricks and stones pelted the road. The fires had burned themselves out.

"Ah, Post One, what is your status? I hear shouting but I cannot see your position from here, over."

Ios suppressed an angry response, "Climate Six, several hundred rioters are approaching my position! We are in danger of being overrun! Request immediate reinforcement!" Stones and bricks hurtled toward Ios. Then another bright orange blossom. "Climate Six, we are being firebombed, repeat, firebombed!"

"Casualties? Over."

Ios took a breath to steady himself. "None, so far, Climate Six, but we cannot hold unless reinforced immediately! What the hell am I supposed to do?"

"Ah, Post One, use proper communications procedure. Use your initiative but hold that gate at all costs. You will be reinforced ASAP. Climate Six out." The staff duty officer, Lieutenant Colonel Poultney Maracay, who only a few moments ago was happily contemplating his position on the promotion list for Full Colonel, had begun to perspire. "Just where in the hell am I supposed to get reinforcements?" he muttered.

"All the line troops are out on Bataan," the staff duty NCO replied.

"I know that!" Maracay responded angrily. Both generals Cazombi and Sorca were out at the Peninsula on Pohick Bay, where the division was billeted. The division hadn't been on Ravenette two weeks yet and already the troops, in the infantryman's age-old cynical way, had dubbed the Peninsula "Bataan." It'd take fifteen minutes or more to get a reaction force back to Main Post and by then . . . he left the thought hanging. All he had at Main Post were supply specialists and, since it was Saturday afternoon, most of them would be out in town or otherwise incapacitated.

"Sergeant," he turned to the staff duty NCO, "I'm going down to the main gate and see for myself what that young stud's got himself into. Inform General—" he thought for a moment. Major General Cazombi was the garrison commander and the senior officer at Fort Seymour but Brigadier General Sorca commanded the infantry division. "—General Sorca and request that he send immediate reinforcements to Main Post. Keep the net open with Lieutenant Ios and keep HQ informed. Jesus, what a mess!" Shaking his head, he strapped on his sidearm as he went through the door. Where'd these people come from? He knew there were tensions between the Confederation Congress and Ravenette and its allies, but that was esoteric, trade-relations crap, not the kind of thing to drive people into the streets, much less motivate them to attack a Confederation military post.

Lieutenant Ios and his men were not at that moment worrying about trade relations. The young officer was so rattled that he couldn't remember if there was a specific command for "unsling arms" so he fell back on the oldest and most reliable method for passing on a command at an officer's disposal: "Sergeant, have the men unsling arms!" he said crisply while unstrapping his own sidearm. As one, the men dropped their shields and unslung their rifles. "Take up firing positions behind the wall!" Ios ordered over the tactical net. "Do not fire unless I give the command! Steady, men, steady! Show them we mean business! Reinforcements are on the way." He said it with a confidence he didn't feel because he knew, as well as the SDO and every man in his tiny guard force, that useful reinforcements were all out on Bataan.

Seeing the soldiers take up firing positions, the mob howled and rushed forward to within fifty meters of the gate. Now rocks, paving stones, bottles, all kinds of junk began raining down on the soldiers. Ios could clearly hear people in the mob shouting for blood. Protected somewhat by their helmets and equipment harnesses, the troops crouched behind the low wall. "Hold on!" Ios shouted into the tactical net, but at that moment a brick smashed into his mouth and he fell to the ground, dazed, spitting teeth and blood.

As he lay there in agony Lieutenant Jacob Ios, "Jake" to his friends, heard only dimly the fatal *zip-craaaak* of a pistol shot.

Panting, out of breath, Lieutenant Colonel Maracay, whose fate it was to be there at that time and in that place merely through the impersonal agency of the post sergeant major's duty roster, gasped in horror at the sight in the street before the main gate.

A driver assigned to one of the blocking vehicles looked up at him, face white, eyes staring. "I-I didn't fire my weapon," he managed at last.

From somewhere off to the right, someone yelled, "Hooo-haaaa!" and began laughing hysterically.

"Open the gates," the colonel said. He stepped out into the street, his now forgotten sidearm dangling uselessly in one hand, and surveyed the carnage. Scores of mangled bodies lay in pools of blood; wounded men and women, even some children, lay moaning in agony. Directly overhead, spanning the gate, incongruously happy and welcoming, a sign announced, FORT SEYMOUR ARMY SUPPLY DEPOT. YOU CALL, WE HAUL.

"Get—get medics!" Maracay screamed into the command net. "Get the fucking medics!" Dimly, he became aware that someone up the street was pointing something at him and instinctively Colonel Maracay raised his pistol, but it was only a man with a vid camera.